WARRIOR ERRANT

WARRIOR ERRANT

HARRY ELLIOTT

GUARDBRIDGE BOOKS
ST ANDREWS, SCOTLAND

Published by Guardbridge Books,
St Andrews, Fife, United Kingdom.

ISBN: 978-1-911486-27-5

To my parents, for their undying support.

ACT I

PARTING

Chapter One

The fist came crashing down.

Light bloomed. The world swivelled through ninety degrees. Hard as a hammer blow, the deck sprung into the back of Private Dalton's head. The tang of iron swelled between his teeth. Groaning, he rolled off his back.

"Still with us, James?" The blur from which the voice was coming resolved into the grinning face of Private Colt Bridger.

"Shove off," growled James Dalton, pushing off the deck. He came to his feet, swaying, and waved off Colt's offer of support. Through the faint ringing in his ears he could hear the corridor echoing with jeers. "Fucking mod can hit."

"Then you better start hitting back, right?" said Colt cheerfully.

Dalton spun on his heel, fists up. The jeers became cheers. He smiled at his opponent through bloody teeth. "What else you got, mod?"

Six foot five, lean and pale to the point of translucence, the mod simply stared back.

"Get him, James," said Colt.

Dalton shouldered in, head low, leading with a hook aimed for the jaw. The mod leaned back, a casual motion, and left the fist to part air. Open-palmed, the mod planted a blow under Dalton's missed punch, and drove the breath from his lungs. James staggered back five paces and would have kept going if not for Colt.

"You're not looking good, pal."

"Do you want to fight the bastard?" spat James.

"Nah, I'm ugly enough as it is," said Colt and pushed, "back you go."

James turned the forward momentum into a charge, shoulder first. The mod caught him under the arms and flung him like a rag doll into the corridor wall. Colt winced at the thud of flesh striking metal. James went down on his hands and knees. Vision blurring, he looked up at the mod. The tall man – if it could even be called a man – hadn't moved a foot. It was still staring, expression unreadable. Through the pallid skin of that immaculately hairless scalp, James could see the traceries of sub-dermal implants.

The jeers were deafening now. He caught Colt's eye and reached up to find purchase against the pipes which lined the wall. Instead, he found a fire extinguisher.

"Fuck it," he said under his breath, and hauled the extinguisher out of its brace. Like a battering ram, he swung it straight for the mod's face. The mod caught it two-handed and stopped it dead.

"Fair enough," said James and shrugged.

He pulled the safety pin and crunched the levers. A plume of dry powder ejected from the hose and coated the mod's face. The mod backed off, groping at its eyes. James dropped the extinguisher and ploughed in with a solid punch to the gut. The mod doubled over, and James put it on the deck with an elbow in the back.

The mods on the other end of the corridor stepped up. In turn, the cheering squad of troopers behind James surged forwards. Colt pulled him back to his comrades, while the mods lifted their own from the deck. The troopers – blood up, bristling – hurled abuse at the silent line of mods. Silent or shouting, both sides looked ready for a fight.

"This is about to get bad," Colt shouted over the noise, still grinning.

There was a loud *thunk* and the corridor lamps blinked from white to red, bathing them all in ruddy light.

"Stand down!" bellowed a voice. Two officers shoved their

way through the crowded corridor. One of them was a mod. The other – the one doing the shouting – was Lieutenant Killian, from the same regiment as Dalton's crowd.

The mod officer went across to its soldiers and silently looked them up and down. Killian was more vocal.

"What is this bullshit?" he barked, already red in the face. "Squabbling in the corridors like academy pups? Straighten up! We're in this together! Do you see two armies here? Because I just see one. One army made up of the hardest bastards from across two moons, shipping out side by side to put the boot to some trouble-makers in our galactic backyard. You don't like it? Deal with it or step out an airlock, because this ship is only going one way, and we're all going together."

Killian let that settle, looking from face to face, then said, "get back to your billets. I'll deal with you all later."

The mod officer dismissed its own soldiers with nothing more than a glance. The corridor emptied, leaving Lieutenant Killian and his counterpart standing under the blood-red lights.

"I thought that was very well said, lieutenant," remarked the mod officer. Killian grunted and crossed to a wall panel. He pulled a lever and the emergency lighting shut off.

"It is good to see the spirit of co-operation being encouraged," pressed the mod officer.

Killian whipped round and made a beeline to the mod, coming up face to face, an inch apart.

"Listen, you mod bastard," growled the lieutenant, "keep your freaks in line and I'll do the same for my troops. Outside of that, we don't need to be friends."

Killian turned sharply and stalked away. The mod officer breathed deeply through the nose and released a small sigh. Then it turned and strode off in the opposite direction.

* * *

The ship was a Gulper–class Military Interplanetary Personnel and Materiel Carrier. No one called it that. Not even the strictest station-operator on the bridge was that prosaic. To the crew and the four-thousand strong complement of soldiers aboard, the ship was known as *The Moongate*.

Nine hundred metres of technological and engineering ingenuity, the carrier had been purpose-built to define a new era of warfare. Distance had never proved an obstacle to men when the time came for killing. When the open plains of Old Earth stretched too far to walk, ancient warriors broke and saddled beasts to carry them to violence. When beyond those plains were discovered seas and oceans that stretched to the horizons, ships were built that would cross the waves and deliver men to war on foreign shores. And now, not even the gulf between worlds could stand before humanity's lust for blood.

The Moongate had been constructed in the orbital shipyards of Landbreak. It was not the first spaceship to be given life above that storm-racked moon; a substantial fleet of ships had been birthed there for the purpose of orbital defence from potential external threats. *The Moongate* was, however, the first ship built above Landbreak with the intention, not to defend, but to attack.

Landbreak's geography had made natural sailors of its population. Hundreds of rocky islands separated by channels of churning water and violent seas had necessitated a society built around sailing. No matter how tumultuous the waters of Landbreak became, travelling by sea was always more preferable to its people than travelling by air. The fierce headwinds and frequent storms prohibited routine flying. Even the sturdiest of shuttles could be plucked from the skies by hurricane-force winds and hurled end over end into the crashing seas. It had not taken the Islanders of Landbreak long to eschew the skies.

Space travel, on the other hand, was perceived by the Islanders as being more akin to sea travel. They had many analogies to describe the similarity and the preference. A favourite went as follows: "If you fall off your boat, you float. If you fall out your spaceship, you float. If you fall out your plane, you just fall." Naturally, floating was always preferable to falling.

Even so, what *The Moongate* represented was unprecedented. It was one thing to sail the seas between islands, but to sail between worlds was another thing entirely. Since the first generation of settlers, no Islander had migrated off of Landbreak. Even the Orbital Defence Fleet was poorly equipped to go beyond high orbit of the moon.

Now, for the first time in two hundred years, Islanders would go not just beyond the gravitational pull of Landbreak, but they would cross the void between moons and set foot where they had never set foot before. They would not be going alone.

The Moongate had broken orbit of Landbreak over a standard week ago. Now it sailed the dark matter seas, cresting the orbital tides of the gas giant Mitera, its course plotted between two of its six sister moons. First it had made the circuit to the moon of Avernus.

The Islanders had laid eyes upon Avernus from afar, through camera displays and observation domes. One soldier had held a keepsake up to the viewing port – a polished Old Earth coin, currency of their ancestors – and made the comparison. It had certainly been appropriate. Avernus was a silver circle against the speckled backdrop of space. Its surface was scored, as if engraved by a metalworker's deft hand.

It had been beautiful and wondrous, at first, at a distance. Then *The Moongate* had docked with one of the orbiting space stations, and a closer look at Avernus had revealed its beauty to be nothing but a mirage. The moon had been barren. Wholly without natural life or the means to sustain it. No water, no plants, not even a breathable atmosphere. Just as Landbreak had shaped its settlers into Islanders, this moon too had shaped the settlers that had come to be known as the Avernii. This change, however, had been a more comprehensive one. A more transformative one.

The Islanders knew about the Avernii, of course. They had heard rumours, passed down from those who had facilitated the first instances of communication between the moons. They had heard about how the settlers – who had become all but stranded on Avernus – had been forced to adapt to the moon's inhospitable environment. Not until that day, though, had an Islander seen an Avernii in person. A regiment-strength detachment of the Avernii Transhuman Forces, as they described themselves, had marched into one of *The Moongate's* mass loading bays. The rumours had not been enough to prepare the Islanders for the truth.

The humans who had settled Avernus had been, physically, no different from those who had settled Landbreak. The humans that had marched on to *The Moongate* two hundred years later, well, it was difficult to be sure whether they could truly be called *human* anymore. The Islanders had all heard about the difficulties of life on Avernus, about how certain compromises had been necessary to survive on such a moon, but nothing could have prepared them for what the Avernii had become.

And what the Avernii had become was difficult for the Islanders to accept.

It wasn't just their freakishly translucent skin. It wasn't just their complete lack of hair or even their unnatural height. It was their uniformity. It was how difficult it was to distinguish between individuals. It was the way they communicated with one another, rarely with words, sometimes with gestures, but mostly with long, blank stares. And most of all it was their eyes.

The iris was no longer present. In its place, extending from the pupil, was a network of lines, like the circuits on a chipset.

It wasn't long before speculation became rampant amongst the Islanders. Some wondered whether those eyes were even real, or whether they were replaced at birth with bionics. Some went further, and claimed that the Avernii had swapped their brains with computers, and that's what could be seen through their eyes. Whatever the truth of the matter was concerning the full extent of their modifications, the Avernii were stoically silent on the matter, evading questions or outright refusing conversation.

That the Avernii wouldn't answer and that the Islanders wouldn't stop asking didn't help to foster trust for either party. It wasn't long before unease had become unrest. The Avernii Transhuman Forces and the 2nd Privateers of Landbreak had barely been sharing the cramped corridors of *The Moongate* for two standard days when the first signs of friction had appeared. It was not a promising start, especially considering that there was still another whole week of travel to endure before they arrived at their destination.

Now *The Moongate* was beyond sight of bleak Avernus. Its thrusters flared, incandescent in the void, speeding the carrier onwards, to distant shores and war.

* * *

"Do you think there are fish on... what's-its-name again?" asked Private Blake Leland, looking up from his tray.

"Ishra," said Dalton, his voice muffled by the ice-pack he was holding to his mouth.

"Eesh-rah," repeated Blake carefully. "Yeah. Do you reckon they've got fish?"

"Hopefully not," said Colt, "that way when we're done cleaning up their mess for them, we can start selling them our catch."

"Thinking of the future, Colt?" asked Dalton.

"I was a fisherman before I signed up, and I'll be a fisherman when I've served the due," said Colt, sitting a little straighter, "just like my Pa."

"I appreciate the vote of confidence that we'll be coming home from this," said Dalton. Blake gave a nervous laugh.

"Well, I'm only speaking for myself," said Colt, grinning. "Can't vouch for the two of you, right? Couple of eel-handed bottom-feeders that you are."

"Don't make me beat on you, Private Bridger," laughed Dalton.

"Yeah, Colt, you saw him put the mod down," said Blake.

Colt raised an eyebrow. "Give me a moment to hide all the fire extinguishers, then I'll be happy to fight you."

Dalton flicked a forkful of gruel across the table. It splattered on Colt's forehead and the three men burst into laughter.

"Enjoying yourselves, privates?"

The three men scrambled off the benches and came to attention. Across the mess hall, the chatter died down.

"Lieutenant Killian, sir," said Dalton stiffly.

"Private James Dalton, that's some nasty looking swelling you've got there. Mod get the better of you?"

"Uh, no sir."

"Oh that's right, because you assaulted a soldier of an allied military force with a fire extinguisher."

"To be fair, lieutenant, mods aren't natural. Private Dalton here was just levelling the playing field, so to speak," said Colt. James really wished the man would stop grinning right about now, and talking, for that matter. He still had a blob of gruel inching down his brow.

"Well, maybe Private Dalton will remember that, the next time he decides to go twelve rounds with a bionically modified transhuman."

"Actually, it was just one round," said Dalton, and then quickly added, "sir."

Lieutenant Killian sniffed. James could see the man reddening at the collar.

"The death sentence might have been outlawed, but I'll make a damn good case for it to High Command the next time you bottom-feeders embarrass me like that."

"Sir, there won't be a next time, sir," said Dalton.

"So you are capable of intelligence after all, what a surprise," sneered the lieutenant. He raised a finger and pointed it directly between Dalton's eyes. "You're a soldier of the 2nd Privateers. Act like it."

Killian turned away so sharply it made Dalton wince. The three men sagged a little, relieved, grinning sheepishly with one another.

"Oh, and you might want to finish up your meal, Private Dalton," said Killian, pausing to look over his shoulder. "You're on latrines from now until we put down anchor. And seeing as your friends are so eager to have your back, they can join you."

They watched Lieutenant Killian stalk away.

Blake raised his hands, incredulous. "I didn't even say anything."

Chapter Two

"Let me explain to you what the Assahi Territory is. It is eight million kilometres squared of dense jungle mass. To put that into perspective, that's just about one tenth of Ishra's entire surface area. If you were to uproot the Assahi Territory and somehow manage to plant it on Landbreak, it would swallow Firstfall, the biggest island we've got, thirty times over. This disgustingly huge swathe of jungle has humidity levels that could suffocate a rock. It's got insects bigger than my boot. It's got local fauna fatter than a tank. I'm told that even some of the plants can kill a fully grown man. This lovely jungle is spread across terrain that makes the sea cliffs back home look tame. It's also the location that the Ishradi Separatists have chosen to make their home in. Lucky us. That means you'll be getting to know the Assahi Territory in intimate levels of detail in just over a week's time. Since none of you have ever seen a jungle, we thought it'd probably be a good idea to do as much basic acclimatisation as we can while aboard *The Moongate*. Now, before we begin, are there any questions?"

The squad were gathered in a corner of one of the ship's many assembly halls. None of them stirred.

"Right. Good. Now, we'll start with something simple—" Sergeant Broden stopped. A hand had gone up in the group. "What's that? A question?"

"Yes, sir," came a voice from between the bodies.

"Who is that? I can't see you," said Broden.

"It's me, sir," said the voice. A couple of the troopers stifled laughs.

"Oh, for crying out loud, just spit it out," growled Broden, craning his neck to see over the front row of heads.

"Will there be fish, sir?"

"What?"

"I think he asked if there will be fish, sir," said another trooper, also concealed in the crowd.

"I've got a couple of fucking fish in this squad is what I've got," said Broden.

"It's just we've got a lot of fish back home, sir," said the voice. The laughter was less easily smothered this time.

"Is that you, Private Leland? I thought I recognised that nasal voice. Up front please, private."

There was some pushing and shoving and Blake was expelled from the group to stand before Sergeant Broden. They were both short men, but Broden was twice as broad with arms thicker than Blake's thighs.

"Private Leland here thinks it's funny to make jokes during briefing. The very same briefing that's going to keep you all from getting killed out there. Who else finds that funny?"

There was silence from the squad.

"Tough crowd today, Private Leland," said Broden.

"Seems so, sir."

Broden smiled indulgently. "It *seems* like you're about to do push ups until you pass out, Private Leland. Isn't that right?"

"Point taken, sir, I'll be quiet now, sir," said Blake, and made to rejoin the squad.

Broden caught him by the shoulder. "You misunderstand, private. The point is, you're *going* to do push ups until your arms give out."

Blake groaned and got down on the deck.

"Now, are there any actual questions?" asked Broden, looking about the squad. The man had the look of a bulldog about him. "Perhaps anyone who is feeling lippy wants to save the squad some time and join Private Leland on the floor? Maybe they can show him how to do a proper push up while they're at it."

"Why are we doing it, sir?" asked another voice from within the crowd. James pushed to the front.

"Why are we doing what, Private Dalton?"

"Going to fight them, sir," said James. "The Ishradi Separatists. What makes them so bad that we have to cross space to kill them on behalf of the Ishradi Government?"

"It's in the name, Private Dalton," said Broden bluntly. "They're *separatists*. They're enemies of the Ishradi Government, and the Ishradi Government is our friend. That makes the Separatists our enemy."

"Yes, sir," said Dalton.

"Good, now, if there is nothing else—"

"It's just, why is it our problem, sir?" asked Dalton.

"Did you sign up to fight, private, or to ask questions?"

"To fight, sir. I'm just saying we've had civil wars of our own on Landbreak," pressed Dalton. "We haven't always been a united people, but we didn't have the help of the other moons to do it."

"That's because we didn't need their help," barked Broden, puffing out his chest. "We're Islanders. We're tough as stone. We're born on the seas, made in the storm. The Ishradi know that. That's why they want the 2nd Privateers to get on a damn starship and cross several hundred thousand kilometres of space to dig them out of a rut. No one better for the job!"

Several troopers in the squad agreed with cheers and hoots.

"Then, why are the Avernii coming too, sir?" asked Colt.

"I don't fucking know!" shouted Broden. "Maybe they want to see the sights. Last time any of them saw a tree was well over two hundred years ago, after all."

There was a thump. Everyone looked down at the deck.

"There goes Private Leland," said Broden. The squad burst into laughter. "Someone help him up for salt's sake."

Dalton and Colt moved up to lift the panting man off of the deck.

"And no more damn questions, either," said Broden. "Don't forget that the lot of you are from the new draft. You've had, what, nine weeks basic training? Some of you probably less than that. And now I've got a week to get you ready to fight a war in an environment you've never even seen before. So shut your mouths and open your eyes and ears and maybe I'll get half of you back to Landbreak at the end of this. Now form up!"

The squad scrambled about, pushing and shoving until they formed a line.

Broden sighed. "I've seen sea-snakes swim in straighter lines. Right, face! Double time, march!"

The squad turned ninety-degrees on their heels and began jogging the perimeter of the assembly hall. All the corridors and chambers of *The Moongate* had a newly finished look about them, plain metal walls and bolted deck-plates, utilitarian support struts and girders. Unlike some of the older and more renowned vessels in the defence fleet, there was no embellishment aboard this carrier. Dalton had once seen pictures from the interior of a defence fleet destroyer. They had layered the steel walls with lacquered panels of wood, and hung ornamental lanterns in the place of fluorescent light-strips. It had resembled the inside of a stately manor more than that of a warship.

Not so for *The Moongate*. She had been finished to a tight schedule and set loose from her berth the moment she was functional and ready to sail. Dalton remembered watching from one of the observatories as the carrier had passed between the arrayed destroyers of the defence fleet. They had assembled to see her off in parade ground fashion. *The Moongate* had dwarfed every one of the destroyers. She was the largest ship that the engineers of Landbreak had ever conceived of. Never before had the Islanders required a ship large and powerful enough to transport an army off-world, along with its support and armour elements.

"Put me in the jungle already," gasped Blake, stumbling along behind Dalton. "I'm ready! Anything to get me away from training."

"I'll remind you of that wish in a week's time, when we're up to our tits in jungle warfare," said Colt, up ahead.

"Hey, Colt, what do you reckon the sergeant isn't telling us?" asked Dalton.

"What do you mean?"

"I mean, he didn't exactly answer my questions," said Dalton.

"My bet is that he doesn't actually have any answers for you," said Colt, glancing over his shoulder and almost tripping over the heels of the trooper in front of him. "Broden is a career soldier. He's in this for the long haul. I don't think it matters to him why we're doing it. Probably easier if he doesn't know. Why the curiosity anyway?"

"You can't tell me you're not even a little curious?" asked Dalton.

"He's right," said Blake, breathing hard. "This is history in the making. No moon has ever interfered militarily with one of its neighbours. You've got to wonder about the precedent."

"Is that why you two signed on then, to play detective?" laughed Colt.

"I signed on to see Ishra," lied Dalton.

"This is history in the making," repeated Blake. "I want to be a part of that."

"What about you, Colt?" asked Dalton.

Colt shrugged. "Yeah, whatever, bit of both."

Dalton looked at the stout trooper's back. Colt Bridger was a classic Landbreak fisherman. Medium-height, stocky, thick-jawed and heavily tattooed with the motifs that were seemingly revered by the fishermen: the waves, the sails and the anchors, the fish, the more obscure patterns of the things that lurked beneath, the things that the fishermen spoke of only when they were really, really drunk.

Colt Bridger was anything but secretive though. Dalton had only known him for the duration of their training, but this was the first time that Colt had given an elusive answer to any question, personal or otherwise. For that reason alone, Dalton decided not to press the issue.

"Still, it'd be nice to know more, about these Separatists, about why they're fighting," said Dalton.

"Are you sure you want to know?" asked Colt.

"Why would I not?"

"Might make it harder to do your job, when the time comes," said Colt. "It's difficult to shoot a man you agree with, after all."

They lapsed into silence after that, but Dalton's mind was unquiet. He found himself thinking back to that day, almost three months ago, when the course of his life had changed forever.

* * *

James Dalton was two minutes ahead of the storm. The thunderheads were rolling in behind him, darkening the sky. The hard wind driving them in was howling through the woods to either side of the road, whipping the branches into a frenzy. Ahead of him, dipping down over the horizon, was the huge, banded sphere of Mitera. Its ember-orange and white bands were bright against the evening sky. Three of the gas giant's daughter moons hung beside her. One was no larger than a golf ball, half concealed by a crescent of shadow. The other two were smaller still, like pearls caught in Mitera's pull.

He rolled on the throttle, building speed, leaning low over his bike as it tore along the road. It had been his father's machine before it had been gifted to James. As a child he had loved to watch his father tending to it in the garage. The pungent smells of machine oil and petrol had become fond childhood associations to him. On occasion he had been allowed to ride on the back, though only when his mother's head had been turned. His father had told him that the bike was a relic of their ancestry, that it had been brought over on the migrant starship that had delivered the first settlers to Landbreak. A heritage curator had once offered a great deal of money for the bike to be preserved in a museum, but Dalton's father had just laughed, claiming that the best way to honour the bike was to ride it till it could be ridden no longer.

The road curved away from the woodlands, bringing him out along the coast. Beyond the tumbled rocks the dark waters foamed and thrashed. The big waves flopped in over the stony shores, sending the spray as far as the road, filling the air with the alkaline smell of salt.

Up ahead, the raised platform of Harrowton, his home town, came into view. Row upon row of five metre thick concrete columns rose up off the coast, supporting the broad platform upon which the town had been built. Landbreak was a moon of storms and shifting tides, wildly effected by the orbital cycles of its sister moons. The tidal range could change by as much as twenty metres along some coasts, and the storms could fling waves higher still. The first Islanders had learned their lessons early on. If a town had to be built on the coast, it had to be built high and sturdy, or Landbreak would drag it away into the depths.

As he sped towards the sloping access roads which led up to Harrowton, Dalton looked out across the water. On the sea's horizon, he could see the lights from a fleet of construction ships, glinting around the base of a colossal pillar, visible even at this distance. It was said that the raised coastal towns would not last forever, not against the constant erosion of the tides. It was said that every year the islands of Landbreak lost another inch off their shores, that one day the moon would be nothing but one immense ocean. It was said that in fifty years they would all be living on floating cities that rose and fell in harmony with the tides. At that moment, Dalton was looking at the foundations of one such city. Even looking at it, he couldn't bring himself to imagine what it would be like to live in a city built on the water, where the floor beneath your feet would never truly be solid.

Dalton looked back to the road as the access ramp joined up with the town platform. He passed by the warehouses and packing factories that reeked of unprocessed fish, the shipyards with their gangly cranes looming overhead and the steepled rooftops of the boathouses. The large workshops of the industrial sector gave way to the streets of commerce, where the shops and market stalls were finishing up their business for the day. James bled speed as the smooth access road was replaced by the cobbled streets of the inner town. As he was passing the Founding Square – the site where the first structure had been raised on the town platform – something turned his head.

That something, specifically, was a tank. A Seahound Class Amphibious Tank. It had been parked in front of the statue of the town's founder, Benjamin Harrow. History remembered Harrow as a pragmatic man, with his eyes always focussed on the road before his feet. The statue had been rendered to respect this in a very literal way, with the founder's eyes downcast. Now it seemed as though Harrow was looking down his nose at the tank, his brow furrowed in disdain.

James slowed to a halt. He wasn't looking at the statue. The tank was ferocity defined. Its angled hull and prow were painted in a dark grey, blue, and black camouflage pattern. Its turret mounted the twin prongs of a railgun weapon, and they had been angled skywards to heroic effect. Draped across the hull was a banner.

"Join the Army! Serve your Home! See the Galaxy!" it proclaimed in bold font.

The storm caught up with him. The rain crashed down over the town without preamble. It hammered on the slate-grey roof tiles and gurgled down the gutters. James throttled the engine and hurried on. Before he turned away from the square he spared a last backward glance at the tank.

He turned onto one of the residential lanes and two minutes later was pulling in to his drive, hefting up the garage door and wheeling the bike in out of the rain. He pulled off his helmet and soaked leather jacket and hung them up before heading in to the house.

The smells of oven-baked potatoes and fried fish filled his nose. They led him to the kitchen, where his mother was leaning against the counter, a book on philosophy in one hand and an oven-glove in the other. She looked up and smiled as he came in. James had inherited that winning smile, along with his mother's thick chestnut hair and green eyes, but his angled jaw, straight nose and brooding brow had all come from his father.

"Just caught you?" she asked, nodding at the rain clattering against the windows.

"Still got soaked," James said, pulling a folder from his backpack and putting it on the kitchen table.

"Your Pa will appreciate that," said his mother, checking on the glowing oven.

"I do indeed," said his father, coming in from the hallway. He stopped in his tracks and made a great show of sniffing the air. "Great salt! That smells something good, Ana."

He went over and gave her a kiss on the forehead, before turning to James. "Thanks son, now we can get an early start on the Whitfield account."

"Right," said James.

"Oh, but you take the rest of the day off," said his father, picking up the folder. "You deserve it for going all the way up to Ridgeton. I'll get started today and you can pick up with me in the morning."

"Yes, Pa," said James.

His father wandered out of the room, flicking through the folder's contents.

"Dinner's in five, John," his mother called after him, and then turned those knowing green eyes on her son. "James, sweetie, one of these days you're going to have to tell your father how much you hate accounting."

"He needs the help," he said.

"No, he doesn't," Ana said, "but you do need to find something for yourself before time gets away from you."

"Have you been into the market today?" he asked, changing the subject.

"Saw the tank did you?" she replied and turned away.

"Is that to do with all this Three Nations business?"

"Probably," she said, "seems a bit counter-intuitive doesn't it? Forming an alliance by starting a war."

"That's the only reason alliances are ever formed," said John, coming back into the kitchen. "Someone has a problem they can't deal with themselves, so they make friends to deal with their problems for them."

"Only slightly pessimistic," said Ana, laughing.

"Well, maybe," he said and started laying the table. "Anyway, this is all a ridiculous business. Raising troops to fight a war on another world that has nothing to do with Landbreak."

"Actually," said James, "I was thinking I might sign on."

His parents went completely still, completely silent. Then his father laughed, as though it was a joke, but when his son's face remained serious he faltered. "What?"

"James, this isn't what I meant when I said..." began his mother.

"When you said what?" asked John. "What ideas have you been putting in his head?"

"John!"

"It's nothing to do with that," said James, cutting across

them. "I just, I don't know, I want to join."

"That's exactly right," said his father, "you *don't* know. You saw a tank and you got excited. I used to be like that as a young man too, but you don't know what you're getting yourself into. This isn't some kind of game, James, this is—"

"I know it's not a game," snapped James, "and it's not about the tank. I'm twenty-four and I've never even been off of Firstfall! I want to see things, Pa."

"Then why didn't you ever say so?" asked John. "We can book a trip, we can tour the islands together, wherever you like. As soon as we finish up work for this quarter I can take some time off, maybe, I mean, probably. We can go somewhere, we can see… things."

"I don't want to…" began James, but stopped himself. "You don't understand."

"Then help us understand," said his mother, coming over and taking his hand.

He pulled away from her, harder than he meant to. She stepped back, shocked.

"I need to be alone," he said. "I've lived my whole life here, in this house. I've been to Firstfall City once and since then never further than Ridgeton. I feel like I don't know who I am. Like I don't know what I'm supposed to be doing."

"And you think that signing on with the army to kill foreigners on Ishra is how you discover that?" asked his father, voice raised.

"Maybe, I don't know," shouted James. "Do you? Do you know?"

"What's that supposed to mean?" asked John.

"This is all you've ever known, Pa," said James. "This life, this house, that stupid accounting job. Maybe that's fine for you, but it's not fine for me. I need something else, something more."

His father looked ready to throw a punch.

"Alright, alright," said Ana, stepping up, "everyone's clearly very emotional, so maybe we should all just calm down, eat dinner, and talk about this tomorrow."

"I'm not hungry," growled James, and pushed past his father out of the kitchen.

"James!" called his mother.

"Leave him, Ana, he's being a child," said John, and that was the last thing James heard his father say.

Later that evening when his mother had come up to his room, she had found the window open – the wind and the rain blowing in out of the night – and his wardrobe half empty.

Chapter Three

"This is a really bad idea," said Blake.

"Shut up, Blake. Act natural," hissed Dalton.

"Act natural? You realise that's a literal contradiction in terms, right?" said Blake between gritted teeth.

"We're just going to have a look, and then we'll leave," said Colt.

"While we're at it you can stop grinning, Colt. You're making us look suspicious," said Dalton.

"What? Was I grinning? Didn't realise," said Colt with a shrug.

"You're still doing it!"

"That's just my face!"

They went silent as a squad of mods came marching down the opposite end of the corridor.

"Just. Act. Natural," said Dalton out the side of his mouth.

The Avernii squad switched fluidly from two columns to one as they saw the Islanders approaching, keeping to the left side of the corridor to prevent obstruction. Not one of them was an inch below six foot three, each clad in a form-fitting, black body-glove. The emblem of either their nation or their military was embossed in silver over the left pectoral. It was an upright hand – as if held in the gesture of halt – and in the palm was the representation of a snake biting its own tail.

An officer of some variation was leading the squad, identifiable by the single, silver line running down the left side of its body-glove. As the mods passed the Islanders, the officer turned its head, regarding the three men with a blank expression. Then the squad was behind them, turning onto a side corridor and moving out of sight.

"He looked at us, he knows we're not supposed to be here," said Blake.

"No, he doesn't," said Dalton. "Islanders come to this side of the ship all the time."

"Yeah, officers, not privates."

"It's not like there's a rule enforcing segregation," said Dalton.

"No, but there is a rule concerning restricted ship access!"

"You worry too much," said Colt.

"He's right," said Dalton. "Besides, we're not in a restricted area of the ship."

"Not yet, at least," said Colt.

"We're going to be on latrines for life," wailed Blake.

"It creeps me out that none of them have any hair," said Colt suddenly.

"None of us have any hair," pointed out Dalton, running a hand over his recently shorn scalp.

"No I mean, no hair whatsoever. It's like they don't grow it. They don't have eyebrows, for salt's sake."

"Here," said Dalton, pointing to a hatch a little further up the corridor. It was labelled "Vehicle Bay 8 Observation". Dalton hit the access pad and the hatch slid open with a whine of servomotors. It led them onto a walkway that overlooked an expansive deck space. A curved pane of thick, transparent plastic isolated the observation walkway from the hangar itself, restricting access to the lower deck. The three men pressed their faces to the plastic, looking down into the hangar.

"Look at those," gasped Blake.

"Salty eel balls," exclaimed Colt, "those sure are something."

Arrayed across the bay's deck were row upon row of statues. Or at least, that's what they resembled. Twice the height of a tall man and five times as broad, they looked like an army of slumbering mechanical giants. Their segments and plates were curved and smooth, matte white and black. Each row of robots sported a different variation of arm-mount. Some had circular saws big enough to cut a man clean in two, paired with chunky flamethrowers. Others had rotary cannons and grasping mechanical claws. One row had rocket pods mounted atop the chassis, with what looked like enough firepower to level a building block in a single salvo.

"Who else is suddenly glad we're not fighting the mods?" asked Dalton.

Blake gave a small, nervous laugh, but Colt just snorted.

"I'd like to see them swim," he said. "You can't beat an Islander on the waves."

"You are correct in that our carapace-walkers have no submarine capabilities."

The three men spun round at the voice. There was a mod standing behind them, also staring down at the hangar deck. It turned its colourless eyes towards them.

"However, I am sure a suitable modification could be devised to enable that function."

"Is that a threat, mod?" asked Colt, stepping forwards, chest out.

"An observation," said the Avernii. "Mod. That is an interesting term you have conceived to refer to my people. I assume it is a contraction for the word: modified?"

"Hah, no," scoffed Colt.

"Actually, um, yeah, it is," said Blake in a small voice.

"Whatever," said Colt.

"I suppose then that it is apt," said the Avernii. "Perhaps in return we should call you nats."

"Did you just call me a gnat?" growled Colt, and turned to Dalton. "Did it just call me a gnat?"

"Nat. A contraction of the word natural."

"You're starting to piss me off, mod," said Colt.

The Avernii looked at Colt for five, long seconds. Then turned its unblinking gaze on Dalton. "Can I assist you? I do not think your superiors would be happy to find three junior-grade soldiers wandering the ship. Perhaps you are lost and require redirecting?"

"This is our ship, mod. We built it and we'll go where we want on it," said Colt.

"That is very impressive," said the Avernii. "I did not realise you personally helped construct this vessel."

"That's not really what he meant," said Blake gingerly.

"Shut up, Blake," Colt said.

"I see. You were using the pronoun 'we' to refer to your people at large."

"Are you simple or something?" asked Colt.

"It would appear that sarcasm is no longer used by the people of Landbreak."

"Find me a fire extinguisher, James. I want to give it a go too," said Colt, not taking his eyes off the Avernii.

"I think we'll be going now," said Dalton, putting a hand on Colt's shoulder.

"You are James Dalton, the Islander who knocked down Zirris?" asked the Avernii.

"Zirris? Who's Zirris?"

"Yesterday you used a fire extinguisher to great effect against an Avernii Transhuman. That was Zirris."

"Uh, yeah, I mean, maybe," said Dalton.

"That is very impressive."

"Was that sarcasm too?" asked Dalton, genuinely unsure. "Because, look, you might not think it was fair, but you mods have got all sorts of… modifications. I was just thinking on my feet."

"Technically, you were on your knees at the time," said Blake.

"Shut up, Blake."

"It was not sarcasm. You displayed resourcefulness in the face of hopeless adversity. That is something we admire very much," said the Avernii.

"Well, I wouldn't have called it hopeless adversity," said Dalton.

"I am Cutra. It is a pleasure to meet you, James Dalton."

"Well, thank you, I guess," said Dalton, entirely wrong-footed.

"Perhaps you would allow me to take you to Zirris?" asked Cutra. "I believe they are eager for a rematch."

"I'm not quite sure our superiors would approve of that," said Dalton, beginning to back away towards the hatch.

"Yes. I heard your commanding officer was displeased. That is strange. Our own officers encourage conflict as much as possible. It is the only way to remain strong."

"That's very clever," said Dalton, hitting the hatch release. "Well, it was very nice to meet you, um, Cutra. Bye for now!"

The three men turned into the corridor and began a brisk walk back towards their billet. Cutra stood in the open hatchway, watching as the three Islanders hurried away. Slowly, Cutra lifted a hand, as though unsure of the gesture.

"Goodbye. For now."

* * *

"I prefer them when they're silent," said Colt, "lippy bastards."

"What's that?" asked Blake, cocking his head.

"Yeah," said Dalton, glancing at the corridor behind, despite now being several junctions away from the portion of the ship given over to the Avernii detachment. "That was creepy."

"You're going to have to watch your back, James," said Colt. "They've got it out for you."

"Guys, what is that?" Blake asked again.

"You reckon it was a threat?" asked Dalton.

"Salt, yes! He as much as said it! His pal is looking for vengeance. His pal is looking for you!"

"Seriously, you two don't hear that?" pressed Blake.

"Hear what?" snapped Dalton.

They rounded another corner and came to an opening where the ship's access ways bled together to form a hub. The small space was clustered with bodies, Islander and Avernii alike. The close air was full of raised voices, coming exclusively from the Islanders. The Avernii present were silent, but tense, like loaded springs.

Dalton and Colt pushed through the crowd, Blake following in their wake. At the eye of the storm were two figures. An Avernii of no discernible rank and a sergeant of the 2nd Privateers. Dalton came up short as he saw the gun. It was a .44 Snapper, the distinctive, sleek, black revolver used by the officers of the Landbreak military. The sergeant had it level with the mod's eye.

"Say it again, you half human freak," growled the sergeant. James didn't know the man by name. His uniform identified him as an officer of the 14th Company, whereas Dalton was part of the 9th.

"You are weak," repeated the Avernii plainly. "In the time that it would take for your primitive brain to send a signal to your trigger finger, I could take that weapon from your hand."

"Do it," said the sergeant, inching the revolver closer. "Make my day, mod."

The Avernii didn't give anything away. It didn't precede with a witty one-liner, it didn't shrug, it didn't so much as blink. It moved like a piston. Its right hand came up with all the speed and precision of a darting sea-snake. It snatched the revolver clean out of its owner's hand.

The sergeant came back like a counter-weight. There was a blur of metal as he swung in. In his fist was the standard issue 2nd Privateer close-combat knife. Its seven inch blade had a black oxide finish, and its grip was worked into the form of brass knuckles. It was with the latter that the sergeant struck. The blow caught the mod across the cheekbone with an audible crunch and hurled it back into its silent comrades.

"Never trust a man that holds his pistol in the left hand," said the sergeant, smiling. "He's hiding something in the right."

"Unless he's genuinely left-handed," whispered Blake.

"Shut up, Blake," said Colt.

"Salt. You freaks don't even bleed right," the sergeant spat as the Avernii righted itself. Its pale skin had been split across the line of its cheekbone, and something like liquid mercury was welling from the cut. An angry murmur spread across the gathered Islanders, something more toxic than just the boisterous encouragement of a brawl. This was genuine disgust.

The Avernii regarded the revolver that was still clutched in its hand. With measured intent, it threw the weapon aside. The revolver clattered across the deck. The Avernii returned its gaze to the sergeant.

"Any second now someone's going to be along to break this up," said Dalton.

With long, slow strides, the Avernii started towards the sergeant.

"Yeah, any second now," said Colt.

"Now, look here," began the sergeant. The Avernii reached out and took a fistful of the sergeant's shirt.

"Bastard!" the sergeant cried, arching back his fist to deliver another brass-plated punch. The Avernii reached out its other hand and closed it over the knife. There was a crack. The blade, snapped from its grip, joined the revolver on the floor. Then the sergeant's boots were scraping at the deck as the Avernii lifted him up by the collar.

"Try again," said the Avernii, turning its face to clearly present the damaged cheek.

"You're sick," choked the sergeant, struggling to steady himself.

"Try again," repeated the Avernii.

The sergeant swung a lousy blow, but a blow backed by brass knuckles nonetheless. He caught the Avernii in the temple and opened up another wound. This time the Avernii didn't even flinch.

"You are weak," it said and whipped out with its free hand. The sergeant toppled backwards as if off of a cliff. His head cracked against the deck. There was blood coming out of his nose and his lips. His eyes were open, staring up at the ceiling.

"He killed him," shouted an Islander in the crowd. "The bastard killed him!"

The simmering anger and disgust boiled over into rage. The Islanders mobbed forwards into the Avernii. Dalton ducked out of the stampede, dragging Blake by the back of his collar. Colt had been swept up in the rush, or had dived in of his own accord—Dalton couldn't be sure.

"This is out of hand!" cried Dalton.

"He killed him," Blake was saying. "He punched him dead. I saw it. I saw it."

Dalton looked about frantically. His eyes fell on a fire extinguisher braced to the wall. He lunged forwards. Fumbling with the cover, James pulled the lever mounted on the wall beside the extinguisher.

Thunk.

The lights went red. The brawling mass of bodies froze. Several Islanders bolted up the corridor, eager to make an escape before the officers turned up. The retreat of these first few spurred on the others, and the crowd began to disperse. The Avernii remained for only a second longer before they too turned about and strode off in the opposite direction, back towards their assigned part of *The Moongate*. Several of the Islanders with more sense than fear tried to restrain the Avernii, but they were shrugged off and pushed down with ease.

"I know your face," screamed one of the 2nd Privateers. "You're done! You'll pay for this!"

The Avernii didn't look back.

Colt jogged over to Dalton, breathing hard. "We need to go, now."

"What? No. We have to stay," said Dalton, nodding to the sergeant's prone body.

"Dalton, you can't be here," said Colt, grabbing James by the shoulders.

"I'm not just leaving him lying here. It's not right."

"There are others, let them stay," urged Colt. "Use your head, James. You can't be present at the site of two fights. You'll be the first one to take the blame. A man is dead, James! A sergeant! We can't be here!"

"He's right," said Blake. For such a skinny man, he was sweating profusely.

"I'm not leaving," Dalton said. His eyes were locked on the sergeant's body. It was sprawled on its back, as if floating on a gentle current, eyes turned skyward, in peaceful repose. But those eyes were bloodshot and too wide, too still.

"I'm not leaving," said Dalton again, but Colt and Blake were already hauling him away. All the way down the corridor Dalton's eyes never left the body, and even when they rounded a corner to make for the billets, he could still see it in his head, lying there, arms spread wide, bloodshot eyes locked to the ceiling. Too wide. Too still.

CHAPTER FOUR

The Moongate went into lockdown half an hour after they had fled the scene. Shipwide announcements were blared from the wall-speakers, ordering all soldiers to return to their billets and remain there until further notice. Any soldier found disobeying these orders would be subject to immediate detention in the brig, followed by a court martial.

No one was in any doubt about the severity of the situation. The ship's security personnel had taken to the corridors in force. They patrolled with their stun batons out, or else stood guard outside the billet hatches.

Dalton had been itching to crawl under a shower when they had arrived back at the billet, as though hot water alone could scour the shock from him. It was at that moment that the announcements had started, and they had been confined to quarters. He had put his back to the wall and slid to the deck. He hadn't moved, not even when his back and haunches had begun to ache.

Blake was lying on his bunk, head buried in his pillow. Colt was pacing furiously. The other six soldiers in the squad were likewise spread about the small billet. Two men were playing a game of shells. Another was reading an infantryman's handbook. Apart from James, Colt and Blake, none of the others had been present at the fight. The six men were either deliberately ignoring the distress of their comrades, or else were blessedly ignorant. Sergeant Broden had been called away to a briefing, along with the rest of the regiment's officers.

"I don't know if this is a good idea anymore," mumbled Dalton.

Colt stopped his pacing. He glanced around the billet. None

of the others had looked up. He went over to Dalton and crouched on his haunches. When he spoke, his voice was low, dangerously so. "You're going to be very careful about you what say, James."

"Did we just witness the same thing, man?" asked Dalton, looking up at Colt.

Colt looked over his shoulder sharply. "Keep your voice down."

"A man died," hissed Dalton.

"No," said Colt, "a man was murdered. There's a fucking difference. One of *our* men."

"Salt's sake, Colt," said Dalton, his eyes wide. "I picked a fight with one of them, for a laugh, because I wanted to look good in front of the others. He could have killed me, just with a punch, just like happened to that sergeant."

"Don't worry. Next time we fight them we won't be doing it for laughs," said Colt.

"What are you talking about?"

"Something big is going to go down because of this," said Colt. That ridiculous cheek-to-cheek grin that Colt so often wore was nowhere to be seen. Now Colt's usual unruly happiness had been replaced with a barely contained fury. His brow was thunderous, so creased with frowning that it looked like it would never go smooth again. "Mark my words, James, our people in charge won't let those freaks get away with this. It's murder. The whole lot of them should be locked up and sent back to that dead world of theirs. Except for the one who did it. Bring back capital punishment for that one. Drowning would be too good a death for that bastard."

"Colt," said Dalton, pressing his fingertips into his temples and squeezing his eyes shut.

"Did you see the way that mod just held him up? He was toying with him. It was sick. They're sick. What they've done to their bodies, what they've become. It's all wrong. This ship is heading in the wrong damn direction if you ask me. Screw Ishra and its separatists; we should be taking this war to Avernus."

"Colt!"

"What's wrong with you?"

Dalton's vision was swimming. His guts churned like they were being turned on a skewer. "Just stop, please."

"Snap out of it, James. You can't go to pieces over this. You've got to stay with it. You've got to stay angry."

"This was a bad idea. This was a mistake," murmured James.

"What are you on about, man?"

"I'm not cut out for this," said James, rubbing his eyes. "I didn't think it through. I don't want to see people die. I didn't want to see it. I don't want to kill."

Colt grabbed him by the collar with both hands. "Get it together! We're in this now. This ship isn't turning back until we've been to Ishra and done the deed. There's no getting out of that, unless you want to sit it out in the brig till it's over and go home a coward."

"I... I..." he stuttered, unable to get his tongue around the words.

"You're not like this, you're not this person," said Colt, giving him a violent shake, banging the back of Dalton's head against the wall. "I'll tell you who you are. You're the man who leaves a cushy life back home to sign on with the Privateers and do something worthwhile with your life. You're the man who doesn't care about going where he's not supposed to. You're the man who picks a fight with a mod and wins."

"None of that's the same," said Dalton. "A man died, Colt. He died right in front of me. I watched it happen and I couldn't do a thing about it. I saw it coming and I didn't stop it."

Colt slapped him hard across the face. The man's hands were like sandpaper.

"Hey!" barked one of the soldiers playing shells, half

standing from his chair.

"Mind your own damn business," shouted Colt. The soldier sat back down. "You're going to deal with this. You hear me? You're going to deal with it because if you don't you're going to get yourself killed, but more than that, you're going to get me killed and I don't feel like dying on some foreigner's moon. Breathe, for salt's sake!"

Dalton forced himself to regulate his breathing, deep and slow, in through the nose, out through the mouth.

"That's right. That's good," said Colt. "Listen. When we're down there, in that stinking jungle, there are going to be people who want to kill us. Salt! There are people on this damn ship that want to kill us. One of them wants to kill you in particular. When that time comes, and it will come, everything gets really simple. All you have to do is kill them first — you get me?"

Dalton nodded.

"Say it! Say you're hearing it."

"I hear it. I'm hearing you."

"Good," said Colt, straightening Dalton's shirt and slapping him on the shoulder. "Now, it's very likely that whoever is investigating this is going to be asking around. Seeing as we've already been involved in one incident, it's more than likely that they'll be coming to us first. When they do, we're just going to play stupid. We were never there. We didn't see a thing. Right?"

"Right," said Dalton.

"Right. Can't go wrong."

* * *

As it turned out the entire incident had been recorded by one of the ship's security cameras. Lieutenant Killian himself came for Dalton, Colt and Blake and assembled them in one of the aquatic training rooms. Other lieutenants did the same for their respective platoons, rounding up every soldier that could be positively identified from the video. Not just that, but they also dragged along the associated squad of every soldier that had been present at the incident.

They were lined up along the edge of the pool. The water reflected strangely on the ceiling, and every little sound echoed with a hollow quality. The temperature in the chamber was low, enough to make them shiver. The water looked even colder.

"Let me teach you a lesson about being in the army," Killian snarled, prowling along the line of men. The other officers present seemed content to let him do the talking. "Everything you do falls on the shoulders of your brothers-in-arms. If you want to go wandering the corridors looking for fights like some gutter turd, then you had best invite along your whole squad, because whether or not you intended it, they're going to suffer the consequences as hard as you are. In case it's not sinking in, this is an analogy. When you're out there in the field, every stupid decision you make is going to cost not just you, but your comrades as well."

Lieutenant Killian paused in front of Dalton, an inch from his nose. "Can someone give me an example of a stupid decision? No? Well, how about this for size? Picking fights with the Avernii Transhumans to prove how much of a man you are."

He curled his lip and then moved on, the volume of his voice rising with every word, his face reddening with with every step. "If that wasn't bad enough, then getting your sergeant involved and subsequently getting your sergeant killed because of what a huge shit you are has got to win the prize for all time stupidity."

Killian stopped in front of a soldier. Dalton cast a sidelong glance down the line and recognised the trooper. He was one of the few who had tried to stop the Avernii from leaving the scene; he was the one who had promised them vengeance.

"That's right, Private Miller," said Killian. "I saw it all. The video was explicit. You provoked one of the Avernii, and when Sergeant Lee attempted to step in and pull your sorry self out of the fire, he was drawn into the fight that you started. That cost him his life. You cost him his life. Remember that until the day you die, you worthless bottom-feeder."

Private Miller was trembling. The hard fluorescent light reflected in the tears that were welling in his eyes. He couldn't have been a day older than twenty-one.

"Retrieve your weapons!" commanded Killian.

The line of men crossed to the tables at the far wall and picked up their rifles.

"Into the pool, now! Up to your chests! Move it!"

They waded in. The water was freezing. It seeped in to their boots and soaked through their fatigues. The shock of it was painful.

"Hold those guns high!" bellowed Killian. "Form up! The first man to lower his weapon sleeps in the pool tonight! You think I'm bluffing? Try me!"

"I can't feel my toes," hissed Blake.

"Shut up, Blake," said Colt.

"Stop telling me to shut up."

"No, seriously, shut up. Before Killian hears."

Blake shut up.

Killian hadn't stopped his lecture, but Dalton could barely hear the man anymore. It was as though someone had spent all night melting ice in the pool. His abdomen was contracting against the cold so much it felt as though his muscles were tearing. He couldn't stop himself from shivering. Barely five minutes had passed and already his arms were burning from the weight of the rifle he was holding above his head.

He realised he didn't care.

"I deserve this," he said under his breath. "I deserve this."

* * *

The investigation lasted another three days, as did the punishments. They ran circuits of the entire accessible length of *The Moongate*, weighed down with packs weighing in at one hundred pounds. Their exercise regimes were doubled in intensity. Blake was not the only soldier to pass out from the exertion. When they were not being pushed to the very limits of their physical capabilities, they were tasked with cleaning every corridor of the ship. On the third day of the punishment Killian had ordered them to paint three hundred metres of corridor wall space on the starboard side of the carrier. He had then ordered them to go back and strip the paint, after they had been forced to watch it dry.

"We'll be dead before we reach Ishra," Dalton had said through gritted teeth, his arms burning from push-ups.

"I don't think he cares," Colt had replied and nodded in the direction of Lieutenant Killian, who had stood vigilant over every second of their suffering. Other officers had been present intermittently, lieutenants and sergeants overseeing their indicted platoons and squads, as well as the stony-faced captain of the 14th Company, to which the murdered sergeant had belonged. Of them all though, Killian had been the most present, not to mention the most vocal.

"I think he enjoys it."

On the fourth day after the death of Sergeant Lee, they had been allowed to rest. Despite the bone-aching exhaustion, it was not enough to keep Colt down when he learned of the investigation's verdict.

He came through the billet hatch and flung his water canteen across the room. It hit the table, shattered a drinking glass and scattered a game of shells across the deck. The three soldiers sitting there jumped to their feet, yelling.

"What's your problem, Bridger?" shouted one of them. Moore was his name. The other two, Harris and Thompson, were silent, but their scowls spoke for them.

"Get out of my face," snarled Colt.

"You get out of my face," said Moore, not backing down. "We've just been through the grinder for your crap and I haven't heard so much as an apology out of you, and you think you can just come in here and pull this shit?"

"Don't mess with me right now," said Colt, his eyes alight with the threat of violence.

"You selfish bastard," said Moore. "It's all about you, is it?"

"We didn't even do anything," snapped Colt. "We were just in the wrong place at the wrong time."

"Just strolling by were you? Didn't join in the fun at all?" sneered Moore.

"I swear by the salt, Moore, I'm going to break your teeth if you don't shut up and sit down."

"Come on then, you fish-herder!" Moore shouted, pushing a chair out of his way.

"Stop it, both of you," said Dalton, getting between the two bristling men. "What does this prove? What do either of you gain? You want Sergeant Broden to come in here and find us scrapping, after everything we've just been through?"

Moore snorted, but turned away. Dalton nodded at the door, and Colt joined him in the corridor.

"What's going on?" asked Dalton.

"They don't care, James," said Colt. "They don't give a shit."

"Who doesn't care?"

"Any of them," Colt said, gesturing helplessly as if to encompass the ship at large. "High Command, the colonel, no one."

"Can we perhaps be a little more specific here, Colt?"

Colt curled his lip. He was moving from foot to foot like a pugilist wired for a fight. His fists clenched and unclenched. "I've just been talking to Broden. He says the investigation is over. He says they're 'compartmentalising the blame'. You know what that means? It's a nice way of saying that the

Avernii are getting away with it. We're letting them deal with their own people. It's fucking criminal, James. You think they're going to punish one of their own? You heard what that mod at the vehicle bay said—their officers encourage conflict. They're probably throwing the bastard a party as we speak."

"Salt's sake," said Dalton, sighing.

"It's political," said Blake. The wiry man had come up to the hatch and had been listening in on their conversation. "They don't want a political fiasco before we've even arrived at Ishra. It wouldn't set a good precedent for the new 'Three Nations' coalition. They'll smooth over this as best they can to keep everything looking good."

"It's criminal," repeated Colt.

"Well, that's politics for you," said Blake.

"Something's got to be done," said Colt. "Someone's got to do something. This isn't right. This isn't justice. I thought being an Islander meant more than this. By doing this we're showing the Avernii that we're weak. We're showing them that we'll throw our own overboard if it means keeping the peace. If High Command won't act, someone has to."

"Colt, you sound like a man on the verge of doing something very stupid," said Dalton.

"Someone has to do something, James," said Colt, shaking his head. "Someone has to act."

Chapter Five

The Moongate's final approach to Ishra was a slow one. Its primary ion drives, burning blue in the void, had accelerated it from the dockyards of Landbreak to the berths of Avernus' orbital station. From there it fell inwards towards the heart of the system, following its meticulously plotted course to bring it onto the path of Ishra's orbit. Inter-planetary travel was a delicate dance made along interlocking circles, where no variable was ever still, and every movement, every thrust and burst of speed had to be made within the parameters of precise calculation. The carrier's secondary drives, mounted to the prow and flanks of the ship, did the bulk of the work now, gently decelerating *The Moongate* so that it would meet Ishra at the time and place of the navigator's choosing.

The slow approach would have also allowed time for another matter: Acclimatisation. *The Moongate's* artificial gravity was slowly adjusted to match that of Ishra, and the air temperature was gradually increased. But equally important as the physical adjustments was the psychological acclimatisation. The military psychologists had warned about the difficulties in integration that the Islanders and Avernii would face. A joint force that couldn't put its differences aside to fight a common enemy was not a joint force at all. The past week had proven that in abundance, but, ultimately, in vain. Following the investigation's conclusion it was strongly *advised* that the Avernii stay to their assigned portion of the ship, and that the 2nd Privateers do the same. The ship's security personnel had formed a cordon of patrols and checkpoints to ensure that this advice was followed.

As such, the distant orb that was the moon of Ishra became

a slowly but steadily looming prospect to the segregated passengers aboard the carrier. Every hour of journey saw Ishra's circumference grow, inch by inch, in the viewing ports of *The Moongate*. It was a remarkably vibrant orb, with great stretches of jade and turquoise colour. It had come to be referred to by the Islanders as the Miteran Jewel, the most beautiful of all of Mitera's daughter-moons.

"Do you know the Trickster?" Colt asked. The three men had left the tense silence of their billet and made their way to one of the dorsal observation domes.

"Is it a type of fish, by any chance?" Dalton ventured, much to Blake's amusement.

"It is," said Colt, nodding, "and do you know how it catches its prey?"

"By trickery?" asked Blake facetiously.

"By trickery, yes," confirmed Colt. "Its face is covered in patterns that can glow in different colours. The Trickster can actually control this. It puts on a light show for the other fish. It's a deep-sea dweller so not many people have seen it in person, but I've been pretty far down on occasion. You should see it. It's really something. It swims up to its prey, real slow, weaving its colourful face back and forth, and these other fish, they don't swim away because they're entranced, right? Then, when it's right up close, its whole face just peels away. Comes apart in four leaves, and underneath there's just teeth."

"That's horrific, Colt," said Blake. "Why would you tell me about that? I'll never get in the water again."

Colt nodded at distant Ishra. "It might look beautiful, but the only thing waiting for us when we get there is death."

"Salty eel balls, Colt, I preferred it when you couldn't get the grin off your face," said Dalton.

"You were right, James, before," said Colt. "You were right to ask why this is our fight. It's clear to me now that this isn't for the Islanders. High Command is willing to overlook murder for this, so I want to know why. What's in it for us? What's down there that's worth Islander blood?"

"Guess we'll find out," said Dalton, "because you were right too, mistake or not, there's no going back now."

* * *

A standard day cycle later, from across the ship's speakers, an announcement called the 2nd Privateers en masse to assembly. They gathered in the prow hangar bay, the only space aboard the carrier capable of accommodating all two thousand Privateers at once.

The atmosphere amongst the soldiers was muted. Every one of them had heard of Sergeant Lee's death, the punishing of those involved and the subsequent decision of the inquest. News travelled fast in the close quarters of *The Moongate*. There was no doubt in anyone's mind as to purpose of this gathering.

Squad by squad, the strength of the 2nd Privateers filed into the hangar. The loading equipment had been shoved to the far corners of the deck and the fleet of drop-ships and fighter jets that normally occupied the space had been redirected to one of the other two hangars, or else ordered to fly alongside the carrier for the duration of the assembly. In front of the sealed blast-doors, a dais had been erected. Embossed in brass on its face was the badge of the 2nd Privateers; the rendition of an anchor, layered over crossed cannon barrels. The number '2' was inscribed on the anchor's head. To either side of the dais a pair of banners hung limp in the still atmosphere of the hangar bay. They were marked with the same badge, against a background of navy blue and black, threaded with gold borders.

They had gathered like this once before, on the embarkation fields before a fleet of waiting drop-ships that had ferried them skyward to *The Moongate*. Despite the tension, the feeling of such a gathering was no less fortifying than it had been almost two weeks ago. To stand in the presence of so many of one's compatriots, to know that every man present had committed himself to the same purpose, it was beyond inspiring. After the tribulations of the past week, just the sight of the assembly restored a measure of Dalton's vigour.

James Dalton, Colt Bridger, Blake Leland and the six others comprising 4th Platoon's 2nd Squad followed Sergeant Broden into the hangar. They linked up with the rest of 9th Company, who in turn joined the five hundred-strong bulk of 2nd Battalion. The regiment was built on the strength of four such battalions. Much of this force had been newly recruited and trained from the civilian population of Landbreak just three months ago. A smaller corps of career soldiers formed the officer cadre and comprised several self-proclaimed "hard-line" squads in the 1st Battalion.

"Fall in," growled Lieutenant Killian, ushering his platoon into formation with a series of angry gesticulations. Given the relatively short training period granted to the majority of the regiment, the 2nd Privateers were not particularly versed in the precise mechanics of parade ground manoeuvres. To the great frustration of the officers, it took almost a full half hour for the two thousand men to be herded into orderly blocks, battalion by battalion, company by company, and so on and so forth.

When at last it was done, the regiment stood in weighted silence. Dalton realised in that moment just how humbling the experience was. To any observer, he was just one face amongst many, just another body in navy blue fatigues. He wasn't an individual here, not really. He was a part of something larger, in the same way that a gun is made up of many smaller pieces that, when combined, serve a greater function.

A man strode up to the dais to look across the arrayed strength of the regiment. He looked larger than life up there, Dalton thought, taller and broader than any man ought to be. He wore a navy blue, heel-length greatcoat with gilded buttons and epaulettes. His face was partially cast in shadow by the bicorn atop his head. Of course, every soldier present knew who this was. He was the highest authority in the 2nd Privateers, he was Colonel Lawrence Hunt, commander of the Landbreak military expedition to Ishra.

"Atten-tion!" barked an officer of the 1st Battalion, and the sound of two-thousand soldiers coming to attention was like a thunderclap in the echoing space of the hangar bay.

"Men of Landbreak, fellow Islanders," began Colonel Hunt. His voice was so powerful and so resonant that it filled the cavernous chamber entirely. He commanded that volume so consummately that it took Dalton a moment to realise that there must have been a microphone concealed at the colonel's collar. "In less than twenty-four hours we will anchor in high orbit of Ishra. I thought it fitting that we share words before deployment. There will be other assemblies, no doubt, once we arrive. The High Shekahn of Ishra has expressed his desire to welcome you in person, and it will be a great honour to be so received. However, this is the last time – until we conclude our operation on Ishra – that we will gather in private, as Islanders only, and speak in confidence.

"Let us be honest with one another then. We do not know these people, these Ishradi. Indeed, we do not truly know the Avernii who even now share with us this vessel. They are as foreign to us as I am sure we are to them. I am not ignorant to the disturbances that this has caused over the last few days, but I will not speak of that directly. That matter, in my mind, has already been resolved."

Dalton could practically feel Colt bristling beside him at those words.

"For the longest time our nation has lived in relative isolation from its neighbours. Long enough, maybe, to have forgotten that our ancestors all came here together, in search of new homes far from the dying Solar System. As history tells it, the migrant fleet decided to settle across three moons rather than all just cohabit one, in the same way that the fisherman has many nets, and spreads them far and wide, so that if one net fails to provide, his venture will not have been a total loss.

"In the days that followed that difficult decision, our ancestors would no doubt have looked up into the night sky and wondered how their fellows were coping. Those first decades were hard, though, and we Islanders fought tooth and nail to make a home amongst the rocky isles of Landbreak. Those trials took all of our strength and all of our focus to overcome. So much so, that it was not until a mere thirty years ago that we first began establishing transmission contact with our far-flung neighbours, who by then had grown into distinct nations of their own, as had we.

"Now, we find that our lives are changing. We turned our focus inwards to survive the challenges of Landbreak, and we proved worthy of our world. We have succeeded in forging a nation that will endure the test of time. But now we must turn our gaze outwards, and realise that we are not alone, whether we should desire it or not. We have a duty to establish Landbreak as a power to be recognised amongst the Miteran Moons, if for nothing else other than the protection of our nation.

"In pursuit of that ideal, our leaders have agreed upon an alliance with the governments of Avernus and of Ishra, upon the creation of a coalition which will be called 'The Three Nations'. Not only will this alliance strengthen Landbreak, but it will provide peace and security between the nations for generations to come. As you know though, all steel is forged in fire. We will have to fight if we wish to realise our ambitions."

The colonel's demeanour was changing now. His delivery was shifting from that of the storyteller to that of the firebrand. His gestures became sharper, the volume of his voice louder and its tone fiercer.

"A great many of you are men of the sea, as is our calling as Islanders. You will understand me then when I say that in order for a ship to be strong, the sum of its parts must each be strong in themselves. Ishra is not strong. Its leaders have called out to us, beseeching us for strength. Their world is plagued by civil war, one that has lasted for many years and crippled the progress of its people. Troublemakers, brigands and traitors; that is who we will be fighting. Those who have no love for order, those who desire only anarchy. If those people are allowed to claim Ishra, it will affect us all. It will not do to have unruly neighbours, not if we want this alliance to work, not if we want it to be strong."

Dalton was suddenly aware of how the atmosphere in the hangar had changed. That muted trepidation had transformed into something else entirely. The air had become electrified with a pent up excitement. Although they stood stock-still at attention, Dalton knew that every man around him shared that charged feeling of anticipation, of eagerness and of pride.

"And so we come to it," said Colonel Hunt, looking across the gathered ranks. "As the first step towards building a sturdy future with our neighbours, we have done the unprecedented. We have made history. We, first amongst the three nations of Mitera, have reached across the gulf of space to provide relief for Ishra and for its people. Let this gesture of kindness and good faith be the foundation upon which 'The Three Nations' is built. Let the Islanders be known as the rock that all turn to for safe harbour against the storm. Let us dispense with foolishness and with squabbling, and be the men we were born to be. Who are we?"

Dalton found himself unable to hold back. He cried out, and realised he had not done so alone.

"Islanders!" came the cry, voiced by two thousand throats with such vigour that he thought he could feel the deck itself tremble beneath his boots.

"Who are we?" bellowed Colonel Hunt again.

"Islanders!" came the response, this time even louder.

"Who are we?"

"Islanders! Islanders!"

* * *

A klaxon sounded. Its wailing filled *The Moongate's* every corridor and chamber.

"That's it," said Dalton, looking up at the restroom's wall-speaker.

"That's it then," said Blake and involuntarily gulped.

Colt triumphantly threw down the mop. Since the speech his grin had returned with a vengeance, and his burning grudge had seemingly dissipated. Even when Lieutenant Killian had gleefully reminded them of their latrine duties, none of the fire in Colt's eyes had dimmed. "Alright then, boys. Time for the real dirty work."

"You can't honestly be excited for this," said Blake.

"This is the first time I've been off of Landbreak," he replied thoughtfully. "You know, it's strange, there's so much of home I haven't seen. Visited a lot of fishing ports, but so many of the famous isles and landmarks, I've never seen them. You know, I've never been to the Site of the First Footfall?"

Dalton shrugged. "It's just an old footprint."

"It's the spot where the first settler, our great ancestor from Old Earth, stepped foot on Landbreak for the very first time. It's not just *an old footprint*," said Blake, aghast.

Colt ignored them both. "And now I'm going to visit an entirely different moon, where an entirely different people live."

"Yup, and we're probably going to have to kill a lot of them, too," said Dalton.

"Yeah, but just the bad ones, right?"

"That's what they say," nodded Dalton.

"We should go," said Blake. Dalton thought there was less colour in the man's face than there had been a moment ago. "We don't want to be late for muster."

"That's the spirit," said Colt, slapping Blake on the shoulder. "It wouldn't do to go and miss the war now, am I right?"

Chapter Six

The Moongate sailed into high orbit of Ishra. Four Ishradi corvettes came out to greet her. The Islander vessel had been designed primarily as a carrier and as such it was a monstrous construction. At three hundred metres wide and nine hundred metres long, she was presumed to be the largest operational starship possessed by any of the three moon-nations.

Only the ancient migrant ships that had ferried the first settlers to Mitera had been larger. They had been gargantuan vessels, designed to support a population of tens of thousands across hundreds of years of space travel. More than that, though, they had possessed a secondary function. Those leviathan starships had doubled as comprehensive starter packs for the settlers. Upon reaching their chosen destinations, each migrant ship had begun an automated disassembly process. Transport modules had detached from the hull, ferrying the passengers to the surface. Once the migrant ship had been evacuated of all life, it had begun to unravel in full, breaking apart into an array of different facilities. Modules stacked with preserved foodstuffs, modules loaded with survival gear and supplies, modules that functioned as greenhouses and medical bays, modules for temporary habitation, modules that unloaded into vehicles, modules that deployed as water purification plants and mining rigs, other modules still that remained in orbit to serve as satellites and ground-to-orbit communication relays. Almost every conceivable necessity had been prepared for. As such, the migrant ships that had brought human life to the Miteran Moons no longer existed as they once had.

The ships that had been constructed afterwards had been

isolated endeavours that had occurred, in Landbreak's case, over a hundred years after the settlers had first descended to the moon. It was from these space programs that the Orbital Defence Fleet and *The Moongate* had been born.

Like the migrant ships, *The Moongate* had been formed to purpose. Slab-sided and blue-grey, like some deep-ocean cetacean, the greater portion of her structure was devoted to the transportation and subsequent deployment of a large military force. She had four primary launch bays. The largest, like a vast rectangular maw, defined the bow of the ship and was capable of disgorging hundreds of drop-ships in a matter of minutes. A second was situated on the broad dorsal side of the ship, where shuttles would soar across hundreds of metres of *The Moongate's* gradually sloping topside, over command centres and observation domes, before clearing the ship's length. The final two primary launch bays were actually one and the same, running the width of the carrier amidships and providing access to both the starboard and port flanks. It was in this hangar that the ship's main complement of fighters was berthed. These sleek, dart-shaped craft were ready to respond at a moment's notice should the carrier come under threat.

They were not *The Moongate's* only defence. Despite being a carrier she sailed alone, without escort, and therefore had armaments of her own. Two forward facing torpedo tubes were situated to either side of the bow launch bay, as well as a battery of rapid firing pin-point defensive turrets, to persuade against unauthorised access to the front hangar. On both the starboard and port-side of the carrier two drum-shaped turrets – sporting dual-barrelled cannons loaded with high-calibre munitions – had been installed for the protection of the ship's flanks. A scattering of rotary cannons and missile pods dotted the carrier's dorsal and underbelly, placed to fend off potential enemy fighters.

The pride piece of *The Moongate*, however, was mounted

a hundred metres aft-wards of the bow. Supported on a command deck dedicated solely to the servicing, control, and recoil management of the huge weapon, the heavy railgun was a fifty-metre instrument capable of a one hundred and eighty degree forward firing arc. These railguns were the pinnacle of Islander weaponry. Their two-pronged rails were capable of electromagnetically launching ordnance in excess of four thousand metres per second. To put this into perspective, the infantry rifles of the 2nd Privateers had a muzzle speed of nine hundred and fifty metres per second, not even a fourth of the velocity achievable by the railgun. That fast even with all the friction and drag presented by a breathable atmosphere. In space, in the hard vacuum where all those hampering forces were no longer present, the railgun's launched projectile would travel even faster. At such tremendous speeds, the ammunition fired by the railguns needed neither propellants nor explosives to be catastrophically destructive.

The four corvettes paled, therefore, in the face of *The Moongate*. A relatively meagre two hundred metres in length, the Ishradi corvette design mostly consisted of a long, tapered hull, along the top and bottom of which was mounted a total of twenty twin-barrelled cannon pods. The bridge and multi-directional thrusters were situated to the aft, and protected by a further four weapon blisters. They were attack craft, designed to strike quickly, hounding their larger foes with torrents of weapons fire before pulling back, only to strike again when their slower-moving target had forgotten them.

There was no hostile intent here, however. The corvettes were representatives of the officially recognised Ishradi government, and had come out to escort *The Moongate* to safe harbour. When the ships met, it was a historic moment. For the first time since settling their respective moons, the Islanders and the Ishradi would share real-time transmissions across a few hundred metres, as opposed to the delayed transmissions that they had initially broadcast to one another, taking place across hundreds of thousands of kilometres.

The ochre-painted corvettes took up position around *The Moongate*, and together they coasted into Ishra's orbit.

* * *

"Remember how much I hated flying up to the ship?" said Colt, teeth clenched.

Dalton didn't even try to respond. It felt as though every fibre of his body was being shaken loose, and he was afraid that if he tried to speak he would shatter every tooth in his mouth.

"Remember how they said flying down would be better?" continued Colt, his voice raised against the roar of blazing thrusters. "They lied."

To his left, strapped into one of the support harnesses like the other sixty Islanders aboard the drop-ship, Blake had developed a subtle green hue to his skin.

"Surely it's not meant to be this... turbulent," shouted Moore.

"Probably not," replied the trooper's friend, Harris. "Islanders can sail, but they sure as shit can't fly."

Dalton shared a grudging laugh with the two men. It occurred to him that he didn't really know the other troopers in his squad like he knew Blake and Colt. Together, the nine of them were a unit under Sergeant Broden. They had all been new recruits and had trained together, eaten together and slept together in the same cramped bunkhouses since the start, but cliques had nonetheless formed in their midst and separated them. Moore, Harris and Thompson were one such circle. Wright, Scott and Nelson were the other.

He wondered whether it was worth trying to get to know them now. He wondered whether it was too late. Right now they were nothing but names to him. Yet here they all were, plummeting to the surface of an alien moon together, looking for a fight that none of them really had a stake in. There was something about that which inspired a measure of unity.

The drop-ship's shuddering eased.

"Are we there yet?" asked Blake. Dalton really didn't want to think about what would happen if the man vomited in the confines of the drop-ship.

"Shut it, Blake," said Colt. "No, seriously, keep it closed, your mouth. If you're sick on me, I can't promise you'll make it to the ground."

"That's a tempting offer," replied Blake.

"Stow it," said Sergeant Broden, one hand pressed to his headset as he received a message from the pilot. "Brace for landing!"

The tone of the engines shifted and the troopers rocked in their harnesses as the deck bounced beneath their boots.

"Out! Now! Double time it!" came the bellowing of Lieutenant Killian. "This flying death-trap has other runs to make, so let's move!"

The embarkation ramp was lowering even as their bulky harness frames disengaged. Troopers staggered free of their cradles, dizzily gathering up their gear. Dalton unclipped his L7 assault rifle from its niche beside the cradle, and hauled his backpack out of the stowage netting. He felt weighed down enough as it was in his combat armour, and the added weight of the pack and rifle almost made him lose his footing.

"Easy there," said a voice, and a hand caught his shoulder to steady him.

"Thanks, Colt," said Dalton, but realised that Colt was already at the ramp. It was Scott who had caught him. "Sorry, Scott. Ride down's got me all turned around."

Scott laughed. The man had a good smile, big and genuine. It was the sort of smile that came with an extra helping of charisma. They moved on, heading for the exit. Along the way Dalton leaned over and helped a struggling Blake to disengage his rifle from its niche. He felt a pang of sympathy as he saw Blake's face. The man looked shaken to his core, as though he could break into tears at any moment.

"Come on, Blake, it looks nice out there," Dalton said, gripping his friend's shoulder and nodding at the warm light that was flooding in through the open hatchway.

Driven on by the berating of the officers, the troopers jogged down the ship's ramp. Coming out of the air-conditioned ship into Ishra's atmosphere was like a wet slap in the face. Dalton stumbled down the ramp, blasted by the sudden heat and humidity, wincing against the brightness of the day. His body felt leaden. There was an unfamiliar weight on his shoulders, and an ungainly gait to his step that he couldn't seem to shake. His feet were striking the metal ramp with greater force than he intended, as though his legs were being sucked towards the ground. He swallowed hot bile as nausea stirred in his gut. The clatter of boots was a storm of noise. Bodies jostled around him, knocking against his shoulders. He was gulping down on air that felt too thick, struggling to get his bearing and keep his footing at the same time.

They were coming down on to a broad, flat expanse of short, yellow grass. The sky was full of Herdsman Class drop-ships. They had straight, broad wings that terminated in VTOL thrusters, allowing the transport craft to come straight down onto the landing fields without the need for runways. Cumbersome and slow in the hot air, their matte grey hulls cast fat shadows across the ground as they hovered over the expanse, coordinating their landings and take-offs with laborious thoroughness. Their own drop-ship was already lifting off behind them, its embarkation ramp still closing. Jets of distorted air blasted from its wing-mounted thrusters, flattening the grass underneath and buffeting the nearest soldiers. Once it had attained sufficient altitude, the main thrusters hugging either side of its bulky fuselage roared to life and punched the drop-ship up and away into the sky.

The ground was swarming with Privateers. They were deploying en masse, all two thousand of them, the drop-ships disgorging the Islanders in lots of sixty and returning to orbit to repeat the process. Many of the drop-ships had tanks and lighter vehicles securely clasped beneath their hulls with claws and harnesses. There were other planes in the air as well. Squadrons of Hurricane Class fighters circled the deployment zone, providing security for the transports. Further afield, Dalton could also make out the Avernii landing craft, their smooth white hulls glaring in the light of Patera, the local star.

He spotted Colt amongst the many bodies and pushed through towards him, one hand keeping his rifle tucked close to his chest, the other locked around the strap of Blake's pack, dragging the man after him.

"I feel like I'm drowning on the air," said Colt. "It's so thick."

"And hot," said Dalton. He was already sweating under his fatigues and combat armour.

"Don't just wander off, you bottom-feeders!" Sergeant Broden was shouting after them, rallying the squad back together. "Stay with me! Follow me!"

The stout sergeant led them through the crowds, and as they walked Dalton began to see a semblance of order arising from the immensity of the landing operation. The squads coming off of the drop-ships were being rallied and led away to make room for more inbound craft.

Along with dozens of others they trekked through the field, the shadows of landing craft passing overhead and washing them with downdraughts of hot air. They left the main area being used for the deployment and started to ascend the gentle incline of the field as it climbed towards a ridge. Halfway up, Dalton looked over his shoulder. Hundreds of troopers were streaming up from the landing field and following them. More still were disembarking from drop-ships.

Far off to his left the Avernii Transhuman Forces were cresting the hill as well. The two regiments were distinct. The 2nd Privateers were in their navy blue fatigues and black combat armour, lugging bulky backpacks and weapons. The Avernii had come clad in fully enclosed suits of segmented armour. Whereas the protection worn by the Privateers consisted of separate pieces – helmet, chest and back plate, shoulder and shin guards – the Avernii possessed an all-encompassing armour system. The glossy black and white plates were layered to facilitate mobility without compromising integrity, and from the glowing blue visors of their helmets it seemed they included some form of integrated power source as well.

"They get all the best toys," mumbled Dalton, feeling meagre and ridiculous in his own gear.

"They've got more to compensate for," replied Colt, sparing a disdainful glance towards the Avernii.

"What, like being physically superior to any man in the 2nd?" asked Blake, making no effort to hide the sarcasm. His colour seemed to be returning, as did some of his composure, though he was now shiny with sweat and flushed from exertion.

"No, like being unnatural freaks," said Colt bluntly.

When they reached the top of the ridge, the line came to a halt. The lay of the land rolled away before them, down across kilometres of uninterrupted, star-bathed grasslands. The grass was short and had the colour of hay. In the middle distance the open fields met the outskirts of a sprawling city of squat, sand-coloured buildings with domed rooftops. A glittering river bisected the city, snaking through from the east and heading out into the west.

"What's that, Sarge?" asked Blake, pointing across the fields.

Sergeant Broden looked up from the thin screen of his data

tablet. "That is Ushura, Private Leland."

"What's there?" pressed Blake.

"Someone very important who wants to say hello to us," said Broden, absent-minded as he returned to the information on his data tablet.

"The High Shekahn?" asked Dalton.

"That's right, Private Dalton," came the voice of Lieutenant Killian as he joined them on the ridge. "Before you ask, because I know one of you will, the High Shekahn is Ishra's equivalent of a president. In other words, he is the most important and powerful man on this planet. I trust none of you are going to pick a fight with him?"

"Why would we do something silly like that, lieutenant?" asked Colt.

"Salt, whatever was I thinking, asking such a question. It's not like the three of you have ever done anything stupid like that in, oh, say, the past week." The lieutenant turned to Broden. "Start moving them up, sergeant."

"You heard the man, move!" barked Broden. The squad started moving down the other side of the ridge, along with the rest of the 2nd Privateers and the Avernii.

"I never picked a fight with anyone," grumbled Blake when the lieutenant had stalked away.

"Good thing you hang out with us then, right?" said Colt. "Otherwise people might think you were a squid-limbed wimp."

Blake ignored him and turned back to Broden. "This city, Ushura, it's the capital?"

"What? No. It's just the closest major city to the Assahi Jungle Territory. The Ishradi have been launching their own counter-offensive against the Separatists out of here, but the front-line is actually a few dozen kilometres to the east."

"Are we going to end up walking there as well?" asked Blake.

"Shut up, Private Leland," said Broden. Dalton and Colt

sniggered.

It was just over five kilometres to Ushura, and took the two regiments less than forty minutes to cross the distance on foot. The vehicles and other armoured support units were still being deployed to the landing field, but along the hike to Ushura a rumour caught on that the Ishradi had forbidden the coalition force from bringing their armoured vehicles and artillery within five kilometres of the city. This rumour wasn't confirmed by any of the officers, but their silence on the issue spoke volumes.

"They don't trust us," said Colt. "We're here to fight their war for them, and they don't trust us."

"To be fair, we've only just arrived," said Dalton. "Would you trust them if they turned up on Landbreak with an army?"

"Firstly, they invited us, and secondly, we've just crossed space to do these people a favour and they can't even drive some trucks out here for us?"

When they reached the outskirts of the city they were brought to a halt by squadrons of dirt-bikes that came out and drove along the length of their line, kicking up plumes of shredded grass and soil. A pair of large-wheeled jeeps came next, transporting a party of Ishradi officials. Colonel Hunt, his Avernii counterpart, and a cadre of officers strode out from the line to make themselves known. The two delegations spoke for some ten minutes before the colonel returned to the line. It was later discovered that he had been offered a ride into the city but had turned it down, stating that if his men were going to walk, then so would he.

The regiments were ordered into a tight marching column and redirected towards one of the thoroughfares that led in and out of Ushura. The Avernii took the lead, their armoured soldiers marching with flawless coordination. The 2nd Privateers followed, somewhat less enthusiastically.

They entered the city via a wide roadway that had been

closed to the public in preparation for their arrival. The streets were lined with short, thick-trunk trees that sprouted broad, waxy fronds. Dalton marvelled at them. There were no trees like that on Landbreak. The buildings were low-ceilinged, with arched doorways and shuttered windows. It was then that Dalton got his first view of the Ishradi people. Many of them had come out of their homes, clustering on the pavements to watch as the regiments marched by. They were a dark-skinned people, an adaptation no doubt to the heavy light exposure on the moon. Their garments were loose and lightweight, baggy cotton shirts, fluted trousers and dresses. Warm, muted colours seemed to be the fashion, beige and ochre, brown and olive green.

This was no triumphant procession accompanied by the cheers of the people. The Ishradi looked on silently, sometimes murmuring to one another, mostly just staring with wary eyes. Husbands held their wives close, and mothers held their children closer. Clusters of people began to follow as the regiments pressed on deeper into the city, through market squares with open stalls and stacked crates of local produce, past compounds of interconnected domes, wider than the ones before but never taller. They crossed a long, arched bridge that spanned the river. The water was a bright turquoise colour, gentle and sparkling in the warm daylight, not like the dark and churning seas back home. Shoals of vividly coloured fish filled the water. Dalton nudged Blake and nodded to the river.

Colt, who had followed their gaze, grinned deviously. "They look small. No good for eating. We'll show them a real fish, after all this is done."

The regiments came into a paved clearing and formed into ranks before what could only be described as a palace. It was the only building with more than one floor that Dalton had seen throughout their march into the city. Low, wide steps led up to the facade, where a row of intricately patterned gates gave access to the atrium. The front seemingly displayed the only straight wall on the palace exterior. The three main halls that comprised the edifice were huge and round, with squat, domed rooftops. The upper floors were fronted with loggias: open, columned walkways that overlooked the city.

A short, portly man with thinning black hair, dressed in red and gold robes, waited for them at the top of the steps. He was accompanied by an honour guard, a squad of soldiers in antiquated brass-plate, wielding long spears with gilded hafts and plumes of red feathers beneath the tips. Dalton noted that, despite their ceremonial weaponry, they also had functional looking side-arms holstered at their belts. Around the perimeter of the square what looked like regular Ishradi soldiers were lining up, dressed simply in dark green fatigues.

"Welcome, welcome! We welcome you to Ishra," said the robed man happily, his voice defined by an accent that clipped consonants and heightened vowels. He beckoned enthusiastically as Colonel Hunt and the Avernii Commander – its armoured suit trimmed with silver – strode up the steps. An aide stepped forward with a platter, upon which were three small glasses filled with an amber liquid. Their host took one, and gestured for his guests to do the same. Colonel Hunt lifted a glass, but the Avernii Commander remained unmoving. Their host's smile faltered as he looked between Hunt and the Avernii, but he recovered with a statesman's grace. He tipped his glass to the two commanders and then to the assembly at large before draining it in a single gulp. Hunt followed his example.

"I, Ar Sarafet, High Shekahn of Ishra, drink with you and accept you as honoured guests in my house," began the robed man, addressing the assembled regiments. "It is both my regret and my blessing that you come as you do, steeled for war. Were it that you had come here simply as tourists to enjoy the beauties and luxuries of Ishra, I would be a happier man. That is not so, unfortunately, but with your help it may one day be possible. For you see, my people are beset by a savage foe, terrorists that lurk in the shadows and strike without honour or mercy!"

As if to prove his point, a rocket twisted over the heads of the assembled Islanders, leaving a corkscrewed trail of smoke in its wake. It arced overhead, and landed like a mortar shell against the palace facade. An explosion engulfed the row of gates, and blasted a wave of flames and rubble across the terrace.

CHAPTER SEVEN

The palace steps were wreathed in smoke. A captain of the 2nd Privateers was leading a band of soldiers up towards the terrace, calling out for the colonel. Dalton could feel the panic setting in. The troopers around him were jostling, casting about, shock and fear etched on their faces. He could hear the chatter of gunfire, somewhere out on the edges of the plaza.

Seconds after the first, another rocket shot into the air. Its trajectory was steeper than the first. It wove into the sky, and for a second appeared to linger, before it begun its downward arc. Soldiers yelled out, pushing and shoving to get away. The rocket buried itself deep in the ranks of the Privateers, and exploded with earth-shaking force. Flames ripped skywards and bodies were flung into the air, turning end over end, slack like rag dolls. Men were screaming, not the sudden yells of fright, but the prolonged howling of agony.

The regiment was breaking apart. Officers were bellowing orders, struggling to be heard over the screams. The gunfire was becoming more frequent now, louder too. A third rocket roared overhead, detonating against the rounded palace walls and showering the heaving mass of soldiers with shattered masonry.

"We should move," yelled Dalton, bracing himself against the scrambling soldiers that surrounded him.

"What the shit is happening?" cried Blake.

"Move!" said Dalton, pushing the terrified man away from the palace.

"Load up!" Colt shouted, slapping a magazine into his L7 rifle. Dalton did the same, sliding a magazine from his webbing and fumbling to slot it home. An Islander shoved into him, and the magazine clattered away amongst the forest of stampeding feet. He cursed as it was kicked from sight, and pulled a second magazine from its pouch, holding it close as he worked it into the slot. With their rifles loaded and pointed skyward, they began pressing through the crowd.

"Get back here!" shouted Sergeant Broden behind them. "Stay with the squad! Stay together!"

"What are we doing?" asked Dalton.

"Move into cover! This way!" said Broden, waving them off to the left of the palace.

The ten troopers forged through the chaos. Other officers were also fighting to rally their men. Isolated stragglers latched onto the bigger groups, desperate to escape the press of bodies. A fragmented semblance of order began to rise from the confusion. Of Lieutenant Killian and the other squad in their platoon, though, there was no sight.

As they reached the edge of the plaza the full extent of the carnage began to show. The bodies of Ishradi regulars lay sprawled about, gunned down with their backs turned, by the looks of them. Dalton faltered as he looked across the corpses of women and men dressed in faded, green fatigues, their bodies twisted and broken by gunfire and explosions. His gaze became fixed on the face of a girl soldier, younger than him, her upturned eyes bloodshot and glassy.

A regular shouldered past Dalton, snapping him from his stupor. More squads of Ishradi soldiers were hurrying down nearby streets, pursuing the unseen attackers.

"There!" yelled Moore. They followed his gesture and saw a group of men and women in civilian clothes, hunched by the outer curve of the palace wall. They had rifles, bandoleers of ammunition and explosives. Balaclavas concealed their faces. It was Dalton's first look at the enemy, at the so-called Separatists.

Broden swung up his L7 to draw a bead on the group,

but there were too many obstructions in his sightline; friendly soldiers and civilians dashing across the plaza seeking cover. This group of Separatist fighters weren't firing into the chaos of the plaza; rather they were hugging the curve of the palace wall, trying to stay out of sight. A second later, Dalton saw why. From the middle of the group came a fighter, the long tube of a rocket launcher braced over her shoulder. They didn't want to give away their position until after they had fired the weapon.

"Clear a space!" bellowed Broden. It took a moment for his squad to realise what he was talking about. The grenade he pulled from his webbing pouch quickly dispelled the confusion. The nine of them went to work pushing and shoving to give Broden the space he needed.

The Separatist with the launcher was bracing herself on one knee, her companions vacating the blast cone. Broden arched back his thick arm and powered the hand-grenade up and over the heads of the swarming crowd. The throw was perfect. The grenade struck one of the Separatists in the nose hard enough to knock him down, and detonated a second later. A geyser of smoke and shrapnel shot into the air, engulfing the fighters.

It didn't entirely have the intended effect. A rocket burst from the swirling dust. Its trajectory was low, thrown off-course by the explosion. Belching a trail of smoke in its wake, the rocket skimmed over the plaza half a metre above head-height. It struck the roof of a building on the far side, scattering chunks of stone and plaster.

"Move up!" ordered Broden. The squad shouldered clear of the thinning crowd. The smoke was clearing by the time they reached the palace wall. A half dozen bodies lay twisted on the cracked tiles. Some of them were still alive, blood and dust-coated shapes writhing on the ground. From the looks of their wounds, they wouldn't stay that way for long.

Movement caught Dalton's eye. Further down the road that bordered one side of the palace, a pair of men were half running, half staggering away. "Separatists!" he shouted and aimed his rifle.

Broden put a hand on the barrel. "We take them alive."

Dalton released a pent-up breath. He could hear blood rushing in his ears. His heart was thundering against his ribs. Beads of sweat were running from underneath his helmet, dripping from his brow, getting in his eyes. He blinked them away and went after Broden.

They left the panic of the plaza behind them. Heavy breathing and the echoing clatter of their boots replaced the screams and the gunfire. The fleeing Separatists were slowed by their wounds, but their head start saw them disappear behind the palace before Broden's squad could catch up with them. When they rounded the palace, the street ahead was empty. The roads that bordered the palace were wide and lined with the stumpy, sharp-leaved trees. Morning shadows stretched long across the tiled pavements and the short, garden walls of the properties adjacent to the palace. There were a hundred places for a man to hide.

"Keep moving—check the alleys," whispered Broden. The squad fanned out down the street, moving quickly, leading with their rifles. The sergeant was pulling ahead with Scott, Nelson, and Harris. The others weren't far off, but Dalton was falling behind.

"Come on," urged Blake.

"Wait," said Dalton. "Look here."

Beside one of the crenelated, garden walls, on the corner of a street that branched off of the palace road, something had been discarded. Dalton inspected it with the tip of his boot. It was a balaclava, coated in dust.

"They went this way," he said, and started running down the side street. Colt followed.

"We found something!" shouted Blake, waving to the others up ahead.

At the end of the street Dalton and Colt came to a stop. Beneath them, the ground level dropped away into an artificial sink. Homes and shops had been built into the layered walls of the deep pit, and flights of stone steps led down from the street level to the sink's base, where a small market of canopied stalls had been erected.

Groups of panicked civilians were hurrying indoors, barring their doors and shutters behind them. From the direction of the palace the sounds of explosions and gunfire could still be heard, but Dalton realised that this was not the direct source of the panic.

"On the steps," shouted Dalton. Clambering down into the pit were the two Separatists, brandishing their rifles to clear the way.

"Stop! Stop! I'll shoot!" warned Colt.

One of the Separatists swung round and opened fire. Dalton grabbed Colt by the pack and pulled. They fell on to the street. Puffs of dust came off of the sink's ledge as solid rounds buried themselves in stone. The wooden balustrades that bordered the ledge splintered and cracked.

"Bastards," growled Colt. The shooting had stopped. They elbowed their way up to the edge and peered down. The Separatists were halfway to the bottom. The two Islanders clambered to their feet and vaulted the balustrade. They thudded onto the steps below, their boots kicking up clouds of dust, and began their descent, more leaping than running, clearing the steps three and four at a time.

They came onto a terrace, halfway down the sink, that connected the stairs from above and those that led further down. The Separatists were almost at the market floor. One of them pointed towards a tunnel in the far wall of the lowest level.

"We'll lose them in there," said Colt.

"Salt to that," said Dalton. He dropped his pack and backed up.

"Don't do it!" cried Colt, but Dalton was already running. He reached the edge of the terrace and leapt. He fell three metres and hit one of the market tarpaulins. It collapsed beneath him, breaking his fall, its wooden support struts splintering.

Dalton fought to free himself from the tarpaulin. The Separatists were lifting their rifles, jogging down the last few steps to the market. His own rifle was caught in the twisted canvas sheet. He hauled on it, but it wouldn't come free. The Separatists had him in their sights now, their rifles aimed. A hail of bullets shattered the tiles in front of their feet. Colt was standing on the edge of the terrace above, L7 braced, firing down.

One of the Separatists bolted left, but the other swung up his rifle, not heeding Colt's warning, and pulled the trigger. Dalton ripped clear of the tarpaulin and barrelled into the Separatist. The two men went down against the stone steps, clawing at one another.

The Separatist got his hands around the rim of Dalton's chest-plate and lurched forwards, smashing him in the face with a brutal headbutt. Dalton reeled, pain exploding across his nose. He tasted blood on his lips. Then the Separatist was on top of him, a curved knife in his hand. Dalton grabbed him by the wrist, halting the blade's descent. They were locked in struggle, each pushing against the other, the blade's edge shivering between them. Dalton looked up into the Separatist's face. This was the one who had discarded his balaclava. The dark-skinned man was young, perhaps the same age as Dalton, perhaps younger. There was desperation in the man's eyes. There was fear.

The muzzle of an L7 rifle pressed into the Separatist's forehead.

"Put it down," came a voice, hard and cold. Colt was standing over them.

The Separatist snarled and yanked on the knife, fighting to swing it free and into Colt's face. The discharge of the rifle's weapon was deafening. Dalton squeezed his eyes shut against the fury of the sound and the splatter of warm blood against his face. He felt the weight of the corpse slumping onto him. His ears were ringing, as though a bell had been struck inside his head.

When he opened his eyes the first thing he saw was the second Separatist – the one who had fled – coming back at them through the market, rifle raised. Colt wasn't looking. The man was too busy fussing over Dalton, making sure he was unharmed. He was saying something, but Dalton couldn't hear him for the ringing in his ears.

He did hear the shot however. It struck Colt square in the chest. He bowled over backwards. Dalton moved. He rolled the corpse off of him and came up, the Separatist's rifle in his hands. He didn't aim. He didn't have time to aim. He just pulled the trigger. The rifle reared in his grip. A spray of bullets cut the second Separatist down, spinning him off his feet.

The man hit the tiles hard, and didn't get back up.

* * *

Blake came into the triage tent. He had a paper bag in one hand.

"You've got to try these," he said, holding up a large, round green fruit. Colt was sitting up in a metal-frame cot, a swathe of bandages around his bare chest. Dalton was in the chair beside him. Both were silent. They had been silent since the rest of the squad had caught up with them in the pit. The whole thing had been over quickly. A sparse matter of minutes. The wider battle had lasted only a half hour longer. The 2nd Privateers and the Avernii Transhuman Forces had pulled out of Ushura three hours later, once all soldiers – dead, alive and wounded – had been accounted for. The Ishradi had provided transportation for the casualties, and the regiments had returned to the landing field, where a base camp was in the process of being established.

"So," said Blake, hesitantly, "what happened?"

Colt and Dalton shared a look.

"You saved my life," said Colt.

Dalton shrugged. "You saved mine first."

"I wouldn't have had to if you weren't balls-to-the-wall crazy," said Colt, flashing a brief grin. "You could have broken both your legs making a jump like that."

"They were going to get away," said Dalton simply. "We had to stop them."

"It was all pointless anyway," said Colt. "We were supposed to take them alive. Might as well have just shot them from the start."

"Salt," whispered Blake, "we haven't been here a day yet and already…"

"Yeah," said Dalton.

"I was right behind you guys, I just, I went to get the rest of the squad and…"

"It's fine, Blake," said Colt. "It was better that you weren't there."

Blake recoiled as if struck.

"There was no need to put more people in danger," put in Dalton quickly.

"Yeah. Right," said Colt. "I mean, look what happened to me. Not even a day on Ishra and I'm already on my arse. Could have been much worse."

"How bad is it?" asked Blake.

"Just bruised. No broken ribs. They haven't taken me off of active duty," said Colt.

"Well then, you'll have to try harder next time," said Dalton.

The three men chuckled, but it was a strained effort.

"Really though, you should eat something," said Blake,

putting the bag of fruit down at the end of the bed. "They're nice, just don't bite down too hard. Someone's already broken a tooth on the pip."

"Thanks," said Dalton.

"Also, Broden's called a briefing in forty minutes," said Blake, checking his watch. "From what I can tell High Command is in an uproar over what happened at Ushura. We could be moving before the day is out."

"Any word on the colonel?" asked Dalton.

"He's fine. So is the Avernii Commander and the High Shekahn from what I've heard," said Blake. "Some shrapnel wounds probably, but the rocket went right over them and into the palace gates. A metre lower and it would have wiped out everyone on that terrace. Stroke of luck, that was."

"So what's the plan now?" asked Colt, shifting painfully on his cot.

Blake shrugged. "Got to wait for the briefing to find that out. My bet is either we'll be put on garrison duty in Ushura, now that there's a confirmed enemy presence there, or they'll be shipping us straight out to the Assahi front-line."

"I didn't come here to stand guard outside some foreigner's hut," said Colt.

"So why did you come here?" asked Blake.

Colt shot him a hard look. "To fight a damn war. To fix someone else's problems so they don't become my problems."

"Are those your words, or the colonel's?" Blake asked.

"Are you getting lippy with me?"

"You two want some privacy to work out all this tension?" Dalton asked, reaching over and taking a fruit from the bag.

"Fuck off, James," said Colt.

"I just think you both need to cool it," said Dalton, inspecting the alien fruit. "People have just been shooting at us. With rockets, for salt's sake. Trying to kill us. That's some serious shit right there, and I reckon you're both pretty tightly strung about it. I know I am. But let's not take it out on each other, alright? Do I have to peel this or something?"

"You don't have to," said Blake, breaking Colt's gaze. "I'm going to go."

"No, you're not," said Dalton firmly. "You're going to pull up a chair and sit here in miserable, awkward silence with us. And then in forty minutes we're all going to go and hear how much worse our lives are about to get, and question our life decisions. Got it?"

Colt snorted. Blake dragged a second chair up to the bed and sat down.

They didn't speak. They didn't need to.

Chapter Eight

"The attack at Ushura was a part of something bigger." Lieutenant Killian had gathered the platoon outside in the clearing at the centre of the camp. Many of the tents were still being put up, and the rumbling sounds of tractors and manual labour filtered back to them through the throng of bodies. A gabion wall, two metres thick, was being erected around the perimeter of the base. The engineering crews attached to the regiments were filling the wire-mesh cages of the gabions with local stone and soil.

The rest of the regiment was gathered in the clearing also, split into platoons for the purposes of briefing. The Avernii were further down. Where the Islanders were clustered in loose groups, sitting or kneeling in the grass, the Avernii were arrayed in strict parade ground formation. They had been standing that way, silently, for an hour now. No one that Dalton had spoken to had any clue as to what the mods were doing.

"Ishradi Military Intelligence claims that they were unaware of the presence of Separatist cells in the city. Allegedly there hasn't ever been Separatist activity this far from the front line before now. What this means is that the Separatists have been building an underground force in Ushura for some time now, arming them with serious weaponry, and managing to keep it all under the radar while they've been at it. The only reason they would do such a thing, is if they were preparing for a large-scale, coordinated strike at a target of opportunity."

"Such as the one we experienced today," said Sergeant Broden.

"Thank you, sergeant," said Killian. "Now, it has been

posited that the assassination of the High Shekahn was the primary goal of today's attack. If that's the case, it means that the Separatists knew not just that the High Shekahn would be in Ushura, but also that he would be giving a public speech. Which means that they also knew we would be here today as well. That they concealed a large, well-equipped force amongst the civilian population is proof of that. To know when and where we would be ahead of our arrival and to have prepared for it to this extent would have required months of preparation on the behalf of the Separatists. All of this points to one revelation."

"The Ishradi regime has been infiltrated," said Broden, nodding sagely.

Killian shot the man an irritated glance. "That's right. As a result we must assume that every piece of information that has been passed between us and the Ishradi has also been received by the enemy. In light of this, High Command has entirely restructured our operation schedule."

A hand went up in the platoon. It belonged to Dalton.

"This isn't time for questions," snapped Broden.

Dalton spoke anyway. "I was wondering whether we could hear about our losses after the events of this morning."

A murmur of assent spread through the platoon. There had fortunately been no casualties across the two squads in 9th Company's 4th Platoon, but many of the soldiers had friends outside of the platoon, friends that they hadn't heard from since the withdrawal from Ushura.

"That can be discussed at a later time—" began Killian, but he was cut off.

"My brother's in 18th Company. I haven't seen him since we deployed." It was Nelson who had spoken.

"And my cousin is in the 6th. I got stopped outside their tents when I went to check on him," said a trooper from 1st Squad. Other soldiers began raising their voices too. Killian waved them down, looking at the other platoons to see if they had noticed the commotion.

"Calm down, for salt's sake," he hissed. Killian tapped the screen of his data tablet a few times. "Alright. Alright. There were fifty-eight casualties across the 2nd Privateers, thirty-four of which were fatal."

The platoon stirred. Troopers shared stern-faced glances and swore under their breaths. Dalton saw the dangerous look in Colt's eye. The man was looking dead ahead, jaw jutting, lips thin. He had his combat knife clenched in one white-knuckled fist. He was dragging its darkened blade through the soil, tearing up the grass.

"Listen, I need you to focus," growled Killian. "We're all angry. I'm angry. Names of the fallen will be made public soon, but the last thing I need is vengeance-thirsty idiots running off and getting themselves killed. I need you to act like soldiers. To do that you need to harness control, up here, in your mind, and here, in your heart."

Killian crouched on his haunches, leaning close and lowering his voice. "We're going to make these bastards pay for what they've done. I promise you that much. And soon, too. But we're going to do it right, the way that makes sure no more of us get killed in the process. For that to happen, I need you all to focus. I need you to listen to what I have to say, to cement it in your heads so you're ready for what comes next. Can you do that?"

The soldiers were looking left and right, agitated, unable to hold a steady gaze, clenching and unclenching their fists, but they fell silent at Killian's words, nodding or else murmuring their assent.

"Good. Damn good," said Killian, standing back up. "This is the plan. We're going back in. Not tomorrow, not the day after. Tonight."

The lieutenant paused, frowning, a thought caught on the

tip of his tongue. He turned to 1st Squad's sergeant. "Banks. Repeat what you were telling me earlier, about how things work on this ball of humidity they call the Miteran Jewel."

"Ah. Right. Well. Ishra goes through four stages of light exposure throughout its rotation cycle of approximately one hundred and twelve days. Each of these mini-seasons, if you will, lasts in the region of twenty-eight days and constitutes—"

"The short version, Banks!"

Sergeant Banks cleared his throat. "Ah. Yes, lieutenant. Right. Well. We're currently in the phase known to the locals as *Parting*, where light exposure from our star is diminishing and the main source of light is reflecting off of the gas giant, Mitera. That means we're going to see gradually lengthening night cycles. We'll be getting roughly twenty hours of light a day, and only about seven hours of night for the next fourteen days or so."

Killian checked his wrist-watch. "Thank you, sergeant. So, that means this operation is time sensitive. We don't want the Separatists in Ushura to know we're coming. To that extent we've communicated our plan with only the highest echelons of Ishradi authority. That, and we're heading in on foot, in the dark. If the Separatists are ready for us, it'll be because the information was leaked, not because they saw us coming. In the event that the information *is* leaked, it will have been from someone high up, and given how few people know the full details, that will narrow down the pool of suspects for a spy in the Ishradi administration. Let me impress upon you the importance of this mission then, as it carries the potential of not just rooting out the Separatist resistance within Ushura, but also of discovering the traitor in the Ishradi ranks."

"That's what we call catching two fish with one hook," said Broden. The lieutenant shot Broden a withering glance, but the sergeant wasn't done. He was an open-faced man, and when a thought occurred to him, one could track the entire cognitive process through Broden's shift in facial expressions alone. "What about the Ishradi rank and file, lieutenant? If they haven't been told we're coming and they catch us sneaking up on them out of the night it might make for some unfortunate accidents."

"That's… actually a good question," said Killian, somewhat deflated, as though he had been looking forward to berating someone, only to have been cruelly robbed of the opportunity. "As information on this operation is classified, Sergeant Broden is correct, the Ishradi regulars won't know we're moving back into the city. However, that shouldn't be a problem. As part of the operation, the Ushura garrison has been pulled back into a defensive position inside the palace. With any luck, the Separatists will see this as a reaction to their attack today, and not catch on to our plan."

"What about the mods?" asked Colt, jerking a thumb towards the precise, unmoving ranks of Avernii soldiers. "They coming with?"

"They coming with, *lieutenant*," stressed Broden, clipping Colt across the back of the head.

"Right. Sorry. Are they, lieutenant?"

"The Avernii Transhuman Forces are going to deploy after us and form a cordon around the city to prevent any Separatists from escaping once we begin our assault," said Killian.

"Wait, High Command is giving perimeter control duty to its most heavily armoured troops?" asked Colt, furrowing his brow. "Surely we'd all be better off if the mods were the ones crawling down the gutters tonight."

The Islanders murmured their grudging assent.

"Shut your mouths for a second and listen," snapped Killian, raising a finger. "You hear that? That hum? That's the sound that comes off of two thousand suits of powered armour. Wouldn't be much of a stealth mission if we sent two thousand armoured mods crunching into the city, would it? Our gear is lighter, our colours are darker. We're the better choice. Besides, I thought you wanted vengeance for the dead?"

Colt fell silent.

"Good." The lieutenant checked his watch again. "Set your alarms. It starts getting dark in five hours. That's when the operation begins. Return to me in four and a half hours from now, combat ready. No backpacks. We'll be moving quick and light. Dismissed! Go and get some rest, eat something if you haven't already. Prepare yourselves. I've got a feeling tonight's going to be a bitch."

* * *

The banded sphere of Mitera and her glaring, yellow star passed beyond the horizon. The Islanders were glad to see them go. Night brought with it a blessed cool, respite from the heat of the day. The 2nd Privateers deployed almost in full, slipping out of the camp through different exits and dispersing in loose formation throughout the fields. Flashlights off, they crept through the low grass, swathed in darkness. When they reached the ridge, Ushura was revealed beyond, its network of squat habitats silhouetted by the warm glow of lanterns.

"Could do with some of that fancy night-vision equipment right about now," muttered Blake. Dalton could barely make the man out in the grass, though his voice was close.

"That's what I'm talking about," replied someone enthusiastically. Dalton recognised the voice as belonging to Wright. "You know, we've got an optical system with full thermal imaging and night-vision capabilities? It's got reticle targeting and distance measuring, the full package."

"We do?" asked Blake. "Because I think I must have missed that queue when they were handing out the toys."

"That's because grunts without proper training don't get expensive, specialist equipment. Just be content that we've given you flashlights," said Broden. "Now shut up and move out."

"Yeah, flashlights that we're not even allowed to turn on," mumbled Blake.

The platoon set off down the hill towards the distant city. At this stage of the operation the Privateers moved alone, with the Avernii Transhuman Forces being held in reserve as they awaited a separate deployment window.

It took longer to reach the city this time, with the officers enforcing stealth over urgency. They came out of the grass and onto the paved roads, melting into the shadows formed by street lamps, avoiding the orange cones of light that shone from doorways and windows. The streets were deserted, perhaps due to the hour, but more than likely because of the day's unexpected violence.

Broden's squad was hunkered down in a small courtyard. It had been some time since they had arrived here, but the sergeant had them waiting in tense silence, checking his watch every two minutes. They had come off of the street and filed down a narrow alley to reach this place. An ornamental fountain babbled gently in the centre of the clearing. A ring of the short, thick trees had been planted along the edges of the courtyard, providing privacy for the surrounding homes. The smells of spiced meats and ground herbs wafted out of the open windows. Muted conversations could be heard beyond the circle of trees, the sounds of families sitting down for dinner or settling in for the evening.

"Now," whispered Broden at last, gesturing to a metal grate set amongst the beige paving stones. Wright and Nelson moved up and lifted the cover aside. The squad collectively winced as the two men fumbled with the heavy grate. It was set down with painstaking care after that, and the squad gathered around the portal. They peered down into the impenetrable, black depth of the maintenance shaft.

"Down there?" asked Blake.

Broden nodded. After the attack earlier that day it had become clear that the Separatists were operating out of the extensive tunnel network beneath the city. The Separatists that Colt and Dalton had chased had been making for the underground, and the same story had repeated itself for other pursuits that had taken place through the streets. Many of the Separatist fighters had managed to escape below ground, into tunnel entrances and storm drains or down through maintenance shafts. At the time, no one had dared follow them.

"So," said Broden, "who wants to go first?"

"You asking for volunteers, sergeant?" whispered Moore.

"You volunteering, private?"

"I'll do it," said Colt, handing his L7 to Dalton.

Dalton pushed it back. "No. I'll go."

"Let me," said Blake, stepping up.

Colt and Dalton both looked at him, eyebrows raised.

"What? I'll do it," repeated Blake, and shoved his rifle into Colt's arms. Before they could stop him, the small man had clambered down onto the rungs inside the lip of the portal, and was disappearing into the narrow hole.

Dalton exchanged a wide-eyed look with Colt. Colt shrugged. He unfastened the rifle's strap on one side and lowered it down into the shaft after Blake. They had lost sight of him almost immediately, but after a moment Colt felt a tug and let go of the strap. It fell into the dark and they heard a muted curse from below. They shared a grin and then Colt was going next, climbing down into the shaft.

After that it was Dalton's turn, and he handed his rifle to Scott-with-the-good-smile. The rungs of the ladder were old and cold. He could feel the rusted metal flaking beneath his fingerless gloves. When he stepped off the last rung, his boots splashed in the puddles that had gathered along the tunnel's floor. He reached up and took his rifle as it was lowered down, leaning out of the way as the loose end of the strap came clattering down.

"I can't see a damn thing," mumbled Colt. Dalton tried to look around, but Colt was right, the tunnel denied sight. None of the light from the street lamps or the night sky stars reached them down here. The clangs of the next soldier coming down the rungs filled the tunnel, echoing from the damp, stone walls.

"Was it that loud when I was coming down?" he asked.

"More or less," replied Blake.

"Then anyone in earshot already knows we're here," said Dalton, and thumbed on the flashlight attached to the barrel of his L7. He played it along the length of the tunnel, past Colt and Blake, illuminating half a dozen metres of rough stone passageway, as far as the light's strength could pierce.

They were being jostled further into that dark space as more and more of the squad descended into the tunnel. There wasn't room for two men to stand abreast, so they would have to advance in the order that they had come down the ladder.

"You're on point, Blake," came Sergeant Broden's voice from halfway down the line.

"There's a door here," he hissed back.

"It leads to the water pump for the fountain above," said Broden, consulting his data tablet. "We have to keep moving until we reach the main drain canal."

Travelling in single file, they followed the tunnel for several dozen metres until it led out on to a more spacious stone walkway that overlooked a wide subterranean canal. The reek of fetid water and sewage rose from the channel with a stomach-churning potency. Several of the troopers gagged and stifled coughs.

"I think there's something moving down there," said Blake, peering over the canal rails into the thick, glutinous river below. Dalton came up to the rail, one hand pressed to his nose.

"Yeah, a legion of turds," said Dalton, after a moment of

staring at the filth encrusted water. He turned to catch up with the squad as it moved away.

Blake shone his light into the river for a minute longer, sure that he had seen something moving through its depths. He gave up and moved on. The beam of his flashlight rose up along the sloped canal wall, briefly catching the walkway on the other side.

He froze. He turned back the torch, shining it again across the canal. There, hunched by the rails on the far side, were three creatures, their wide, glossy eyes reflecting the light. They spread their wings and reared up.

Private Blake Leland screamed. He levelled his assault rifle and wrenched the trigger. The muzzle flare lit the tunnel with rapid, bright flashes that threw sharp shadows against the walls. The throaty, staccato chatter of the L7 echoed loud in the close, stone tunnel. He screamed all the while, tearing up the far side of the walkway with a stream of hard rounds, filling the air with chips of shattered stone, and didn't stop screaming even after his rifle clicked dry.

Chapter Nine

"Hold fire!" bellowed Broden.

The squad was racing back down the walkway, back towards Blake. The trooper was no longer screaming, now fumbling for the magazine pouches at his belt with trembling fingers.

"What in all the salty depths of the great blue sea are you doing, boy?" roared Broden.

"Things! Things! Over there! The size of a man!" cried Blake.

"Secure the far side!" ordered Broden, jabbing a finger at Dalton.

James nodded to Colt, and the two men clambered up onto one of the long, narrow bridges that spanned the canal. Their boots against the metal rang loud in the sudden silence of the tunnel. They reached the far side, flashing their torches rapidly about the walkway. It didn't take long to find one of Blake's creatures.

The man was on his back, his thick, black cloak sodden with blood, the round-eyed gas-mask askew on his face. There was a rifle beside him, one of the local Ishradi designs, with its decorative wooden casing and stock.

"Separatist?" Colt asked.

"The Ishradi would have told us if they had men down here, so yeah, Separatist is my guess too," said Dalton.

They cast around the area, looking for further hostiles. Blake had unloaded thirty rounds into this patch of wall. His first shots had been accurate or lucky enough to put down one of the fighters, but the recoil of sustained firing had seen most of the rounds hit nothing but the curved stone wall above and behind them. The clatter of boots on metal drew their attention. Broden and the rest of the squad were coming across the bridge now.

"Separatists," said Dalton, gesturing to the downed man.

"I… I did that?" Blake stuttered, his eyes wide and his lips trembling.

"Damn right you did," said Colt, grinning and slapping the small man on the shoulder. Blake leaned over the canal rail and loudly threw up. Broden inspected the corpse quickly and turned back to Blake, grabbing him by the chest-plate and pulling him round.

"How many did you see? How many?" he shouted.

"Three!" cried Blake. He looked pale as a corpse in the light of their torches, the skin under his eyes drawn and dark.

"Then at least two of them got away," said Broden. "We need to get on them, now, before they get back to their base and warn the rest."

"You reckon they were a guard detail?" asked Moore.

"No, they were clearly just enjoying this fine locale," snarled Broden, shoving past the trooper and lighting up the back wall. He illuminated a tunnel entrance there, wider than the one they had come through on the other side. "Here. They must have gone this way, or else we would have seen them heading up or down the walkway. Scott, with me. Wright, bring up the rear with Blake. Let's move, eyes peeled!"

They hurried down the tunnel in two lines. Visibility was low, the beams of their torches lighting snatched glimpses of the stone walls, of clattering boots, and of armour-bulked soldiers. There was just the thud of their boots and the chorus of their breaths in the low-ceilinged tunnel, and the wild bobbing of their torches.

"Do we even know where we're going?" asked Dalton between ragged lungfuls of cold, subterranean air.

"Towards the enemy," grunted Colt.

"We have no idea what's ahead of us," said Dalton, "no idea what we're running into."

The explosion lit the tunnel with one brief, violent flash. Dalton felt the pressure pop in his ears, felt the sudden wave of heat, right before he crashed into Harris up ahead. Moore crashed into him in turn. The whole squad came to a tumbling halt. Someone was screaming. A horrible, shrill screaming.

"What happened?" one of them cried.

"Back up! Back up!" Broden was yelling.

Silhouettes shifted in the tunnel ahead of them. Then a rifle was firing, its muzzle flare painting the walls with swift splashes of orange light. The man in front of Colt went over backwards, his arms swinging wildly as he reached for support. Colt tried to catch him, but lost his footing and was dragged down.

Broden went to one knee, rifle at his shoulder, and snapped off a burst of return fire along the tunnel. There were yells from further up. The sergeant kept firing, one controlled burst after the other. The acrid reek of ammunition propellant stained the air.

Dalton stumbled past Harris and over Nelson. Scott was curled up in a ball by the sergeant's boots, his face buried in his hands. The man was still screaming, or trying to at least. It sounded like something was choking him. Dalton pulled him from the floor. The soldier's hands fell away and in the light of flashing rifles Dalton saw the bloody ruin of Scott's face. There wasn't an inch of skin that wasn't covered in slick red.

"Get him out of here!" yelled Broden as his magazine clicked empty. "Get everyone out of here!"

Dalton lifted the suddenly slack trooper over his shoulder and began staggering back down the tunnel. Colt stepped around him and took up position next to Broden, opening up with his L7 as the sergeant reloaded.

"Nelson's hit!" Harris shouted, hunched over the other

fallen trooper.

"Get him up! With me! With me!" called Dalton.

The eight soldiers staggered and stumbled back the way they had come, carrying their two wounded between them. Barks of gunfire hounded their backs as Broden and Colt kept up the covering fire. There were other noises too, echoing strangely against the stone walls, distorted over distance into some cacophonous amalgam.

They burst out of the corridor and into the vaulted canal tunnel. The walkways were no longer quiet, like they had been when the squad had first moved through this way. Now each side was lined with soldiers, hunched and crouched by the rails, exchanging volleys of fire across the murky river.

The squad stumbled back into the cover of the corridor. Dalton put Scott down as gently as he could manage and unslung his L7. He looked around the group of men. They all looked terrible, their skin pale and shiny with sweat, eyes wide and bright with fear. Broden and Colt had yet to return. In the depths of the corridor he could still see the occasional flash of gunfire.

"How is he?" asked Dalton, nodding at Nelson.

"I think he fainted," said Harris, fumbling at the man's throat as he tried to check for a pulse.

"Don't bother with that, Harris," said Dalton. "Just check for wounds and keep these two safe. The rest of you, come with me."

"We should wait here, until the sergeant gets back," said Thompson.

"Look," said Dalton, jabbing the muzzle of his L7 out towards the main canal tunnel. "We're behind the enemy. You know who that is on the far side? Those are our boys! Those are Islanders! We can help them win this, but only if we act now, before we're discovered."

"He's right," said Blake. "We should listen to James."

"What do we do? What if we get hit by friendly fire from the other side?" asked Wright.

"Who has the emergency flares?"

The men looked at each other, nonplussed. Dalton sighed and began patting down Scott's webbing and pouches, feeling for the flares. He tried not to look at the man's face. There was so much blood. He found what he was looking for and worked one of the flares out of its strap.

"This is the plan," said Dalton. "We go out behind the Separatists, I light this up and then we start shooting. Hopefully our boys on the far side will realise it's us once they see the flare. We'll sweep along the walkway and cut these bastards down as we go. They'll never even see us coming if we do this fast. Alright?"

"Alright," said Moore, though his face was uncertain.

Thompson and Wright nodded in unison.

"I'm with you," said Blake.

Harris was stripping off Nelson's chest-plate to see if any of the rounds had gone through. Dalton left him to it and went back into the main tunnel. The four others came with him, rifles at the ready. Arrayed along the rails in front of them were dozens of Separatists in their black cloaks and gas-masks. They were so focussed on the Privateers across the river that they hadn't even noticed the ones behind them.

Dalton thumbed the cap off of the flare and struck it across the end, like he would to light a match. A red flame burst into life. He thrust the flare over his head.

"Open fire, Islanders!" he yelled. "Kill them all, for Landbreak! For Landbreak!"

The Separatists were turning, confused and caught off-guard, when the four soldiers opened up with their L7s. They roared as they fired, pumped up on terror and adrenaline. The Separatists nearest to them went down in a hail of bullets. Several of them pitched over the rails, bounced off of the sloping canal wall and splashed into the filthy water below.

Dalton dropped the flare and brought up his own rifle. He loosed a burst down the length of the walkway. The Separatists were reeling, caught between two fronts. The sweeping crossfire enfiladed the enemy, cutting them apart and sending them fleeing for the shadows. James Dalton led his companions after them, driving the Separatists off of the walkway with punishing fusillades of rifle fire. The survivors scuttled away down side-alleys and branching corridors.

The Islanders came to a halt, leaning on their knees or against the rails, breathing hard as the last bursts of gunfire echoed away in the tunnel. Dalton turned and raised a fist to the Privateers across the canal. In return, they raised their rifles and let out a bellowing cheer. Dalton found himself laughing, half from shock and half from a savage joy that he felt pounding through his veins. Moore, Wright, Thompson, and Blake joined the cheering. They looked surprised to even be alive. As he watched them, Dalton realised that these men had expected to die, but now here they were, still alive, and the potency of that was like a drug coursing through their veins. So they cheered, loud and wild, happy to be alive, entirely oblivious to the carnage that littered the ground.

"What the fuck is going on?" called Broden. The sergeant was jogging towards them along the walkway, with Colt in tow.

"Your men here just executed a grade-A flanking manoeuvre is what just happened," came another voice. A lieutenant was striding across one of the metal bridges to their side of the canal. His platoon was spreading out across both walkways to secure the tunnel. "Lieutenant Hayes, 12th Company, 5th Platoon. Ashamed to say we got lost down here and ended up by this canal when the whole place exploded with Separatists. I've a feeling we've really kicked the eel's nest now."

"Sergeant Broden, 9th Company, 4th Platoon. It's good to

run into some support down here."

"You're kidding me, right?" laughed Lieutenant Hayes. "You were *our* support, coming out behind the enemy like that. They had us pinned to the fucking wall out here. Who was that, with the flare, roaring like a madman?"

Blake shoved Dalton forwards. "It was him, sir, Private James Dalton. The whole thing was his plan."

"You've got real Islander blood in you, private," said the lieutenant, holding out his hand. Dalton shook it. "I think you might have saved our scales out here. I appreciate it."

"What's the overall situation looking like, lieutenant?" asked Broden.

Hayes turned away from Dalton. "To be honest, I've not got a damned idea. Comms are shot to shit down here. I haven't been able to get through to my captain since we came underground. If this is any example though, then tonight's only just getting started."

"Sounds like a mess," said Broden.

"The Separatists are down here in force, more so than we expected. I can't figure it out though. They've got an army down here, so why didn't they use it earlier when they attacked the palace? They could have done ten times the damage."

"Look, lieutenant, I've got two wounded on me," said Broden, glancing back in the direction of the side-tunnel where they had left Scott and Nelson.

"I've got wounded of my own," said Hayes. "I'll task a detail to get them all top-side, but we've got to keep pushing. We've got to stick to the plan, form up our side of the cordon and link up with the rest of our troops down here. I'm not going to be the weak link in the chain tonight."

Broden nodded and the two officers strode off down the walkway. The lieutenant waved over his field medic as they made plans to get the wounded to the surface. The rest of the squad clustered around Dalton.

"Salt! Fucking salt, man! Did you see that?" Thompson was saying, bouncing on his feet. "We just cut through these bastards, bang-bang-bang! They didn't know what fucking hit them!"

"You just can't help getting yourself into trouble, can you?" said Colt, giving Dalton a comradely shove.

"The trouble finds me, I swear. I don't go looking for it," said Dalton, still light-headed with shock and adrenaline.

"You joined the damn army, James," said Colt, grinning. "Of course you're looking for trouble."

"Let's move!" yelled Broden, waving them over.

"Come on," said Dalton, "we're not done yet."

* * *

The 2nd Privateers had spread through the city under cover of dark. Split into platoons and squads, each task force had its entry point, a designated entrance to the subterranean layer of Ushura's infrastructure. Maps had been provided by their Ishradi allies, detailing each and every tunnel entrance, maintenance shaft, river overflow, storm drain, sewer hatch, catacomb gate and so on and so forth.

At the appointed minute to which all officers had synchronised their watches, the 2nd Privateers had gone underground en masse. The plan had been simple and brutal. Hit the hidden Separatist cells with overwhelming force from every possible angle and provide no opportunity for them to consolidate their forces for a concentrated counter-offensive.

Execution of the plan had proved more difficult than it had appeared on paper. Ushura had been one of the very first settlements developed on the surface of Ishra. In the two hundred years since its founding, its infrastructure had been built and rebuilt. Its sewers and tunnels and maintenance ways had developed, overlapped, become redundant and forgotten, been redesigned and rerouted. It quickly became clear that the maps they had been provided with did not account for the many changes that had warped and restructured the city's underground layer into a dark and winding labyrinth.

The Separatists, on the other hand, had become more than acquainted with this underworld since their forces had infiltrated Ushura. They knew which corridors and pipes to retreat down when they wanted to regroup, which catwalks to use to get behind their enemy; they knew the tunnels best suited to bottleneck the Islander advance and which sectors provided the best locations to dig in and defend from.

They were like spectres in the dark, with their cloaks and round-eyed gas-masks, striking from every shadow and branching tunnel, withdrawing at the first sign of resistance only to return when least expected.

Their fight was a dogged one. They did not give mercy nor did they expect it, they did not yield a metre unfought, and not one of them surrendered. They did their damage. The 2nd Privateers suffered four hundred casualties that night. Half of that number would not return alive from Ushura's underbelly. Together with the casualties from the ambush at the palace, almost a fourth of the Regiment's fighting strength had been maimed in just the first day of their deployment.

As fierce as their fighting spirit was, however, the Separatists could not have hoped to win the day. Set upon at every angle, with individual combat cells and outposts cut off from one another, outnumbered and outgunned, their guerilla tactics could only win them so much.

At one point, a Separatist captain had rallied a substantial force and fought free of the cordon. They had broken out of the underground into Ishra's cool, night air and made to escape the city via a broad overflow channel. They had found the Avernii Transhuman Forces patiently awaiting them. One of the Avernii war machines – a carapace-walker – had thumped forwards on its mechanical claw-feet. A high-pitched whine had filled the night as its rotary cannon had spooled up.

With the Privateers closing the noose tunnel by tunnel, the guerilla tactics of the Separatists had eventually failed them. One cannot fight a war from the shadows, after all, when one runs out of shadows to hide in. Without recourse or a means to escape, the bands of Separatist fighters had been pinned down and wiped out. They fought like cornered beasts and chose death over capture.

In the post-operation report, tacticians surmised that ninety-five percent of the Separatist fighting force in Ushura had been destroyed, with a negligible few having gone into hiding. Finding a force of hundreds in those tunnels and sewers was one thing, but if a single man wanted to hide in the depths of the city's underground, he would never be found.

The 2nd Privateers re-emerged three hours after they had gone below Ushura. Wearily, covered in filth and in blood, they pushed up manhole covers and pulled aside tunnel grates, and staggered back out into the small hours of the night.

Chapter Ten

In his dreams he walked in a city made of sunshine. He leapt out of the sky and landed gently on golden streets, lined with pools of sapphire-blue water and emerald-green trees. Happiness welled in his chest, but as he walked, long shadows crept down the streets that he left at his back. Hands reached up out of those shadows, clawed and dripping with darkness. Soon the shadows raced ahead of him and the city of sunshine became a city of night. Grinning cadavers pulled themselves up out of the tunnels and sewers beneath his feet. Their eyes were hollow and round, and the night clung to their skeletal frames like cloaks of tattered shadow. They said his name as they clawed across the ground towards him, chanting it, screaming it, howling it like a curse. Their twisted, bony fingers dug into his ankles and calves. He looked skyward and thrust up his hands but he could no longer leap back into the sky. The grinning cadavers dragged him down, through the paved street, through the rock and soil, until the mantle of the world gave way to a bed of bones, and upon every one of them was carved his name.

* * *

Colt offered him a bottle as he stepped out of the tent. He took it and tipped it back. The drink was crisp and fresh and the subtle kick of alcohol lurked beneath its fruity palette.

"What is this?" he asked, handing back the bottle.

"Local brew," replied Colt. "Sarge got us a crate of the stuff. Was going to give it to us in the morning, but seems there's more than one of us that isn't sleeping tonight."

"I'm bone-tired," said Dalton, nursing the ache in his neck.

His whole body ached.

"Too tired to sleep," nodded Colt.

"Salt, Colt, did all that really just happen?"

"Yeah," said Colt, knocking back another gulp and then looking at the bottle in disgust, "and this shit is too weak to make me doubt it."

"I feel like every nerve in my body is about to explode," he said.

"Try one of these."

Dalton jumped. He hadn't noticed Blake standing beside him. The skinny man was smoking a brown-paper cigarette between two fingers, and was offering Dalton a packet filled with more of the same.

"Drink, smokes," said Dalton, "is Broden trying to win sergeant of the year award?"

"It's not just Broden," said Colt. "I'm pretty sure the colonel had a truck-load of the stuff brought in from the city."

"Our reward?" asked Dalton sarcastically.

"For a battle well fought," said Colt, utterly serious.

"Seriously, try one," said Blake, drawing in a lungful of smoke. "It takes the edge off."

Dalton waved the offer aside. Blake shrugged and pocketed the packet.

"Has anyone been to see Scott, or Nelson?" Dalton asked.

"They've had to put up new med-tents just to keep up with the casualties," said Blake. "They aren't letting anyone near who isn't wounded or a medic. It's a madhouse."

Dalton nodded and fell silent for a second. "I keep thinking about that group we cornered, towards the end."

"The ones who rushed us?" asked Colt.

"Those ones, yeah," he said. "They were out of ammo, backs to the wall, but they came at us anyway. What were they thinking to do that? What did they think we were going to do to them if we took them alive?"

Colt shrugged and took another bottle out of the crate by his foot. He handed it to Dalton. "They're crazy. Fanatics. You can't apply reason to their actions."

Dalton took the bottle and worked off the cap with the edge of his combat knife. "Still. That sort of behaviour… you've got to be completely fucking wired to throw your life away like that. You've got to be sure that the alternative isn't worth living through."

"Don't think about it, James," said Colt. "It'll only make it harder to pull the trigger next time."

Dalton said nothing. Instead, he lifted the bottle to his lips and drank deep. He wondered just how many of the slender, tinted bottles he would have to empty to find a dreamless sleep.

* * *

Dawn came less than two hours later and sleep yet evaded them. They were not the only ones to go restless out into the early morning, seeking distraction. Three hours dodging death in the darkness beneath Ushura could do something terrible to a man's nerves. The camp murmured with activity in those small hours. Men drank and smoked, sat out in the open and played shells or recounted their stories from the battle. They did the latter loudly and with bravado, as though doing so would detach the terror from their memories.

By the time Mitera emerged over the line of the horizon, with Patera glinting at her shoulder, the soldiers were dead on their feet, the lingering adrenaline having at last drained from their bodies, leaving them hollow and exhausted. Mercifully, High Command had put all operations for the 2nd Privateers on hold to allow for rest and recuperation. The Avernii, in tandem with the Ishradi military, would sweep and secure the city, ensuring that the Separatist presence was truly broken.

The Islanders dragged themselves back into their tents to escape the rising warmth of the coming day, and fell on to the thin mattresses of their metal-frame cots. Even then sleep did not come easily. The heat became oppressive faster than anyone had expected, and the morning brought with it other annoyances. A legion of critters and bugs dug themselves up from their night-time burrows in the soil, and filled the air with their incessant buzzing and chirping. Those tents with flaps left open soon became infested with leaping insects, many of which turned out to be capable of delivering a stinging bite.

Dalton's platoon had sealed up their tent to keep out the encroaching light, and so fortunately escaped the wrath of Ishra's insect kingdom. Though, between the humidity and the commotion caused outside by the disturbed soldiers, sleep was still fitful and restless.

After a couple of hours Dalton gave up. The others were still groaning and twisting in their cots as he made his way outside. Wispy clouds formed a lattice across the morning sky, gilded from Mitera's reflected light. The air was thick and sticky. As he walked towards the triage centre, insects scattered from the grass beneath his boots, bounding and hopping away in deft arcs. They seemed to move slowly in the hot air, more gliding than jumping.

A pair of medics were sitting on crates outside one of the triage tents. They looked utterly drained. There were smears of blood on their fatigues. They looked up at him as he approached, heads heavy on necks, and simply waved him through without a word. Dalton thanked them and went through the two flaps, dutifully zipping up the one behind him before progressing through the next.

The long medical tent reeked of antiseptic. Row upon row of cots had been jammed side by side into the space. There wasn't a single unoccupied bed. Men lay swaddled in bandages, hooked up to drips or with fractured limbs locked in splints. The groans, mewling, yelps, and cries of wounded men all merged into one droning background noise of shared pain.

Dalton walked down the aisle of beds, looking from face to face, trying to make out Scott or Nelson. There were so many faces, each one twisted in agony or ruined by war. Here was a man who had "got lucky" and been grazed by a bullet aimed for his head. The round had gouged out his cheek and torn through his ear. There was a man who had accidentally triggered an improvised bomb. Now his legs ended in stumps above the knee. After twenty paces, Dalton realised he had stopped looking. His eyes had become locked to the exit at the far side of the tent. His pace had picked up.

"James?"

The voice drew him up short. Reluctantly, he swept his gaze across the faces of the men nearest to him. All he saw was more of the same, bloodied bandages and eyes squeezed tight against the pain.

"James? Here, I'm here, right here. It's me. Scott."

At last, Dalton saw him. He was in the bed right beside Dalton, his face almost entirely hidden behind thick bandages. Dalton faltered. He had come to visit the man, but now that he was here…

"Don't recognise me?" asked Scott, still managing to put across the humour in his voice.

"Scott," began Dalton, but words escaped him.

"I hear you were quite the hero down there," said Scott. There was a slur to his words that hadn't been there before, as though his lips weren't quite working as they used to. "Heard you carried my sorry self to safety and then led a glorious charge behind enemy lines. Apparently there was even a battle cry involved?"

"I just…"

"Don't be modest," said Scott, attempting a chuckle but producing a phlegm-clogged cough instead. "Sarge was just in here. Told me the whole story. Don't tell him I told you this, but I think he's a little bit proud of you."

"How are you feeling?" managed Dalton. There was a nausea rising in his gullet.

"Better than ever," replied Scott through a slit in the bandages where his mouth ought to have been. A memory from yesterday flashed before Dalton's eyes, a memory of Scott reaching out to steady him on the drop-ship, a memory of the man's big, charismatic smile. The tone of Scott's voice made it sound like, were it not for the bandages, that smile would be plastered across his face even now.

"Oh, come on, don't give me that look," said Scott. "I practically signed up with the hopes of acquiring a dashing scar for myself. I'm sure it'll look quite roguish when the bandages come off."

"It was so dark, in the tunnel. I didn't see what happened. One moment we were running and the next, there was a flash, an explosion?"

"Yeah," sighed Scott. "Turns out I tripped a wire and ate a chunk of shrapnel to the face. Sarge got lucky and took it across the chest-plate. That's messed up, isn't it? One moment you can be enjoying a rigorous jog and the next moment, *splat*, your face is on backwards. You know, I had a nickname back home. Sexy Scott, they used to call me."

"Salt, Scott, I'm so sorry," said Dalton.

"Don't be. You carried me out of there. I could have been shot if you hadn't. I could be dead."

"We could all be dead," said Dalton. "I led the squad out there like it was a game. Like a scene from one of those war films. Like we were invincible."

Scott shrugged. "Turns out it was the correct move. You're right though, it could have just as easily been the wrong move, but I think that's war. You judge the moment, and either you get it wrong and you die, or you get it right and you live."

"You get it wrong and you die. You get it right and you kill."

"Salt, you'd think you were the one lying in the triage tent without a face," said Scott, attempting another laugh.

"How's Nelson?"

"Couple of beds down," said Scott. "Sarge says he'll be fine. His chest-plate took the worst of it. Couple of broken ribs and some internal bleeding. Bastard got off lucky!"

"You take it easy now, Scott," said Dalton. "I'll bring the others by later."

"Oh yeah, you've got to be around when the bandages come off," said Scott. "That'll be a laugh."

Dalton made his way back down the aisle of beds. He let his feet lead him out, his fingers fumbling on automatic at the tent flaps. The brightness and the heat of the day washed over him. He sank to his haunches, buried his face in his hands and drew in a deep, trembling breath.

* * *

That night, several kilometres east up the Sadari River that ran through Ushura, a figure slipped along the bank, moving through the tall, red reeds. They moved close to the water's edge where the ground was muddy and treacherous beneath the boot. Slipping posed a greater threat than just getting wet, for there were things that swam in the river, creatures known to possess an appetite for human flesh.

The figure moved without concern though. They went nimbly over the mud, weaving between the reed stands, never stumbling or catching themselves in the tangled roots that clogged the banks. A shadow parted from the dark, appearing suddenly between the tall, lanky stalks.

"Eskela," said this second figure.

"Ajati," replied the first, in her thick Ishradi accent. "You are taking an unnecessary risk being out here."

"I will be at the front of the fight, wherever I lead it," said Ajati, his eyes glinting in the dark.

"There is no fight at Ushura, not anymore," said Eskela,

bitterness on her tongue.

"The off-worlders?"

"They arrived earlier than we anticipated, only marginally, but the Ushura cell moved without us. A few of them, at least. From what my contact tells me, there was a... disagreement. Some argued that with or without support, the opportunity to strike at the High Shekahn could not be wasted. Most wanted to delay the plan until we arrived. In the end those who wanted to strike, did so, and those who wanted to wait, did so."

"To the detriment of both sides, I imagine?" sighed Ajati.

Eskela nodded. "The Ushura cell is all but gone. I was lucky to make contact with even one of the survivors."

"What do we know of our new enemies?"

"They will turn the tide of this war against us, Ajati," said Eskela. "Thousands of soldiers from both Landbreak and Avernus. Not just men, but fighting machines too, things we have never seen before. They are here on the warpath. They did not hesitate to go beneath Ushura and I do not believe they will hesitate to come to Assahi either."

"The tunnels beneath Ushura were defensible, but they are not comparable to Assahi. The jungle will not only protect us, Eskela, it will win this war for us. We fight for it, and it will fight for us."

He turned and disappeared back into the rust-red reeds. Eskela went after him. The growth was thick here and hid wide stretches of the water from view. They trekked through a dense patch of reeds and emerged on the other side of a bend in the river. A fleet of boats awaited them. Long, low and slender, each boat was laden with men and women. They were wrapped in thick leathers to protect against the frosty night air, and were armed with rifles and rocket launchers. There were hundreds of boats, drifting silently in the river, stretching for as far back as could be seen.

"Ushura was a loss, it is true," said Ajati as they drew near to the closest boat, "but not a permanent one. We will not allow shame or rage to shape our actions. We will not drive blindly into an enemy's strengths. Instead, we shall withdraw."

He signalled to the lead boat with broad gestures, and word swiftly travelled down the fleet. There was no question or argument. Rowers simply turned and made ready to take their boats back east.

"We shall draw the enemy to us. The battlefield will be of our choosing and the war fought on our terms," said Ajati, splashing through the mud and climbing into the lead boat. "If these foreign invaders believe they have the measure of us, then I welcome their arrival in Assahi. This war is far from over, Eskela. In truth, it is only now beginning."

ACT II

SPLIT

Chapter Eleven

"Now, I remember the first drink I had on Ishra," Colt said, waving the little glass clutched between his meaty forefinger and thumb. The clear liquid inside hugged the lip of the glass, somehow not spilling over the edge with the Islander's wild movements. "Let me tell you, I was not impressed. Woman's drink was what it was. Isn't that right, James? James?"

"I'm right next to you, you lubber," said Dalton, elbowing the stout man sitting beside him at the bar.

"Well, it was, right?"

"Was what?" asked Dalton idly. He was fiddling with a radio on the bar-top, delicately turning the dials. A vilifying news report about Separatists murdering children was being broadcast, but every few sentences a burst of static would interrupt the signal.

"A woman's drink!" roared Colt.

Dalton shrugged and downed the contents of his own shot glass. He screwed up his face and thumped the little glass down on the bar-top. Colt laughed and drained his own.

"But this," he declared, holding up the little glass. "This is a real drink! A man's drink!"

A local came up to the bar. "Serek," she said to the bartender, and held up two fingers. Her skin was the colour of olives, her long hair as black as jet. Her curves were wrapped in an airy fabric, the same deep green as her eyes.

The bartender put down two fluted glasses and filled them with a dark liquid from a tall, thin bottle. The woman looked Colt in the eye and slid one of the glasses towards him. Colt stuck out his chest and snatched up the glass. They raised their drinks and knocked them back, neither one breaking eye contact. For a moment they held each other's glare. Then Colt recoiled, making a face like he had sucked a lemon.

Dalton and the rest of the squad around the bar burst out laughing.

"That," she said, pointing at the tall, empty glass, "that is a woman's drink. Too much for you?"

Colt's grin spread. "I believe this may be the start of a beautiful relationship."

The woman frowned at him and walked away, disappearing amongst the press of bodies that crowded the watering hall.

"She'll come around," said Colt with a shrug, flagging down the bartender for more drinks.

"Right, because you've got such a way with women," said Dalton, still laughing.

* * *

It was on the twenty-first day of their deployment to Ishra that the word came.

Twenty days since the events of moonfall, when they had descended from orbit and on that same day been given their first bitter taste of war. Events had calmed down after that, at least for those still stationed at Fort Alliance. That had become the official designation for the camp that had sprung up around their landing zone. It was now the main base of operations for the coalition forces on Ishra, overseeing the many smaller, forward bases that had been established thirty-seven kilometres to the east, along a stretch of the Assahi Jungle Territory.

Over half of the two regiments had been deployed across those bases, to begin laying the groundwork for the push into Separatist-held territory. Reserve forces and a garrison had been kept behind at Fort Alliance, mostly consisting of those companies that had taken heavy casualties on Day One and required time to recover and reorganise.

Sergeant Broden's squad was part of the reserve, assigned to patrol duties in Ushura to assist the Ishradi military in keeping the city safe. Although no further attempts at a welcome ceremony had been made, the High Shekahn had opted to remain in the city, purportedly as a show of defiance to the enemy. The presence of their nation's leader meant that the Ishradi were taking the security of Ushura very seriously, so much so that they had requested support from Fort Alliance.

The assignment had widely come to be considered a blessing for those squads on rotation. After the first week it had become clear that the enemy presence in the city had been crushed, and that any potential hostiles who had survived the assault were in hiding, with survival having taken priority over retaliation.

Patrol shifts were defined by long, casual strolls through the shady avenues and paved streets of the city. Squads from the 2nd Privateers often diverted from their assigned routes to pass through market squares or enjoy street fairs, where local delicacies and trinkets could be purchased. The Avernii patrols, on the other hand, were observed to be considerably more strict in their duties. The Islanders did their best to steer clear of the transhumans whenever they saw them marching their way.

When their shifts ended they would retire to the lodgings that had been provided for them inside the city. The local government had commandeered several hotels to house the coalition garrison. Many of these establishments had been built into the sides of the artificial sinks that dotted the city. With the war front being so close, Ushura had lost its attraction to tourists and to travellers, so its hotels were largely abandoned anyway. Compared to their billets aboard *The Moongate* or the tents of Fort Alliance, the lodgings provided in Ushura were luxurious in the extreme.

As comfortable as the accommodations were however, the

Islanders used the rooms only sparingly. They would clean off the day's sweat and rest a little, before heading out to visit the drinking houses and restaurants. Some of the local establishments regarded the foreign soldiers with great esteem, proclaiming them to be saviours from above, and serving them complementary food and drink. The Islanders were quick to capitalise on this favour. It came to be that a night would not pass where roaming bands of off-duty soldiers could not be seen in the streets.

Then, on the twenty-first day, it happened. They had all known it would, eventually, but with each passing day in Ushura they had lulled themselves deeper and deeper into a false sense of complacency and comfort.

In the end it had only made it more difficult to swallow when finally the call had come.

* * *

They came out of the watering hall, swaying and tottering as they fought to find their legs. Ishra's dawn was only a handful of hours away. They milled about in the street for a moment as they struggled to figure out the way back to their assigned lodgings. Sergeant Broden—who had surprised them all by being the first to suggest these late-night drinking sessions—was fumbling with his data tablet's GPS function.

"James, James," Colt was saying, flexing his hands in front of his face. "I can't feel my fingers. Is that normal? Can you feel your fingers?"

Dalton held up his own hands and regarded them quizzically. "That's… a good question, Colt. You know, it's just occurred to me, fingers are strange."

"Yeah," said Colt, his expression distant.

"Come on, you louts," slurred Broden. "We're going this way. No, this way!"

The squad started off down the street, helping each other

along, stumbling and tripping. From up ahead came the thud of boots marching in synchrony.

"Look, boys," said Broden, "it's the mod brigade! Salute our fearless companions! How well they march, look, look!"

The Islanders jeered and laughed as the Avernii patrol came down the street. In their identical suits of powered armour they looked even more uniform than normal, as though they had been pressed from a factory mould. The transhumans didn't so much as turn a head in Broden's direction. They just marched on in single file, faces hidden behind their glowing, blue visors.

"Uptight bastards," said Colt. "They ought to have a drink sometime. Relax a little."

"Hah, I doubt they could handle it," said Broden, and waved them onwards.

As they stumbled on, Scott wandered up to them and grinned. He had only recently been released from the care of the medics at Fort Alliance. His smile was no longer the charming sight it had once been. Now the scars that criss-crossed his face contorted hideously at the slightest change in expression. Many of his stitches had yet to be removed, and some of the wounds were still covered in wadding.

"You know," he said, putting an arm around Dalton's shoulder, "I have decided that the women of this moon are very... very... beautiful. I am very... very... sure that I was flirted with a great deal tonight."

"You and Colt both," laughed Dalton.

"Tomorrow I will find that woman," declared Colt, "and I will challenge her to a bottle of... what was it called? That horrible, black stuff?"

"Seck? Senek? Serek!" said Blake.

"Sea-wreck?" asked Colt. "Well, that's sure what it felt like. But never-the-nevertheless, I shall drink a whole bottle of the stuff!"

"To impress a woman whose name you don't even know, a woman who humiliated you and then walked away from you?"

"That's just how women show they like you," said Colt dismissively.

The loose formation of drunken soldiers came to a blundering halt. Broden had come to a sudden stop, the data tablet held up to his face.

"Well, fuck," he said after a moment.

They clustered around him silently. Broden lowered the data tablet, the stark white light of its screen throwing shadows up along his face. His lip curled and one of his nostrils twitched.

"We've been called," he said, his voice hoarse. "We're going back to war."

* * *

Fortunately, their transports were not scheduled to arrive until later in the morning. As the days had progressed and the moon of Ishra had continued its rotation around its celestial host, the gas giant Mitera, they had all noticed the difference in light exposure. This was the change in "mini-season" that 1st Squad Sergeant Banks had described to them all those days ago, before their descent into Ushura's underworld. Ishra had shifted to the far side of its parent body from the star Patera. The moon lurked in the shadow of its mother, hiding its face from the glaring light of the system's star. Mitera provided a source of illumination in itself though, its strong reflective power and churning internal gases giving Ishra a day-side even away from the light of Patera. It was a different quality of light, albeit, not as clear, not as bright, but it was a light nonetheless, gentle and warm. The comparison was akin to that of a fluorescent light to a candle.

This also meant that the durations of night and of day had equalised. The nights were now more than twice as long as they had been and the days shorter by about seven hours. The Islanders were grateful for it. The nights provided respite from the soaring temperatures of the day and although it could become bone-achingly cold, the soldiers could always put on another layer of clothing, whereas during the day there was only so much that they could remove.

In this case, the longer night also meant more hours to sleep before the transportation arrived to ferry them back to Fort Alliance, which was another reason to be grateful. When it was time, they awoke with much groaning and complaining. They had indulged in the night's activities entirely too much. Dalton's head pounded and his tongue and throat felt as dry as paper. He forced himself to sit up in bed before silencing the annoying bleeps of his wrist-watch, something he had trained himself to do so that he wouldn't drift off to sleep again.

The room smelled wretched. Someone had probably thrown up during the night and decided it was easier to go back to sleep than to clean it up. It wouldn't have been the first time. There were five of them in this one room, with the rest of the squad in the room next door. Cots had been set up to accommodate the extra bodies, as the rooms had originally been designed for no more than two people at a time. Who got to sleep in the two comfortable beds was decided by the outcomes of the many, creative drinking games that only drunk minds could conceive of.

Dalton opened the windows, slid back the insect nets and threw open the shutters. It was something he immediately regretted doing, for although the morning light was gentle, it was still too much for his sensitive eyes. It earned him no praise from his comrades either. They cursed him, twisting away from the light, burying their heads beneath pillows.

"Get up," he said, deciding it was unfair that he should be the only one to be awake on time. He went by their cots, shaking them and dragging back the sheets.

"I'll fucking slay you if you touch me," grunted Colt, as he neared the man's bed. Dalton decided against it, and began gathering together his gear instead. He took a clean set of fatigues from his duffel, along with his wash bag, and made for the en suite. "Well, I guess I'll just use all the hot water then."

That roused the men from their beds, with yet another torrent of expletives, but Dalton, cackling, had already locked the en suite door behind him. He was merciful and showered quickly. He ran a razor across his face for fear of Lieutenant Killian, and towelled himself down before dressing in fresh fatigues and relinquishing the bathroom to be fought over by his squad mates.

He strapped on his combat armour. Even though they wouldn't be in a danger zone for some time yet, it was easier to wear than to lug about separately, and between his backpack, bedroll and duffel bag he already had enough to carry as it was.

Broden turned up ten minutes later to make sure they were awake, his round, clean-shaven head appearing in the window. The man looked miserable and didn't speak much. It had been good to spend these last three weeks in Broden's company, not as their sergeant, but just as a fellow man. There was a separation in the 2nd Privateers, between the new recruits and the career soldiers who formed the officer cadre. It was often cause for tension, but their time in Ushura together had bonded the squad to their sergeant through more than just training.

Forty-five minutes later the squad was assembled in full on the steps at the base of the hotel's sink. There was a round swimming pool set into the paved floor. It hadn't been used in a while, at least not since the majority of 9th Company had been bunked here. Empty bottles, grease paper from take-away food and other bits of rubbish floated in the water. On the tiered walkways and steps that led up and down the depth of the sink, the other squads were slowly beginning to assemble. They all had the same look about them, the look of men who have been woken from a blissful dream only to realise that it was just that, a dream.

"I'm too hungry to be dealing with this," said Colt. He was watching one of the other squads, who had woken much earlier than them and gone out to get breakfast from a nearby street vendor. The thick, round breads stuffed with spiced meats and colourful vegetables made Dalton's mouth water.

"Reckon there'll be time to get something along the way?" asked Dalton.

"Probably not," said Blake. "But I'm sure there will be food at the fort."

Dalton and Colt gave a joint groan.

When the company was assembled they went up to street level and walked a couple of blocks until they reached one of the main roads. A convoy of Ishradi trucks awaited them, beige-painted vehicles with canopied cargo beds. The air was full of the stink of diesel as the trucks were refuelled by a fat tanker that trundled slowly alongside, stopping by each vehicle so that a crewman could link up the pipe and open the valve. These trucks were fresh from the front line it seemed, low on fuel, their tyres caked with dirt and clumps of grass, their paintwork scuffed. One truck even had a line of what were most certainly bullet holes in its canvas covering.

There were other companies present, and more still coming in from nearby parts of the city. The other Privateers were already loading onto the trucks, slinging their bags ahead of them and helping each other to climb into the high cargo beds. The officers of the 9th began directing them towards their designated transports.

"Where are the mods?" asked Harris, looking about.

Colt shrugged. "Probably marched off the moment they got their new orders, being the unnatural and uptight bastards that they are."

"They're quick, I'll give them that," said Moore. "Organised, efficient. More than us."

Following the perpetually angry gesticulations of Lieutenant Killian, the platoon mounted up in their assigned truck. The convoy came to life, engines revving throatily, and the air filled with the acrid reek of combustion engines. The trucks pulled away down the road and headed out of Ushura. Dalton, Colt, and Blake sat at the back of their transport, staring out at the city as they drew away.

"Well, that was nice…" said Blake, "while it lasted."

Chapter Twelve

"I don't believe it," said Colt. "That's her, that's definitely her."

"I don't know," said Dalton, frowning. "She looks different."

"She looks different because she's in a fucking military uniform," said Colt excitedly. "She's military. I don't believe it."

The force that had been activated for front line deployment was assembled in the clearing at the heart of Fort Alliance. Eight hundred soldiers from between the 2nd Privateers and the Avernii Transhuman Forces. This much was nothing new to Dalton, but the small division of Ishradi soldiers present in the camp came as a surprise to them all.

They were a scruffy bunch, in their star-faded, green fatigues. Many of them wore their jackets tied about their waists, standing in t-shirts and vests, tanned arms and necks exposed in the morning light. Unlike the off-world forces, the Ishradi military was comprised of both men and women. On Landbreak, it wasn't even considered that women could be a part of the army's fighting strength.

"What do you reckon they're doing here?" asked Thompson.

"Deploying alongside us to the front most likely," replied Blake. "After all, we're here to support the local military, not replace them."

"They're pathfinders," said Sergeant Broden, striding into their midst, having returned from conference with the other officers of the 9th. "Jungle specialists. One of them will be assigned to each squad to help us survive and navigate the Assahi Territory."

"Do we get to choose our pathfinder?" asked Colt, grinning.

Broden followed his gaze. "Hold on, isn't that the girl from the bar, last night?"

"Told you," said Colt.

"I didn't deny it," shrugged Dalton.

"Women in their army," scoffed Broden. "No wonder they're losing this war."

"I wouldn't say that too loudly if I were you," said Blake. Dalton thought the man was right. They didn't seem like the sort of women who would take a comment like Broden's without challenge. Every one of them looked to be in peak condition, their bodies lean with hard muscle. Most of them had shaven off their hair, but others wore it up in tight tails or braids. Either way, they had a severe look about them, like they would sooner break a hand than shake one.

Broden didn't seem intimidated. "I'll make sure we get a man."

"I wonder whether there are any women under those armoured suits," said Colt, peering over at the Avernii detachment. "Salt, can you imagine how ugly a mod woman must look?"

"So, what's the plan, Sarge?" asked Wright, ignoring Colt's boorishness.

"We're going straight to the front," said Broden. "Can't tell you much, because I wasn't told much. I think High Command is on edge with so many potential Separatist infiltrators in our midst."

"Salt, you're telling me any one of them could be an enemy in disguise?" asked Nelson, nodding towards the Ishradi soldiers loitering across from them.

"We know their security has been compromised — we knew that much on Day One. High Command doesn't want to take too many chances. We'll get our intel and orders piecemeal from now on, to minimise the damage of any leaks."

"So, we're going in blind," said Dalton.

"Stow it, Dalton. The hand doesn't need to know what it's doing so long as the brain does. We're the hand. Not the brain.

Got it?"

"Yes, sir," Dalton said.

"Look sharp," said Broden, nodding to where a group of officers were making their way through the assembly. Colonel Hunt was at the front. It was the first time Dalton or any of the squad had seen the man since he had disappeared in smoke and fire on the palace steps, three weeks ago. He was in his usual regalia, looking tall and broad in his heel-length coat, with his iconic bicorn casting his long face in shadow.

The colonel walked amongst his men, sharing words and nods of encouragement. After a few leisurely minutes of mingling, he strode away from the men of his regiment and crossed over to where the Ishradi pathfinders were grouped.

"If there is an infiltrator amongst them, is it really a good idea for the colonel to be so close?" asked Scott.

"That's Colonel Lawrence Hunt, son," said Broden. "You'd need more than a hopeful assassin to take him out of the game. You'd need a whole damn army and then some. They call him The Storm of Landbreak for a reason, you know?"

"Do they?" asked Harris, nonplussed.

"Don't tell me you haven't heard the story," said Colt.

"Salty eel balls, call yourself an Islander, do you?" said Broden, his voice dripping with scorn. "Alright, listen. Thirty years ago during the Boyle Insurrection, when you were still tucked up tight in your daddy's ball-sack, Colonel Hunt was a commodore in the Confederation Army, back when there still was a confederation. Tell me you've at least heard of the Battle of Ironsea?"

"That was the big one, wasn't it?" said Harris, uncertain.

"The big one," scoffed Blake. "That battle is the reason Landbreak is a globally unified republic now and not a confederation anymore."

"Anyway," continued Broden, "you know what they say about Ironsea, right? You'd sooner smash a boat on those waves than float one. It's a no-go. Ships just don't sail through that stretch of water. The storms are too fierce and the waves too high. You have to stick to the coasts if you want to cross the Ironsea Gulf. Thing was though, the main fleet of the Boyle Insurrectionists were a day out from Firstfall City, and the Confederation reinforcements were on the wrong side of the gulf. It would have taken them three days to go around and by then the Insurrectionists would have already taken Firstfall City and that would have been the end of that. Well, Commodore Hunt wasn't going to have any of that. He commanded his reinforcement fleet to go straight through the middle of Ironsea and cut the Insurrectionists off before they even reached the harbour.

"Turns out that night was one of the biggest storms to ever happen. Half the ships in the reinforcement fleet were lost never to be recovered, even to this day. Commodore Hunt didn't so much as blink. He sailed out of that storm like he was a part of it, and slammed right into the middle of the Insurrectionist fleet. They didn't know what hit them. No one could have expected a fleet to come out of the Ironsea, let alone in a storm like that. Even battered and outnumbered, Commodore Hunt defeated the Insurrectionists at sea and put an end to the war then and there."

"And that's why they call him The Storm of Landbreak," said Colt proudly.

"Enough chatter," came the raised voice of Lieutenant Killian, striding down the line of Privateers to reach his platoon. "Form up in squads, side by side."

Other lieutenants were doing the same, lining up their platoons with the sergeants standing up front to distinguish individual squads. One by one, the Ishradi pathfinders crossed over and joined the Privateers, taking up positions by the sergeants. Colt nudged Dalton as the woman from last night began walking over. She headed towards them, then veered and joined a squad further up the line.

"Damn it," grumbled Colt.

Their pathfinder turned out to be a slender man with long, slicked-back hair. The bone structure of his face seemed unnaturally prominent, and his eyes were bright and wide, lending him a startling appearance.

"I am Ilom," said the pathfinder, nodding so deeply that it was almost a bow.

"Sergeant Broden," he replied stiffly, barely glancing at the man.

Ilom regarded the sergeant for a moment before turning his big eyes on the rest of them. That look made Dalton feel acutely uncomfortable, as though he was standing out here naked and being inspected with intimate levels of attention.

"See something you like?" asked Colt, jutting out his jaw.

"Just deciding," said Ilom.

"Deciding what?"

"Deciding who amongst you will survive the jungle."

* * *

They left the camp in an armoured convoy that stretched for almost two kilometres before its tail end cleared Fort Alliance. Setting the pace at the front of the line were thirty Avernii carapace-walkers, marching in two columns of fifteen, their mechanical, back-jointed legs carrying them at a speed of thirty kilometres per hour.

Behind them came a single column of one hundred Wave-Rider Class Amphibious Armoured Personnel Carriers. These enclosed, Islander vehicles carried the eight hundred-strong task force, along with their complement of Ishradi pathfinders. Those vehicles not transporting manpower were laden with supplies, munitions and rations. The Wave-Riders had eight thick wheels beneath their angled hulls, and churned up the grass and soil in great plumes as they forged a path east towards the Assahi Territory.

Twenty Seahound Class Amphibious Tanks followed, and behind them, bringing up the column's rear, were ten Striker Class Self-propelled Rocket Artillery pieces. The latter, to put it simply, were rocket boxes on tracks. The Striker had a forward cabin for the crew, while its cargo bed was dominated by the armament itself. The rocket box consisted of twelve firing tubes capable of loading and launching an array of specialised warheads, ranging from submunitions to air-burst payloads and everything in between.

The convoy was conspicuous as it drove out of Fort Alliance and made its own road across the open fields. The leading carapace-walkers gleamed with their glossy white and black plates, and the 2nd Privateers had kept their iconic colours of navy blue, black and grey. Ploughing across the low, yellow grass it was clear that the convoy had no intention of hiding its presence.

This was to be a war of domination, High Command had declared; a theatre of battle that would witness a technologically superior force overwhelm and pacify a poorly armed and equipped adversary. It would be done swiftly, with maximum application of force. Hit them hard and hit them fast and they'll stay down, had said Lieutenant Killian, explaining the overriding philosophy behind their attack strategy.

The enemy had already shown their hand during the palace ambush. Their weapons were basic, poorly maintained assault rifles and low-powered rocket launchers that operated more like mortars than true rocket-propelled grenades. It wouldn't matter if the Separatists could easily recognise the tanks and fighting vehicles of the Privateers, because they possessed nothing in their arsenal capable of harming them.

The 2nd Privateers would go forth proudly, hoisting their colours openly and without fear. The enemy would see them coming and be stricken with fear. The psychological assault of such a bold advance would weaken the enemy resolve and see them routed shortly after the first shots had been fired.

That, at least, was how Lieutenant Killian had described it to them.

"Sounds like a good way to get shot," had grumbled Dalton, keeping his voice low.

"I'll just paint a big, red bullseye on my chest while we're at it," Blake had added.

The convoy pressed on east, keeping the Sadari River a kilometre to the north of them. There were no true roads leading from Ushura to the front-line, and so they crossed the open countryside instead. There had been some discussion about using the river itself to reach the Assahi Territory – seeing as all the vehicles of the 2nd Privateers were amphibious – but the deep bends of the Sadari would have made the journey three times as long than travelling over ground, even off-road.

As it turned out, their destination was not directly east anyway. Halfway to the front line, the convoy drivers received new orders over the radio. The armour column began a gradual turn to the southeast, putting more distance between them and the Sadari River. Sealed away in their transports, without windows to look through, the troopers had no idea about their change in direction.

That was not all that the passengers missed. They did not see the herds of squat, leathery-skinned grazers that waddled about on their hind legs, gathering up the short grass in bunches with their three-fingered claws and feeding it through blunt-toothed mouths. When the convoy passed too close, the stubby grazers would hop away and disappear down burrow holes, emitting high-pitched squeals as they went.

Nor did they see the colourful flocks of wide-bodied birds – patterned in aqua blue and electric purple – which flew on featherless wings so slowly in the thick, hot air of Ishra that they seemed almost to hover. They congregated over the river, their long, black beaks angled downwards. Without warning they would collapse those bright wings, like a ship drawing in its sails, and plummet towards the water, unfolding them again only at the very last second to climb effortlessly back into the sky, their beaks full of fish.

The column's bearing steepened until they were heading almost wholly south. When finally the convoy drivers were close enough to see the distant, eastern face of the jungle, they were running nearly parallel to it. It was an abrupt, green wall, stretching north and south for such a distance that it appeared to be infinite in its breadth.

Two hours after setting off, the convoy pulled into Camp Golf. It was a small base, perched on the edge of an escarpment that overlooked the jungle two or three kilometres away. Too small even to accommodate the thirty Avernii carapace-walkers, let alone the one hundred and sixty armoured vehicles of the 2nd Privateers.

The convoy was arranging itself outside of the camp's gabion perimeter when their new orders came in. Ten Wave-Riders, five Seahounds, two Strikers and six carapace-walkers were instructed out of the formation. They pulled away from the rest of the convoy and, as per their instructions, began heading further south at a furious pace.

* * *

"What's happening?" Blake asked, fumbling to re-buckle his harness as their transport's engines revved back up. "I thought we were stopping!"

Two hours in the back of a Wave-Rider, trundling over untamed terrain with the continuous growl of its monstrous tyres grinding up the soil, had left the squad weary and disoriented. The prospect of stopping and stretching their legs had been a glorious one, but no sooner had they begun to unstrap themselves than the transport had set off again.

"Wherever we're going, we're sure in a hurry," said Moore, gripping the bench and bracing himself against the growing momentum.

Dalton looked along the cargo hold to where Broden was pushing off of the bench, using the overhead rails to steady himself. The sergeant stood so that he could see down the aisle, on either side of which were seated the men of his squad, now with the addition of Ilom, their Ishradi pathfinder.

"Pay attention," he said, his voice raised over the din of the closed space. "We've just been selected as part of a strike force that's heading to a place called Kura Valley, south of Camp Golf. Intel has it that the Separatists are using the valley to smuggle supplies and soldiers into the jungle. Spotters in the valley have reported that one of those supply operations is underway right now. We're going to hit it, stop it from reaching Separatist territory. That means it's time to get ready, boys, combat ready. Let's show these bastards Islander steel!"

Chapter Thirteen

The Wave-Riders hit the valley ridge at eighty kilometres an hour. Their tyres left the ground, just briefly, before the heavy transports ploughed down onto the north slope of Kura Valley. They ripped up clouds of soil and dust in their wake, coming over the ridge like a steel avalanche pouring into the valley.

A kilometre wide and five times as long, Kura Valley was a deep corridor that led northeast out of the grasslands and scored a path into the jungle depths. The strike force came over the valley's northern lip at speed, six hundred metres from the jungle wall.

They acquired their target, a convoy of eight Ishradi cargo trucks, escorted by squadrons of dirt-bike outriders and jeeps with mounted guns in their cargo beds. They had been moving slowly along the valley floor, cautious not to kick up a dirt trail that would give away their position. At the time the spotters had relayed word of the Separatist convoy, the column of vehicles had just been entering the valley mouth five kilometres to the southwest. By the time the coalition strike force actually arrived, the Separatist convoy was just over half a kilometre from entering the Assahi Territory.

When they noticed the armoured transports coming up over the ridge though, they put on speed, racing to pass through the jungle wall before they could be caught in the open. Once they were in amongst the trees, catching them would be nigh impossible. Drivers on both sides floored their accelerators. The Wave-Rivers powered hard and fast down the valley side.

Inside the armoured hulls of the transports, the soldiers were being tossed back and forth like rag dolls, only just kept in their seats by the harnesses they had tightened around their chests. Blake was screaming like a child on a water slide. Colt was roaring with a madman's glee. That was making Dalton laugh. Across from them, Scott and Nelson were bracing one another against the violent juddering. Harris was hanging limp in his harness. Either he had passed out, or hit his head against the hull hard enough to have been knocked out.

Behind the line of transports, the Seahounds and Strikers crested the valley ridge. The tank crews had been briefed along the way with a set of plans to cover the eventualities upon reaching the valley. When they arrived, if the Separatist convoy was still in the open, they were to deny ground and impede them only. If the convoy was destroyed outright then the supplies could not be captured for the coalition. That, and the value of prisoners with strategic information was not to be overlooked. Only in the event of the convoy's imminent escape would the tank crews be authorised to act with extreme prejudice.

The Striker crews went to work at once. The rocket boxes craned upwards on their mounts and rotated to face the jungle. Integrated computing systems calculated distances and plotted trajectories. Auto-loading servomechanisms cycled the desired munitions, thudding the warheads into place. The Strikers opened fire. One by one, the firing tubes discharged their payloads. The rockets cleared the launchers on streams of smoke and fire, splitting the air with high-pitched screeches that echoed the breadth of the valley.

The volley went arching overhead, streaking the sky with bright propellant trails, passing over the pursuing Wave-Riders and outpacing the fleeing convoy. The rockets came down less than fifty metres ahead of the Separatists. The warheads struck the earth and in the same instant detonated into huge sheets of liquid fire that splashed out in every direction. In a matter of seconds, the last stretch of dirt road leading into the jungle was set ablaze. The open-sided jeeps and trucks with their canvas tarpaulins didn't dare drive through the flames.

Bike squadrons kicked up waves of soil as they peeled away from the sudden conflagration. The rest of the convoy braked hard. The lead truck was rear-ended by the vehicle behind. One jeep lost control of its abrupt deceleration, wheels skidding, and flipped over its side, tumbling into the raging chemical fire. Its exposed fuel tank went up a second later, and the jeep disappeared in an expanding fireball that rained shards of burning metal across the convoy.

The rest of the escort turned about. With the prospect of escape denied, the Separatists had only one choice left to them. They would fight. A horde of jeeps and bikes charged the approaching line of Wave-Riders. Separatist fighters climbed up into the backs of jeeps, racked the slides on their heavy-calibre mounted guns, and opened fire. The long-barrelled weapons chattered and bucked as they unleashed torrents of 15.3mm rounds. The bullets tore up the ground around the advancing Wave-Riders and blew craters in the thick armour of their hulls, sending cascades of sparks along their dark flanks.

The Wave-Riders had armaments of their own. Sleek, angled turrets mounted 8.6mm chain-guns capable of firing five hundred rounds per minute. In the face of the enemy fire, the Wave-Riders responded in kind. Long gouts of flame licked from the chain-gun barrels as they opened fire. Hundreds of spent shell casings jettisoned into the air. The turrets traversed left and right, raking their fire across the approaching enemy. Jeeps were perforated, their hoods punctured by dozens of rounds, their engines destroyed. Windscreens shattered beneath the hail, the drivers riddled with bullets. Bike riders were knocked clean off their saddles, torn apart by the massive rates of fire, their bikes flipping out from underneath them.

Then the two lines collided. The ten Wave-Riders and the

Separatist escort met in a crashing storm of gunfire, each side dragging clouds of dust behind them. One jeep slammed into the front of a Wave-Rider. It was flung up and off the side of the armoured transport, its rusty metal framework coming apart with the force of the collision. Another Wave-Rider passed between two bikers, who hurled firebombs at its hull as they raced by, engulfing the vehicle in rippling flames. A jeep managed to steer clear of one of the big transports at the last second, and strafed its flank with gunfire. The 15.3mm rounds peppered the side of the Wave-Rider with fist-sized craters, but failed to pierce the thick armour plating. The squad in that transport watched in horror as a line of dents were hammered across the inside of the hull.

The two lines came apart. Those jeeps and bikes that survived the clash drifted round to come in again, only to be torn apart in a second fusillade of high velocity rounds. The Wave-Rider turrets had tracked them through one hundred and eighty degrees and re-engaged, dealing the killing blow and destroying the escort in its entirety.

Some of the trucks had tried to use the escort's sacrifice to back out of the line, to try to find a way around the chemical fire into the jungle. There hadn't been enough time. The Wave-Riders cut them off, surrounded the supply convoy and came to a halt, smoke drifting from their tyres.

* * *

"Out! Now!" barked Broden, as the rear-hatch to their transport dropped open.

They piled out, unsteady on their feet, and followed their sergeant around the transport towards the convoy. Two Ishradi fighters leapt down from the back of the nearest truck. They were dressed for the heat and the jungle, green vests and baggy trousers.

"Put down your weapons!" shouted Broden.

The Separatists didn't seem inclined to obey. They lifted their rifles. Broden killed one of them with a quick burst from his L7. Colt, always a step behind the sergeant, took down the second with a solid body shot. Other fighters were coming out of the trucks, putting up what resistance they could. Surrounded and outgunned, their efforts were futile. A force of one hundred soldiers, split evenly between the Privateers and the Avernii, closed a noose around the eight cargo trucks and swiftly put an end to the fighting.

Dalton caught sight of the transhumans prowling around the convoy. With their fully enclosed suits of powered armour and their triangular-barrelled rifles, the Avernii were distinct on the battlefield. The L7 assault rifle used by the Privateers was an adaptation of the rifles that had been brought with them on the migrant ship from Old Earth. Its casing was sleek, matte black and built for prolonged battlefield use, weighing in at less than six pounds. It was gas operated and chambered a 5.56mm round, capable of both burst and fully automatic fire. There was a vertical foregrip for manoeuvrability and a slot for scope attachments.

It did not in the slightest resemble the rifles used by their Avernii allies. From the white casing and triangular barrel to the blue flash and high-pitched drone of its discharge, the weapon was entirely alien to the Islanders. Its ammunition type and firing mechanism were unknown. All that could be determined from observation was that whatever rounds it fired were caseless, as no spent shells were ejected from the weapon upon firing.

"Hands on the wheel! Now! Where I can see them!" Broden was shouting. The squad had moved up to the driver's cabin of the nearest truck. Two men were seated there, sweat beading on their dark skin, their eyes wide. Trembling, they did as they were told.

"Harris, get the door," ordered Broden. The trooper moved

up and took the door handle, but it wouldn't budge. The sergeant brandished his rifle at the driver. "Unlock it! Unlock it now!"

The driver nodded frantically. He reached down behind the door to disengage the lock. Harris tried the handle again. The door swung open. He stared down the barrel of the pistol gripped in the driver's hand. It barked once. Blood splattered across Dalton's face. Harris went down, clutching at his neck. Blood was pumping up between his twitching fingers.

Colt shredded the cabin with a full magazine of rounds, shattering the windows and killing both men seated within. Broden was howling curses. Thompson was screaming for a medic. Moore went to his knees, throwing down his rifle and fumbling to help his friend. Harris was choking, spitting up blood and writhing in the grass.

Somewhere in the distance, someone was shouting. Dalton reached up to touch his face. He felt the blood there, still warm. 'This is not my blood,' he thought, 'this is Harris' blood. This is Harris' blood on my face.' The thoughts came slowly, mired in shock. Someone was still shouting in the background, but Dalton couldn't make out the words.

The first mortar shell came out of the sky, tore through the tarpaulin of one of the convoy trucks, and blew out the entire contents of its cargo bed. The tarpaulin came apart in ribbons. Crates full of processed foodstuffs were shattered and flung upwards and outwards on flaming trails. Islanders ducked and dived aside. The Avernii turned their heads towards the jungle, ignoring the debris that pelted their armoured bodies.

"Take cover!" roared Broden.

A second mortar shell howled out of the sky. It hit the prow of a Wave-Rider and detonated, a fountain of flame and smoke billowing into the air. A third came down on the far side of the convoy and hurled a dozen men off their feet. A fourth and a fifth fell short of the mark, digging up clods of grass and soil.

"Back! Back to the transport!"

Moore and Thompson lifted Harris between them. The man was covered in his own blood, more blood than Dalton knew was in the human body. They dashed back towards their Wave-Rider, mortar shells howling out of the sky and exploding all around them. The wounded trooper was manhandled up the ramp. The rest of them followed, taking cover beneath the transport's armoured hull.

"Separatist mortar crews in the damned tree line," said Broden.

"What do we do?" asked Nelson.

"We stay put. I'm not about to charge headlong into the jungle for a welcoming party."

"Did they know we were coming?" asked Wright.

"How the fuck am I supposed to know?" Broden snapped.

"I do not think they were waiting for you," said a voice from the back of the transport. The Islanders twisted round, rifles snapping up. Ilom raised his hands slowly, an amused expression on his face. "I believe this is standard operating procedure for them. They smuggle supplies into the jungle and have a team waiting to receive them, or to cover them, should the need arise."

"And how the salt do you know so much about Separatist procedure?" asked Broden.

Ilom shrugged. "It's what I would do."

"How is he?" Broden asked, turning his attention to Harris. Moore had found a first aid kit and was fighting to wrap a bandage around the thrashing soldier's neck. The bandage was already soaked in blood. The sergeant tried to raise a medic over his headset, but the channel was clogged with frantically shouting voices.

"Dalton! Blake! Find a medic!" ordered the sergeant.

"Out there?" asked Blake, watching as another mortar shell dug up a crater in the soil just two dozen metres away.

"I'll go," said Colt, following Dalton back down the ramp.

"For salt's sake," cried Blake and went after them, throwing a fearful glance at the sky.

They slipped round the side of the Wave-Rider, hugging its hull. Squads of troopers were still dashing around in the open. They saw a lone Avernii soldier limping out of the smoke and the fire, his armour scorched, his visor cracked, revealing a slash of the pale face beneath.

"Medic!" called Dalton as they made their way along the semi-circle of transports. "Medic!"

"Here! Here!" replied a voice. A Privateer detached from a huddle of soldiers and ran over to them, half crouched. He had a red cross on his helmet.

"Where?" asked the medic, straight to the point.

"Come with me!" shouted Blake and immediately headed back towards their transport. The medic followed, but Dalton lagged behind.

"Colt, look," he said. The stout trooper stopped and followed Dalton's gaze. The flames from the incendiary bombardment were dying out now, and beyond the scorched earth they could see the jungle face. The six carapace-walkers attached to the strike force were sprinting down the valley. They had held back in reserve, out of sight, but now they were powering down the slope on their back-jointed legs, making a beeline for the trees.

"It's about time," said Colt.

Two of the walkers opened fire on the move, their rotary cannons spooling up and unleashing rapid torrents of gunfire into the tree line. The rate of fire was so high that it chewed through the trunks of several trees, sending them creaking and snapping to the jungle floor. A second pair of walkers brought up their flamethrowers. They sent long tongues of ignited napalm hissing into the tree line. The last two walkers hung back, panning their long-barrelled cannons back and forth, providing overwatch for their companions.

The rest of the carapace-walkers didn't stop or even slow. Atomising the jungle facade with a withering onslaught of high-velocity rounds and sheets of dripping napalm, the walkers surged into the collapsing tree line, going to work with their mechanised claws and huge buzz saws. Even from a distance, Dalton could hear the screams.

"Well, fuck me," said Colt, staring dumbfounded at the ensuing carnage.

"Let's get back," Dalton said, and the two men set off towards their squad.

The mortar bombardment had ceased and, other than the distant grinding of huge saws and the crackle of flames, the clamour of combat was finally subsiding. Smoke and dust was swirling in the air, drifting down the length of the valley and blanketing the grass in a broad shroud of ash.

Chapter Fourteen

Mitera was on the horizon, dragging with her all of the warm light out of the sky, when they arrived back at Camp Golf. The strike force brought with it the surviving seven trucks of the Separatist supply convoy, along with a dozen prisoners. The operation was being hailed as a success, but as they rode back in their Wave-Rider, coated in blood and dust, with Harris out cold and strapped to a stretcher, it didn't much feel like victory.

"He was lucky, we all were," Broden had said, picking up on the low mood.

"Lucky," Dalton had murmured. He had thought about those mortar shells that had come hammering out of the sky. If one of those had come down even eight or ten metres from him, he would be like Harris right now, pale and delirious from blood loss, clinging to life by a thread. If he was lucky, that was. More likely he wouldn't be alive at all, but scattered in bloody chunks in the low, yellow grass of a moon that was not his own.

He had wondered just how many more times they would get "lucky".

The wounded, of which there were always too many, had been rushed to the medical tents, leaving the rest of them standing beneath the darkening sky. Broden, along with the other officers, had been called off for debriefing. The smells of cooking stew were wafting from an open eating area, where long tables and benches had been arranged beneath the shade of a sheet-metal roof. Food wasn't being served yet, but some of the soldiers had already taken seats, as though sitting down for dinner would hasten its arrival.

Broden's squad, along with most others, were standing and sitting about in the camp's assembly clearing, filling the air with the low murmur of half-hearted conversation. New tents were still being erected by those soldiers who had not been a part of the strike force sent to Kura Valley. Until then, they had nowhere else to be, having been ordered to stay within the camp's protective perimeter. With eight hundred new arrivals packed inside of its high gabion walls, Camp Golf was uncomfortably overcrowded.

"James," said Colt, tugging on his sleeve to stir him from his thoughts. "James, is it just me, or is that mod looking at you?"

Dalton looked up. Sure enough, just across from where their squad was huddled, a trio of the transhumans were staring their way. They had their helmets off, not that it did much to distinguish them from one another, each being pale to the point of translucence and devoid of even a single hair anywhere on their heads. Once Dalton had seen them, the three Avernii began striding their way.

"Oh, what now?" sighed Scott.

The Avernii came close and quietly regarded the Islanders.

"I'm really not in the mood for this," snarled Colt. "Something you want, mods?"

"Hello," said the lead Avernii, looking directly at Dalton. "It is good to meet you again."

"Do I know you?" asked Dalton.

"You do not recall our exchange," said the Avernii plainly. "I am Cutra. We met aboard *The Moongate*. At the vehicle bay."

"Oh! Right," said Dalton, narrowing his eyes as he hunted for anything distinguishing about the transhuman's face that he could commit to memory. Between his fatigue and the fading light it was too difficult a task. "Small world."

"These are my companions, Rolay and Zirris," said Cutra, indicating in turn to the other two transhumans. "You will recall your exchange with Zirris."

"I do," said Dalton slowly, unsure exactly what was happening. He could practically feel Colt's anticipation. The man was rolling out his shoulders and stretching his neck. "Look, sorry about all that business, you know, with the… fire extinguisher."

"I consider it a valuable lesson, James Dalton," said Zirris.

"Ah? Well, good. I guess," said Dalton. The group lapsed into silence. The three Avernii stared at them plainly. Dalton looked away. Blake cleared his throat loudly. Scott let out a low whistle.

"So, were you at the valley?" asked Dalton, when the silence threatened no end.

"We were not part of the strike force," said Cutra.

"It is regrettable," added Zirris.

"Regrettable? How's that?" sneered Colt.

"We have seen the battle data," said the third transhuman, Rolay. "There were opportunities for trial. Potential for distinction."

"Distinction? You're talking about fame?" asked Blake, frowning.

"Distinction," repeated Rolay. "The recognition of one's strength as a warrior."

"Do you not also strive for distinction?" asked Cutra.

"Mostly I just try to stay alive," laughed Dalton.

"Then why do you fight in the first place?" asked Zirris.

"It does seem counter-intuitive," admitted Blake. Colt glanced at him, but Blake held up a warning finger. "Don't tell me to shut up. Don't do it."

"We fight to end the war on Ishra. That's the mission," said Dalton firmly.

"But why do *you* fight, James Dalton?" asked Cutra.

"I just told you why," said Dalton.

"No. You have told me why our governing authorities have shipped a fighting force to this moon. That is their fight, but what is *your* fight?"

"What are you talking about?" asked Dalton, his patience

wearing thin.

"Every warrior must know their fight," said Zirris.

The three transhumans promptly turned around and began marching away.

"Salt, don't just walk away," Dalton called after them.

Only Cutra paused and turned back. "I apologise. It is easy to forget that you are not connected. My kin and I are summoned."

"Summoned?" asked Wright. "I didn't hear anything."

There had been no audible announcement of any kind, but sure enough the Avernii were congregating at the far end of the clearing, drawn as if by instinct alone. Cutra raised a finger and placed it against his temple. "You are not connected."

The transhuman strode away.

"What the salt was that about?" asked Nelson.

"Freaks," said Colt, as if by way of explanation.

* * *

"There's home," said Dalton, lying in the grass and pointing up at the sky.

By the time they had eaten – a richly flavoured stew cooked with local vegetables – the new tents had been raised. Most of the squad were too wired to sleep though. Thompson and Moore had gone to see Harris, who had survived his injury and been stabilised after a full hour of surgery. Colt and Scott had gone to see if they could scrounge up more food. The rest of them were lounging outside of their tent. The pathfinder, Ilom, was sitting with them.

Landbreak hung in the sky. It was a dark orb of stone-grey and midnight-blue, obscured in part by huge swirls of clouds.

"It must be strange," said Ilom, "to see your home from so far away."

"It is," agreed Dalton. "I keep thinking about all the people I know there, going about their lives as normal."

"Tell me about Landbreak. What kind of moon is it?" asked Ilom.

"Colder than here," said Dalton, running a sleeve across his sweaty brow. "More water, from what I've seen at least. Seems everywhere on Landbreak is along one coast or another. Tides are a problem. Most of our cities and towns are raised above the ground, or else they'd spend half the time underwater. Lots of rocky sea cliffs. Forests further inland, but not so much open land like you've got. Nothing like the Assahi Territory, that's for sure. There are no jungles on Landbreak. There are storms, too. Big storms that blow in off the sea."

"We have storms on Ishra."

Dalton raised an eyebrow. "You do?"

Ilom laughed. "You have been fortunate, Islander. Ishra has welcomed you with tranquillity, but it will not last. Sooner or later, her calm will pass. Then you will see. Ishra has storms."

"They sound bad," said Dalton.

"There is a reason nothing taller than mole-grass grows in the plains west of Assahi. There is a reason we build our homes short and round. It is said that our ancestors tried to build cities in the image of the Birthworld, very tall and all made of glass, but the Scour of Ishra does not abide such hubris. This moon has taught us to live in humility, close to the earth, that we do not forget from where it is we come."

"The palace in Ushura is pretty big," said Blake.

"And claimed many lives and many years in the making," said Ilom, curling his lip in distaste. "The pride of some men will never be satisfied, even with sacrifices made in blood."

"Are you talking about the High Shekahn?" asked Dalton.

"Ar Sarafet, the current High Shekahn, did not commission the palace in Ushura, but it was a man much like him, a man of great arrogance and self-importance."

"You don't sound like a fan of the High Shekahn," Dalton said.

Ilom sniffed derisively but looked aside, saying nothing.

"What about the Assahi Territory?" asked Blake. "Why don't the storms blow those trees down?"

"It is protected," said Ilom, "by The Jungle Spider."

"The… Jungle Spider?" asked Nelson, sitting up suddenly from where he had been lying in the grass.

"That is what we call the mountains of the Assahi Territory," said Ilom. The pathfinder shrugged at the wary stares of the squad. "It is not as sinister as it sounds. From above, the mountain ranges resemble a spider's body and legs. They act as natural wind-breakers. The storms blow up and over them, leaving the jungle untouched."

"Are there spiders on Ishra?" pressed Nelson.

"Not like the ones you may have seen in the pictures from the Birthworld," said Ilom, "but yes, there are insects here that we call spiders. They grow very large. Some of them even fly. Pay them no mind; you will see worse things when we enter the jungle."

"Wonderful," said Nelson. Subconsciously, he had begun scratching at his legs.

"You know, I never thought I would meet a person from Ishra, let alone come here," said Dalton.

"And what do you think, now that you are here, surrounded by my people?" asked Ilom.

Dalton gave the question some thought. "You look different. You sound different. You build differently, dress differently. Your food is different. But, despite all that, we still speak the same language. We still understand one another. The Avernii too."

"There are a few other languages on Ishra also, used mostly by the older generations," said Ilom. "Again, it is an issue of pride. Some people find it important to remember the Birthworld cultures that their ancestors came from."

"But not you?" asked Blake.

"Ishra *is* my culture," replied the pathfinder. "I am Ishradi. I speak Standard simply because that is the language that was pre-loaded into the systems of the migrant ship that brought us here. Those same systems were used as the basis for our historical archiving, our documentation, our education and so on. If the purpose of language is communication, then it is best that we all speak the same words, no?"

Dalton nodded. "I guess we all come from the same place, when you think about it."

"Perhaps," said Ilom, "but we did not end up in the same place."

"Oh, I don't know about that," said Dalton with a small smile, spreading his arms to gesture to the moon at large. "Aren't we both here?"

"You are being trivial," said Ilom. "The migrant ship of your ancestors went to Landbreak. That makes you an Islander. The migrant ship of my ancestors came here. That makes me Ishradi. Look also to the Avernii. We have all changed from what we once were. We speak the same language to understand one another, but we are not the same. I think it is important not to forget that."

"Very philosophical. What did you do, before the war?" asked Dalton.

"Before?" Ilom asked. "This war has been happening since before I was born. I have never been anything else. It is the same for my sisters and my brothers. This war is what defines me; it is what defines Ishra."

"Wars don't last forever, you know," said Dalton. "That's why we're here."

Ilom shrugged.

"What will you do when the war is over then? You don't have plans for the future?" Dalton asked.

"We Ishradi have a saying. It is not the stone ahead that trips you, but the stone at your toes. You understand? If all we can think about is what is to come next, then we will never win this fight. The war is happening now, and so that is what we must focus on. Everything else is distraction."

"Surely you're looking forward to it being over though?" asked Blake. "Surely that's why you fight, for a peaceful future?"

"We fight to win this war," said Ilom. "No one can say what will come after."

"That's sort of the point of making plans," said Dalton.

"Plans," scoffed Ilom. "Plans are just words."

Dalton and Blake shared a glance. It did not go unnoticed by the pathfinder.

"You see?" said Ilom. "We speak the same words, but we understand the world differently. You do not understand my perspective, and to be honest, I do not understand yours."

"Our peoples have been isolated from one another for two hundred years. I suppose a little miscommunication is to be expected," said Blake.

"Going forwards from this though, our cultures won't be separate any longer," said Dalton. "After this war there will be no going back to isolation."

Ilom laughed and stood up, shaking his head. "More talk of plans. I am tired."

"Goodnight then," said Dalton.

The pathfinder made a strange clicking noise in the back of his mouth, and disappeared through the tent hatch.

"Can't seem to get along with anybody today," said Dalton.

"Don't take it personally," Blake said. "After all, we are at war."

* * *

They were woken at the very crack of dawn. Emerging heavy-eyed from their tents, they battled through the swarms of leaping, chattering insects and ate a rushed breakfast of leftover stew, accompanied by the round, flat-breads that the

Ishradi were so fond of.

The Avernii were already standing silently in formation off to one side of the assembly field. Either they had already eaten, or didn't need to, which wouldn't have surprised anyone. As Dalton thought about it, he realised he hadn't actually ever seen a transhuman eating or even drinking.

When their fifteen minutes of breakfast were over, they were shepherded into platoons and directed out of the camp towards their transports. There was no briefing nor explanation, just officers mercilessly barraging them with orders. As the platoon dragged their feet through the grass, checking their hastily assembled gear on the move, Dalton sought out Sergeant Broden in hopes of getting at least a hint about the day's agenda.

"You know the drill, private," said Broden irritably. He looked just as groggy and confused as the rest of them. "Our orders are need to know. Keeps us safe from enemy spies. The less we know, the less they can find out."

"How long is it going to be like this?" complained Blake, fumbling with his webbing. "Loud mornings give me headaches."

"Suck it up," snapped Broden. "This is how it is until it isn't."

"Do you at least know where we're going?" asked Dalton. They had filed out through the corridor-gate of the gabion wall and were heading towards the Wave-Riders.

"That much is no secret," said the sergeant. "Only one place to go once you're at the front line."

Broden lifted one muscled arm and pointed out over the ridge on which Camp Golf was perched. Dalton followed the sergeant's gesture. Two kilometres distant was the tree line, a solid wall of dense green. The face of the Assahi Jungle.

Chapter Fifteen

"It's a baby-sit," Broden was saying, raising his voice to be heard over the roar of the transport's revving engine. As was quickly becoming their tradition, they were receiving the specifics of their assignment ten minutes out from the target destination.

"The Ishradi have been trying to establish several logging industries along the jungle edge. The Separatists have stalled these operations by sabotaging the machinery or openly attacking the work sites. Now that we're here, the Ishradi have plans to move up a fresh batch of workers and equipment. Our job is to secure the work site and the surrounding area. Following that, we will establish a perimeter and begin constructing a defensive line to keep out any hostiles."

"Construction detail," grumbled Colt. "Fantastic."

"The lot of you are jungle virgins, and that includes me too, so I want heads on swivels," Broden continued. "The moment you're past that first tree, consider yourself to be deep in enemy territory. Keep your wits about you, stay together and follow the pathfinder. If you do those three things, I guarantee that each man here will walk out of that jungle alive."

"How long are we out here for, Sarge?" asked Dalton.

"Until the job's done," replied Broden. "You're not being paid by the hour, so the faster we get this done, the better."

"We're being paid?" asked Wright. The squad gave a bitter laugh.

They deployed in force. Eighty Wave-Riders, ferrying between them eight hundred soldiers, formed the centre of an armoured, arrowhead formation that powered towards the jungle face. Bringing up the flanks on each side were two Seahound tanks, their pronged railgun turrets locked ahead.

Coming in behind them were all thirty of the Avernii carapace-walkers. The ten Strikers and the rest of the Seahounds had remained at Camp Golf. Once through the tree line there would be very little room for large, tracked vehicles to manoeuvre, and the dense jungle canopy would make precision artillery strikes impossible.

As they neared the jungle face, the Wave-Riders cut speed and allowed the four Seahounds to pull ahead. The tanks formed up in a single column and throttled down their engines, stopping just short of a wide dirt road that had been opened in the tree line. The transports widened their formation, spreading out across a broader stretch of the jungle face and disgorging their troop complements.

The squad followed Broden out of their Wave-Rider and towards the tree line. To their left was 4th Platoon's 1st Squad, forming up around Sergeant Banks. Lieutenant Killian was at the head of the platoon, waving and calling orders. Off to the right, a squad of transhumans was advancing alongside them. The same was occurring all across the line, with alternating platoons between the 2nd Privateers and the Avernii Transhuman Forces.

"In we go," called Killian.

They trudged up to the staggered facade of trees and pressed in. Dalton fought through a bushy fern, stumbled as his boot caught a protruding root, and came to a stop. It took him a moment to find his bearing. The world had changed around him. The open fields of low, yellow grass and the warm, morning light were gone. He had passed into a clustered realm of shade. Ferns blanketed the floor, their long, drooping branches lined with wide, waxy fronds. The trees, crooked and wrapped in tendrils of creeper, were packed so closely that in some places it was difficult to differentiate one trunk from the next. Thick ropes of glossy vines hung from the canopy above, the dark, green fronds interlaced with trails of red and purple flowers. Explosions of twisting lianas – like the thrashing tentacles of storied, deep-sea horrors – clasped and climbed up and over the tree trunks, fighting to reach the light.

Creatures buzzed and chirped all around, concealed by the dense undergrowth. Above, other things lurked in the branches and the tree-tops, screeching, tweeting, singing, and hooting. The canopy rustled with life, sending a near constant rain of dislodged leaves drifting and twirling to the ground. Only narrow shafts of light pierced the jungle roof, so thickly entwined were the tree-tops.

"People are going to get lost in this."

Dalton started at the voice behind him. "Shitting salt-bricks, man, don't creep up on me like that."

"Sorry, didn't realise," said Wright. "Where's the rest of the squad?"

"Over here," called another voice, off to the right, from behind a cluster of tall, thin trees that were covered in colonies of fuzzy moss. At the same time, two Islanders came crashing through the ferns to the left, cursing and fighting to stay upright. Dalton vaguely recognised them as troopers from 1st Squad.

"Get some damn cohesion, you squid-legged bastards," shouted Lieutenant Killian, coming out from behind a contorted mass of roots. "Two feet into the jungle and already the lot of you are flopping about like beached gulpers!"

Broden, Colt, and Scott appeared from the right, leading with their rifles, as if they were wary of enemies around every tree.

"I can't see two metres in this mess," Broden was saying. "Where's everyone else?"

"Here, here!" called Blake. The pathfinder, Ilom, was looping back from somewhere up ahead, with Moore, Thompson, Nelson, and Blake in tow.

"Don't stray ahead," said Broden. "Stick together."

"We should move in single file," said Ilom, looking between Broden and the lieutenant. "The soldier behind keeps his hand on the soldier ahead. Best way to stay together in the jungle."

"Also the best way to get enfiladed," said Killian. "No. We have to keep the cordon intact and cover as much ground as possible. Single line, one metre spread. Don't lose track of the man to your right. Let's move out! The rest of the cordon has probably already pulled ahead of us."

"Shouldn't we be listening to the pathfinder?" asked Blake quietly, as the squad stretched out in a loose line.

"Oh no, I'm sure Lieutenant Killian has years of experience traversing the jungles back home," said Dalton.

"There are no jungles on Landbreak," said Colt.

"That was called sarcasm, for future reference."

"Lowest form of wit, they say," retorted Colt.

"Only idiots who don't get sarcasm say that," Dalton replied.

"No one would ever find your body in this jungle, James, not ever."

The three men laughed. Blake caught his boot on a cluster of vines and tripped headlong into the undergrowth. That made them laugh even more. Dalton stopped laughing when Killian's red face filled his vision. The lieutenant grabbed him by the lip of his chest-plate.

"Let me hear one more noise out of your mouth, private. You'll be posted in this jungle until the day it kills you," growled Killian. The lieutenant shoved him hard and stalked back to his position at the head of the line, snarling as he went. "Children."

Colt raised his eyebrows at Dalton. They stifled their laughter and helped Blake to his feet. The platoon moved on, crunching over dead leaves and rustling ferns, snapping twigs underfoot and stubbing toes on root clumps. Dalton saw Ilom draw level with Sergeant Broden.

"You're making too much noise," said the pathfinder.

"There's eight hundred of us moving into this stretch of

jungle," replied Broden. "If there are Separatists nearby, then they saw us before we even reached the tree line."

"It's not Separatists I'm worried about," said Ilom.

Broden gave the man a look. "What's that supposed to mean?"

"There are predators in the deep jungle, creatures that I would not face even with eight hundred men," said Ilom.

"We're not going deep," said Broden. "Half a kilometre, at most. Is that going to be a problem?"

Ilom shrugged. "I cannot say."

"What do you mean you can't say?" asked Broden, losing his patience. "You're the damn pathfinder."

"Things move unpredictably in the jungle. There are many factors. Let's say there is a food shortage one day, well, a predator may hunt further from its den than normal."

"These… things, they don't scare easy? There's a lot of us moving in one direction and we're making a lot of noise, like you say. That won't drive off anything ahead of us?"

"Some things," agreed Ilom. "Other things? Not so much."

* * *

Three hundred metres into the jungle they came across the work site. Crossing even such a short distance through the tight-packed trees had taken the line close to an hour. There had been constant halts and delays as the officers co-ordinated up and down the line of eight hundred soldiers, ensuring that all elements were advancing at a level pace and that no section was falling behind or drawing too far ahead. From end to end the line spanned a width of over a kilometre. Keeping so many bodies in formation over such a distance – with no direct line of sight and the constant diversions offered up by the jungle – was an undertaking to drive even the most patient man to frustration.

Then there were the casualties. The ground was

treacherous. Wading through the knee-high undergrowth, a man was hard-pressed to see where his feet were going. Surface roots, stones, and uneven terrain were ubiquitous features of the jungle floor. Privateers would trip, stumble, and slip with every few steps. Most would press on, grumbling but unhindered. Others were not so fortunate. Some men would lose their footing entirely, disappearing into the ferns like a man sinking beneath the surface of a rustling, green sea. Ankles were strained, calves were gashed and in the worst cases bones were fractured. Medics raced up and down the line, toiling to carry those who could no longer walk back to the transports.

The terrain was not their only enemy. At one point they had come across a tree that had been split down the middle. A white, foul smelling sap was oozing from the crack and had attracted a swarm of flying, finger-length insects. Their bodies were glossy and red, with segmented tails that curled beneath their wings, and overly long mandibles hanging from their heads. Each insect had two sets of wings, and the sound of hundreds of them in the air was a head-ache inducing buzz that set the teeth on edge.

Ilom had made to voice a warning, but Lieutenant Killian had cut the pathfinder off and waved them through. His stoicism won him no favours. As it turned out, the big, red flies didn't take kindly to being disturbed. The swarm had set upon them as they had advanced. The insects would grip with their barbed mandibles and strike repeatedly with the twin barbs of their tails. Their sting proved to be not only sharp, but long-lived also, as they injected some venom that resulted in a burning rash. The squad had broken into a mad scramble, fighting through the trees to escape the enraged swarm. When at last they had put the vicious insects behind them, Ilom had appeared through the trees up ahead, without so much as a scratch on him. He had shrugged at them, exasperated. The lieutenant had shoved by the pathfinder, snapping at the squad to reform the line.

The screecher swarm, as Ilom had referred to the angry insects, were not the only example of local fauna that they had encountered. Dalton had seen a worm-like creature looped around a low hanging branch, strings of gluey saliva dripping from the hook-toothed maw that dominated its face.

"Salty eel balls," Blake had exclaimed when Dalton had pointed out the creature. "It looks like someone's intestines."

Dalton didn't think the analogy was far off. Flesh pink, thicker than a man's arm and maybe two metres in length, the worm-creature was nothing short of disgusting.

"Do not walk beneath it," Ilom had instructed them.

"Don't say that," Scott had replied quietly. "If the lieutenant hears you he'll dive right under."

"Fine by me," Moore had replied bitterly, nursing a rash-covered arm. They had curbed their laughter and given the worm-creature a wide berth.

Now they stood at the edge of the work site. The trees – which had become thicker and taller further into the jungle – had been cleared in a wide circle. Around the edges of the clearing were rings of tree stumps, but towards the centre the trees looked to have been torn whole from the soil, leaving craters where the roots had dug deep into the earth. Several tractors dotted the clearing, abandoned and blackened by fire. The remains of a work-camp could be seen at the middle of the site, charred and dilapidated. Cut logs had been piled in preparation for shipment, but the work site had been attacked before that could happen.

Their platoon set off around the edge of the clearing. Further back, other squads in the line were picking their way through the ruins of the work site.

"Let's watch the trees," Broden told them, gesturing ahead with his L7. "If this is bait I don't want to be caught with my pants down."

"What do you think, Ilom?" asked Dalton.

"I think your sergeant is correct to be cautious," replied the pathfinder, "but I would keep one eye on the ground also. The Separatists are fond of traps."

"That's a lesson you don't want to learn first hand, trust me," said Scott, pointing to his scarred face.

"You heard the man," Broden said. "Keep your eyes peeled for anything on the ground that doesn't belong."

That was an easier task out here in the clearing. Along with the trees, the undergrowth had been torn up, leaving bare the rich jungle soil. They worked their way across the curve of the cleared ground, the far end of the platoon travelling along the tree line. Now that they had arrived, Dalton could feel the tension building in the men around him. In the jungle, surrounded by trees, there was a sense of safety from prying eyes, no matter how much noise they made. Out here, in the open, with the shadows of the tree line ahead of him, he felt vulnerable and exposed.

"Hold up," called Killian, raising a fist and slowing the platoon to a halt. A few metres in front of the line, a gulley had been revealed in the soil. Either a particularly large and deep-rooted tree had been ripped out here, or the efforts of the workers had uncovered a natural defile in the jungle floor.

Broden jogged over. "Lieutenant?"

"There," said Killian, pointing to the lip of the gulley. They followed his finger. Just shy of the edge was a shape heaped in the earth. It took a moment for Dalton to make sense of what he was seeing.

"Shit!" cried Blake, taking a step back, his face painted with horror.

Broden went forwards, slowly, as if treading on thin ice. He reached down and pulled at the heap. As the torso was lifted from the ground, hundreds of small flies swarmed into the air. The hard-hat slipped from the body's head.

"One of the workers," called Broden, dropping the corpse to swat the flies away from his face.

"Half of one, at least," said Killian.

Whatever had killed the Ishradi worker had done so violently. From the waist down the corpse no longer existed. Something had torn him clean in half.

"You think it was a mine?" asked Broden.

None of the soldiers were paying attention. They were too fixated on the thing that was rising up behind the sergeant, dragging itself from the gulley on sinewy forelimbs. The sharp-ended spines that lined its back bristled as it drew itself up from the depths of the defile. Its small, black eyes were locked on Broden. It drew back its head, teeth parting in lipless jaws.

Chapter Sixteen

There are sounds that some men go their entire lives without hearing. There are sounds that a man should never have to hear. A mouth full of three inch teeth clamping down on human flesh and bone was one such noise. The way Broden screamed was another.

The monster had the sergeant in its mouth, like a dog with a toy. It thrashed its head back and forth. They heard meat tearing and joints popping. Beads of blood caught the light as they splashed into the air. The sergeant's face was locked in a grimace, his teeth clenched so hard it was a wonder they didn't break. Somehow, Broden was still conscious, still screaming.

Rifles aimed, but not one of the soldiers dared to risk a shot, for fear of hitting the sergeant by mistake. Those of them not rooted in horror by what they were seeing began to fan out, struggling to get a clear line of sight on the beast's flanks.

It reared up on its hind legs and thudded down hard, slamming Broden's writhing body into the dirt. It raked its claws over him, scoring armour plates, shredding fatigues and flesh, rolling the sergeant onto his back. Colt seized the opportunity before any of them. He snapped the rifle to his shoulder and fired a single shot. It punched into the beast's midriff with a wet smack. The creature recoiled, yowling, snarling. Its sinewy legs buckled, but it kept its footing and recovered. Its mewls of pain became a low-pitched growl that made every man's hair stand on end.

Colt went for a second shot, but pulled up his rifle as a roar split the air. It was the sound of pain and of hatred. As bestial as the roar was, it was ripped from a human throat. Broden swung himself up out of the dirt with every scrap of strength left to his savaged body. There were seven inches of sharpened steel in his hand. He drove the combat knife through the beast's eye. He buried it up to the hilt.

The beast jerked back off the blade, wounded and howling, a trail of dark gore splattering from its ruptured eye socket. The sergeant collapsed on his back, the blood-slick knife held close to his heaving chest. They didn't wait to see whether Broden had killed it. With the sergeant out of their sights, the platoon opened fire. They hit the beast with so many rounds that it reared on to its hind-legs and toppled over backwards, disappearing into the gulley it had crawled from.

"Medic!" bellowed Lieutenant Killian.

They raced over to the sergeant. Broden was twitching in a blood soaked patch of soil. His breath was coming in wet, rattling gasps, as though something important had been dislodged in his chest. He was writhing, his chest rising and falling as he fought to climb to his feet. His eyes were wide, his lips twitching like he was trying to say something. The beast's bite had punctured all the way through the sergeant's breast-plate, but beneath his bloody fatigues the extent of his wounds were hidden.

"Stay still, you damn idiot," said Killian. "Give him some space, for salt's sake! Secure that gulley! Make sure that thing is dead! Make sure it's got no friends nearby!"

Colt dragged Dalton to his feet and shook him. "Come on!"

The eight Islanders still active in the squad went over to the gulley's ridge. Creeping up, they peered hesitantly over the edge. The smell hit them then, the awful stench of putrefaction. Corpses had been dragged into the defile and heaped in a charnel mass. Much of the flesh had been consumed, leaving a pile of splintered and broken bones protruding from a mess of stinking entrails.

Sprawled across the mound of viscera was the beast, its sinewy, black skin cratered with dozens of bullet holes. It was like nothing that existed on Landbreak, like nothing they had seen in the data archives from Old Earth. Its limbs were long and jagged, taut with wiry muscle. Its skin was like polished obsidian. A forest of spines coated its arched back, running from the nape of its neck, over its powerful shoulders and down to its rump.

"There are many names for this animal, and many myths as well," said Ilom, joining the squad at the lip of the defile. "Spineback, Night Hunter, Shadow Lurker. It is the Swift Terror of Assahi. The old jungle pathfinders say it is a guardian of the Shadow Hall, to which all souls make their final journey. They say that makes Assahi Death's Gateway."

"Shut up," snapped Colt. "You think anyone cares about that shit? A good man almost just died. He still might. No one wants to hear your superstitious rambling."

Ilom shrugged, unperturbed. "They are not pack animals. They meet only to mate. Often they might compete in the hunt. Otherwise they are highly protective of their territory, and this is the beast's den, without doubt. There will not be another one for some distance of this place."

"Good," said Colt, and spat into the defile.

The rest of the line, trailing behind to make a thorough sweep of the work site, was rushing to catch up with them, alerted by the gunfire and the screams. Behind them, the four Seahounds were pulling into the clearing, followed by the marching column of thirty carapace-walkers. Dalton watched as Captain Patton, 9th Company's commander, jogged over to Lieutenant Killian to receive a status update in person. The two officers left the groaning Sergeant Broden in the care of a medic, and came over to the defile.

"Salt from below," said Captain Patton as he laid eyes on the spineback. Patton may have been the captain of their company, but Dalton rarely found himself in the man's presence. Captain Patton was a man who appreciated the chain of command. He had a reputation for dealing only with his lieutenants, leaving the direct handling of the rank and file troops to his subordinates. The captain was a tall man, with narrow shoulders and an even narrower face. A thin goatee framed his slit of a mouth.

"Which one of you men will bring me that monster's head?" he asked, looking about the soldiers of 4th Platoon. "I will return it to Landbreak after our victory and mount it on my wall. A commemoration of Islander triumph over the horrors of this wretched moon."

The troopers looked dubiously into the gulley. When none of them responded and the captain's expression began to sour, Colt drew his combat knife.

"I'll do it."

* * *

"What's this?" asked Wright. He was standing at the foot of a thick tree, gesturing to a cross that had been carved in its bark.

"There it is," said Lieutenant Killian, fighting his way through the underbrush. Sergeant Broden had been kept behind at the clearing, where a forward base was being established to protect future work efforts by the Ishradi logging crews. For the duration, Killian had assumed direct control of 2nd Squad. The lieutenant tapped the cross with the muzzle of his L7. "I've been looking for this. It's a depth marker. A scout squad from Camp Golf did the initial sweep of this area. They put down marks like this to indicate the farthest that any of our forces have been into the jungle. Past this point is uncharted territory."

Someone laughed. The Islanders looked round and laid eyes on the pathfinder.

"I don't remember making a joke," said Killian.

"All of the Assahi Territory is uncharted," said Ilom. "Just because you walk amongst the trees does not mean you know them. Tomorrow you could walk these very same steps and not know it."

"Well, that's why we put a great, big, fucking cross on this tree, isn't it?" snarled Killian. "I'm beginning to doubt your usefulness, pathfinder."

"That is not how you navigate the jungle," said Ilom, nodding at the cross.

"I'm losing my patience, pathfinder," said Killian.

Ilom shrugged. "There are no permanent paths in the jungle, no roads, no landmarks. We can only borrow routes between the trees, routes that close even as we tread them."

Killian was going red at the neck. Before he could reply, a voice crackled across his headset. Amongst the dense trees, the quality of signal on their short-range radios was suffering. Killian had to ask for the message to be repeated three times.

"We're lagging behind," he snapped. "Pathfinder! Do your damn job."

Ilom went ahead, knees slightly crouched, moving through the undergrowth with sure-footed steps. Compared to the bumbling Islanders, the pathfinder barely made a noise as he went, the shrubs and the ferns whispering around his legs. The soldiers went after him, crunching dried twigs and crisp leaves beneath their boots.

"You alright, Moore?" asked Dalton, giving the trooper a sidelong glance. The man had an unhealthy sheen to his skin, and his breath was laboured. They were all sweating, but whereas most of them were flushed with exertion, Moore was pale.

"I'm good," said Moore, forcing a weak smile.

"You sure?" Dalton asked. "Because you don't look it."

"Damn bugs got me good," Moore confessed, gingerly probing the arm where a screecher had stung him several times.

Dalton pressed ahead and drew level with Ilom. The

pathfinder greeted him with an indignant look.

"You need to learn how to walk, Islander," said Ilom. "Heel to toe. Crouch your legs. Move with your eyes first, then your feet."

"What?" asked Dalton, baffled. "Never mind that. Those flies we ran through earlier, the screechers? Any chance they're poisonous?"

"Of course they are," said Ilom.

"Well, that's a problem, because there's not one of us who wasn't stung," said Dalton, looking back at Moore.

Ilom spared him another swift glance, looking him up and down, eyes narrowed. "You will be fine."

"The poison isn't lethal, then?" asked Dalton.

"Not usually," said Ilom, having returned his gaze to the way forward.

"I would really appreciate a straight answer, Ilom," said Dalton. "I'm worried for a friend."

"The issue is not the venom," said Ilom. "The issue is the man. Some feel very little, others suffer more. A few do not endure."

"Salt's sake," Dalton cursed, and jogged down the line.

"The fuck are you doing, private?" snapped Killian. "Keep formation!"

"I think we need to get Moore back to the camp, lieutenant," said Dalton. "He's having a bad reaction to the screecher sting."

"What the salt's a screecher?"

"Those flying bugs, the red ones, from earlier," said Dalton.

"You tell Private Moore to suck it up and keep marching," said Killian.

"Lieutenant, please, the pathfinder says some people don't survive the sting," said Dalton.

Killian pulled back his collar to show a furious rash creeping up his neck. Dalton realised it wasn't the man's customary angry blushing, but a result of the screecher sting.

"You don't see me complaining, do you?" asked Killian. "If I can deal with it, so can he."

"It's not the same—"

"I'm done talking, private," Killian said, cutting him off. "Get back in line."

Dalton returned to his place beside Moore. The man didn't look any better. If anything, he was looking worse with every passing minute.

"Stay strong, buddy," said Dalton. "We'll get a medic down here to have a look at you as soon as we can."

"That's what the lieutenant said?" asked Moore.

"Yeah," lied Dalton, "he'll look out for you. We all will."

"You're alright, James, you know that?"

"We're not going much farther, anyway. We'll be back at the camp before you know it."

* * *

For the next two hours they continued deeper into the jungle. There was no accurate way of telling how much ground they were covering. Killian and Sergeant Banks had data tablets with GPS and mapping functions, but they had given up with them shortly after passing through the tree line. Travelling in a straight line was impossible with the density of the trees and the sheer volume of undergrowth, so thick in some places that it acted as a physical barrier. A man could cover ten metres of ground and only have actually advanced four metres forwards.

Moore was not the only one who was suffering. Blake's pace had slowed so much that the lieutenant had begun berating him about it every ten minutes. Thompson had hurt his ankle at some point and was walking with a slight limp. Nelson had started to have sneezing fits so severe that he physically had to stop moving until they subsided. With Harris recovering from his neck wound at Camp Golf, and Broden back at the work site, their squad was looking less and less capable.

They were getting jittery, too. At one point a pack of creatures had passed overhead, swinging and leaping through the tree-tops, hooting and cackling, too fast to make out the shape or size of them. The squad had instinctively ducked into cover. Somewhere along the line, a soldier in another platoon had discharged his rifle into the canopy. The gunshots had echoed strangely in the jungle, the tight-packed trees distorting the sound's origin. The creatures had gone out of earshot and the squad had recovered cautiously, eyes turned skywards. They had found Ilom watching them, subtly shaking his head, arms crossed over his chest.

Far from quickly becoming accustomed to this alien environment, the deeper the soldiers ventured into the jungle the more astounding it became. The array of flora on display was bewildering. There were trees with thick, ridged trunks whose roots surfaced from the underbrush in tangled knots, other trees still with pale bark and broad, drooping fronds. A hundred different varieties of fern could be distinguished with every kilometre walked, differing in size and colour and in the shape of their leaves. Mosses and fungal growths thrived on every surface. A plethora of flowers and fruit-bearing plants grew in the midst of it all, streaking the jungle green with wild rashes of colour, lapis blues, sangria reds, and pineapple yellows.

This profusion of flora was home to an abundance of creatures. If one wasn't perceptive it was easy to overlook the presence of life in every corner, but a moment's inspection of a tree's bark or the inner folds of a fern would reveal the hidden denizens of the jungle. Armies of many-legged, hive insects journeyed industriously up and down the boles of trees, labouring to stockpile small nuts and berries. Larger, more alarming looking insects with needle-ended limbs and sickle-shaped mandibles lurked in the shadows of root clumps or on the undersides of low-hanging fronds. Scaled creatures with long, serrated tails darted over moss-blanketed boulders, or out from bolt-holes in weed-entwined banks of earth.

The line of soldiers travelled northeast into the jungle, with the ridge of Kura Valley in the south hemming them in on one side. It was difficult to remember that they were moving as part of a much larger force. Dalton could barely see the entirety of the squad at any one point, let alone their platoon. The rest of the line was entirely out of sight.

"Hold up, hold up!" called Killian, bringing the platoon to a halt. The lieutenant was looking around, angrily swinging his head left and right. "Where the salt has that bastard got to?"

"Problem, lieutenant?" asked Colt.

"If anyone can see the damn pathfinder, speak up!" shouted Killian.

Dalton started as he realised that Ilom had indeed gone missing. "I was literally just looking at his back."

"Me too," replied Blake. "How does a man disappear like that? I didn't even notice I wasn't looking at him anymore."

"He's probably just behind a tree somewhere," said Wright. "Probably just taking a piss."

Dalton was looking at Wright's face when it was blown out the back of the trooper's helmet. There was no slowing of time, no intricately detailed view of his collapsing face as it was dragged through the back of his skull. One moment it was Wright's face, enthusiastic and good spirited, his skin flushed and his bushy, blonde beard dripping with sweat, and the next it was nothing more than a bloody crater.

His helmet toppled off of his obliterated head, and his body pitched over backwards, hitting a tree and falling sideways into the ferns. The crack of the gunshot that had killed Private Wright bounced off of the trees in echoing waves, dislodging dozens of avian creatures from the canopy above in a panicked flutter of wings.

"Down! Get down!" shouted Killian. A second shot split the bark of the tree beside him. The lieutenant jerked involuntarily, leapt off of his feet like a spooked cat and crashed down into the undergrowth.

Dalton twisted behind the trunk of the closest tree as the rest of the squad rushed into cover. Other shots were sounding now, the dislocated echoes making it impossible to determine where they were coming from. Soldiers began shouting up and down the line, the clarity of their words lost to the jungle. Bursts of semi-automatic gunfire joined the solitary blasts of distant sniper rifles. Dalton had no idea whether this new shooting was from their side or the enemy's.

"Who's hit?" yelled Killian from the ground, several metres away.

"Wright! Wright's down!" shouted Dalton, thumbing off the safety on his assault rifle.

"Dead?"

"Dead!"

"Anyone see a target?"

"Not a fucking thing!" roared Colt.

"I need a damn target!"

"I think I see something!" bellowed someone else.

An L7 went live. From behind cover Dalton couldn't see who was doing the shooting. The rifle fell silent. A single gunshot replied, loud and echoing.

"Fuck!"

"What the shit is going on?!"

"Who's hit?"

"No one! I'm good! I'm good!"

Another shot boomed from the shadows. A tree behind Dalton had a fist-sized crater blown out of its bark.

"They're close!"

"Where? Can you see them?"

"I can't see anything!"

"Who's got a fucking target?"

Dalton didn't even know who was speaking anymore. He strained his neck, trying to look left and right without exposing himself. There were shapes bundled behind trees, or lying prone in the underbrush. He couldn't see faces. One trooper got to his knees and opened up on full-auto, lashing the jungle ahead of them with a volley of rounds. Ferns rippled and thrashed as bullets flew. Another sniper shot whined out of the shadows. This one cut through the side of a tree, splitting the bark into threads. The trooper dived back down into cover.

"We've got to move!"

"I'm pinned, damn it!"

"If we stay here, we're fucked!"

"If I move, I'm fucked!"

"On my mark!"

"Wait! Wait! Where are we going?"

"Three!"

"He's looking right at my position, for salt's sake! I'll get shot!"

"Two!"

"This is fucking crazy!"

Dalton tensed, holding his rifle close.

"One!"

Chapter Seventeen

The jungle was a blur. Dalton crashed through the undergrowth. Giant ferns and tree trunks whipped by. Soldiers were coming out of cover around him, hurling themselves headlong into the unknown. Many of them were screaming. Not in agony or in rage, but to vent themselves of the fear-induced adrenaline that was flooding their bodies. Death lay ahead, and they were running towards it.

Lieutenant Killian was in front, half standing, half kneeling on a bank of roots and clumped soil. He had his rifle in the crook of one arm and with the other he was pointing forwards, into the endless trees and the shadows that pooled between them. A bullet hit the tree behind him, sending a shower of splintered bark spinning into the air. Killian didn't even notice. A bullet had come half a metre shy of killing him and he would never know.

Gunfire en masse was shuddering the jungle now. Hundreds of L7 assault rifles were blazing up and down the length of the line, joined by the high-pitched drone of the Avernii weapons. Dalton watched as a tree collapsed, its bole creaking and snapping, cored through with the hundreds of shots that were being blindly loosed forwards of the line.

Smoke filled the air, swirling around the trees like a fog. It reeked of ammunition propellant and ozone. The sharp blue and orange flashes of pounding rifles were caught in the smoke and softened, so that the colours seemed almost to linger in the air. The jungle became a place of distorted hues and echoing sounds, of racing, screaming bodies, of whirring death in the air.

They were going blindly towards the enemy, an enemy that

Dalton had yet to even see. He staggered and stumbled, bouncing off of the trees, leaping from stones and ploughing through ferns. Ahead of him a Y-shaped bole loomed. Dalton launched himself off of his feet and sailed between the forked trunks. Something hard smacked him across the shins, sending his balance spiralling away. The rifle tumbled from his grip. He slammed front first to the ground, the momentum rolling him a few metres more.

Dalton choked, sucking air into breathless lungs. He pushed off of his front and slumped to his back, groaning at the pain in his ribs. His vision was swimming. A figure was approaching, detaching itself from the shadow of the forked tree. The man's skin was smeared with mud, a hooded cloak of woven leaves darkening his face. He had a long-barrelled rifle in his hands. He dragged back the bolt. A spent shell casing spun free of the chamber, trailing wisps of smoke. The man was lowering the rifle now, aiming it down at Dalton's face.

Dalton's hands were fumbling in the underbrush. His fingers closed around something hard. He didn't think twice. His arm came up, flung the stone across the distance. It struck the sniper as he was aiming, caught him across the temple hard enough to spin him off his feet. The rifle fired. Dalton's eyes squeezed shut, his head jerked back. The crack of the weapon firing was close, so close it left his ears ringing. When he opened his eyes, he saw the cluster of roots two feet from his head. The round had split it clean in two.

With a roar of effort he hauled himself to his feet. He didn't have time to look for his L7. The sniper was stirring on the ground, coming to his senses. There was blood running down the side of the man's face. Dalton's hand went to his thigh and ripped free the combat knife sheathed there. He fell on the sniper, the blade raised in his fist. The knife stopped two inches from the sniper's throat. The man had got his hands around Dalton's wrist.

Dalton looked into his enemy's eyes. They were wide with desperation, almost bulging from the man's skull. The veins in his neck were taut with exertion, his face contorted as he poured his strength into keeping the knife at bay. Dalton put his other hand behind the grip, piling his weight behind the blade. The sniper's teeth were gritted with strain, a miserable whine emitting from his throat. His strength gave out all at once. The knife went through his neck, tip to hilt, in less than a second.

The sniper spat blood in Dalton's face. The man was gurgling and choking, his face creased in an undignified expression of pain. Dalton looked into the face of a dying man. Nausea reared in his gut, rushed up his oesophagus, stole away his breath. He rolled off of the burbling, weeping man. The muscles in Dalton's neck and arms were burning. He could barely draw air into his lungs, let alone rise to his feet.

There was no respite. More Separatists were coming out of the trees, camouflaged with mud and improvised ghillie suits. They saw their comrade sprawled at the foot of the forked tree, the combat knife buried to the hilt in his jugular. The sniper still wasn't dead, choking out his final breaths with wet, rasping gasps.

A second later the Separatists saw Dalton.

They didn't have time to raise their rifles. The Avernii hammered into view. Dalton saw the first of them land with two feet on a moss-heaped boulder. The transhuman bent at the knees, channelling its momentum to power itself into a second pounce that carried it three metres through the air. The Separatists barely had time to turn their heads. The first transhuman collided with the nearest fighter, armoured knee to the face, and ploughed the Separatist flat into the ground.

The other transhumans followed, bounding and leaping between the trees in their armoured suits. Their rifles were secured across their backs. They crossed the distance in a blur of movement and crashed into the Separatists with their fists and their feet. They killed with brutal efficiency, snapping necks, crushing throats, collapsing legs and crumpling chests. The group of fighters were dead in under ten seconds. Not a single shot had been fired on either side.

One of the transhumans turned its visored head towards Dalton. It walked over, looking between the Islander and the sniper, who had finally fallen silent. The transhuman reached down and pulled the combat knife free. It made a wet, slithering sound as steel parted from flesh. The transhuman flipped the blade in its armoured gloved, catching it by the tip between forefinger and thumb.

"A good kill, James Dalton," said the transhuman, offering the knife back to Dalton, grip first.

"Cutra?" asked Dalton, taking back the blade. The transhuman simply nodded its helmeted head. Dalton struggled to his feet. He took a moment to find his balance. His head was light, his heart pounding. The pain in his chest was throbbing.

"I don't think I'll ever get used to that," he breathed, pinching the bridge of his nose. His vision kept swimming out of focus.

"Get used to what?" asked Cutra. The transhuman had pulled the white-cased rifle from its back and was scanning their surroundings. The other Avernii were doing the same.

"People trying to kill me," Dalton replied, retrieving his own weapon from the ground. "Killing people."

"This is good," said Cutra. "The close kill is the finest kill. This environment provides unique opportunities. One does not often find themselves with the luxury of closing with one's enemy."

Dalton looked at Cutra, his expression incredulous. "Are you serious? Do you really enjoy this so much?"

Cutra turned back to regard him, face hidden behind the

steely blue of the backlit visor. "You cannot see yourself, James Dalton. You are alive. There is blood on your face. It is not yours. Your heart is beating two hundred times a minute. This is your purest aspect. The warrior in you is awake."

Privateers came crashing through the trees behind them, their weapons at the ready. Dalton recognised the men of his platoon. Each and every one of them looked ragged, as though they'd been dragged by the feet through the underbrush. Their fatigues were ripped and bloodied, their faces were scratched and bruised.

"James!" cried Blake, and rushed over. He slowed as he came near. Dalton's face and chest-plate were streaked in blood. He had a dripping combat knife in one hand, his rifle in the other. "Salt, James, what happened?"

"You overstretched, private," snapped Killian, striding over. "Remember your training. Stay with the damn squad! Don't just run off to play with your mod friends."

Colt was inspecting the dead sniper. "I think this is the bastard who killed Wright."

"James Dalton killed that one," said Cutra. "A close kill no less. That sniper was perfectly positioned to target each and every one of you along your approach. If James Dalton had not advanced, it is entirely possible that the sniper would have killed many more of you."

"I don't remember asking for your opinion, mod," snarled Killian.

"You lucky bastard, James," said Scott. "How didn't that sniper stop you dead in your tracks?"

"He is a warrior," said Cutra. "Warriors are not so easily stopped."

"How romantic," said Killian. "Fall in line, damn it. This isn't over yet."

Cutra looked back at its companions. The other transhumans were already advancing. "Follow us. We have a lock on the enemy."

"Just don't get in our way," said Killian.

***

"The whole line is in disarray," Sergeant Banks said, talking quietly with Killian. Dalton was off to the left of the two officers. He could see the Avernii up front, moving quickly between the trees. They didn't stumble like the Islanders, but nor did they move quietly like the Ishradi. Their crunching footsteps were making Dalton wince. The sounds of battle had been reduced to the occasional burst of gunfire echoing from afar. In the sudden calm, every small sound was amplified tenfold.

"This whole operation is eel-handed," hissed Killian. "High Command has marched almost a quarter of its fighting strength blindly into this jungle. We don't have a salty idea what else the Separatists have in store for us."

"You! Pathfinder!" yelled Banks. Dalton cringed at the loudness of it. In his head, Wright's death replayed itself. Smiling one second, a bloody, red mess in the next. He looked around at his friends, struggling through the thick vegetation. The close-packed trees offered no comfort to him anymore. Now every tree hid an enemy, every shadow concealed a gun barrel pointing his way. They were all so exposed.

"Still no sign of Broden's pathfinder," Killian was saying, as the Ishradi assigned to Banks' squad trotted over. "I've half a mind to think he betrayed us, disappearing like that just before the attack."

"Salt," murmured Banks, "that's the last thing we need."

"Yes, boss?" asked the pathfinder.

"What do you know about this area?" the sergeant asked. "Anything we should be aware of?"

"It's the jungle, boss," said the pathfinder. "Everything is something to be aware of."

"Specifics, please."

"I don't know what you want me to tell you," the pathfinder confessed. "The jungle is vast. I can tell you that the Sadari River is about four hundred kilometres north of here. I can tell you that Kura Valley is maybe two kilometres to the southeast. The closest branch of the Jungle Spider Mountain Range is about five hundred kilometres to the east. Those things I can tell you. Where this is, right here, what is immediately around us? No one can tell you those things."

"Wonderful," sneered Killian.

The platoon came to a halt.

"What's going on?" asked Thompson. "Why have we stopped?"

Colt pointed ahead. The transhumans had abruptly gone still.

"Dalton," said the lieutenant. "Go and find out what your friends are doing."

Dalton sighed and forged ahead. As he approached the Avernii he realised he had no way of telling them apart. He remembered from *The Moongate* that the officers were denoted by a silver line on their body-gloves, but in their glossy, black and white armour plating they all looked identical.

"Cutra?" he said, trying to keep his voice low and still be heard. "Cutra?"

One of the transhumans turned its head to look at him. Dalton went over, suddenly feeling the need to stay low as he moved, despite the Avernii standing proud and unafraid at well over six foot.

"Cutra, what's—"

The transhuman's chest exploded in a fizzing shower of sparks. The warrior looked down at its torso. There was a crater in the chest-plate, its sheared edges glowing red hot. Through the hole Dalton could see a splattered mess of organs and shattered bones, but where an Islander would bleed red, the Avernii had insides like liquid mercury.

"Oh, shit," said Dalton.

The undergrowth came apart, shredded ferns and bark fragments spinning into the air. Small arms fire rattled from the armoured transhumans, denting segmented plates and cracking off of hardened visors. The transhumans were moving a second later, lifting their rifles and filling the air with blue flashes as they riddled the canopy with caseless rounds.

"The trees!" bellowed Dalton, turning back to find his squad. "They're in the trees!"

A line of shots tore across the ground in a straight line towards him. Dalton watched the little fountains of dirt rising up off the jungle floor, one bullet impact after the other. By the time the muscles in his legs had engaged to hurl him clear, he felt the impacts thudding into his body. He went over backwards, the air around him filled with grains of soil and severed fronds.

The trees loomed over him, stretching towards the hidden sky like hideously long fingers. Even as he watched, writhing on his back, the transhumans began to climb. They leapt onto the trunks and scuttled upwards like big spiders, their armoured shells glinting in the shafts of light that filtered down through the canopy. One of the transhumans jerked sideways, a cascade of sparks bursting from its midriff. It came off the tree, turning once end over end before thumping into the ground. The transhuman half rose from the mangled ferns, then collapsed again and lay still. Another Avernii warrior reached one of the wooden platforms high up in the trees. It swung over the ledge and began taking apart the Separatists, breaking their bodies with swift strikes and hurling them over the platform's side.

Colt's face filled Dalton's vision. The man looked him over and then grinned.

"You really are a lucky bastard," he said, rapping his

knuckles on Dalton's chest-plate. "Your armour took the shots."

"I don't feel lucky," gasped Dalton. His chest burned like it was on fire, like every rib had been broken into a thousand shards.

"You sure won't be for much longer if you don't move!" said Colt, grabbing him by the arms and hauling him to his feet. The world span. Light bloomed before Dalton's eyes. Then the jungle slammed back into focus, so hard that he almost lost his footing again. He felt hot sick in the back of his throat and his eyes stung as he swallowed it back.

Privateers were jogging up, necks craned, rifles trained above. A trooper from 1st Squad came forward, a fat-barrelled, cylinder-fed grenade launcher in his hands. He swung it up, sighting the tree-tops through the scope. The high-calibre sniper round that killed him went first through the forearm that was bracing the weapon. It severed the arm above the wrist and continued through the chest, piercing both the front and back plates of his armour and coring his ribcage. The soldier kicked backwards, his grenade launcher tumbling to the ground.

"Stay here!" yelled Colt, pushing Dalton into the cover of a tree. The stout trooper dived forwards and scooped up the grenade launcher in his arms. He came to one knee, the barrel aimed high. He sighted one of the platforms secured about the tops of the trees. Each one housed four or five Separatists, who were strafing the ground with rifle fire from their high perches. Colt pulled the trigger.

Thunk!

The 40mm burst from the launcher and sailed into the canopy. It went between the heads of two fighters and hammered into the bole at their backs. A blistering fireball ripped apart the platform, sending the fighters tumbling seven metres to the ground, trailing flames from their flailing bodies.

The pressure wave billowed out into the surrounding trees, knocking back their trunks and stripping them of their branches, sending severed fronds crashing down around the Privateers.

"How do you like that, you bastards?" roared Colt, swinging the grenade launcher round to target another tree.

"Colt, wait!" cried Dalton. He was looking up into the tree that Colt was aiming for. There were two transhumans scaling the trunk, working their way up towards the platform. Colt wasn't listening. He pulled the trigger. The grenade hit the second platform, shattered it into splinters. More burning Separatists rained out of the canopy. They hit the floor bodily, with the wet impact thuds of meat and bone.

The Separatist fighters weren't the only ones who fell. One of the Avernii was dislodged by the shuddering tree as it groaned under the pressure of the explosion. The armoured figure slammed back-first into the ground. The second Avernii slid down the trunk, gouging trails in the bark beneath its fingers. The first transhuman came out of the undergrowth, seemingly unharmed, and the two of them looked up at the burning wreck of the tree-top. They turned their heads to find Colt, who was still totting the grenade launcher, the revolving chamber locking another shell into place. Even with their faces hidden, the transhumans were all threat, their shoulders hunched, their legs planted wide.

"Make my day, you freaks," growled Colt.

The two mods broke into a run, coming straight towards the Islander. Colt braced himself, lowering the grenade launcher's aim. There was a killing light in his eyes.

"No!" yelled Dalton, trying to push himself off the ground. Pain flared in his ribs and his back, keeping him down.

The sniper round hit one of the transhumans in the back of the head and exploded its visor in a shower of glass shards and glistening grey matter. The transhuman's legs went out from under it. Without hesitation, the second Avernii skidded to a halt and bolted in the opposite direction, tearing across the undergrowth towards where the enemy sniper had fired from.

Up on the platforms, the remaining Separatist fighters were abandoning their positions, leaping on to ziplines and plunging out of sight between the trees. Colt let the grenade launcher fall slack in his hand. He turned to look at Dalton. That big grin was slapped across his face again.

"Thought I was a dead man," Colt said, and started to laugh.

Chapter Eighteen

The detachment returned to the jungle work site. Separatist resistance had faded following the initial ambushes, and the jungle fighters had melted away into the trees. The Privateers and the Avernii had pursued for a while, but it soon became clear to the officers that their soldiers were battered and weary. What was more, the battle line had lost its cohesion early on in the fighting, and if they had proceeded any further they would have risked being cut off and surrounded. Instead, they had gathered up the wounded and the dead, and struggled back towards the work site, where a team of army engineers from Camp Golf were establishing a forward base.

Scott and Nelson had insisted on carrying Wright's body back to the camp, accepting no help even though the journey had been long and difficult. They had been close friends, the three of them, having bonded in basic training and then further cemented that friendship aboard *The Moongate*. Dalton knew that the death would be particularly hard for the two men to bear, not that they didn't all feel the loss.

Wright was the first of their squad to die. Many of them had faced mortality already. Even Dalton had not been spared death's glance. After the Separatists had fallen back, Colt and Blake had stripped him of his combat armour. There had been two rounds lodged in his left thigh-plate, four more buried in the chest-piece. Beneath his fatigues Dalton's entire chest was bruised red and purple. His friends had taken him under the arms and supported him the whole way back to the work site.

All of those close calls, all of that pain, now seemed trivial in the face of Wright's death. It was one thing, to dally briefly in the shadow of death, to escape and flaunt your scars to the world as proof of your defiance. There was a stupid sort of pride in that. At the very least, it was something to be laughed at over drinks. No one could laugh at Wright's passing. There was nothing to be relished in it. It was just loss, hollow and bitter.

When they had arrived back at the logging site, the bodies of the fallen had been taken away. The squad had been told that every dead Islander would be put into cold storage and returned to Landbreak. If it could be helped, a sober-faced medic had promised them, no soldier of the 2nd Privateers would be forgotten in the nightmare realm of the Assahi Territory.

The seven men still standing in 2nd Squad had gathered a little way off from where the camp was being constructed. Platoons and squads were still filtering into the clearing, their weapons dangling from straps or held loosely in exhausted arms, every man dragging his feet with heavy legs. The buzz and whine of power tools carried across the open space, from where the engineers were erecting a radio tower and entrenching gun emplacements. Tractors were being powered up to dig trenches and pile mounds of soil to serve as barricades.

Dalton insisted on being with them for this, even though Blake had wanted to take him straight to the medics. He sat on one of the tree stumps, clutching at his bruised ribs. None of them spoke for a long while. They didn't even make eye contact.

"Did anyone see it?" asked Nelson, finally breaking the silence.

"I saw it," said Dalton.

Nelson swallowed. "Was it… was it quick?"

"He didn't even… he wouldn't have…" started Dalton, struggling to find the words but giving up. "Yeah. It was quick."

"Good. He didn't deserve to suffer," said Scott. Dalton still hadn't got used to the man's scars. They were so brutal that it was difficult to see anything else when looking at him. Sometimes, Dalton struggled to remember what Scott had looked like before the explosion that had stolen away his face.

"We should all say some words. To honour him, to remember him," said Blake. There was a murmur of agreement. "Scott, do you want to start?"

"Salt. When I met Wright I never thought I'd be giving his eulogy," said Scott. He searched for the right words to say. "Shit, I don't know. He was a good man, alright? He was never a prick to me. He was easy-going. Good drinking buddy. He liked redheads. He didn't deserve to die in this sweaty shithole."

"We should have drinks for this," said Colt.

Thompson nodded. "Strong drinks."

"Drinks would be for us," said Blake, "this is for Wright. Nelson?"

"He was a smart man. Properly smart though, you know? He was studying to be a ship engineer, did anyone know that? He once explained to me how the artificial gravity generators in starships work. Tried to explain, at least. Didn't take in a word of it. Knew then he was leagues smarter than me. He only joined up to pay for his studies. And so he could get aboard *The Moongate*. This wasn't supposed to be the end for him."

Blake nodded solemnly. "Moore?"

"I… I'm sorry, guys. I barely knew the man. I wish I'd taken the time to get to know him. There was a time, back in Ushura, when he'd tried to talk to me while we were out drinking. I was too busy chasing tail and I brushed him off. I keep remembering that moment now."

"That's alright, Moore," said Blake. He looked at Dalton.

"Yeah, to be honest, I didn't take the time either," Dalton said. "I remember he was with me that night in the tunnels beneath Ushura. He was one of the four who followed me into battle. He didn't have to, he had no obligation to, but he was brave. He had my back. That makes it harder. He's gone now and I didn't know him. He was a person, you know? A whole other person, with his own history, with people who loved him, with a home back on Landbreak just like the rest of us. Now he's gone. He was an Islander; he was a brother. He fought alongside us. It's only hitting me now just how important that is. None of us are here because we're career soldiers. We're all here for our own reasons, but we're here together. We have to take care of one another out here. We have to watch each other's backs, just like Wright watched my back that night under Ushura."

"Hear, hear," said Scott. Nelson nodded and squeezed Dalton's shoulder.

"How about you, Colt?" asked Blake.

"Salt to this," murmured Colt. "There's got to be a damn drink somewhere in this camp."

The trooper turned his back on the circle and skulked away.

"Think I'll join him, actually," said Thompson, swiping at his nose and doing his best to avoid eye contact with anyone. He pushed off of the tree stump he was sitting on and went after Colt.

"Guys, wait!"

"Shut up, Blake," Colt said over his shoulder.

"Leave them," said Dalton quietly. "They'll deal with it in their own way."

* * *

There were over a hundred wounded waiting outside of the medical tent. Engineers were racing to put up extensions, but until then those with injuries that weren't immediately life-threatening were clustered in the open. Those who couldn't stand took places on the folding, metal benches that had been brought up with the construction materiel. The rest stood or sat in the dirt.

Dalton noticed that there were no transhumans amongst the waiting wounded. He looked about the growing camp. Some of the engineers were still labouring to secure the radio mast, supporting it with steel cables. Others were operating tractors, or bolting together sniper towers on the perimeter. He couldn't see a place where the Avernii might be treating their wounded. The thirty carapace-walkers were standing guard at the edges of the jungle clearing, and there were transhuman patrols marching about, but there were no gatherings of Avernii wounded. He wondered what they had done with their casualties.

"What was that, James?" asked Blake. Along with Scott, he had helped Dalton to the triage centre. Scott had wandered off, but Blake had stayed at his side.

"What?"

"You said something. You said, 'they're really not like us'."

"Did I?" asked Dalton. "Don't mind me."

"You're talking about them, aren't you? The mods," said Blake.

"They're just... so different. Not just physically, but mentally too. The way they speak, the way they interact. They're so far from us."

"I hate them, sometimes," admitted Blake, staring off at one of the carapace-walkers, its shell-like body segment rotating on its leg mount as it surveyed the tree line. "I think it's because they frighten me."

"Did you know Colt almost killed two of them today?"

"What?"

"He put a grenade into one of the trees that they were climbing. Knocked them out of it. They came straight at us. I swear they were going to kill him. Colt wanted to kill them, too. I could see it in his eyes. It's like he was baiting them. It's like he wanted a reason. Like he's still looking for revenge, for Sergeant Lee's murder."

"What happened?"

Dalton shrugged. "We got lucky, I guess."

"You've been having a lot of that lately," laughed Blake.

"Do you think it's a finite thing? Do you think a person's luck can run out?"

"Everyone's luck runs out eventually, especially out here," said Blake, then waved a hand dismissively. "Don't think about it."

"I think I'm going to have to talk to Colt," said Dalton. "I think he's getting lost."

"I don't blame him," Blake said, looking around at the many wounded. "You know, every time I wake up, before I open my eyes, I hope that I'm not really here. I came here to be a part of history, but the more I'm out here the more I realise history can go and get stuffed. It was a mistake. It was a stupid, stupid mistake. I had everything back home. Too much, maybe. I took it for granted. My Pa encouraged me to sign up. Said it would do me good. He's not a cruel man—I just don't think he had a damn idea what he was talking about."

"Remember back on *The Moongate*?" Dalton asked, changing the subject. "Remember how much I wanted to know what the reason was behind this war?"

"Yeah, well, now we know," said Blake bitterly.

"Do we?"

Blake gave him a blank look. "Of course we do. We're here because these murdering, Separatist sons of bitches are sneaking about in the jungle and in the sewers, making life difficult for the Ishradi. Their entire culture has suffered because of it. You heard how Ilom was speaking, about knowing nothing but a lifetime of war. Look at their technology too: they're decades behind us because of this war."

"I've been thinking about what Cutra and his friends were saying, back at Camp Golf," said Dalton. "They said that every warrior has to know his fight. Everyone fights for a reason, after all. So, why are the Separatists fighting? What's their fight?"

"Are you fucking kidding me, pal?" snarled a voice beside him. Dalton looked at the trooper on the bench beside him. The man's face was a mess of blood and dirt. He was clutching his arm to his chest. "I'm not out here getting fucked up so that I can figure out why some of the locals are having a tantrum. We came here to stop Ishra's crap from spilling out and over onto Landbreak, to enforce some damn peace. What do we get for our efforts? The bastards bombed us on the parade ground, on the very first day. They had their chance to talk and they decided to shoot first. Dishonourable shits. I'll kill them all. I saw friends die today. Have some damn respect and keep your stupid, fucking philosophy to yourself."

Dalton shook his head, but said nothing. There was no point trying to argue reason to an angry man. His father had taught him that. He wondered what his parents were doing right now. He wondered whether they were worrying about him. He wondered whether they hated him for the childish stupidity that had brought him to Ishra.

Every warrior must know their fight.

That's what Zirris had said. That's what Cutra had been trying to help him figure out. Frustration and fear had driven him from his home, but was that a real reason? Was that a fight? He had wanted to make something of his own, coming from a generation whose parents could provide everything. When a person is provided for so entirely, what do they do with their lives? What do they make of themselves in the world?

He might not have come here with the best of intentions, but Dalton realised that didn't mean he couldn't find a reason. In that moment, Dalton decided that he would discover a purpose for himself here on Ishra. He would *know* his fight.

Chapter Nineteen

There was no respite from the jungle. The days dragged on, one blurring into the next, the time made indistinct by the constant cloying heat and dense humidity of the Assahi Territory. The jungle had become their prison. Only the dead and the dying earned passage beyond the tree line. For the rest of the detachment – now numbering less than seven hundred – the work site had grudgingly become home away from home.

Their camp, at the heart of the clearing, had been designated Fort Resolute. The dilapidated remains of the Ishradi logging camp had been demolished to make room for the closely clustered tents and sandbag-reinforced command huts. Four watchtowers marked the outermost points of the base, linked together by banks of soil that had been piled up to form a defensible perimeter. At night, spotlights mounted in the towers would strafe their beams back and forth along the edges of the clearing, keeping watch for Separatist sharpshooters and raiding parties.

It wasn't long after the completion of Fort Resolute that the Ishradi work-crews had arrived. Patrols were dispatched to protect the loggers, and during his shifts Dalton found his curiosity piqued by the work. The crews would move amongst the trees, methodically working their way out from the clearing's edge. They would subject each and every tree to a test, probing into the bark with long, thin drills and then marking them with either an 'S' or with a 'W'. Those trees marked with the latter were simply cut down, but those marked with an 'S' were plucked intact from the soil. To this purpose special tractors were brought up, with arm attachments that locked around the base of a tree and tore it clean from the ground, roots and all.

"What do the markings mean?" The platoon had been out on patrol, combing through the trees ahead of the workers, when Dalton had asked the question of 1st Squad's pathfinder. Their own pathfinder, Ilom, had been missing since their first foray into the jungle and most of them had begun to assume that he was long dead. A few others had darker thoughts about the matter, quietly claiming that Ilom was a double agent who had abandoned them prior to the ambush.

"Stay focussed," the pathfinder had replied. "They do their job and you do yours."

The jungle had not been kind to their squad. Sergeant Broden had been shipped off of the front line to receive extensive medical care for his wounds. Harris was still incapacitated at Camp Golf. The day after the ambush, Moore had succumbed to a fever, suffering an allergic reaction to the screecher sting. Moore's condition became so severe that eventually he had been sent to join Harris. Along with Wright's death, that left only six of them.

Fortunately, Dalton's injuries had not been crippling and he was back on his feet after five days of recuperation. His left leg and ribs still ached, but he had escaped without broken bones and quickly been marked fit for active duty. The medical tent at Fort Resolute had been a grim reminder of his visit to Scott, after the battle beneath Ushura. There had been that same shroud of misery and mortality hanging over the cramped cots, that same reek of antiseptic that nonetheless barely masked the fetor of blood and infection. His release couldn't have come soon enough and he had been happy to rejoin his squad, even if it meant a return to the jungle.

Events had not calmed down following their arrival in Assahi. The Separatists were relentless in their resistance, but worst of all, they were fickle. Their sharpshooters – who were quickly becoming infamous – would lie in wait for hours only to fire a single shot before fading away. Groups of fighters, ranging from anywhere between three to ten Separatists, would scale the trees and anchor themselves there until a patrol came by, at which point they would drop grenades and strafe the ground with rifle fire. Solitary runners would reveal themselves just so that they could lead their pursuers on a frantic hunt through the trees. Sometimes there would be traps along the way, tripwires, makeshift explosives and concealed pits filled with sharpened stakes. Other times there would be nothing, leaving the hapless pursuers rattled and exhausted. When one sergeant had refused to give chase, the runner had passed on information of that squad's patrol route, and returned with a full complement of Separatist fighters to ambush the Privateers along the way.

It was psychological warfare at its most chilling. The Separatists were toying with them. Each course of action seemed to play directly into the hands of the enemy. Every time an Islander patrol would go out, they would do so with fear in their hearts, feeling as though they were being watched from the moment they left Fort Resolute. It drove down morale and spiked the nerves, making soldiers jittery and trigger-happy. As a result, accidents and incidents of friendly fire doubled in less than a week.

No matter which tactics the coalition forces chose to adopt, the Separatists always seemed to know exactly how to counter them. When officers ordered their troops to advance in spaced formations, so as to minimise the damage from explosives and ambushes, the Separatists changed their approach and began hunting the thinly spread soldiers one by one, using close combat knives and machetes to strike from the undergrowth. When the alliance forces were instead ordered to reel back their patrol routes and advance alongside the logging efforts, the Separatists took the opportunity to strike at the vulnerable work-crews, sabotaging tractors and murdering workers.

The Avernii, with all of their physical and technological advantages, fared no better against a foe that refused to be brought to open battle. The transhumans could move with awesome speed and agility in their servo-enhanced armour, but it counted for nothing when the Separatists knew the battlefield in intricate detail. Their grasp of the jungle's layout made the alliance pathfinders look like blind men.

In one case, a squad of transhumans had come under sniper fire. They had rapidly closed in on the position of the sharpshooter, only to have then been fired on by a second enemy further away. Of the first sniper, there had been no sign. When the surviving Avernii had at last driven off the Separatists and retraced their steps, they had discovered abandoned bolt-holes and camouflaged coverings that the snipers had used to hide themselves from sight, drawing the transhumans in a wild chase from one sharpshooter's scope to the next.

Even with the thermal imaging equipment built into their helmet visors, detecting the hidden Separatists was no easier. It quickly became apparent that the usefulness of that technology in Ishra's jungles was limited. The background heat trapped amidst the dense tree concentration played havoc with the accuracy of their sensors, making it nearly impossible to distinguish a warm body's heat signature from those of the jungle that it was standing in.

News of the nightmare fighting conditions travelled out of the jungle via the grievously injured, and Fort Resolute swiftly gained a reputation for being the worst posting on Ishra. Despite the heavy resistance and the steadily mounting casualty rate, High Command refused to pull its forces out of the Assahi Territory. They maintained that the fight had to be taken to the heart of the enemy, and that heart was buried deep in the hidden depths of the jungle.

* * *

"What day is it?" asked Dalton, stopping to remove his helmet and wipe the sweat from his forehead.

Blake shrugged. "I don't even know what that means anymore."

"I mean, how long have we been out here?"

"On Ishra? What is it now, forty-one days? Forty-two? Local time, that is," said Blake.

"Is that all?" asked Dalton. "Feels like so much longer."

"Guys," hissed Nelson, from up ahead. He pressed a finger to his lips for silence and waved them over. They caught up with the rest of the platoon, who were deep in cover, pressed against trees or crouched behind a line of tumbled rocks. With casualties across both squads, the platoon now numbered thirteen men, as opposed to the twenty it had started with.

Dalton shifted into cover alongside Colt, behind a stand of thin, close-packed boles. "What have we got?"

Colt pointed over his shoulder. His lip was curled in disgust. Dalton peered around the trees. He immediately wished he hadn't. Beyond was a shallow basin in the jungle floor. A bloated mass of pink flesh was writhing within. Dozens of the fat worm-creatures that they had seen before had congregated here, squirming and twisting over one another. More of them were hanging from the branches that overlooked the basin, wriggling their slimy, intestine-like bodies in the air.

"Fuck this jungle," muttered Colt.

"Wait," said Dalton, catching a glimpse of something between the contorting creatures. "Salt. There's a body in there. More than one."

"He's right," snarled Killian, watching from behind the stony ridge that bordered one side of the basin. "Those are Privateer fatigues. Those slimy bastards are eating our own."

"We can't just leave them here," said Sergeant Banks.

"You're damn right we can't," said Killian. "Thompson, light these shits up."

Thompson handed his L7 off to Moore and unslung a long pipe from beside the twin tanks that he wore strapped to his back. The weapon was not one that was native to the arsenal of the 2nd Privateers. The Ishradi work-crews had brought the flamethrowers with them for clearing out critter nests, and Killian had eagerly commandeered one for his platoon. When it had come to deciding who would carry the weapon, Thompson had drawn the short straw.

"Go on, Tanker Thompson, burn the bastards," said Colt, grinning.

"If that name sticks, I'll be coming for you, Colt Bridger," warned Thompson, adjusting a valve on the pipe. He ignited the pilot flame at the tip of the nozzle and pulled the trigger. A jet of flame washed over the rocks and splattered across the basin. A wave of hot pressure rippled in the air. The nest of feasting worms began to jerk and spasm as the liquid fire hissed over their bodies. They shrivelled under the heat, their pink flesh blistering and peeling away in layers. The reek of cooking fat filled the air. The worms hanging from the trees pulled away, coiling their glistening bodies tightly about the branches.

"Flamethrower in a jungle seems like a bad idea to me," said Dalton, wincing against the roar of the flames and the backwash of the heat.

"This stinking jungle could do with a million more flamethrowers, in my opinion," said Colt.

"There's too much moisture in the trees for them to burn easily," Blake said. "The bark, the ferns, none of it's dry enough to catch."

"That's not what I'm worried about," said Dalton, and pointed to the greasy, black smoke that was rising from the pit of roasting worms. "That's a great, big signal pointing right to our position."

"Salt, it reeks!" said Moore, gagging as the smell of burning flesh assaulted his senses.

"They must have something foul in them to burn like that," said Scott, covering his nose.

When the basin had been cleansed, Sergeant Banks led a few of his men down the scorched slope to pull dog-tags and weapons from the three dead Islanders. The worms had stripped the bodies almost down to the bone and the flames had done the rest, making the corpses ghoulish and unrecognisable.

"Where's the rest of the squad?" asked Sergeant Banks. "I didn't think there were any other patrols in this section."

"There aren't," said Killian, standing at the lip of the basin. "We're the only platoon assigned to this area. Whoever these boys were, my guess is they got chased off of their section and ran straight into this nest of ugly fuckers."

"What do you want to do?" asked Banks.

"Where's the pathfinder? Ah, you there. Can you find their tracks? Maybe we can locate the rest of their squad if we know where these three came from," said the lieutenant. The pathfinder nodded and started off along the edge of the basin, inspecting the ground for footprints and other signs that someone had moved through the area.

"Here! Here!" called the pathfinder, when he had reached the far side of the basin. "They came from this way."

The platoon followed the pathfinder through the trees, glancing up as they went, fearful of more worms slithering along the branches. They trekked through the undergrowth for two dozen metres until they came across the next body. It was another dead Privateer, lying face down in the ferns. It seemed that no opportunity to eat was wasted in the jungle. Two dog-sized creatures were clawing at the corpse, fighting to get through the combat armour and dig their three-part mandibles into the flesh. Their skin was scaly and horned, mottled dark green and yellow. As the Islanders approached, the creatures turned to look at them with hooded eyes. They flared the three, toothed mandibles that made up their triangular mouths, emitting a rattling growl from the backs of their throats.

Killian fired a burst into the canopy and sent the creatures scampering away. "This jungle is eating us up."

"Bone-dogs didn't do this," said the pathfinder, moving up to inspect the corpse. He gestured in the direction that the creatures had fled. "Bone-dogs are scavengers. They only eat what is already dead. Look here. His neck is broken. Something else killed this man."

"Why do you call them bone-dogs?" asked Blake.

"Because they roam in packs, like the dogs of the Birthworld. And because they consume whatever they can find, even the bones."

"Lovely," he replied.

"Shut up, Blake," said Colt. He ignored Blake's scowl, and pointed ahead. "There's another body."

"That's not one of ours," said Killian, as they closed in around the prone figure.

"He's alive!" yelped Nelson as the body stirred. The man was dressed in the green fatigues of the Ishradi military, and as they rolled him over they immediately recognised his distinct facial features.

"It's Ilom," said Scott, leaning over the bruised and bloodied pathfinder.

"Step aside, private," said Killian. The lieutenant had drawn his .44 Snapper and was aiming the sleek, black revolver over Scott's head.

"What are you doing?" asked Dalton, stepping up.

"I'm putting down a spy, now get out of my way," growled Killian.

"You don't know that," Dalton said.

"He's awake, he's trying to say something!" said Scott.

"Out of the way, private!" barked Killian and thumbed back the hammer.

"Stop!" yelled Dalton. He lunged forwards and grabbed the barrel of the revolver, yanking it aside. Killian looked as though he had been slapped. The lieutenant swung round with his fist so hard that it put Dalton down sideways on one knee. He came straight back up again, right into Killian's face.

"Please!" came a strained cry. The two men, their faces an inch apart, looked down at Ilom. The pathfinder was holding up a thick and battered folder in one trembling hand. His knuckles were scratched and scabbed with dry blood. His eyes flickered on the edge of consciousness. When he spoke, Ilom's voice was hoarse and broken, as though he had spent the day screaming out his lungs. "We have to... get this... to safety. Separatists... behind... me."

Scott took the folder and opened it up. He flicked through the wad of documents inside.

"Salt below, this is military intelligence," he said, his scarred face twisting in shock. "There are troop dispositions here, movement reports, mission briefings, there are maps too!"

Killian shoved Dalton aside and snatched the folder from Scott. He holstered his revolver and scanned through the sheaf of papers.

"Right," he said and nodded at Ilom, who had passed out again. "Get the pathfinder off his backside and let's double time it back to base. We have to get this intel to High Command before we're caught out here with our pants down. Let's move, you bastards!"

Chapter Twenty

"This presents an opportunity," declared Captain Patton.

The entirety of 9th Company, seventy-eight Privateers, had been gathered at Camp Golf. In the two days since they had returned to Fort Resolute with Ilom and the information, there had been a great deal of excitement. The strike force deployed into the jungle to protect the loggers had been redeployed en masse. Some companies had been separated by platoon and dispersed throughout the eight forward camps that punctuated the seven hundred kilometre front-line. Other companies, such as the 9th, had been withdrawn in full and put on standby as they awaited new orders. It had become clear that something big was in the works. Now, on the forty-third day after moonfall, the company had been summoned in full for mission briefing.

"The aim of this campaign was always to secure a swift victory over the Separatist forces and usher in a new age of peace and security for the Three Nations," said Patton, addressing his assembled troop. "We've had our fair share of hurdles along the way, but thanks to the information retrieved by our own 4th Platoon's 2nd Squad, we now have the means to strike a decisive blow against the enemy and end this wretched war in one fell swoop!"

The captain paused and glanced awkwardly about his soldiers. He lowered the fist that had been triumphantly raised at the end of his sentence and cleared his throat.

"I think he was expecting a cheer," mumbled Dalton. Blake smothered a giggle.

"Time, however, is of the essence," Patton continued. "We have yet to resuscitate the pathfinder who acquired the intelligence, and without his report on how he obtained the data we must assume the enemy already knows that their security has been compromised. In order to capitalise on our advantage, High Command has authorised an immediate, surgical, airborne assault into the heart of the enemy territory, which our new intelligence reveals is beyond the westernmost mountain range. Hurricane Fighters will clear the air, allowing a flight of bombers to move in and take out several key enemy locations. An infantry vanguard of three companies will then follow in drop-ships to clean up what's left, preceding a second, larger wave to secure ground. If we pull this off we'll be toasting victory aboard *The Moongate* before the week's out."

"Hear, hear," grumbled Lieutenant Killian. A half-hearted murmur of assent rippled through the assembled troopers.

"Well then, excellent," said Patton, clearing his throat again and checking his wristwatch. "Take note. The mission commences in exactly four hours and fifty-seven minutes. You're all to remain on standby and be fully prepared to deploy at a moment's notice. Dismissed."

The soldiers dispersed. They dragged their feet as they went, their limbs heavy and their backs bent. They had all been glad to leave Fort Resolute behind, but news of this fresh assault was an unwelcome irony. They had been withdrawn from the shallow edges of the Assahi Territory, only to discover that they were about to be cast deeper still into the jungle.

"By the salty depths of the deep blue sea," said Colt loudly, shocking them from their dark thoughts. "It's Bullseye-Fucking-Broden!"

"What's that?" barked the sergeant, limping towards his squad. None of them had seen him since that first day in the jungle, when the spineback had come out of the shadows and torn him almost in two. Most of them had not expected to see him ever again. They had all witnessed the extent of his wounds. That he had survived at all was impressive. That he was on his feet was miraculous. They jogged over to greet him.

"Bullseye Broden," said Colt, grinning. "Respectfully, that's your name from now on, sir."

"And why is that?" asked Broden.

"Because even after that thing tried to make you its snack, you got up and stabbed it right in its fucking eye," said Colt proudly.

"Well then, that's *Sergeant* Bullseye Broden to you, private."

The squad broke into laughter. Dalton could tell that many of them were refraining from getting too close or from giving the man a comradely slap on the back. Broden looked stiff, as though he was being held up by something other than his legs. Every little motion sent a hint of discomfort shooting across his face. Dalton wondered whether the medics had even discharged him, or if he had just got out of bed and left of his own accord. The latter wouldn't have surprised him.

"Listen, I heard about Wright," said Broden, his expression sobering. "Damn shame, was what that was. I'll have you all know that I hold myself personally responsible for it. If I hadn't gone and got myself chewed on, I would have been there in the jungle with you all. I would have had my eye on the situation. I could have stopped it. I'm sorry for that, boys, but I won't let it happen again. I might have missed the briefing, but that doesn't mean I'm not coming with you. We're going to finish this thing together and then I'm going to get you all home safely at the end of it."

"I'll drink to that," said Colt.

"Unless it's water, you won't be drinking a damn thing," said Broden, and they laughed again. This time Dalton didn't join in.

"Are you sure that's a good idea?" asked Dalton hesitantly. "No offence, sergeant, but you don't look like you're at your best."

"I've been lying on my back with medics telling me what I

can and can't do for twenty-two sodding days," said Broden. "I had to walk out of there just to stop myself from killing one of them. Are you going to tell me what I can and can't do, Private Dalton?"

"No, sir," said Dalton, smiling despite himself.

"That's damn right," said Broden. "Now, one of you go in there and get Moore and Harris for me. Then we'll be ready for this thing."

"How are they?" asked Thompson.

"Moore's fine. Harris sounds horrible, his vocal chords are all messed up, but that won't stop him from fighting. Don't take any shit from the medics. Go and get me my troopers, private."

Thompson nodded eagerly and ran off in the direction of the medical tent.

"Not going back in there yourself?" asked Colt wryly.

"Salt no. I don't think they've even noticed that I've left yet," said Broden. "Hopefully we'll be en route by the time they do."

* * *

War was in the air. Dalton had come to recognise it. Like the pungent zing of ozone before the coming of a storm, there was a charged quality that electrified the camp and all of its inhabitants. It was a collective understanding at a physical level of the inevitable violence to come. Every mind was turned towards it, every thought occupied by the imminence of battle. The building adrenaline, the anxiety, the restless energy, the fear, all of it combined into one shared emotion that suffused the men of the 9th Company.

Every man reacted differently. Some went utterly silent, focussing on tasks that they had completed a dozen times over, cleaning the barrels of their rifles, checking the rounds in their magazines, securing equipment to their webbing, packing and re-packing their backpacks. Other men were the opposite, overflowing with an almost manic energy. They would fidget endlessly, unable to sit still or stay quiet, speaking in overly loud tones about anything and everything that came to mind.

With the squad reunited for the first time since their deployment to the front line, Wright's absence was sorely pronounced. They had gathered loosely beyond the gabion wall of Camp Golf. They were one squad amongst many, each consumed by the flurry of activity that preceded a combat operation. Thompson was struggling with his flamethrower tanks, ceaselessly readjusting the straps to make them more comfortable on his back. Blake was sitting quietly in the grass. His face was pale. He was pretending to study the new thermal imaging goggles that they had all been issued for the coming mission. Harris and Moore had got hold of some camouflage paint, and were covering their faces in streaks of green and black paste. Standing to one side, Scott and Nelson were engaged in quiet conversation, their expressions sober.

In the middle of them all was Colt, down on one knee, his broad shoulders hunched as he hand-loaded his magazines. With a care that bordered on reverence, he would lift each bullet to his eye, turn it in his fingers to inspect it, and then press it into the magazine with his thumb. Every time he filled a magazine, Colt would tuck it into one of the pouches on his webbing and give it a gentle pat. An alarming light was creeping into the man's eyes, the same light that Dalton had seen out in the jungle, when Colt had turned the grenade launcher on the transhumans.

"I should have spoken to him when I had the chance," Dalton murmured.

Blake, sitting beside him, followed Dalton's gaze. "He isn't an easy man to approach. Not for a subject like that."

"I put it off," said Dalton, shaking his head. "There were opportunities and I passed them up. Now it's too late."

"Don't beat yourself up about it," said Blake. "When a man has his mind set on violence, there isn't a thing in all the universe that can keep him from it."

"He wants vengeance, for what happened on *The Moongate*, for Sergeant Lee. I thought he would forget about it, or at least get over it, but it's clung to him like a sickness."

"I think it's about more than just that," said Blake. "Yes, vengeance is a motivation, an excuse, but in truth I think it's simpler than all that. I think he just hates the Avernii. He's disgusted by them. Maybe a little threatened too, by their strength. Hate drives men to do irrational things."

"When the time comes, will you help me stop him?" asked Dalton.

"When the times comes, I'm not sure we'll be able to."

"He's our friend. We have to try. For his sake."

* * *

They watched as the ships came out of the sky. Twelve Herdsman Class drop-ships with their broad wings and matte grey hulls descended directly from *The Moongate*, the carrier hidden from sight somewhere high above in orbit. They came down in formation, their heat-resistant skins enveloped in sheaths of burning atmosphere, scoring trails of smoke in the midday sky. As their descent levelled out, the flight of drop-ships separated into pairs, each duo heading for a different camp along the front line.

The next wave was comprised of twelve Avernii drop-ships, their smooth white hulls, curved backs and compact VTOL thrusters making them distinct from the broader Islander craft. They too broke formation to pursue pre-designated landing zones. The first wave would deliver approximately three hundred soldiers into battle, but with the amount of drop-ships allocated to this operation it was evident that the second wave would be at least a thousand strong.

"Form up, form up!" yelled Lieutenant Killian, striding into their midst, flanked by his sergeants. The platoon gathered before him. The air was full of the roar of thrusters as two drop-ships came down in the field beyond Camp Golf. Hot wind gusted across the Privateers, whipped up by the cycling engines.

"This is it!" shouted Killian, striding up and down the length of the platoon. The man's blood was up, his skin reddening at the neck. His vigour was infectious. "This is the hammer blow! This is what we came here to do! Each and every one of you has been through the storm since we arrived here. You've survived it. It's made you into men. It's made you into soldiers. Every horror you've endured up until this point has been in preparation for this final battle. Take comfort in that knowledge. You are ready for this. You are ready to end this!"

Colt beat a fist against his chest-plate. Islanders yelled and cheered, brandishing their rifles in the air. Dalton looked around at their faces, feeling oddly dislocated from their zeal.

"We're about to impart some righteous fury on these jungle-loving bastards! Fury from the skies, like a storm from Landbreak itself! We're going in hot on the heels of a precision bombing run. That means those Separatist cowards will be burning even as we descend on them from above. This is going to be fucking glorious, mark these words! Come on, Islanders! Let's end this!"

They howled at the sky like dogs, punching the air with balled fists, thrusting their rifles above their heads. All the fear and the stress that had built up inside of them over the course of the day was moulded into anger and hate, and vented in cries of rage that billowed away in the hot wind.

"Load up! Load up!" ordered Killian, as the drop-ships lowered their ramps and 9th Company began moving towards the transports. 4th Platoon fell into two columns and jogged across the field, leaving Camp Golf behind them. The updraught blasted them as they joined the other soldiers, queuing to take their places in the belly of the drop-ship. Squad after squad, platoon by platoon, the 2nd Privateers split across the two transports, along with their accompanying pathfinders and field medics.

Dalton locked his L7 into its niche and swung his backpack into the stowage netting. Troopers nudged by him as they fought to get to their cradles and stow their gear, struggling in the cramped aisle of the fuselage. The faces around him were grim, and Dalton knew that his was the same. Not only were they going to fly, something that Islanders hated with a superstitious vigour, but they were going to fly into the heart of the Assahi Territory, a place that was fast becoming a new pet hate for the sons of Landbreak.

He forced the thoughts from his mind, pressing his back into the padded cradle and hauling the harness down over his head. It juddered against his chest, locking him securely into place. To his left was Colt, to his right was Blake. The rest of the squad were strapping in around them. As he looked up and down the aisle he caught a glimpse of Broden. The sergeant had slipped a small syringe from his webbing and was pressing the needle into his forearm. He tilted back his head and released a small sigh, his face awash with relief. Dalton recognised the syringe; he had seen medics administering the same medication to wounded soldiers to ease their suffering. Broden caught him watching and nodded his way, gaze firm. Dalton returned the nod and looked away, pressing his head back into the cradle.

The embarkation ramp sealed them in, muting the rushing shriek of the thrusters as they surged with power and lifted the drop-ship from the ground. The troopers lurched in their cradles as the drop-ship punched forwards, speeding over the lip of the jungle and towards the mountain range five hundred kilometres distant. The swarming, green canopy was a blur beneath them, unseen by the soldiers who were sequestered away in their dimly-lit drop-ships.

It took them approximately half an hour to reach the westernmost mountain range. Carving a ragged scar through the jungle, the mountain line stretched for almost three-thousand kilometres, fully matching the entire length of the western edge of the Assahi Territory. These were not the snow-capped peaks of Landbreak. These heights were barren, their exposed flanks scoured by the legendary storms that the off-world soldiers had yet to witness. It was by the sacrifice of the mountains that the jungle was allowed to exist. That was what Ilom had told them. Dalton glanced around the fuselage again. Ilom was no longer with them, still recovering from his wounds at Camp Golf, but he saw a number of other pathfinders.

Dalton smiled and nudged Colt. He nodded down the aisle, at one of the pathfinders. It was the woman from Ushura, the one who had scorned Colt at the watering hole. Colt grinned and said something that Dalton couldn't make out over the roar of the drop-ship.

"What?"

"I said, this might be worth it after all!" replied Colt. They laughed, barely able to hear the sounds coming from each other's mouths.

* * *

As the flight of drop-ships approached the mountains, they were preceded by squadrons of dart-shaped Hurricane fighters. These sleek jets plummeted from orbit at near-vertical trajectories. They veered out of their dive a mere thousand metres from the mountain tops, shooting ahead of the drop-ships on narrow contrails. A second wave of craft came down from orbit after the fighters had levelled out over the jungle. These flyers had broad, sloping wings, like the fins of an Old Earth stingray. They came down from *The Moongate* with much gentler trajectories than the agile fighters, flying with a degree more care than their sharp-winged brethren. These were Herald Class bombers, and each craft was carrying twenty tonnes of ordnance. They maintained a higher altitude than the Hurricanes, capable of accurately dropping their payloads from a height of up to fifteen kilometres.

The wave of fighters skimmed over the jungle ceiling, trying to bait a response from any enemy capable of retaliating. There was no intelligence to suggest that the Separatists had anything capable of a land-to-air strike out of the jungle, but the Ishradi had nonetheless maintained a strict no-fly zone over the Assahi Territory. Without precise coordinates of enemy locations, there had never been any point in waging an air campaign against the Separatists. The jungle canopy was impenetrable to the eye from above, keeping its secrets protected from the air. Until now.

Following the fighter screen, the Heralds came in, breaking their formation and closing in on their designated targets. They opened their bellies and began to sow death upon the jungle. Rotating racks turned within the bombers, releasing shell after shell into the air. They fell like seeds from the farmer's hand, lines of little, black shapes that rushed down towards the distant canopy.

They crashed through the branches and ignited in plumes of fire that jettisoned straight back up into the air. Trees in the immediate blast zones were simply atomised, torn fibre from fibre, shredded into splinters and blasted away. Those trees further out were stripped of their bark by the rapidly expanding fireballs, and ripped from the soil, sent tumbling end over end like scattered toys. At the furthest edge of a blast radius, the trees, creaking back with the force of the explosions, were ignited, swallowed up in rippling tongues of fire.

The bombing campaign targeted over seventy individual locations throughout the inner region of the Assahi Territory, culminating in the deployment of over fourteen hundred tonnes of explosives. From above it looked as though Ishra's mantle was tearing itself apart, releasing twenty metre gouts of flame that boiled into the air.

With their bombing run complete, the Heralds followed the fighter escort back into orbit, leaving swathes of fire and destruction in their wake. The drop-ships came in next, soaring towards the fat pillars of smoke that were rising from the wounded jungle.

* * *

"Down in five!" bellowed Killian, gesturing to clarify his words against the thrum of the engines.

None of them had seen the bombing run, save the pilots in their cockpits. Even the sweeping pressure waves that pounded the air with percussive booms did not reach the troopers in their drop-ships.

Dalton looked along the row of cradles. He saw the faces of Islanders and Ishradi, all of them tensed against the turbulence, teeth gritted and brows furrowed. There was so much stress in those faces, both physical and mental. He looked to his own squad, leaning against his harness to better see their faces.

There was Scott, now unmistakeable for the ruin of his face. Next was Harris, his neck still wrapped in bandages. Then Colt, pressed back in his cradle, his mouth moving as he uttered unheard words to himself, his eyes gleaming in the red light of the fuselage. Dalton turned his gaze right, past a queasy-looking Blake, and met Nelson's eyes staring back at him. The man was doing the same as him, pushing against his harness, taking in the faces of the soldiers around him. He grinned at Dalton, held up a thumb and winked.

The drop-ship lurched. The impact snapped Dalton's head against the side of his harness. A brief drumming sound cut through the roar of the engines, each staccato beat sending violent tremors ripping through the fuselage. The drop-ship was shuddering, shaking the troopers in their cradles. Men were screaming.

Something exploded. Light and heat tore its way into the troop hold. Then the world was spinning. Dalton was being crushed into one side of his cradle, his vision a wheeling blur. He saw the jagged tear in the hull, saw the flashes beyond, blue sky, green jungle, blue sky, green jungle.

Blue sky.

Green jungle.

ACT III

RETURN

CHAPTER TWENTY-ONE

A trickle of light danced against Dalton's face, seeping through the shadow and the smoke. Somewhere, something was burning. There was the reek of fuel and the crackling of flames. Someone was weeping; long, shuddering gasps of agony and despair.

Dalton realised he was on his back, still locked into the cradle. He groaned, struggling against the padded bar over his chest. Dark silhouettes resolved above him, limp figures dangling from their harnesses, their arms and legs hanging over him. They reminded him of animals on the butcher's hook, suspended and swaying.

"Hello?" he asked, his voice weak and croaking. There was blood in his mouth. He cleared his throat and tried again, but there was no answer. He looked up and down the length of the drop-ship. The fuselage was torn in several places. Entire panels of the hull had been split and bent aside. Fronds and branches were tangled in amongst the wreckage. Vines hung down through the breached metal.

He braced his hands against the harness and pushed, gritting his teeth and groaning as he poured out the strength of his aching muscles. The harness jolted to the side as a broken hinge gave way. It gave him enough room to slide out from underneath the bar.

"Blake?" he called. "Colt?"

On his hands and knees, Dalton crawled to the next cradle along. In the gloom he could barely see a thing. He groped blindly, feeling along the harness and finding the man heaped within. He came to his senses and fumbled at his helmet, activating the small flashlight that was mounted there. The beam lit up Blake's face. There was a trickle of blood running from the man's nose.

"Blake, wake up, come on, man, wake up now," he said. When there was no response he put his hands around the bar of the harness and heaved. He sagged, unable to pull it free.

"Hello?"

Dalton looked round. "Who's that?"

"Help me," said the strained voice.

"Where are you?" asked Dalton, scrambling around on all fours, the beam of his torch flashing about in the dark.

"My harness, it's stuck," said the voice. "I can't move."

"Sergeant? Sergeant Broden, is that you?"

"Yes, help me, salt damn it."

Dalton crawled across to where he remembered the sergeant had been seated, stumbling as he stepped on the arms and legs of unconscious soldiers. He reached Broden. The man looked pale under the light of the torch. His pupils were dilated, the whites of his eyes shot through with blood. Dalton pulled at the harness.

"Not like that, you idiot," said Broden, "there's a manual release. I can't reach it like this. It's just there, above my head. That's it, you've got it."

Dalton activated the manual release levers and the harness popped free. He dragged it aside.

"Are you hurt?"

"I've got no damn idea," said Broden, laughing. "Too much morphine in my blood. Lucky me."

"You look alright," said Dalton, checking the sergeant with his flashlight. "From what I can see, I mean."

"I'll take your word for it, doc," said Broden, and pushed himself upright. He immediately leaned over and unclasped his rifle from its niche.

"What happened?" asked Dalton.

"What the salt do you think happened, private?" Broden

replied. "We got shot down."

"Intelligence said they had nothing to shoot us down with."

"Well, that's the thing about intel, private, it's never right when it counts. Come on, we have to get the rest of these lazy bastards up. Rise and shine, you bastards!" he shouted, clambering unsteadily to his feet, bracing himself on what used to be the drop-ship's ceiling.

Dalton went along the line, hitting the manual releases and pulling aside the harnesses, giving each man a shake as he went by.

"Oh, no," said Dalton, freezing in his tracks. "Oh, salt no."

Broden came up beside him. He swore and pushed past Dalton, hunching over the cradle and ripping aside the harness.

"Nelson! Nelson, you bastard, come on, talk to me."

"Sergeant," said Dalton, his eyes distant.

"Nelson, say something, move, *come on*!"

"Sergeant, he's…"

"No! No! Get me a damn medic, private!"

Dalton got down next to Broden. He shone his light over Nelson's body, down from his slack face where his eyes were locked open, still and glassy, to the ragged shard of hull that had punched through his back and up out of his chest. The trooper was sodden in his own blood.

"He's gone, Broden," Dalton said, his voice quiet.

The sergeant slammed his fists against Nelson's torso, howling like a beast. Dalton pulled him away.

"You didn't do this, this wasn't your fault," said Dalton.

"I can't keep you alive," said Broden through gritted teeth. "I can't keep any of you alive."

"You couldn't have stopped this. No one could have."

Broden pulled away, his face set hard. "He won't be the only one. Let's get the living free, and quickly. The Separatists will be expecting us, and I don't intend on making them wait."

* * *

Of the forty-five soldiers who had been aboard the drop-ship, just over half of them made it out alive. Two lieutenants, three sergeants, sixteen rank and file troopers and two Ishradi pathfinders. Once the survivors had been roused and freed, they had gathered all the supplies they could carry between them and climbed out of the hole in the drop-ship's flank.

The craft had come down spinning and shredded a path through the canopy, bulldozing several trees before coming to a crashing halt on its side, tangled in the debris of mauled vegetation. The pilot and co-pilot had been killed before they had even hit the ground. A hail of anti-aircraft fire had perforated the cockpit, obliterating the two men inside.

They had put a kilometre or so between themselves and the crash site, not wanting to be present for a Separatist search party. Ragged and aching from the crash, panting and sticky from the heat and the humidity, the band of soldiers had come to a halt, surrounded once more by the dense jungle. The rustling of ferns and the chirping of insects formed a constant background noise.

Dalton noted that the trees were thicker in this part of the jungle, and more spaced, though their branches and fronds were still so broad that the canopy remained an unbroken layer, blotting out the sky above and casting them in a murky twilight.

"It's useless," said the lieutenant of 5th Platoon, a man called Graham Evans. He had been trying to raise a friendly channel on his short-range headset for the last fifteen minutes, without luck.

"Too much interference," said Killian, glaring up at the looming boles. "We'd need to get above the trees for it to work."

"That would mean in order for someone to receive our signal they would also have to be above the trees, no?" asked Evans, gingerly feeling along his scalp. The lieutenant had taken a head wound during the crash, and his forehead was wrapped in bandages.

Killian gave an irritable shrug.

"Well, this is just fucking lovely," said Colt. "We're stranded a thousand kilometres from the front line with no way of contacting friendlies. And to top it off, this area is probably swarming with Separatists."

"Put a lid on that shit, private," snapped Killian.

"There might be another reason to get above the trees," said Dalton.

"Speak up then," said Broden.

"There are a few things we don't know," Dalton said, turning to address the group. "Firstly, we don't know where we are. Secondly, we don't know whether the other drop-ship in our strike force got shot down."

"Stating the obvious, trooper," said Killian, impatient.

"Well, we do know where we were going, right?" pressed Dalton. "We were going to secure one of the bombed Separatist camps. I reckon that from above the trees we'd be able to make out that site from the smoke alone."

"And the same applies for the other drop-ship," said Blake, catching on. "If it came down nearby, there might be a smoke trail we can home in on."

Killian scoffed and pointed up at the towering trees that surrounded them. "And which one of you is going to make the climb?"

"I'll do it."

All heads turned towards the voice. One of the Ishradi pathfinders had spoken. It was the woman from Ushura. She ignored their stares and picked out what she gauged to be the tallest of the immediate trees.

"Hold on," said Moore, stepping forwards, "surely there's a safer way of doing this."

The pathfinder was too busy pulling off her boots to pay him any attention. She put both hands on the trunk, securing her fingers on the ridged bark. When she was braced, she leapt up in one deft movement, finding purchase against the tree with her toes. In this manner she scaled the tree, handhold after handhold, leap after leap.

"If she falls," said Moore, staring up at the pathfinder with an expression stuck somewhere between horror and awe.

"Try not to think about it," said Thompson. "Try not to stand too close to the bottom of the tree, either."

Moore shuffled back a step. They watched as the pathfinder reached the top of the trunk and then disappeared into the thickness of the canopy.

"How's she going to get back down?" asked Blake.

"I'm still not sure how she managed to get up," replied Scott.

Five minutes later the pathfinder returned to sight, gently working her way down the tree with all the ease of a person descending a ladder.

"He's right," she said, nodding at Dalton. "I can see where our drop-ship came down, a kilometre to the north of here. Then there's a much larger smoke trail, six or seven kilometres to the east. That's definitely the site that got bombed. In between here and there I saw where maybe the other drop-ship came down. I can't be sure, but it's worth checking out. I might have to go back up a couple of times to keep us on track, but I can lead us there."

"Well, that's a damn fine thing, it being your job and all," said Killian. The pathfinder shot him a glance. There was venom in that look. Killian flicked his wrist at her. "Let's move."

* * *

"How are you holding up?" asked Dalton, falling in next to Scott. The man turned his scarred face to regard him.

"You're talking about Nelson," he said flatly.

"Yeah," said Dalton. "He was a good man."

Scott gave a wry, little laugh. "They're all good men to

someone, James. Doesn't stop them from dying."

"We never really got to know each other as a squad until Ushura," said Dalton. "I was always with Colt and Blake. Moore, Harris and Thompson had their own thing. Then it was you, Wright and Nelson."

"Seems my little band got the worst of it," he said, flashing a brittle smile. "Two down and one without a face."

"I'm sorry, Scott."

"Don't be. Salt, I hate it when people apologise for stuff like that. I'm okay."

"You don't have to be, you know?" said Dalton.

"Of course I do," snapped Scott. "Look around, James. We're in the thick of it. We're soldiers. Some of us die. The rest move on. We have to, otherwise none of us survive. This is just what we have to live with now. This is just how it is."

"It's wrong," Dalton said.

"How are you still alive with that mentality?" asked Scott. "You're still thinking like a civilian. Sure, from that perspective it is wrong. But from a soldier's point of view? In this life, the military life? It's not wrong. It's the only way there is."

"And you're okay with that?"

"Do I have a choice?"

"I guess not," said Dalton. "Not exactly what we signed up for, right?"

"I don't think anyone really knows what they're signing up for when they join the army."

"But we did it anyway."

"Why did you do it?" asked Scott.

Dalton looked down the staggered line of soldiers to Blake and Colt. The three of them had once discussed their reasons for joining up, aboard *The Moongate*. He remembered that he had lied to them then. He had told his friends that he had joined up to see Ishra. He also remembered that Colt hadn't given a straight answer that day either.

"We've all got our reasons," he said, distantly.

"Do you know why Nelson joined up?" asked Scott.

"I don't. Why?"

"He has a younger brother, here on Ishra. In the 18th Company."

"That's right, I remember," said Dalton, recalling the briefing before the battle beneath Ushura.

"They joined up together," continued Scott, "but it wasn't Nelson's idea. His brother had a hankering for it. Got the idea in his head and couldn't get rid of it, no matter how much people told him it was a bad idea. In the end, Nelson realised his brother was going to join with or without his family's consent, so he joined up with him, to keep him safe. Ironic, isn't it?"

"When we get out of here, we'll have to find Nelson's brother. We should be the ones to tell him."

"Assuming he's still alive," said Scott. "Assuming we get out of here at all."

Dalton looked sidelong at Scott. It was unusual for Scott to be so grim. Normally, he was light-hearted and difficult to anger. Now, he was pessimistic and on the brink of anger at every sentence. Dalton couldn't blame him. Scott had lost so much and so quickly. His amiable demeanour was just the latest casualty.

"We will get out of here," said Dalton firmly.

"Maybe you will," laughed Scott. "James 'Lucky' Dalton. Since we've been giving out nicknames lately, that can be yours."

"I like it," said Colt, striding up behind them. "You can be Scott 'The Scar' Williams."

"I'd probably take offence to that if I wasn't so surprised that you know my surname," said Scott.

"Why would you take offence?" asked Colt. "Your scars are what make you."

"Was that a bit of philosophy, Professor Bridger?" Dalton asked, chuckling.

"I'm being serious," said Colt. "I know you think those scars have taken away your face, Scott, but that's not true. They've given you a new face. A war face. It's something your enemies will fear. When they see you, they'll see a man too hard to kill."

"That's all very well," said Scott, "but we're not going to be at war forever."

Colt sniffed and pulled ahead of them. "That's where you're wrong. This is all there is."

* * *

The group stopped three times after that and waited as the pathfinder climbed above the canopy to make sure they were on the right track. When she came down the fourth time she was breathing hard, her skin shiny with sweat. Every climb seemed to be more difficult than the last.

"We're almost there," she announced, slumping against the tree to pull on her boots.

They kept moving. Dalton pressed up the line to walk alongside the pathfinder.

"There is a problem with my plan," said Dalton quietly, glancing over his shoulder.

"I know," she replied, not taking her eyes off of the way forward. "When we get to the downed drop-ship, if it is the drop-ship, it's likely that any survivors will have moved on already, as we have."

"Right," said Dalton. "I was just wondering whether you could track them, if it came to that."

"I could," she replied.

"But?"

"But it might not be the best idea. In the jungle you do not move simply from point A to point B. There are no roads, no straight lines to walk. If we follow a group that has no understanding of this, it will run us into trouble. If there are survivors from the other drop-ship and they don't have pathfinders with them, they are probably dead already."

"We're doing alright," Dalton pointed out.

"That's because you have me with you," she said.

Dalton laughed. "I haven't seen anything dangerous yet."

"Exactly," she said, shooting him a cocky smile. "You can thank me later."

"We won't leave anyone behind. If our brothers are out there, it's our duty to find them," said Dalton.

"You Islanders think you can come here and survive without changing your ways," she said. "Look at you, in your blue uniforms, and your metal covered friends in their bright, white armour. It's arrogance. Worse, it's stupidity."

"You don't sound very grateful," said Dalton.

"Should I be?"

"We came here because your government asked for our help. We're bleeding and dying on Ishra's soil to end your war."

The pathfinder said nothing.

"I don't even know your name," said Dalton.

She spared him another glance. Her eyes had a bewildering depth to them, as green and wild as the jungle itself.

"My name is Eskela."

Chapter Twenty-Two

The second drop-ship had not fared as well as their own. Either the anti-aircraft fire or its crash impact had shorn it clean in two. Its split halves lay twenty metres apart, linked by a stretch of splintered trees, burning ferns and mangled corpses. There were no survivors in sight.

"Fan out," called Killian, "and search the wreckage for anyone alive and anything we can use."

Cautiously, the troopers began spreading out around the drop-ship, picking their way through the ruined heap of the fuselage. They stepped around the small fires that gnawed at clumps of ferns, and checked on the corpses that lay strewn across the charred ground. The trees surrounding the crash site were blackened and in some places still smouldering. It looked as though the drop-ship's tanks had ignited and doused the area in a wave of burning fuel.

"You coming?" asked Dalton, glancing back at the pathfinder.

Eskela ignored him. Her head was cocked, her gaze turned outwards where everyone else was looking inwards at the downed craft. Dalton followed her lead and glanced around, searching for whatever it was that had the pathfinder so distracted. He couldn't see anything.

"Something wrong?" he asked, coming closer and speaking quietly.

The pathfinder looked at him, almost quizzically, as though she didn't recognise him. "We're not alone."

Dalton felt the hairs stand up on the back of his neck. As discreetly as he could, he checked the perimeter again, straining his peripherals, trying to see anything at all that might be lurking behind the trees. "I don't see anything."

"You're blind," she said. "You also don't need to worry."

"Why not?"

"Because if it were Separatists watching us right now, you'd already be dead." Eskela put two fingers between her lips and produced a shrill whistle.

The troopers around the drop-ship turned sharply. Killian's head came up, like a hound on the scent. Before he could say anything, a figure emerged from the trees, appearing amongst the ferns without so much as a whisper to announce his presence. The man was an Ishradi pathfinder, his green fatigues tattered and scorched. It didn't stop Killian and the rest of the Privateers from whipping up their weapons. Eskela waved them off dismissively.

"Sarash, I saw you right away. You should be ashamed of yourself," she said to the approaching pathfinder.

"Eskela, you are alive," he said and embraced her.

"Were there any survivors?" she asked.

Sarash nodded and looked back the way he had come. "It's safe! You can come out!"

There was a loud rustling and then several curses. Five Privateers stumbled out of the foliage. Captain Patton was amongst them. Lieutenants Killian and Evans immediately jogged over, helping Patton to untangle himself from a string of vines.

"Merciful salt," gasped the captain. "I had feared we were the only survivors."

"There's so few of you," Killian said, looking over the five ragged Islanders.

"It was a bad crash," said Patton, leaning on Evans and pulling himself free from a cluster of weeds that had ensnared his boot. "This is all of you? Any contact from the rest of the vanguard?"

"Nothing," said Killian, "but the second wave should be

coming in soon."

Patton shook his head. "They'll have turned back the moment they saw us get shot down. Either they'll have returned to the front line or they'll have set their troops down further back, to move up on foot and neutralise those anti-aircraft positions. They won't risk more losses."

"What are your orders, sir?" asked Lieutenant Evans.

"I… well, we should…" said Patton, faltering as the survivors gathered around him. His eyes went from the ruin of the drop-ship to the jungle that enclosed them on every side. Dalton realised just how shaken the man looked.

"If I could make a suggestion, sir?" said Broden. "I think we should press on and complete the mission. Our original target is only, what, three or four clicks from here?"

He looked to Eskela, who nodded.

"We've taken losses, but the Separatists will have suffered worse in the bombing run. We can still turn this into a victory. We can still do what we came here to do."

Dalton looked at his sergeant. Broden's rage had yet to subside. At this point, Dalton reckoned it was the only thing that was still driving Broden onwards. That, and the drugs. Dalton had seen the sergeant inject himself with another dose of painkiller on their way through the jungle. His skin had an unhealthy shine to it and his eyes were bright with zeal.

Captain Patton saw none of this, because he wasn't looking. He was too desperate to appear in control to pay attention to anything else. "We are of a like mind, sergeant! I was about to suggest the very same thing. Yes. Yes. We will complete the mission. There's also a chance that we can link up with more allies at the target site and work out how we're going to get out of here."

"That's the plan then," said Killian. "Form up around the captain! Let's move out! Pathfinders, get to it!"

* * *

"How long do you reckon it would take to walk a thousand kilometres?" asked Blake.

"Why? Planning on turning around and making your way back on foot?" said Colt, sneering.

"I'm just thinking it may come to that, if the drop-ships won't fly out here to get us," Blake said. "How else are we going to get back?"

"I'm not walking a thousand kilometres," grumbled Colt.

"More likely, once we've secured our objective we'll double back and try to link up with the second wave," said Broden. "Taking out those anti-aircraft positions is our best bet at getting airlifted out of here."

"Yeah, if there even is a second wave," muttered Scott.

"Stop sulking, the lot of you," growled Broden. "If you want to get out of here alive then I suggest you muster some damn fight."

"I don't like it, Sarge," said Thompson quietly, glancing over his shoulder at the pathfinder bringing up the rear. Eskela and Sarash were at the front. "Being out here, cut off from support, relying on *them* to see us through. I don't trust them."

"We don't have a choice," Broden said.

"Think about it though," continued Thompson. "We get all this intel off of Ilom, right? Real detailed stuff, enemy dispositions, camp locations, supply routes, but nothing in there about anti-aircraft guns. If that's not a trap, then I don't know what is."

"Keep your voice down," hissed Broden. "Besides, it doesn't make any sense. If our pathfinders were double-agents, then why would they willingly come out here with us, knowing we were going to get shot down?"

Thompson shrugged. "You don't see Ilom out here."

"Then, by all means, don't trust Ilom. He's no harm to us from a hospital bed," said Broden. "If it turns out he purposefully fed us fake information, then you can shoot him yourself when we get back."

"Oh, I got something better than shooting in mind," he said, shifting the weight of the flamethrower on his back.

Sarash held up a fist, bringing the group to a halt. He shared a few quiet words with Eskela. She nodded and went forwards alone, disappearing between the trees.

"What's going on?" demanded Killian, striding to the front.

"A possible obstruction," said Sarash calmly.

"Explain."

Sarash nodded diplomatically and gestured to the trees in front of them. There were scratches in the bark, long and deep. Whatever had caused these grooves clearly did not lack for claws. "Spinebacks. If we're lucky."

"If we're lucky?"

"There are worse things this deep in the Assahi Territory."

Eskela reappeared. "We're close. The bombing has disturbed a great deal of the wildlife in these parts. That may be to our benefit. I've already seen a dozen abandoned lairs and dens along the way. Everything has fled. They will return, eventually, but for now the way is clear."

They smelled the target destination long before they saw it. The scent of burning wood permeated the jungle, carried on winding tendrils of smoke that curled between the trees. As they advanced further, the signs of destruction became more and more apparent. Branches, torn up plants and root clusters, even entire sections of shattered tree trunks, had all been blasted away from the site. They stepped around chunks of splintered bark that were still smoking and glowing with embers.

Then the trees fell away entirely, presenting a clearing in the jungle at least a hundred metres wide. The ground had been scorched clean, every shrub and fern and weed incinerated by the bombs that had opened this apocalyptic wound in the jungle's body. The remains of felled trees existed as nothing more than piles of charcoal, still hot to the touch. Oily, black smoke drifted in columns across the clearing, merging overhead into a huge cloud that rained ash across the canopy.

The group crunched out onto the blackened ground, their boots kicking up puffs of ash and embers that swirled in the air around their calves. Dalton dragged his wide-eyed gaze from one end of the clearing to the other, his lips parted but bereft of words. It was difficult to reconcile the verdant jungle at his back with the ash-ridden wasteland that stretched before him. All it had taken was a single second, and this stretch of Ishra had been transformed in a monumental display of violence.

Broden was striding ahead, plumes of smoke dragging behind his boots as he scattered the burned remains of trees in his wake. His head was snapping angrily from side to side as he surveyed the devastation. Dalton and the rest of the squad caught up with him. The sergeant turned towards them. His face was thunderous.

"Where is it?" he snapped.

"Where's what, Sarge?" asked Scott.

Broden held out his arms, gesturing to the clearing at large. "Take a damn look around, Private Williams. What do you see?"

"Not a lot, to be honest," said Scott.

"Exactly," growled Broden. "You were right, Thompson. We've been played for fools!"

"What's going on, sergeant?" asked Lieutenant Killian, moving up with the rest of the group.

"No bodies, sir," said Broden, "no guns, no signs of any destroyed buildings. All our bombing run did was kill a fuck-load of trees."

"That can't be right," said Captain Patton, pushing to the front and stumbling as he did so. "I want this area searched, right away! Don't stop until you've found me evidence of some damned Separatists!"

"Captain, with respect, Sergeant Broden is right," said

Killian. "If there had been an enemy encampment here on the scale that our intelligence suggested, we would be seeing something else here. Ruins, foundations, bodies, anything."

"Isn't it possible that the bombardment just, you know, destroyed the lot?" asked Patton hesitantly. "I mean, look at this place. They bombed it flat."

Broden stared at the captain for a moment and then wandered off, muttering to himself and kicking through the ash.

"Military hardware, materiel, those sorts of things would have survived the bombing, captain, maybe not fully intact, but we would be seeing some evidence of it, at least." As Killian patiently explained things to Captain Patton, the rest of the squad went after Broden.

"The man's a damn idiot," mumbled Broden, glancing at his troopers as they joined him. "Got his rank through his family connections. We would all be better of if…"

"Sarge?" pressed Moore, as the sergeant trailed off.

"Life has a sick sense of humour. Good men die – the sort of men you'd want with you in a mess like this – while the morons get spared."

"I don't suppose it's possible that the bombers just missed their mark?" asked Dalton. "After all, they were only relying on coordinates for their targets. There was no other way to verify it."

"Or maybe the Separatists just moved fast once they'd discovered we knew their positions," suggested Moore.

"No," Broden said bluntly. "Thompson was right. The Separatists have played us. They leaked that information to us knowing we would storm out here to put an end to things. They saw how quickly we responded to their attack in Ushura. They've figured out that High Command wants a swift conclusion here. They've learned how to use that against us."

"They knew we would take the bait," said Dalton.

"Exactly. They laid a trap right in the heart of their home turf, and we ran straight into it."

"Salt," said Blake. "You reckon they got every drop-ship in the first wave?"

"Three hundred soldiers, just like that," said Moore.

"You can bet the second wave will be in for a surprise or two as well," Broden said. "The Separatists will have been prepared for us moving in with force. It's what we've been doing this whole time. On the first night here we flung the whole regiment at Ushura, then we pushed eight hundred soldiers into the jungle to protect a damn logging operation, basically to bait an enemy response. High Command has been predictable and bullheaded, and now the Separatists are making us pay for it."

"So much for overwhelming force," croaked Harris. They all looked round at him. The man had barely said a word since his return to the squad and they hadn't pestered him about it, knowing that it would take a long time for his throat to heal in full.

"Salty eel balls, Harris, you still sound horrible," said Broden.

"Hey, that's not half bad. 'Horrible' Harris," Colt said, chuckling.

"I swear, I'll fucking shoot you, Bridger," said Harris. They burst into laughter.

None of them were ready for the mounted machine gun that opened fire from the edge of the blast site. Nestled in the shadows of the tree line, the weapon's operator pulled the trigger and strafed the clearing with a stream of rounds. The volley fell short of their squad by a single metre, ripping up the ground and filling the air with ash. As the gunner swept the weapon across the clearing he adjusted his aim, so that when it reached Patton and the rest of the group, it cut across the Privateers at waist height and sent them juddering to the floor.

"Down!" screamed Broden.

The squad hit the ground, burying themselves in a foot of ash and crumbling charcoal. Dalton choked on the stuff, spitting it from his mouth and blinking to clear his eyes. He was fighting to get his rifle into a position that he could aim from, but he had fallen awkwardly, trapping his weapon beneath him.

Survivors of the group that had been with Patton were returning fire, peppering the tree line with bursts of fire from their L7s. The mounted machine gun came back for a second pass, silencing the return fire. When the hail of bullets returned to Dalton's position they chewed up the ground behind him, so close that he could feel the rounds whining through the air above his head.

"Thompson!" yelled Broden. "Can you burn them from here?"

"This close to the ground?" replied Thompson, struggling to pull the nozzle from his back. "Not sure I can get an angle!"

The machine gunner returned his aim for a third strafe. Rounds cut a path through the dirt, closer this time, showering them with ash and dust. There was a fleshy thud amidst the impacts. Someone yelled out.

"Moore's hit!" cried Scott. Broden howled and stood up, emptying his magazine in the direction of the muzzle flare that was lighting up the tree line. Small arms fire came back his way, forcing him down. Dalton used the sergeant's distraction to roll over to Moore. The trooper was thrashing in agony, heaving in painful lungfuls of air even as blood splattered from his mouth. Three or four high-calibre rounds had lashed across his back. His combat armour hadn't stopped them. Moore had been punctured through flesh, rib and lung. Blood was spreading through his fatigues, oozing into the ash.

This was how all men died in war, Dalton realised, down in the dirt, choking on their own blood. There was no final moment of clarity, no dignity, no poignant chance for last words. There was only the panic and the pain, the body's last futile throes in the face of death.

Dalton knew Moore was dead even as the man gasped out his final breaths. There was nothing to be done for him, nothing that would help. Instead, Dalton rolled away and crawled forwards, hoping to be clear of the machine gunner's line of fire when it inevitably returned.

The squad was pinned, face down in the ash, unable to move for fear of being shredded by the mounted gun. There was no way of telling how many men were still alive in the rest of the group. No one was returning fire now. One by one, they would be picked off as the torrents of gunfire whipped across the clearing. There was no true cover, nowhere to run to, no way to escape nor to retaliate.

They were all going to die.

Chapter Twenty-Three

Dalton inched his way across the ground, dragging himself on his elbows, pushing with the caps of his boots. He kept his head low, despite the ash that was clogging his eyes and nose and sticking to his lips. It was preferable to a bullet in the brainpan.

"Sarge," he said. "If we're going to get out of here, someone's going to have to draw their fire."

"You'll die, you idiot," growled Broden.

"As soon as I get up, I'll start running that way. Give them a second to see me, then take the rest of the men and run in the opposite direction."

"I don't take orders from you, private. This is a shit plan and we're not doing it."

"Sorry, Sarge," said Dalton, tensing the muscles in his back and his thighs as he prepared to rise. "I'm not giving you a choice in the matter."

"James, you bastard, no!"

Dalton roared as he pushed himself to his feet. The cry was not intentional. Every atom of his being railed against the action. The body always flinched from danger. It was a directive ingrained into the human psyche as deeply as the need to breathe. Self-preservation was the most difficult of instincts to ignore. Dalton did so anyway. He strained against his own body, lurching out of the ash, rising like a revenant from the grave. The roar ripped his throat ragged, but he could not stop it. He hurled himself across the clearing, his legs staggering beneath him.

The end did not come. That fatal hail of rounds did not strike him from his feet and leave him bloody and holed in the dirt. Still running, he realised he was alive when by all rights he should not have been. He slowed, stumbling to a halt, the muscles in his legs burning. Blinking, he turned his eyes to the tree line. There was no muzzle flare, no bullets from the mounted machine gun, not even any small arms fire from the gunner's companions. The clearing had fallen quiet.

A figure emerged from the shadows. Tall and clad in armoured plates of glossy white and black, its cracked visor flickering with blue light, the transhuman strode out of the trees. A second emerged, followed by a third and then a fourth. Nine of them in total appeared from the shadows.

The lead Avernii raised a hand in greeting. The gesture was stilted and awkward. "Hello, James Dalton. It seems that your fight and mine are yet entwined."

"Cutra?" asked Dalton, incredulous. "I thought you were dead!"

"And why is that?"

"I saw you, in the jungle, before the ambush," stammered Dalton. "You looked at me when I called your name. You took a sniper round through the chest."

"That was not me," said Cutra simply. "You possess poor eyesight, James Dalton, if you cannot tell me apart from my companions."

Dalton looked between the transhumans, each one of them identical in their suits of powered armour, save for the damages that none of them had managed to escape. He wondered just how differently he and Cutra saw the world, that the transhuman perceived such defining separations between individual Avernii.

"Whatever. I'm just glad you're here," he said, slumping as a sudden fatigue gripped him. The survivors were clambering to their feet and trudging over.

"Why are you here, exactly?" asked Lieutenant Killian. The man's face was almost entirely black with ash.

"This is our grid," said Cutra. "When our transport was

shot down we opted to continue with our directives. We were nearby when we heard gunfire. We came to investigate."

"We are glad that we did," said a second transhuman. Its armoured gloves were dripping red with gore.

"So are we," said Dalton.

"You mad, lucky bastard," said Broden, storming over and catching Dalton in a headlock. "If you ever do something like that again, I'll shoot you myself."

"It might have worked," said Dalton, struggling free of the sergeant's grip. "I'm just relieved it didn't have to."

"We need to move, now," snapped Killian. "If this was part of a trap then there will be more Separatists, and nearby."

"Where's Captain Patton?" asked Broden.

Killian nodded over his shoulder, to where several Privateers lay slumped in the dirt. There were just nineteen of them left standing now. Killian, Sergeants Broden and Banks, fourteen troopers and two of the pathfinders, Eskela and Sarash.

"Evans too? Well then, I guess that puts you in charge, lieutenant. What are your orders?"

"Right now, we focus on getting away from here. The long-term plan can wait until we're safe."

"There is a fault in your plan." They turned to look at the transhuman that had spoken, the one with the bloody gauntlets. There was a diagonal crack in the segmented armour of its chest that distinguished it from the others.

"And who the fuck are you?" said Killian.

"I am Zirris," said the transhuman.

"I don't actually care, and I don't have time to argue, mod."

"Nonetheless, our mission here is to kill Separatists. This location is the one most likely to have the highest concentration of Separatists. If we leave this location, our chances of being able to find and kill Separatists is significantly reduced. We should remain. So that we can kill more

Separatists."

"You psychotic mod son of a bitch," hissed Killian. He turned away from the transhumans and addressed the rest of the group. "First, we're getting out of here. Then we find a way to link up with the second wave. There's a better chance that they'll be in contact with High Command and we can relay what we know about the trap. Now let's move."

"Come with us," said Dalton, as Killian and the others began to move off.

"I agree with Zirris," said Cutra.

"As do I," said a third transhuman. Dalton assumed it was Rolay, the only other transhuman he knew by name. "If we wait here there is a high chance that more Separatists will appear. We could kill them, but we could also follow them back to their base."

"That would give us more opportunities," said Zirris. "I like this plan."

"You can't kill them all by yourselves," said Dalton.

"Regardless, I think it would be good to try," said Cutra.

Dalton glanced back at the Privateers. They were moving off towards the tree line. He had to think fast. "Yes, maybe, but, hear me out, where is the distinction in that?"

The transhumans seemed to consider this carefully.

"Elaborate," said Zirris.

"If you stay here, the nine of you, and you try to fight the Separatists alone, you're all going to die," said Dalton, speaking quickly. "Granted, you will probably kill a great many of them, but there are certainly hundreds of them out there, and eventually they will overwhelm you. One by one you will die in this jungle, and although you will die fighting, there will be no one to remember your battles. How can a warrior's strength be recognised if there is no one left to speak of it?"

The transhumans were quiet and utterly still. Lieutenant Killian and the rest of the group had reached the tree line and, soldier by soldier, were being swallowed up by the shadows beyond. If Dalton didn't catch up with them soon, he wasn't sure he would be able to find them in the jungle.

"On the other hand," continued Dalton, when the transhumans remained silent, "if you come with us, we'll find the second wave and together we'll get this operation back on track. We'll find the Separatist positions, and I can assure you that there will be many, many, um, opportunities."

He looked between the transhumans. They were like statues, unmoving, unspeaking. Cutra's cracked visor flickered.

"We have decided that you make sense, James Dalton," said Cutra at last. "We will come with you."

Dalton breathed a sigh of relief and glanced back at his squad. The last of the Islanders was leaving the clearing. "Come on!"

Dalton set off after the group, the nine transhumans in tow. They left the dead behind them, heaped in the ruin and the ash, to bleed out what little was left in their ruptured veins.

*　*　*

They travelled without stop for three hours after that, relying on Eskela and Sarash to guide them safely as far away from the downed drop-ships as possible. The pathfinders took them on a winding route west through the trees. The silence of the jungle was remarkable, even though Eskela insisted that these stretches of the Assahi Territory were amongst the most densely populated. Whatever creatures lived in these parts must have gone to ground, rattled by the sudden violence of the bombing run.

When Killian was finally satisfied that they were out of any immediate danger from the Separatists, he called off the march. The troopers gratefully dropped their weapons and packs, finding places to sit amongst the roots and the trees, pulling off their boots and massaging aching feet. They broke out their canteens and ration packs.

"Go easy," said Broden, gingerly lowering himself off of his feet, sliding his back down the bole of a curved tree. He looked drawn and pale. "We don't know how long it's going to be until we find friendlies, let alone until we can resupply. Conserve your supplies. Starvation, dehydration, these things will kill you surer than any enemy will."

"Is it just me, or are the days getting longer?" asked Blake, chewing on a dry biscuit as he stared up at the daylight filtering through the canopy.

"They are," said Sergeant Banks. "We're in the season that the Ishradi call *Return*. This moon is coming out from behind Mitera, so we're going to be getting brighter, longer days as we're re-exposed to the star's light. The same as when we arrived. Actually, that reminds me, there should be an eclipse coming up in a week's time or so, if I'm recalling the intelligence briefings correctly, that is. Ought to be a sight."

"Permission to ask you a question, sir," said Blake. Banks nodded. "What did you do before you signed up?"

Banks gave a chuckle. "Don't strike you as the military type, private?"

"That's not what I meant, sir!" said Blake quickly.

"Sergeant Arnold Banks has been military longer than you've been sentient, Private Leland," said Broden, winking at Blake. "He's not some green bastard fresh out of basic, unlike some."

"I started off in logistics, moved up to intelligence," said Banks. "When they were putting together this expedition though, there was a demand for field officers. Well, I'd had my fill of desk work and decided it might be fun to stretch my legs a little."

"To bad decisions," said Broden, lifting his water canteen.

"It could be worse," replied Banks, attempting nonchalance.

"Yeah, you could be lying dead somewhere in this shithole

of a jungle, forgotten by your brothers without so much as a backwards glance, let alone a funeral, left as a snack for the wildlife."

They looked at Scott. The man was sitting on his haunches, staring at the ground. He had pinned a long insect with his combat knife. It was still squirming on the end of the blade, the translucent layer of jelly-like flesh that covered its back rippling with mesmerising motion. Scott lifted the knife to inspect the impaled creature. His eyes were full of cruelty. He looked monstrous in that moment, with his scarred face and hate-filled eyes, nothing like the charming man who had helped Dalton on deployment day.

"He's dead," said Colt bluntly. Where Scott's eyes were alight with bitter malice, Colt's were dull, as though all the emotion had been hollowed out of them. "Moore's dead. Nelson's dead. Wright's dead. That's all there is to it. It doesn't matter whether they're dead above the dirt or below it. They're still dead. They don't care one way or the other, so why should you?"

"Fuck you, Colt," Scott spat. He pointed his knife at the man, the insect still curling on the end of it, and twisted his ruined face into a sneer. "Moore never liked you, know that? Never trusted you. Not since *The Moongate*, when you dragged the rest of us into your mess. He always used to say what a brute he thought you were, strutting around like you were entitled to the world and everything in it. Selfish bastard is what he thought you were. I'm inclined to agree."

Colt grinned his big, iconic grin, but it didn't reach his eyes. He looked like a shark, teeth bared, eyes dead. The stout trooper just sat there, his eyes never leaving Scott, his grin never wavering.

"Enough of that," said Broden, but there was no strength in his voice.

"And you," said Scott, turning his gaze on the sergeant.

"Look at you. You're a fucking mess. Thought you could lead us like this, propped up on an overdose of painkillers? Going to get us all home safely, were you? *All* of us? Pathetic."

Broden looked away. His face was sour.

"What are you doing, man?" asked Banks. "Take a look around. The men you're insulting are the only people you've got to rely on out here. I know you're angry. I know you're bitter. This is how it is though. Private Moore wasn't the only good soldier who died out there. Moore's wasn't the only body we left behind. Carrying them would have just slowed us down, and we couldn't risk the time it would take to bury them. That's just the way it works. They died so that we could live. I'll honour them by remembering that and by making the most of the time they bought for me."

"Bullshit," said Scott. "Moore didn't die for some heroic reason. He was pinned in the dirt with the rest of us and his luck ran out. If it wasn't for the mods the same would have happened to the rest of us."

"Harris and I knew him best," said Thompson. "Better than you did, Scott. While I appreciate what you're trying to say here, I know that Moore wouldn't have wanted us to be at each other's throats over this. Let's not taint our memories of him."

Scott said nothing more. He scraped the insect from his knife and flicked it into the dirt. It skittered away, seemingly unaffected by its wound, and disappeared between a cluster of roots.

"When we were down in that valley and I got shot," said Harris, his voice hoarse, "I remember it was Moore who came to me first. Salt, but I was terrified. I thought I was done for. Do you have any idea what it's like, to be covered in your own blood like that? To know you're an inch from death? To be honest, I barely remember it myself. I do remember Moore though. He got down next to me, put his hands over my neck, and he told me it was going to be alright. Salt, I didn't believe the bastard, but in that moment I felt glad that it was me who was going to die, and not him. Not any of you. Just me. But now I'm still here and he's gone. That's twisted, isn't it?"

Before any of them could answer, one of the transhumans came into view. The Avernii had refused the prospect of rest and had gone out on patrol instead, to scout the perimeter. Dalton turned to get a better look at the transhuman. He saw the cracked visor and its flickering blue light.

"Cutra," Dalton said, nodding.

"Get up," said Cutra. The transhuman had its rifle armed and at the ready. "Something is coming."

Chapter Twenty-Four

"This way!" hissed Eskela, waving them towards her. They dashed between the trees, moving as quietly as they could. The thunder of dozens of clawed feet pounding the ground filled the air. Dalton caught glimpses of the creatures as they raced by. Their forelimbs were long, unnervingly so, slender and jointed in four places. They had three lengthy digits at the end of each arm, which they used to wrap around the trunks of trees and speed themselves along with thudding leaps. Their hind-legs were back-jointed and powerfully muscled, terminating in feet that possessed a single, curved claw. They looked emaciated – waxy, grey skin drawn tight over bones – their bodies overly big in comparison to their gangly limbs. Their necks were hunched and their heads were small. A pair of wide ears sprouted from either side of their narrow faces, where side-facing eyes and beak-like mouths were situated.

"Are they dangerous?" asked Blake.

"If cornered," said Eskela. The pathfinder wasn't watching the stampeding herd of long-limbed creatures though. She seemed more interested in where the herd was coming from. The rest of the group were spread out in cover behind her, peering out at the passing creatures with a mix between horror and curiosity.

"What are we doing?" hissed Killian. "We should be moving!"

Eskela held up a hand to his face, refusing to break her concentration. Killian's hand went to the grip of his holstered .44. Dalton moved up beside the pathfinder, getting between her and the lieutenant.

"These men are seriously on edge, Eskela," he whispered. "I

know you're doing your thing, but you need to keep us in the loop."

The pathfinder rolled her eyes and whipped round to face the group. She jabbed a finger at the passing herd. "Those are jungle crawlers. They're herbivores. They're *prey*. And they're running. What do you think that means?"

"Oh shit," said Blake.

"Exactly," snapped Eskela.

"No, I mean, *oh shit*," said Blake, pointing in the direction that the herd was fleeing from.

The spineback exploded from the shadows, leaping between the trees like it was spring-loaded. Its spines were pressed flat against its back. The lipless skin of its mouth peeled away. Its teeth parted as it stretched open its jaws. There was a squelch and a crunch, the sound of flesh being crushed and bones being snapped. The spineback ploughed into the ground, a jungle crawler clamped in its mouth. It thrashed its head side to side, mauling the fight from its catch.

They heard the spineback's growl. The sound made the skin crawl, made the hairs at the back of the neck stand on end. It twisted the gut and stirred the instinctual urge to flee. It disturbed them so much – Islander, Ishradi and Avernii alike – that it took them a moment to realise that the sound was not coming from the spineback ahead.

The sound was coming from behind them.

Dalton spun on his heel, bringing up his L7 as he moved, safety off, finger on the trigger. His rounds chewed up bark and foliage. The second spineback was a blur, a smudge of black against the trees. It rammed into Zirris. The transhuman was crushed against the tree at its back. The beast juddered to a halt, even as its hind legs scrambled in the dirt and its claws clattered against the transhuman's armour. Somehow, in the scant seconds it had taken the spineback to cross the distance, Zirris had managed to catch the beast by its jaws, stopping its snarling maw a second away from clamping shut.

Sergeant Banks stepped up, pulled free his .44 Snapper and unloaded three booming shots into the spineback's flank. The beast lashed out even as it lurched aside. It raked a claw over Banks and sent him tumbling into the undergrowth.

Cutra came up behind the spineback at a run. The transhuman leapt onto its back, feet first, knees crouched. In one hand Cutra grabbed at the beast's spines for purchase, and with the other punched the rifle muzzle into the back of its neck. The shots blew out the spineback's throat. It collapsed snout first into the dirt.

The first spineback charged through the trees. It took one of the Privateers off of his feet and trampled the man into the ground. His screams were cut short as the spineback closed its teeth around his skull. Bone shattered. Every soldier opened fire at once. The spineback came apart in ribbons of sinewy, black flesh.

"Let's move!" cried Eskela.

"You heard her!" yelled Killian. "Move!"

The group scrambled after the pathfinder. Broden was on his knees, dragging at something on the ground. Dalton came down next to the sergeant. Banks was limp in Broden's arms, four deep gouges opening his body from throat to gut. The man's blood was pumping out in liberal quantities, soaking into Broden's fatigues and trickling into the soil.

"He's dead! We have to go!" pleaded Dalton.

Broden dragged hopelessly at the corpse. His face was twisted in shock. He looked utterly lost, as though the world was slipping away beneath his feet, entirely beyond his control.

"Come on, damn you," shouted Dalton, pulling the sergeant to his feet. Side by side, they staggered after the group, covered in the blood of beasts and men.

Somewhere, off in the distance, a roar echoed in the hot, cloying air.

* * *

"The Ishradi might be several decades behind modern civilisation. They might live on this sweaty, stinking, death-trap of a moon. But you've got to give it to them, their women are something to behold."

Dalton looked sidelong at Colt. The man was grinning, his eyes on Eskela's backside as she led them through the jungle. They had put less than half an hour's distance between them and where the spinebacks had attacked. Sergeant Banks' blood hadn't fully dried on Dalton's fatigues yet. Every one of them was mired in grim silence. Every one of them except Colt. Colt was grinning.

"I get that you're dealing with this in your own way, but try to keep it down," said Dalton quietly, glancing at the pathfinder ahead. He was sure she had heard them.

"Dealing with what?" asked Colt. He didn't wait for a reply, turning instead to look up at Cutra. The transhuman had been striding alongside them for a while now. "What about you, mod? You hit up any tail since we've been here? Maybe you've got a lady waiting for you back on that airless ball you call home?"

"There will be things that you will struggle to understand about society on Avernus," said Cutra.

"Please, please don't tell me some weird shit right now," said Colt, "like you don't have women, or something else equally sickening."

"Technically, we don't have men either," replied Cutra, quite calmly.

"What the salt are you talking about?" asked Colt. "Don't tell me you're a woman, because I've seen your face, and if you're not a man, then you're the ugliest damn woman ever to blight the face of the galaxy."

"I am transhuman," said Cutra, as if by way of explanation.

"Try to stay on track here, mod. We're talking about gender, not race."

"You do not understand. I am *trans*human. The Avernii have transcended humanity and all of its inefficiencies. Such as gender. We are both and we are neither. We are more."

"Wait," said Dalton, fumbling with the concept. "You're neither a man nor a woman?"

"Correct."

"And this is the same for all of your people?" asked Dalton.

"It is."

"So… how do you… procreate?"

"All new Avernii are developed from a cultivated mix of genetic material sourced from a variety of specimens. In this way, all Avernii are created without flaw or weakness."

"You don't have your own children?" asked Dalton, nonplussed.

"Each new Avernii is a child of the species as a whole. It is just one of the many aspects that unites us as a people. We owe our loyalty and our love to the entire race, not just to a select family."

"Let me get this straight," said Colt, his face rich with mocking amusement. "You're not born, you're *made*, probably in vats, right? You don't have genders, which means you don't fuck. I'm not even going to ask what's between those legs of yours. But more than that, when your ancestors got together and decided on all of this, the look that they arrived at for the future of their flawless species was a giant snowflake? That's the look you stuck with? Six and a half foot, bald, gender neutral albinos? Really?"

"The semi-translucent nature of our skin is actually an unintended mutation of the melanocytes in the epidermis, caused by the nano-constructs in our blood and the sub-dermal implants that we all receive during development. It also induces a strain of alopecia universalis, thus our lack of hair. We have decided that efficiency is senior to aesthetics."

"Salty eel balls, you're all robots," said Colt, incredulous. "I'm done with this shit."

Dalton and Cutra watched the trooper stride ahead.

"I could be mistaken, but I don't think he likes me," said Cutra.

Dalton reached up to pat the transhuman on the arm. "Don't take it personally. I think he's insane."

* * *

"Hold up," said Lieutenant Killian, bringing the group to a halt. He confronted Eskela, brandishing his data tablet. The screen had a web of cracks in it and several patches of dead pixels. "Just where are you leading us? Because we're supposed to be moving to link up with the second wave, and by any estimation that means we should be heading directly west, but you've been leading us on a path that would make a drunk man's wandering look sensible."

"Your little computer tells you that, does it?" asked Eskela. "So tell me, if your little computer there is so accurate, why did your High Command see fit to deploy you alongside us pathfinders?"

"Don't dodge the question," growled Killian. "I want to know where you're taking us, and you're going to tell me, right now."

Eskela sighed. She crouched down on her haunches and beckoned for them to join her. She tore up a fern and smoothed over a patch of soil. With the stem of the fern she drew a circle in the earth.

"This circle is the inner jungle of the Assahi Territory. The edges of this circle represent the ring of the Jungle Spider mountains."

"You know I have a map here, right?" asked Killian, holding up his data tablet. Eskela waved it away dismissively. She drew a second circle inside the first, off centre to the west.

"Now, this area here? This is the Spider's Eye."

"And? What about it?" snapped Killian.

"We don't go there. You don't go there. No one goes there. It's a dead zone. No one that's ever gone in there has ever come out."

"Have you considered that it could be the Separatist headquarters?" asked Broden.

Eskela laughed. "As far as I know even the Separatists don't go in there."

"Why?" pressed Killian. "Give me something that doesn't sound like superstition."

"Haven't you been listening to me? How can I tell you if no one knows? People go into the Spider's Eye and they don't come out. Maybe there's a high concentration of spinebacks in the area? Maybe there's a poisonous plant that grows in dense quantities there? I don't know. No one does."

"Why exactly are you telling us this?" asked Killian.

"Because we're here," said Eskela, pointing to the side of the inner circle that was farthest from the mountains in the west.

"Ah," said Dalton.

"It's directly between us and where we need to get to," said Blake.

"So I've been trying to get us around it," said Eskela. "The thing about the Spider's Eye is it's not a well documented area. No one can tell you exactly where it begins or for how far it stretches. We just roughly know where the edges are. Which is why navigating around it is so difficult. I've heard stories about parties that thought they were skirting the edges, only to realise that they had ventured into the area itself."

"That doesn't make sense," said Cutra. Eskela shot him a glare. Cutra continued, unfazed. "If no one who enters that region ever comes out, then there would be no one alive to have told that story in the first place."

"You don't believe me?" asked Eskela, standing up sharply.

"Go ahead. Test it for yourself."

"So, what do we do? If we don't know exactly where this forbidden region begins, wouldn't the safest option be to track back east and then give the whole area as wide a berth as possible?" asked Dalton.

"I'm guessing because that would take us straight back into Separatist territory," said Broden.

"Exactly," said Eskela, and turned on Killian. "So either you let me do my job or I might as well just shut up and let that little computer of yours lead us out of the jungle."

Killian looked as though he was going to press the issue. He was reddening at the neck, one hand squeezing the data tablet so hard it looked as though it might snap clean in two, and the other at the grip of his side-arm, from which it never seemed to stray too far.

"I agree with Eskela," said Dalton. "Our information on the Assahi Territory comes from orbital pictures only. That's worthless if all our maps show us are the tops of trees. The pathfinders know how to get us safely through the jungle."

"Safely? Tell that to Sergeant Banks," snarled one of the troopers from the remnants of 1st squad.

"Just the latest Islander we've left to rot in this jungle. And for what? For these ungrateful bastards," said Scott, jabbing a finger at Eskela and Sarash. Several of the Privateers murmured in agreement. Amongst them were Thompson and Colt.

"Shut it, Williams," barked Broden. The sergeant was glancing warily about the group. Eskela and Sarash were slowly edging closer together. Their rifles were held at their chests.

"Why haven't we heard about this so-called Spider's Eye until now?" asked Killian, eyes narrowed suspiciously. He was drumming his fingers against the grip of his revolver.

"Are you kidding me?" asked Eskela angrily. "If your High

Command had thought for a second to coordinate with us, we could have provided in-depth detail about the whole inner region. I didn't know we were coming out here until I was being ordered onto the drop-ship."

"I suppose if you had known, you might have found a reason not to be on that drop-ship, just like your friend, Ilom," said Thompson.

"Who the fuck is Ilom?" asked Eskela.

"Come on, Thompson, there's no need for that," said Dalton. "Eskela has done everything we've asked of her. If she was an infiltrator, wouldn't she have just led us straight into a trap?"

"Who's to say she hasn't been trying?" asked Scott. "She did lead us to the objective area where a Separatist ambush was waiting."

"A Separatist ambush which fired on us indiscriminately," said Dalton, stressing the point.

"They probably don't care if a few of theirs get caught in the crossfire," muttered Colt.

"How is this bickering going to help?" asked Blake.

"For once you're speaking some sense, Private Leland," said Killian, tearing the .44 Snapper from its holster. "It's time we stopped talking about this and took action."

"That's not what I meant!" cried Blake.

"Hold on now, lieutenant," said Broden.

"We're going to shoot our pathfinder, in the middle of a jungle that is actively trying to kill us, really?" asked Dalton.

"Shut your mouth, private," said Killian. "I've had it with your insubordination."

"We need to be rational about this," said Harris.

"I'm done playing their game," said Killian, pointing his revolver at Eskela. Several of the Privateers were also turning their guns on the pathfinders. A few were hesitating, looking with uncertainty from face to face, as though they no longer knew who to listen to. The transhumans, as ever, stood quiet and unmoving.

"What's that noise?" asked one of the Privateers, glancing up at the canopy. Then they all heard it. The unmistakeable wind-roar of afterburners. The rushing howl of a supersonic, fighter jet carving up the air. Then the bone-jarring crash of air pressure as the sound barrier was broken.

"Hurricane fighters," said Killian, lowering his revolver as he looked up.

A second sound shuddered the jungle a moment later. The thudding boom of rapid-firing cannons sent shivers through the undergrowth and set the vines and hanging tendrils to gently swaying. The soldiers could feel the vibrations coming up through their boots. Instinctively, the group turned towards the source of the sound.

"That's close," said Killian.

"Within two hundred metres," added Cutra.

The cannons fell silent, but the group could still hear the trailing roar of the Hurricane's afterburners as it powered away. Further out, other cannons opened fire, the explosive discharge of their hammering barrels echoing through the jungle.

"They're flying the gauntlet," said Broden, realisation in his voice. "They're making passes to bait the Separatists into opening fire."

"So that they can reveal their positions to the second wave," said Dalton.

Killian holstered his revolver. The tension eased. Then the lieutenant struck. He slung the L7 from his back and in the same motion cracked the stock into the side of Sarash's head. The pathfinder went over sideways. Eskela had her rifle up in a heartbeat, trained on Killian.

"Don't," said Colt. The trooper was standing behind Eskela. He nudged the muzzle of his rifle into the back of her head.

"Restrain them, sergeant," said Killian.

Broden hesitated. He looked around the group. Dalton met his eyes, silently imploring him to resist. The sergeant gave him an apologetic look and fished a loop of zip ties from his webbing. He trudged over and tied Sarash's hands behind his back, then did his best to prop the unconscious pathfinder into a more dignified position. Next, he approached Eskela.

"This will go better for all of us if you don't try anything foolish," said Broden.

Eskela shot Dalton a venomous look. When he couldn't meet her gaze, she snarled and threw down her rifle. Broden fastened her wrists behind her back.

"Thank you, sergeant," said Killian, and turned to address the group. "Now that we're not in any danger of being betrayed, this is the plan. We're going to find that Separatist anti-aircraft position, and we're going to hit it hard and fast. All we need to do is wipe out the crew and sit tight while we wait for the second wave to move up and find us. Chances are the Separatists will have long-range communication equipment on site, and we can use that to make sure our allies know where we are."

Killian swept his hard gaze across the group. It lingered on Dalton.

"Anyone got a problem with that?"

Chapter Twenty-Five

Nightfall came. To the survivors, it was as if an age had passed. In reality, it had been a single day, a day that all of them were eager to leave behind. There is only so much trauma that the human brain can process before it begins to recoil against the onslaught of pain. It withdraws all emotion behind bolted gates and leaves a person numb, but protected from further injury.

That was what Dalton had always heard, at least. Looking around the ragged group as they huddled together for comfort and protection, he could believe it for the hollow stares that many of them wore. For him though, there was no truth in it. There was no mental respite from the agony and the stress, there was no escaping the exhaustion of body and of mind. Every wound and every loss was simply layered over the last. He was raw from it.

He put his head against the trunk behind him and closed his eyes.

* * *

Blake was sitting across from Dalton, watching his friend in the fading light.

"He's in bad shape," said Harris quietly, following Blake's gaze.

"Aren't we all?" asked Blake.

"He has a nose for trouble, that one," said Harris, nodding towards Dalton. "Whenever there's conflict, he always seems to be at the heart of it."

"I don't think he chooses it," said Blake defensively.

"Don't you?" asked Harris, and began ticking off fingers on his hands. "He chose to get into a punching match with that mod back on *The Moongate*. He chose to chase those Separatists after the palace ambush, instead of staying with the squad. He chose to lead us against the enemy flank in the battle beneath Ushura, instead of waiting for Broden. He chose to run ahead and find that sniper on our first day in the jungle. He consistently chooses to challenge the lieutenant. He—"

Blake held up a hand. "You've made your point. Abundantly."

"My point is, it's not some abstract concept like destiny that's hurling him into these scenarios. We're all faced with the same choices that he is. Beneath Ushura, do you know what I was doing when he was leading you behind enemy lines? I was back in the tunnel with Scott and Nelson. They were wounded, sure, but they would have survived without me being there. I *chose* to stay behind."

"Are you just labouring the point, or are you going somewhere with this?" asked Blake.

"He fights. More than the rest of us do. I don't mean in the same way that Colt or Broden fight, he doesn't seem to have an actual joy for combat or for killing. I mean, it's as though he's fighting against the world, as if he has something to prove to himself."

Blake frowned and looked back at Dalton.

"Maybe he does."

"A man with something to prove is one of two things in my experience," said Harris. "Incredibly stupid, or incredibly dangerous."

"Which one do you reckon he is?"

Harris shrugged. "We've all got our trials. We've all got things that haunt us. But whatever those things are for James, they seem to drive him, more than they do for the rest of us. That's either going to save him, or it's going to be the death of him. But that's not what concerns me."

"What does?"

"What concerns me is whether it'll be the death of us as well."

* * *

The Separatist anti-aircraft position lay ahead of them. They had found it before nightfall, and sat in wait as the last of the light had faded from the jungle. A clearing had been made in the trees and in the centre of that space a large, three-barrelled turret had been assembled. Camouflage netting had been secured across the gap in the tree canopy, to conceal the position from aerial scans. Around the turret were three log cabins and several smaller tents, that provided shelter for a garrison estimated to be in the region of thirty fighters.

Their group numbered twenty-four. Fifteen Privateers and nine Avernii. Killian had expressed his lack of concern about being outnumbered, and more or less everyone had agreed with the lieutenant. For the first time since they had arrived on Ishra, the element of surprise was fully in their favour. They could see their enemy, and their enemy was unaware. It felt good for the tables to be reversed. It filled the men with a savage excitement and a bloodthirsty eagerness to be unleashed upon the foe.

Cutra took his transhumans and moved off to flank the enemy from the far side of the clearing. The Privateers split into five groups of three and spaced themselves out along one face of the enemy position. Dalton lay in the undergrowth alongside Harris and Blake. Colt had chosen to group with Scott and Thompson, and Dalton knew that the decision had not been a random one. The friendship that had once bonded the three men had become strained, and the cracks were beginning to show.

"I can't see a damn thing in these," hissed Blake, fidgeting with the specialist, thermal imaging goggles that had been issued to the vanguard.

"You have to adjust the contrast, or you won't be able to distinguish between heat signatures," said Harris. The dry rasp of the man's voice made Dalton wince.

"I read the manual, thanks," snapped Blake.

Dalton was more preoccupied with another piece of gear that they had been issued. He thumbed the button on the colourless laser sight attached to the barrel of his L7. A wireless signal connected the device to his goggles, and a digital reticle blinked into life before his eyes. He shifted the barrel of his rifle and the reticle travelled in unison with the motion. Wherever he aimed his weapon, the reticle would show him precisely where his rounds would strike, allowing him to fire quickly and accurately from the hip.

"That's cool," murmured Dalton.

Radio silence was to be maintained for fifteen minutes, to allow all fire teams to move into position. When the count was done, Killian would issue a single command. If the enemy was listening in on the frequency, it would be too late even if they heard it. The fire teams would fall on the Separatist position from every angle, ensuring a swift end to any resistance.

"It's got to have been fifteen minutes by now," said Blake.

"It's been five. Be patient," said Dalton. "Focus."

"How are you not shitting yourself right now?" asked Blake, giving him a sidelong look.

Dalton paused to think about it. He hadn't realised just how calm he was until that moment. "I don't know. I guess we've just been here before."

"What do you mean—"

A fern rustled. The three Islanders froze.

"What the fuck?" said a voice behind them, thick with the Ishradi accent.

Dalton glanced over his shoulder. There were two Separatists standing behind them, a woman and a man. They wore the same green fatigues as the Ishradi regulars, but those were barely recognisable for the modifications that the fighters had made. They had strips of cloth wound about their lower legs and forearms, bandoleers of ammunition fastened over their chests, and cloaks woven from leaves and fronds. They had their rifles slung across their backs. One of them had a string of small, dead creatures slung over his shoulder.

The fighters were hesitating, caught off-guard. They were a hunting party on their way back to camp. They had not expected to find enemies lying in wait at their doorstep. Dalton realised all of this in a second. His instincts were screaming at him to act. So he did.

He twisted round, springing to his feet and launching himself shoulder first into one of the Separatists. Dalton crashed into the fighter and knocked him clean off his feet, driving the breath from his lungs. The fighter unclasped his rifle at the strap and pulled it clear, but Dalton kicked it from his grasp. He put his knee in the fighter's gut and pressed the stock of the L7 into his throat.

A second behind Dalton, Harris and Blake went for the other Separatist. She was fast. She pivoted on her heel, bent sideways at the waist and delivered a booted kick to Blake's stomach that put him on his back. Harris stepped up and cracked her in the side of the head with the butt of his rifle. He rotated the L7 in his hands and aimed it at the downed fighter.

"No," hissed Dalton. "If you fire your weapon, every Separatist in that camp will hear it."

Harris made the mistake of lowering his rifle. The fighter scissored her legs, crashing them against Harris' ankles and sending him toppling to the ground. She fought to free her rifle from its strap. Dalton moved to intercept her, releasing his hold on the other Separatist. The man lashed out, grabbed Dalton by the helmet and pushed him into the dirt. Dalton swung his rifle, but his momentum was poor and the fighter stopped it with both hands. They grappled, fighting for control of the weapon.

The other fighter freed her rifle and clambered to her knees. She braced the weapon and pointed it at Harris, who was scrambling to regain his feet. Blake barrelled into her from the side, sending them both crashing to the ground in a tangle of limbs. The rifle clattered away into the ferns.

Dalton was pushing against the Separatist, fighting to keep the man from driving the rifle into his neck. The fighter stopped pushing and pulled instead, catching Dalton off-guard and tearing the L7 free. The momentum sent the Separatist staggering back. He waved his arms as he fought to find his balance. Dalton rolled sideways and snatched up one of the wooden-stock rifles dropped by the fighters. He twisted round and levelled the weapon. The Separatist was staring back, aiming Dalton's L7.

"We don't have to do this," said Dalton, breathing hard. "There's another way."

The Separatist's eyes were wild with adrenaline. His nostrils were flaring.

"Please," urged Dalton. "We have your base surrounded. In less than ten minutes my commander is going to give the order to attack. None of your people will survive."

The Separatist bristled.

"That doesn't have to happen though," said Dalton quickly. "I will radio my commander right now and tell him to call off the attack. I will do that, if you stand down and agree to be my hostage."

"Why the fuck would I do that?" snapped the Separatist.

"Because if you do, we don't have to attack your camp. No one here has to die. We can arrange a ceasefire, using you and your friend as leverage. We have your camp surrounded, outnumbered and outgunned. You're going to lose this battle one way or another, no matter what happens here, but you have a chance, right now, to save lives. If your camp stands down when they see that we have prisoners, I personally guarantee that none of you will come to any harm."

Dalton could see the conflict in the man's eyes, could see the doubt chipping away at his anger.

"What's the alternative?" asked Dalton. "We shoot each other? My commander will order the attack anyway. Then your camp burns, along with every man and woman inside. It doesn't have to be that way. You can save them."

The Separatist swallowed. The weapon wavered in his grip. Harris stepped up behind the fighter and drove his rifle into the back of the man's head. The fighter collapsed face first, out cold.

"He was going to surrender, damn it," snapped Dalton, retrieving his L7.

Harris shrugged. "I wasn't so sure."

Blake gave a muffled cry. The second Separatist had managed to draw a blade from her hip and had dragged it up across Blake's front, scoring his chest-piece and nicking his jaw. She kicked Blake aside and rolled, scooped up her dropped rifle and came to her feet in one fluid motion. Dalton saw her bring the rifle round, saw her finger sliding to the trigger, saw the hard look in her eyes.

The shot echoed against the trees and into the clearing. The fighter's legs gave out beneath her. Dalton lowered his L7, a tendril of smoke curling from the barrel. Killian's voice crackled across their handheld radio.

"What the fuck was that? Attack! Attack now!"

Gunfire exploded across the clearing.

* * *

Harris thudded into a tree on the edge of the clearing. He leaned out of cover, brought up his L7 and began to snap off short bursts of fire into the camp. His rounds hit the back of one of the log cabins, tore up tufts of grass and soil. The four

Separatists, who had been moving up and strafing the tree line with rifle fire, ducked away to safety.

Dalton tore from cover. Blake came after him. They crossed the open stretch of ground between the trees and the camp. To either side more Privateers were breaking from cover and storming the camp, firing short, controlled bursts as they closed the gap. From the far side of the camp, he could hear the high-pitched drone of Avernii weapons discharging.

A Separatist fighter swung out from behind the nearest log cabin. Dalton was faster, carrying his rifle high and at the ready as he ran. He snapped the L7 to his shoulder and dropped the fighter with a burst of three shots to the chest. Blake fired a second later. Dalton flinched and glanced at his friend. He followed the angle of Blake's gun and saw a Separatist lying on the ground, a Separatist that had been about to catch them in enfilade. He nodded to Blake.

They barrelled into cover behind the log cabin. A dozen metres off to the left Broden arched a grenade over the roof of a second cabin and scattered a cluster of fighters. The detonation was sudden and loud, a percussive bang Dalton felt in the air. The sergeant's fire team moved up, gun barrels flashing in the night. Dalton leaned round the side of the cabin and started laying down covering fire. Blake was watching his six.

Harris moved up from the tree line and joined them. They slipped around the side of the cabin and into the heart of the camp. Ahead of them squatted the anti-aircraft gun, its three long barrels silhouetted in the dark by the repeating flash of weapons fire. To their right a cluster of tents had caught alight. Shadowed figures burst from those tents, flailing and howling. Fire clung to their limbs like swarms of enraged screechers. They collapsed to the dirt, beating their bodies into the earth in an attempt to douse the flames. Three Privateers came through the burning huddle of tents and shot the Separatists where they lay.

Two fighters burst from the doorway of the cabin. For the last few seconds of their lives they looked shocked and confused. Dalton, Blake, and Harris opened fire simultaneously, riddling the fighters with bullets. Killian strode out of the shadows and the smoke.

"Fire in the hole!" yelled the lieutenant, and the three Islanders leapt aside as he bowled a grenade through the open cabin door. The flash of the detonation lit the cabin from within, briefly filling the cracks between the stacked logs with fiery, orange light. Flames and debris billowed from the doorway.

"Move on!" shouted Killian. "Secure this camp!"

On the other side of the anti-aircraft emplacement, the transhumans were surrounding the third and final cabin. One of the Avernii moved up to the closed door. As the warrior came near, the door cracked open. The barrel of a shotgun protruded from the opening. In casual response, the transhuman reached out to grab the weapon. The first blast shredded the transhuman's arm to the elbow. The second shattered the visor and pulverised the head within.

The rest of the Avernii opened fire in the same second that the door slammed shut. Their barrage splintered the cabin's facade, but the logs were too thick to be penetrated by rifle fire alone. They ceased fire. Little wisps of smoke curled from two hundred bullet holes in the cabin's front. Silence fell across the camp, broken only by the crackle and creak of burning tents.

"How many do you reckon are in there?" asked Killian, pushing his way to the front of the group that had gathered in front of the cabin.

"Five or six, at most, judging from a rough kill count and our original estimate," said Broden.

"Solutions?"

"I'd say breach and enter, if we had any det-packs," said Broden.

"We could always burn it down," suggested Thompson, lugging his flamethrower.

"Take too long to catch. I've got a better solution," said Colt. The stout soldier moved across to the anti-aircraft gun and hauled himself into the operator's seat.

"What are you doing, private?" barked Killian.

"Can't be too difficult," said Colt thoughtfully, taking hold of the turret's controls. "These are to fire, so this must be for elevation?"

Actuators whined as the emplacement rotated on its axis and the barrels shuddered down to the horizontal plane. Men yelped and jumped out of the way as Colt brought the weapon round to bear on the cabin.

"Salt below, man!" yelled Broden, diving for cover.

"Brace yourselves!" bellowed Colt gleefully, and depressed the firing studs.

The roar was ear-splitting. The pounding of the three gun barrels reached down into the earth and shook it so hard that several Privateers lost their balance. The muzzle flare was blindingly bright. It seared long shadows across the breadth of the camp. The cabin simply came apart. It exploded in a storm of splinters, the high velocity rounds stripping the logs into their constituent fibres.

Colt kept firing long after he had obliterated the cabin. His eyes were bright, reflecting the harsh light of destruction. His mouth was stretched wide in a scream that couldn't be heard over the pulsing crash of the three barrels. A huge plume of dust and smoke was rising up over where the cabin had once stood. It danced and rippled as tracers of anti-aircraft fire punched through and continued on to rip up the jungle beyond.

As Dalton watched, he realised it was not a scream that was issuing unheard from Colt's mouth. It was laughter.

Chapter Twenty-Six

"There is definitely movement," said Zirris.

"In the west?" asked Killian. "That's got to be the second wave."

Zirris said nothing. Cutra was striding back into the smoke-wreathed remains of the camp, alongside the second scouting party.

"Movement, headed our way," the transhuman said, rejoining the group.

"From the east, as well?" said Broden. "Salt. There's no way that's friendly."

"So, we've got allies moving to our position from the west, and enemies approaching from the east," Killian said.

"We're sure those are allies at our back?" asked Dalton.

"We all heard the Hurricane," snapped Killian. "There's no way High Command would risk a fighter jet to unmask an enemy position, unless they were going to move on it immediately."

"We should at least consider the worst case scenario," replied Dalton, "that we're about to be caught in a pincer movement."

"I've got your worst case scenario, right here," said Colt. The trooper was still sat in the operator's seat of the anti-aircraft gun.

"You've done enough damage as it is," snarled Killian, glancing at the smouldering ruin of the cabin. "Literally and figuratively."

"The Separatists heard us one way or another," said Colt. "We rolled in here guns blazing. They would have heard that long before they heard this baby."

Despite the loathsome insouciance plastered across Colt's face, Dalton knew the man was right, and so did Killian.

"I say we sit tight. Let them come to us, whoever they are. I'll watch the east side, the rest of you hold the west," Colt said.

"There's no need to defend on the west," said Killian. "We just have to hold the Separatists in the east long enough for reinforcements to arrive. We might not have the numbers, but we've got the gun. That makes the difference."

"I'll drink to that," said Colt. The emplacement whined and whirred as the trooper swung it round to bear east.

"This could be a huge mistake—" Dalton began.

Killian shouted over him, pointing to the fortifications that were piled around the base of the anti-aircraft cannon. "Start re-arranging these sandbags! I want an east-facing wall, right now! Come on, move!"

The troopers set about the work, hauling on the sandbags. Dalton strode over to Killian. The lieutenant turned his head to half look over his shoulder. He rested his hand on the grip of the .44. Before Dalton could speak, Killian cut him off in a low voice.

"This is the last chance I'll ever give you, Dalton. You've become the itch in my arse lately, and I'm this close to scratching you out. Keep your mouth shut and get to work, and maybe, just maybe, you'll get out of here alive."

Dalton tensed. The grip on his rifle tightened.

"Make my day, private," growled Killian.

Dalton breathed out slowly. He slung his rifle and joined the group. Blake hefted a sandbag and gave Dalton a sidelong look, eyebrows raised. Dalton shook his head, but said nothing, lifting one of the sacks and thumping it into place.

"We're out of time, lieutenant," called Broden, pointing to the tree line in the east. There was movement there, figures shifting in the dark spaces between the trees.

"Defensive positions!" yelled Killian. "Private Bridger,

prepare to unleash havoc!"

"Roger that, lieutenant," said Colt, grinning.

The group rushed into the cover of their half finished wall, digging their backs into the sandbags and keeping their heads low.

"Defence is our least favourite strategy," said Cutra, crouched beside Dalton.

"Bit late now," said Dalton.

"I thought it appropriate to inform you," said Cutra.

"Inform me of what?" Dalton asked, narrowing his eyes at the transhuman.

"If this goes poorly, my companions and I will charge the enemy," said Cutra. "We will seek to inflict maximum damage before we are overwhelmed. It is—"

"A better way to die?"

"Precisely. It is because you understand this that I am telling you, James Dalton."

"Wait, are you… inviting me?" asked Dalton.

"It will be a good death."

"Let's just see how things go first, shall we?"

Cutra stared at him with that blank, cracked visor. The transhumans had switched the settings of their visors from the glowing blue to a dull black that reflected no light. It was a shame that they could not do the same for the white segments of their armour, though many of them were smeared with dirt and ash. Dalton doubted it was intentional. Somehow, camouflage didn't strike him as something that the Avernii would countenance.

He became aware of the dense silence that had seeped in around them. Blake was holding his breath. Dalton realised that he too had stifled his breath. Every tiny noise was emphasised against the stillness. The rustle of a soldier rearranging his weight. The clatter of a rifle being adjusted. The gentle whine of the anti-aircraft gun as its servos made fractional movements under Colt's tight grip.

"We can talk!"

The voice had not come from any of them. It had echoed out from the trees. No one behind the line of sandbags moved. No one said anything.

"I have a man here," continued the voice, when no response was given. "One of ours. One who you spared. He says there are reasonable men amongst you. Men who are willing to talk!"

"What the shit is he talking about?" hissed Killian.

"We didn't shoot him," whispered Harris. "The Separatist I knocked out, before the attack. We just left him there."

Dalton shot the man a warning look, but Killian wasn't listening.

"He says you gave him an ultimatum," called the voice from the jungle. "He says you told him that you had the camp surrounded, and that he would lose one way or another, but that he had the chance to save lives by surrendering. I am returning that courtesy to you now."

"Fuck off!" shouted Colt.

"Is that your final answer?" returned the voice.

"Wait! Wait!" called Dalton.

Killian drew his revolver and pointed it straight at Dalton's head. "You don't talk, boy."

"Allow me to clarify," said the voice. "This is mercy. We outnumber you, and if you do not surrender we will not hesitate to attack. With or without that gun, you lose either way. Many soldiers will die. Yours. Mine too, yes, but the difference is, your deaths will achieve nothing. They will be in vain. They do not have to be."

"You stupid bastards," yelled Killian and laughed. "You really have no idea, do you?"

There was silence from the tree line.

"Any second now and you're about to be let in on the bigger picture," continued Killian. "You think you have us outnumbered? You think you have us outgunned? Allow me to clarify! You lost this war the moment we stepped foot on this moon!"

Still, no response came from the dark.

"How about this?" proposed Killian. "You surrender, throw down your weapons, step out into the open, and when our reinforcements arrive, we'll put in a good word for you."

"Which reinforcements would those be?"

The group froze. This voice had come from the tree line too, but not from the east side. This new voice had come from the west.

"Ah, good," called the first voice. "Took you long enough to get into position."

"Sons of bitches," growled Killian.

"We need to take their offer," said Dalton.

Killian still had the .44 levelled at Dalton's head. The lieutenant said nothing, he just watched as figures began peeling themselves from the shadows on the west side of the clearing.

"You would surrender, James Dalton?" asked Cutra. There was an edge to the transhuman's voice. Dalton didn't like the sound of it.

"There's no point in dying here, Cutra," he said. "It won't be a good death. There will be no glory in it, no distinction, no one to remember it."

"It is preferable to surrender."

"No," said Dalton firmly. Most of the group had turned their heads towards him now. "It really isn't. If we die here, then that's it. We don't achieve anything. We don't matter. If we survive this though, if we can live to one day fight again, then that's a victory worth surrendering for."

Cutra was silent. After a second, it was Rolay who spoke. "You are full of many strange ideas, James Dalton, but they appeal."

"A victory worth surrendering for," repeated Cutra, tasting the words.

"Enough of this bullshit," snapped Killian. "You are not the one calling the shots here. We are not surrendering. The second wave is coming. It's just a matter of time."

Cutra made a strange sound. It took Dalton a moment to realise that the transhuman had sighed. In the time that realisation took, Cutra's hand had darted out and snatched the revolver from the lieutenant's grip. Killian cursed and went for his rifle. Someone clamped a hand on the weapon and stopped him from raising it.

"It's over, lieutenant," said Broden, forcing the L7 down. "Don't get your men killed for this."

"Fuck this," growled Colt. He hunched his shoulders, moved his thumbs onto the firing studs.

"Colt, look!" cried Dalton.

Colt paused. He had seen it too. A red dot was shuddering on his chest. It was the bead of a laser sight, shining from the rifle of a concealed sniper who even now had Colt in his cross-hairs.

"Well, shit."

* * *

"This is treason! This is insubordination of the highest level! I'll have them bring back the death sentence for this, Dalton, you hear me? You'll drown for this!"

Dalton watched as Killian was dragged away by two of the Separatist fighters. The lieutenant raged and struggled the whole way, until he disappeared into the trees and his voice was swallowed by the dark.

"You gave your word," said Dalton, turning to face the Separatist who had first addressed them.

"And I intend to keep it," said the man. "None of you will be harmed. Ranking officer or not though, that man does not represent a reasonable voice. I cannot speak to him. But I think I can speak to you, yes?"

Dalton narrowed his eyes at the Separatist. The man was young, perhaps the same age as Dalton or possibly younger. Once the group had put down their weapons, this Separatist had been the first to approach them. A hundred fighters had followed him into the clearing, and Dalton suspected there were twice as many waiting beyond the tree line. For the most part, the Ishradi Separatist was not exceptional in appearance. He was a head shorter than Dalton, wiry and narrow of frame. His curly, black hair hung to his shoulders and was held out of his face with a green bandanna. Like all of the Ishradi, his skin was dark from exposure to the light. His face was narrow and plain, but his eyes were a startling blue. They had a piercing quality to them, the sort that could make even the most stoic of men feel uncomfortable.

"Who are you?" asked Dalton.

The Separatist smiled. "Just another soldier in this war. Like you."

"Yeah, somehow I doubt that. You're an officer? A leader? You speak for these men?"

"Surely the right to ask questions is mine, you being the surrendered party," he said, not losing his polite, close-lipped smile for a second.

There was a ripple of movement amongst the fighters as two people were brought forwards. It was the pathfinders, Eskela and Sarash. Their hands were still bound as they were escorted into the clearing.

"We found these two tied to a tree nearby," said one of the escorts.

The young man's face lit up as he laid eyes on Eskela. Dalton saw her shoot the man a warning look, but he waved away her concerns. "Untie her, untie her!"

"And him?"

The young Separatist spared Sarash a dismissive glance. "Not of the cause. Put him with the others."

"What are you doing?" hissed Eskela, glancing at the Islanders and the Avernii, who, save for Dalton, were sitting in a group under armed guard.

"I am so happy to see you, Eskela," said the young man and warmly embraced the pathfinder.

"I fucking knew it," spat Thompson.

"Eskela?" said Dalton. She met his eyes for a brief moment before looking away, her expression unreadable.

"Well, that's my cover blown," she said.

"That's not important now," said the young man. His eyes widened as he looked at her. "Don't tell me you were aboard one of those drop-ships?"

"I knew the risks," she said. "We all knew the risks. It wouldn't be the first time I've been mistakenly fired upon by my own. I just hadn't realised your plans had advanced so quickly."

The young man shot a glance at their prisoners and pressed a finger to his smile. "Let us not say too much in the presence of our guests, yes?"

"You're going to keep them alive?" asked Eskela, glancing at Dalton.

"I gave my word."

"Of course. Why are *you* here, anyway? This is too close to the enemy. Too close to the Spider's Eye."

The young man's eyes glinted in the dark. "I will be at the front of the fight, Eskela, wherever I lead it."

* * *

The Separatists did not blindfold or bind them in any way. Even the transhumans – who could have been considered armed even without their weapons and armour – were left unhindered. The group was made to walk in single file, with the hands of the man behind on the shoulders of the man in front. Ahead, behind and to either side the enemy fighters travelled in loose formation.

Dalton was at the front of the line. The Separatist leader – who had introduced himself as Ajati – had seemed to have placed him there on purpose and chosen to walk beside him. Ajati did not appear concerned to be walking side by side with an enemy. If they saw merit in it, Dalton reckoned the transhumans could leap from the line and wreak havoc across the Separatist ranks before being gunned down. They could certainly make it to the front of the line and kill Ajati before any of the fighters could even bring a rifle to bear. Either the young Separatist did not know this, or he was simply unafraid.

"I cannot imagine how it must feel," said Ajati, after they had been walking for fifteen minutes. "You have done what no human under Mitera has done in two hundred years. You have travelled in space and set foot on another moon. The history of our nations will remember this for all time, you understand? Children will be told stories of it in school."

"You realise we're here to kill you, yes?" asked Dalton.

"Well, that is why you *were* here, yes," said Ajati. "Now you are here to be our guests until this war is over. Then, when Ishra is free of its doom, you will be released to your starship and be allowed to go home, as a gesture of goodwill to your people."

"I don't mean to aggravate you, given my current circumstances, but do you really believe the Separatists can win this war?"

"I can comprehend no future in which we lose," said Ajati, fixing Dalton with his piercing blue eyes. "Do you know why that is? It is because there is no future for Ishra if we lose."

"There are a lot of people on this moon, your people, who believe otherwise," said Dalton. "That's why we were asked to come here in the first place."

"Strange, I do not recall a vote amongst the people for off-world assistance," said Ajati thoughtfully. "You see, in truth, it is only a very small group of people who we oppose: The High Shekahn and his administration. The people who live under the authority of his regime do so because they have not yet seen the truth. That is our mission, Mister Dalton—"

"Just call me James."

"As you like. That is our mission, James. To bring the truth to Ishra. No, more than that. To bring the truth to all people who live under Mitera."

"And what truth is that?" asked Dalton.

Ajati smiled. "That, James, is something which is better seen than heard."

Chapter Twenty-Seven

The Separatist camp was a city in the shadow of the jungle canopy. Hundreds of ladders made from wound vines hung from enclosed platforms that hugged the upper reaches of the thick trees. Open walkways and vine-ropes crossed between the structures, forming a network suspended six metres above the ground. The place swarmed with activity. There were hundreds of fighters garrisoned here, walking ground patrols, climbing and swinging between the trees, crossing the planks and bridges that linked one platform to the next.

Each suspended hut was lit from within by a combination of electric lamps, glow-sticks and even candles. In the gloom of night the effect was mesmerising. Hundreds of raised platforms, stretching away between the trees, each emanating a different quality of light. Dalton noticed that the pitched camouflage-netting and sloping rooftops had been carefully constructed to overlap the platforms, guarding against any light that might penetrate the jungle canopy and be visible from the air.

"Are you insane?" asked Eskela, striding up beside Ajati.

"My dear Eskela," said Ajati, his tone light. "We have been reunited against impossible odds, yet you have been nothing but cruel to me since then."

"Please don't tell me here is where you have encamped the main force? Here, of all places?"

"It is precisely because of where we are that motivated my decision," replied Ajati.

"If I'm judging this correctly, and I'm damn sure I am, this location is right at the edge of the Spider's Eye. How did you ever manage to convince the army to make base here?"

"I told them that the enemy is in the west. I told them that the Spider's Eye is also in the west. I told them that the only way any force from the west could ever reach us, would be by marching *through* the Spider's Eye. That, my dear Eskela, is what I told them."

"Oh," said Eskela. "So you are insane."

"But also somewhat brilliant, can we not agree?" said Ajati, throwing her an endearing smile.

"Theoretically it has its merits," conceded Eskela. "I don't like it though. I can feel the difference, in the trees, in the air. It's not right, being so close to that place."

"Those not of the cause have a great deal more to fear from Assahi than we," said Ajati.

"Not of the cause," said Dalton. "You've said that before. What does it mean, exactly?"

"What did they tell you, I wonder; your commanders, the High Shekahn, those loyal to him? What did they tell you about us? About why we fight?"

"Very little," admitted Dalton. "That you're anarchists. Malcontents. Terrorists."

"How pitiful, that all it takes are such thin accusations to demonise us, to rouse armies from across the very breadth of the void to smite us," said Ajati. "Is that why you are here, James? Were you incited by our anarchy and our terrorism?"

"I had my doubts, my questions," said Dalton, hesitant to speak openly with the other Islanders so close.

"Then I deduce – from the fact that you are still here fighting and killing my brethren – that you never found the answers to those questions."

"What if I did?" asked Dalton. "What if the answer was that the Separatists are wrong. That the civil war you've been fighting has left your nation crippled, both socially and technologically?"

"Then you found the wrong answer," said Ajati. He paused

and signalled to one of his men. "Take the others to the stockade."

"What about him?" asked the fighter, nodding at Dalton.

"This one is coming with me," said Ajati, putting a hand on Dalton's shoulder. "He has something to see before he joins his friends."

The fighter nodded and began shepherding the prisoners onwards, deeper into the camp. Dalton watched them go by. Blake gave him a worried look. Harris just nodded. Scott shot him a venomous glare, and Thompson refused to meet his eyes at all. Colt held his stare, his eyes hard, until he was jostled onwards and could look over his shoulder no longer. Broden gave him that same firm gaze as he had done aboard the drop-ship, when only Dalton had seen the sergeant injecting himself with morphine.

That look alone imparted something more than emotion. The sergeant expected something of him, as he had expected his discretion aboard the drop-ship. What was it now? What was Broden trying to tell him? What was he asking of Dalton?

"Come," said Ajati, extending his hand in invitation. Along with Eskela and two guards, they walked away from where the prisoners were being taken. The air became thick with the buzzing of insects in the undergrowth. Ajati led them to a rope ladder and began to climb. The vines twisted and creaked as they bore his weight. Dalton followed and clambered onto the platform of a surprisingly large structure. Inside the treehouse every item of furniture had been hand-crafted, the low, round table and the bowl that sat upon it, filled with fruit, the three-legged stools, the crates padded with short-grass and the hammock in its carved frame. It did not look like a soldier's billet as much as it did someone's home.

"This is where you live?" asked Dalton, looking around.

"If by this, you mean the jungle, then yes," said Ajati, going over to a side-table and filling three wooden cups from a gourd canteen. "If by this, you mean the specific location that we currently inhabit, then the answer is: for now."

"You're on the move a lot. It makes sense, given that you're being hunted," said Dalton, accepting one of the cups. It was filled with a white, sour smelling liquid.

"That is correct," said Ajati pointedly, "and I would like you to remember it. If by some stroke of utter luck you were to somehow escape here, survive the jungle and return to one of your bases, any information you provided on our whereabouts would have long since become outdated. That is why I did not bother to have you blindfolded, not that you have the faintest clue as to where we currently are in the vastness of the Assahi Territory."

"Point made," said Dalton, "but you don't think I'm going to escape, do you?"

"No?" Ajati asked. "Please, tell me, what exactly is it that I think?"

"I can't presume to know that much," said Dalton, "but I know I'm more than just a prisoner to you. The way I see it, if that were the case, I'd be in a cage with the rest of my friends right now, and not standing here in your house, having a drink and a chat."

"Very perceptive," said Ajati, giving his polite, close-lipped smile. "Is he always like this, Eskela?"

Eskela shrugged and said nothing. She was holding her rifle close, her eyes locked on Dalton.

"Speaking of, what is this?" asked Dalton, looking dubiously at the contents of his cup.

"This?" said Ajati, swirling the liquid in circles. "This is simply the key to everything."

"If it's alcohol I know a few people who would agree with you," Dalton said.

Ajati chuckled. "Your forces conducted a major operation on the westernmost edge of the Assahi Territory, yes?"

"Protecting the loggers and baiting a response from the Separatists at the same time, yeah," confirmed Dalton.

"And, tell me, did you see much of the work that was being done?"

Dalton thought back and recalled that he had never discovered why the workers had been marking the trees or why some were cut down and others pulled up at their roots.

"Yes, you saw it," said Ajati perceptively. "The answer is tree sap."

"Tree sap?" asked Dalton.

"There is a specific type of tree that grows in the Assahi Territory, and within its bark can be found a sap. The properties and applications of this substance are astounding. Right now it's in your cup as a beverage, mixed with the juice of the satacia fruit. Consumed in this way it has medically proven restorative effects on the human body. You can do more than just drink it, though. Depending on how you mix it and what you combine it with, the uses are seemingly limitless. It can be made into a cream for maladies of the skin. It can be worked into a poultice to draw bacteria from a wound, or even cleanse the blood of impurities. There are industrial uses, as well. It can be worked into a powerful adhesive, used as a lubricant, even burned as a clean fuel. I could go on. I could write a damn book."

"That's very impressive," said Dalton, "but I don't see a connection to the war here."

"The government quickly realised the huge economic benefits that they could reap by controlling such a resource. They forcibly seized all companies that were making a living extracting sap. An edict was passed declaring that the Assahi Territory, in its entirety, was to become private government property. They justified this by claiming that they were protecting the people of Ishra from the dangers of the jungle. Their true agenda was to establish a monopoly over all products derived from the sap, and then sell it at extortionate prices to the common man. They hoarded the wealth, a wealth that they had stolen from the people. It could have been used to enrich the nation, to ease the burden of the poor and the suffering, to develop the infrastructure of our cities, to build houses and schools and hospitals."

Eskela put a hand on Ajati's shoulder. The man had worked himself into such a rage that he was trembling. He steadied himself with a deep breath.

"Instead," he continued, speaking now almost in a whisper, "the High Shekahns used the wealth only to glorify themselves. You have seen the palace in Ushura? It is a lesson in hubris. Did you know that over three hundred people died in its construction? No compensation or gifts of commiseration were granted to the bereaved families. The workers themselves were paid so little that they might as well have been considered slaves by another name. What choice did they have though, when the wealth of the nation was so firmly in the hands of the High Shekahn? The choice was no choice at all. Accept the meagre payment the government was offering, or die from starvation.

"Every year when the Scour of Ishra blows hard, that palace and all those like it across the moon suffer the most. You cannot build high on the open plains of Ishra – it is arrogance and it is stupidity of the most appalling order – but the High Shekahns believe their authority to be beyond nature itself. It costs millions in repairs and renovations, and results in the deaths of more people who are forced to accept the work because they can find it nowhere else."

Eskela was nodding, her face creased with anger and disgust. "That's just the tip of the tree. When they're not wasting our money aggrandising themselves, they're using it to ensure that they can never be dislodged. They poured billions into the development of the space fleet, so that they could lord their authority over Ishra from beyond the skies."

"And so that they could protect their interests against our neighbours," Ajati added, giving Dalton a pointed look. "The line of High Shekahns have long been preparing their defences for an inter-moon war. If your people or the Avernii were to realise the truth of the atrocities taking place on Ishra, the High Shekahns have always feared that it would provoke an intervention. Ar Sarafet, the current High Shekahn, is a more cunning animal than his predecessors. Instead of preparing for a war against your nations, he invited them to partake in the atrocities alongside him, no doubt promising your leaders a share in the profits."

"Hold on," said Dalton, staggered by the sheer volume and passion of the argument that he was being presented with. "This whole war, you're telling me it all boils down to tree sap?"

"Don't be simple," snapped Eskela. "Haven't you been listening to us? It's about ending the tyranny of the High Shekahns. It's about justice for our people!"

"Eskela speaks true," said Ajati, "but it's about so much more than that as well. It's about the whole moon. It's about the survival of Ishra as we know it. I am convinced that the sap is vital to the life of the jungle. Four years ago I was at one of the logging sites, north of the Sadari. We drove off the workers, but not before they had dragged up every sap tree in three kilometres of their camp. They had been at work for several months, and I noticed that the trees and plants at the edges of the work site were withering. There was no explanation for it, until I realised that there could be some link between the sap trees and the rest of the flora. I thought, perhaps they exude their sap into the soil, enriching it and providing succour for the other plants?"

"You don't sound sure," said Dalton.

"It's just a theory," said Eskela. "No one has done the science to prove it. Not that the High Shekahn would ever concern himself with such a thing. If it got out that pulling up the sap trees was draining the life out of the Assahi Territory, it would undoubtedly cause problems for the High Shekahn's agenda. Even without Ajati's theory though, there is plenty of justification behind our fight."

"So, what's your agenda here?" Dalton asked. "You've told me about how amazing this sap is, but you disagree with mining it?"

"I did not say that," said Ajati. "I disagree with how the government goes about the work. Before the civil war, when the government was free to conduct its operations without our defiance, they would tear up thousands of trees a day. They would even cut down those trees without sap to be used as lumber. Do you imagine they replant that which they cut? The Assahi Territory produces just less than fifty percent of the oxygen in our atmosphere. If we had left the High Shekahn unopposed, at the rate his operations were tearing up trees the jungle would be eighty percent smaller than it is today.

"It is not possible to drain the sap trees without killing them, but it is possible to bleed them, slowly, so they can regenerate that which is taken. Does that not make more sense? As a boy, I read a cautionary tale in one of the relic books brought from the Birthworld. It was about a bird that could lay golden eggs. A pair of fools kill the bird to get at the gold in its belly, only to realise that it would lay eggs no more. That is what Ar Sarafet is so short-sightedly condoning. He is killing the very source of the wealth he so desires. And why? Because it is faster. More profitable in the short-term. Would you abide such a thing, James? To destroy your home out of laziness and greed?"

"This is the first I'm hearing of any of this," said Dalton. "How do I know you're not just spinning me a tale to convince me to act in your interest?"

"Of course this is the first you're hearing of it," said Eskela.

"I don't suppose you get much time off from shooting at us to ask about our moral values?"

"As I recall, it was your people who opened fire on us first," Dalton retorted. "Rained missiles down on our heads on the first day of our arrival. Excuse me if I'm not immediately won over by your argument here."

Ajati raised his hands and stepped between Dalton and Eskela. "Please, please. Has there not been enough fighting this night already? I believe we are all tired. Perhaps it was a mistake to bombard you with so much information and so soon, James, and for this I apologise. I will allow you to return to your friends, so that you may rest. Hopefully, in the days to come we can speak more. I truly believe that there is much we can do to help one another."

Dalton eyed the young man warily, but said nothing. He followed the man's gesture and descended the ladder. Two guards were waiting to lead him away. Ajati and Eskela stood on the edge of the platform and watched as Dalton was led to the stockades.

"Do you really believe he is the one who can help us?" asked Eskela.

"If he is not," said Ajati, turning away, "then I will find another."

Chapter Twenty-Eight

Dalton awoke to the creaking and clicking of the sharp-winged creatures that lived in the canopy. The gentle light of morning filtered in through the tops of the trees. His body ached in a hundred different places, but for the first time in what felt like an age he awoke with a feeling of peacefulness. Ironic then, that he should feel so at ease, being that he was a captive of the very people he had considered to be the enemy since his arrival on Ishra.

He sat up, groaning as he stretched his back. Along with five others, he occupied a cage that had been built high up on one of the trees. The platform was divided into four cells, with half a dozen prisoners in each quarter, separated by thick wooden bars. Dalton had been put with Blake, Harris, Rolay and two other transhumans whose names he did not know. The three Avernii were sitting with their backs against the broad trunk, cross-legged, eyes closed. They looked formidable even without their armour, their body-gloves emphasising the lean and powerful musculature of their enhanced physiques. Blake and Harris were still asleep.

Beyond the bars of the stockade, the Separatist camp murmured with quiet activity. In the undergrowth below, hunters and foragers were heading out to find food for the day. Snipers in camouflaged cloaks watched them from the platforms above, cradling their long-barrelled, high-calibre rifles. Men and women went about their work, moving deftly between the raised huts via narrow walkways, ascending through the tiers on creaking vine-ropes.

It was strange to see the Separatists this way, as people simply going about their lives, detached from the violence and the war with which he had come to associate them. Before today they had been phantoms in his mind, killers cloaked in shadow that lurked behind every tree. To watch them now, especially in the light of Ajati's words last night, Dalton was not sure he could bring himself to call them his enemy anymore.

"Have a nice chat last night?" Colt was leaning on the bars of the cage adjoining Dalton's.

"I think you should hear what they told me," said Dalton, coming up to the bars that separated them. "If there is truth in it, then we all have a lot to think about. We all have a decision to make."

Colt scoffed and looked away. "I should have known."

"Should have known what?" asked Dalton.

"From that moment aboard *The Moongate*, from how you reacted to Sergeant Lee's death. Pathetic. Weak. That should have been the first warning. I should have known they would turn you so easily."

"You stubborn bastard," said Dalton. "You haven't even heard what I have to say and already you've refused."

"You don't get it," Colt said, "but then again, you never have. This is war, James. You do know what that means, right? Let me try to spell it out for you one last time, in the hopes that you'll see the truth of it. From the moment that first shot is fired, a line is drawn, a line between your enemy and you. After that, anything that crosses that line is a weapon. Bullets, missiles, *words*. We don't speak to our enemies, Dalton. We kill them."

"We came here to put an end to a civil war," Dalton said, "and in your mind the only way to do that is to exterminate everyone on one side?"

"You say that as though it isn't logical," said Colt, "as though it's something to be frowned upon. It's only when no one is left alive to fight you, that you find peace."

"I don't believe that you could actually be this bloodthirsty," said Dalton. "Look around you, Colt. These are people, just like the ones you met in Ushura, just like you and me. They're not fighting because they're evil. They're fighting because they have a cause that they believe in. We should have considered that long before we turned up to fight on the High Shekahn's side."

"Salt, you're still in that place," said Colt, shaking his head.

"What place?"

"The place you were in on *The Moongate*. Asking questions that don't matter, trying to figure out why we're fighting instead of being a soldier."

"Does being a soldier have to mean blindly following orders?"

"This is exactly what happens when soldiers don't follow orders," shouted Colt. "We're in this mess because you questioned the lieutenant, because you put doubt in the minds of your brothers. You might as well have just shot us all yourself."

"If we hadn't surrendered we'd all be dead," said Dalton.

"Is that what you tell yourself?" asked Colt, his lip curling. "Is that how you excuse your betrayal?"

"Were you always this hateful?" Dalton asked in return. "Has this war changed you so much, or simply shown you for what you always were?"

Colt's hand shot between the bars and locked around Dalton's throat. "You have no idea what I am."

Dalton forced Colt's hand away and stepped back from the bars, his eyes burning with anger and shock. Colt snarled and turned his back, moving to the far side of his cage and out of sight. Dalton rubbed his neck. There had been no restraint in Colt's outburst. That killing light had surfaced in his eyes, that maddened gaze which could not tell friend from foe.

"He's not the only one who feels that way," said Blake. The man was awake and had been watching.

"You too, Blake?" asked Dalton.

"Salt no," he said. "I know the score. If we'd listened to Killian out there we'd all just be meat for the bone-dogs. And Colt would've been the first to go. He's just too angry to see it."

"And not the only one?"

Blake nodded. "Scott, Thompson, obviously the lieutenant. They've got him in the quarter on the far side. He'll spit poison about you to anyone who'll listen."

"And what about...?" Dalton asked, nodding his head to the three Avernii in their cage, whose eyes were still closed. The transhumans hadn't moved an inch this whole time. Blake shrugged.

"What's the game here, James?" asked Blake. "What's the plan?"

Dalton sighed and turned away. He put his hands on the wooden bars and stared out across the Separatist camp. "I'm working on it."

* * *

Patera rose eight more times before Dalton saw Ajati again. They were left in peace, brought food and water twice a day and watched at all times by the snipers on the surrounding platforms. The camp was a pocket of calm, shielded from the ripples of war by the sheer density of the jungle. They heard the occasional roar and boom of air pressure as speeding Hurricanes tore overhead – daring anti-aircraft turrets to unmask themselves – but other than that no sounds of battle reached them. It was impossible to gauge the progress of the coalition's second wave, let alone the status of the overall war. Even when they had been stranded and wandering they had not felt so isolated, so cut off from the bigger picture.

In that time, Dalton spoke to the group as best he could about what Ajati had told him. In Colt's quarter there were no willing ears. Scott and Thompson had sided with Colt in their anger towards Dalton. The other Privateers in that cell were too scared of Colt to be seen speaking with Dalton. The transhumans in his own cell only stared at him when he tried to speak with them, deigning neither to reply nor to move. In fact, they only ever moved to take water and eat sparingly from the food bowls provided. At one point, Blake commented quietly that he had yet to even see them move to relieve their bowels.

Fortunately, Dalton didn't have to contend with Killian. The lieutenant was hidden from view in the quarter of the cage on the far side of the tree. In the final quarter of the prison were Broden and Cutra, along with a second transhuman and three Privateers. Sergeant Broden took a practical approach to their discussions, treating what Dalton had to say as tactical information. Perhaps because of this, Dalton couldn't bring himself to raise the topic that had lodged itself in his mind since his conversation with Ajati. To discuss with Broden the idea that they might be fighting for the wrong side terrified Dalton, not out of fear that the sergeant would lash out like Colt had, but because of that look in his eyes, that expectant gaze which seemed to say "I know you'll do the right thing. I know you won't let me down."

In those quiet moments when Broden wasn't listening, Dalton would speak with Cutra. Their whispered exchanges through the bars of the cell were the closest thing that Dalton got to a true debate. Blake and Harris supported him with eager nods whenever he spoke with them, but it was only Cutra who really seemed to listen with the intent of discovering the truth behind Dalton's quandary.

"You have heard me speak of the unity of my people," said Cutra, during one of their late night discussions. "I admit that it was not always so. The early years of settlement on Avernus are defined by decades of conflict. There were a number of issues that fragmented our society. We were a nation of factions, warring amongst ourselves like the tribal clans of Ancient Earth. Some opposed the modifications that have made us what we are today. Some argued that we had not gone far enough in our forced evolution. One faction wanted to leave Avernus behind altogether. Others fought simply for power and for control. There always seemed to be a reason, an excuse to kill one another."

"Don't worry, I think that's just a human condition," said Dalton.

"Perhaps," conceded Cutra, "but I believe that in my society we have refined that instinct. We have distilled it into a culture of its own."

"Your culture determines that you should kill each other?"

"You must understand that on Avernus everything is about survival," said Cutra. "The moon rejects life itself. To the unmodified human, the air is poison. The land is barren. The atmosphere is too thin to absorb the worst of our star's radiation. Do you see? On Avernus, even the light will kill you. If you do not harden yourself in every way, if you do not resolve to be as strong as possible, you will not survive."

Dalton nodded. "Survival of the strongest. Life on Avernus demanded it and so it's become a part of your culture."

"Our unity is a recent thing," Cutra continued. "It was only when we established contact with Landbreak and Ishra that we began to unify as a people."

"Against a common enemy?" asked Dalton, raising an eyebrow.

"Potentially, yes," said Cutra without shame. "You cannot say different for your own government, or that of Ishra's. A nation does what it must to protect itself from anything that could threaten it. As much as we have modified ourselves, as far as we have come from our original humanity, we have never been able to override that most basic of instincts. The preservation of self and kin."

"And what does fighting a war on behalf of someone else have to do with preserving your nation?" asked Dalton. Cutra didn't reply. The transhuman just stared at him with those unblinking, circuit board eyes. "Zirris said a warrior has to know their fight. What's your fight, Cutra? Why are your people here? It can't just be to prove yourselves, it can't just be for distinction. Why are the Avernii really here?"

"The point I was making, James Dalton, was that I understand the disunity that grips Ishra," said Cutra. "Every victory on Avernus shaped what became of our nation. It will be the same here. If the Separatists are true about their intentions and about the accusations that they have levelled at the High Shekahn's government, then the outcome of this war will have ramifications beyond just a change in regime."

"If the Separatists win, Ishra lives. That's what Ajati says. Which means that if the High Shekahn wins…"

"Then Ishra dies," said Cutra, "and becomes barren and lifeless, like Avernus."

"So… you agree with me? That we have to consider the possibility that our forces here aren't fighting for the right side?"

"I agree that Ishra cannot be allowed to die," said Cutra. The transhuman turned. "I will converse with my kin."

"You didn't answer my question," said Dalton. "Why are the Avernii here? What's your fight?"

Cutra walked away.

* * *

On the ninth day of their captivity, Dalton was escorted from the cell and led along the creaking walkways between the trees. He looked over his shoulder and saw Colt. The trooper was pressed against the cell, his thick arms hanging between the bars. He was watching Dalton's every footstep, his face half lost to shadow.

Ajati was in his hut. He was splashing his face with water from a basin and running his fingers through his hair. His fatigues were filthy, tattered and crusted with dark stains. He straightened up as Dalton was brought in. Ajati looked weary, but that small, polite smile came to his face all the same.

"James, I am happy to see you," he said, and gestured to a pair of stools by the low table. Ajati groaned as he took the weight off of his feet. In that moment, the man seemed decades older than he was.

"You've been fighting," said Dalton.

"That is the occupation I find forced upon me," said Ajati. "So, as with all things in life, I will make the best of it."

"The second wave is near?" asked Dalton.

Ajati waved off the question. "I said I was happy to see you, James. Don't make me regret it."

"Why? Why are you happy to see me?"

"Because you remind me that when this war is over there can still be friendship between my people and yours," said Ajati. Dalton frowned. Ajati sighed. "I've been out there for seven days, fighting your people, fighting the Avernii and their damn war machines. I've killed many men. Islander men. Nothing about it satisfies me. None of their deaths bring us any closer to Ishra's salvation. So, coming back here, to this place I consider my home, it is good to see the face of an Islander who is not trying to kill me, and who I have no need to kill in turn."

"And that's why you called me here today?" Dalton asked. "To enjoy my company? To divest you of your guilt?"

"I have no desire to kill my own people, let alone yours, but it has been made necessary. I have no guilt. If Ishra is to survive, we must make difficult decisions."

"Then why?"

"I told you that the truth was something better seen than heard," said Ajati, "and I was being quite literal. I want to show you the truth. I want to show you why our fight here is so important."

Ajati stood up and crossed over to a small chest beside his hammock. When he returned, he had a data tablet in his hands, an older version of the device that Dalton hadn't seen before. Ajati brought it to the table and slid it across to Dalton.

"It's a planet," said Dalton, looking at the image on the cracked screen.

"Which planet?" asked Ajati.

Dalton shrugged. He traced his fingers over the image and the representation of the planet turned. It looked like a beautiful world, with sweeping tracts of vibrant, green land, sprawling, snow-capped mountains and vast ocean bodies.

"You don't recognise it, do you?" Ajati asked.

"I don't think I've ever seen this world," said Dalton.

"Not a person that lives under Mitera has, not with their own eyes, at least," said Ajati, "but at some point or another, we've all seen pictures of this planet."

Dalton narrowed his eyes. "What are you talking about?"

"What about this one?" asked Ajati, swiping the screen to bring up a different image.

"That's easy," said Dalton, recognising the arid and craggy world at a glance. "That's Old Earth."

"The Birthworld, the planet that all humanity stems from," said Ajati, nodding.

"Sorry, I'm not quite sure what you're trying to show me here."

Ajati smiled, but there was no joy in the expression. "They're both pictures of the Birthworld, James. They're both Earth."

"They're clearly not," said Dalton, switching back and forth between the two images.

"It is difficult to see," Ajati admitted.

"This planet has completely different landmasses," said Dalton, pointing to the first image. "Look at the oceans. Earth doesn't have water like that and, well, it's not as green either. You're seriously telling me that both these pictures are of Earth?"

Ajati reached over and displayed a third image. This one was both planets, the first rendered translucent and imposed over the second. Dotted lines traced the outlines of landmasses and major geographical aspects. Dalton stared at it for a long time.

"How?" he asked at last, unable to move his eyes from the cracked screen.

"I think you know how," said Ajati.

"We did this?"

"Our ancient ancestors did, yes. They had everything, and they threw it all away. They cut down the forests and the jungles, they polluted the skies and boiled away the oceans with their nuclear wars. They scarred the Birthworld until all that remained was the dry and barren world which you recognise today."

"How is it that I've never seen this picture of Old Earth before?"

"The colony ships which brought our people to Mitera were not equal in design, nor, I believe, were they intended to have been separated from one another. Our colony ship held a sizeable repository of knowledge, a culture bank brimming with millions of records on every detail of the Birthworld's history. Remember that people were living on the Birthworld as you and I recognise it for hundreds of years before the exodus. Our ancestors who boarded the colony ships wouldn't have known their planet for the garden that it once was, nor is it likely that they would have had pictures. War has a way of erasing history, and the final wars of the Birthworld were particularly thorough. The repository on our ship must have been a truly special thing, one of the last remaining archives of intact human history."

"You said you didn't believe the colony ships were supposed to have been separated. Why?"

"From the records I also learned of the unique qualities of each vessel. They were never designed to operate alone, but rather to complement one another in the creation of a perfect society. Somewhere along the line, our ancestors who made the long voyage lost sight of that ideal. Human conflict, no doubt, got in the way of a brighter future, as it always does."

"The unique qualities of the ships, what were they?" asked Dalton.

"Your colony ship had more in the way of industrial infrastructure, and the one which went to Avernus was fitted with advanced scientific installations. Can you see now why Landbreak and Avernus developed as they did?"

"And Ishra?"

"Our nation was not shaped by its colony ship, because our people never had access to its unique resources," said Ajati. "As my ancestors descended to Ishra for the first time and the colony ship began to detach into its constituent modules, history tells us that a terrible accident occurred. Dozens of modules fell into orbit, only for their guidance systems to fail. They crashed to the surface and were lost. Amongst them was the repository, the digital library that contained the history of our species on the Birthworld."

"But it was found?" asked Dalton.

"Some of it," said Eskela, coming in from the walkway. She looked just as tired as Ajati. "A boy found the remains of the module buried deep in the jungle, and in doing so validated every belief that the Separatist cause has ever clung to."

"You were the boy," said Dalton, looking at Ajati.

"I was," he replied. "The civil war was already past its twentieth year by then. Mitera be praised that there were those among us who had no need of history to know that we should respect the world on which we live."

"With the information that was salvaged from the module, our cause swelled with recruits," said Eskela. "One of the primary missions back then was the distribution of that information. In the rural areas, with the small towns and villages, it was easy. The larger population centres, on the other hand, aren't so simple to infiltrate. Tighter security, endless checkpoints, kilometres of fencing, even minefields. Eventually one of our operatives got captured and the government found his copy of the data. They realised the damage it could do if it got into the main information network. Since then they've been stamping it out, destroying it wherever they can find it and monitoring the network, censoring anything they don't like. We don't have the technology or the expertise to spread the information globally."

"We don't even have the resources on hand to make endless duplicates," said Ajati, tapping the data tablet. "This is the last copy we have left."

"What about the source?" asked Dalton.

"Immovable, but safe," said Eskela. "It was all we could do to secure and preserve the site, but without launching a full scale excavation that module is never leaving this jungle."

"Not that it would matter. The module ran out of power years ago," said Ajati. He sat up and fixed Dalton with those piercing, blue eyes. "Getting this information to *my* people is no longer the primary concern."

"Then what is?" asked Dalton.

"Getting it to *your* people, James. The common men and women of Landbreak, and the Avernii too. If we can spread this truth to the other moons, then surely the people will rise up in support of us. Your government and that of Avernus will face overwhelming public pressure and have no choice but to align themselves with us against the High Shekahn."

"That's a serious gamble," said Dalton.

"It will work. I know it will," said Ajati.

"How can you be so sure?"

"Because today I saw an Islander witness the truth," said Ajati, smiling. "I watched him as revelation dawned behind his eyes, and in that moment I knew that if you could see the truth, then so could a nation, especially if that truth were delivered by one of their own."

"You want me to do this?" asked Dalton, incredulous.

"Yes, James," said Ajati. "I want you to be my messenger. I want you to go home."

Chapter Twenty-Nine

Dalton's eyes snapped open. He lay still for a second, surfacing from the fog of sleep, struggling to identify what had woken him. It didn't take long. A second explosion thundered across the camp, muffled by the trees and the distance. He bolted upright. Blake and Harris were coming to their feet. Rolay and the two other transhumans in the cage sat unmoving, but their eyes were wide open now.

Hard flashes were lighting up the jungle, out to the east. Dalton recognised the sharp muzzle flare of gunfire when he saw it. The camp was coming to life with hurried activity. Whistles were filling the air, summoning patrols and rousing fighters from their sleep. Every Separatist in the area was running towards the fight. There was a third detonation, this one closer than the last. Dalton glimpsed arcs of flame tumbling between the trees at the far edge of the camp.

"The second wave?" asked Harris, coming up beside him.

"No, not in full, at least," said Dalton. "If High Command knew about this place they'd make sure to hit it with everything they had."

"So what's going on?" Blake asked.

"I don't know," said Harris. "A scouting party must've found the camp by accident."

"Doesn't make sense," Dalton said. "How did they get so close without the Separatists sounding the alarm?"

The three of them turned their heads towards Colt's cell. They had heard a sharp crunch that sounded all too much like splintering wood. Lieutenant Killian appeared, alongside Zirris and the others of his cell.

"Break us out of here," Killian ordered. Zirris strode up to the bars, pulled back a fist and hammered it into the wooden beam. It split under the blow. Two other transhumans stepped up and began pounding at the bars, cracking them open and tearing them free. They made a gap big enough to pass through and escaped onto the outer walkway of the prison. Colt, Thompson, Scott and four other Privateers went with them.

Killian stopped at the bars of Dalton's cell and sneered. "I'll see you branded a traitor for this, Dalton. If you try to return and spread your sedition, you'll be shot before you so much as open your mouth. Stay in this jungle. Rot with your new friends."

The lieutenant turned on his heel and stalked away across the bridge, leading his group towards the sounds of battle. Colt moved up beside Killian and pointed in a different direction. The lieutenant nodded and they hurriedly changed their course, switching onto a bridge that ran parallel to the fighting.

"They're going for Ajati's hut," said Dalton.

"How do you know?" asked Blake.

"Colt watched where I was taken when I went to see Ajati," he said. "They're going to kill him."

"Maybe this is a good thing, James," said Harris, though his voice wavered. "Maybe this is how it was always going to end."

"No," said Dalton firmly. "I can't allow it. If Ajati dies, if the Separatists are beaten, then this moon dies as well. If Ishra, the Miteran Jewel, can be so easily allowed to wither, then what chance does Landbreak have? What happens on this moon affects us all. There will be no future for any of us if we don't learn from the past. Ajati has that past."

There was a sharp crack. Cutra was ripping open the bars that separated their cells. The transhuman came through, followed by Broden and the other prisoners.

"I agree that Ishra cannot be allowed to die," said Cutra, and began laying into the outer bars.

"You're telling me we've been trapped in here, and you mod

bastards could have just broken us out with your bare hands this whole time?" asked Broden.

"A considerably more difficult feat when being watched," said Rolay, gesturing to the sniper nests that surrounded the prison platform, all of which were now empty.

"Why didn't Killian break you out?" Dalton asked, looking to the sergeant.

Broden nodded at Cutra. "Probably because I was in a cell with the mod that helped you negotiate our surrender."

"You realise we're going to stop him, don't you?" said Dalton. "You realise what that might mean."

"I do," Broden replied, sighing. "I can't stop you, but that doesn't mean I agree with you, James. You're starting down a path that will lead to war against your own brothers. I can't be a part of that."

"I didn't want this," said Dalton. "I'm not choosing a side here, I'm not choosing to betray my brothers, but if Killian gets away with that data, then he'll paint us all as traitors. There'll be no going back for any of us then. Look, the discussion can wait. Right now all that matters is stopping Killian."

"Stopping Killian *is* choosing a side," Broden said.

"I don't have time for this," snapped Dalton, turning away

"Just try not to get killed," Broden muttered.

Dalton followed Cutra out of the cell. Blake and Harris came with him, as did Rolay and three other transhumans. He set off across the walkway, retracing his steps towards Ajati's hut. He glanced at Cutra, leading them across a platform and onto the next bridge. "Zirris was with them, and two more of yours as well. If it comes to a fight…"

"Zirris is a fine warrior," said Cutra. "I will relish the opportunity."

The sounds of battle were at their loudest as they approached the hut. A high-pitched whine had been echoing through the trees continuously for the past two minutes.

Dalton knew what kind of weapon made that sound. He also knew that only carapace-walkers were outfitted with rotary cannons. If one of those things was in the fight, then the situation was worse than he had thought.

They clattered across the final walkway and burst into Ajati's hut. The platform was empty. Furniture had been overturned and shattered, boxes had been upturned and sheets of paper were scattered across the deck.

"Ajati wasn't here," said Blake.

Dalton moved through the wreckage of the hut and came to the chest beside Ajati's bed.

"It's empty," he growled, hurling the container aside.

"What was in it?" asked Harris.

"The key to ending this war," said Dalton. "If Killian gets it back to the front-line then the High Shekahn will do everything in his power to see it destroyed. We have to get it back before they can escape."

"It's too late."

Dalton looked round. Ajati was in the doorway, ragged and panting. He was bleeding from a shallow cut across his temple.

"The fighting has stopped," said Blake, cocking his head. True enough, the sounds of battle had abated.

"I saw a group of prisoners link up with the attackers. They broke off their assault only seconds later," said Ajati. "I feared you had betrayed me, James. I came to make sure you hadn't taken the information with you."

"They took it," said Dalton.

Ajati pushed through into his hut and began rummaging through the upended contents of a set of drawers. "That's not all they took. I had a map detailing the boundaries of the Spider's Eye. If they have that, then their escape is assured."

"They managed to get here without a map, perhaps they already know the way," said Harris.

Ajati sighed and slumped against the tree around which his

hut was built. "No. The truth is your second wave is as stranded as the first. We let them air-drop into the jungle and we've been breaking them apart ever since, raiding them and disappearing, denying them air-support with our turrets.

"This group though, they tailed us here. Other than blind luck, it's the only way they could have found us without getting trapped in the Spider's Eye. We, no, *I* underestimated them. They must have followed our safe route back to the camp and waited for nightfall to attack. They even managed to kill our sentries without raising the alarm. I never thought we could be outplayed, not in our jungle."

"Did you send men after them?" asked Dalton.

"Their damn war machine made close pursuit impossible, but I sent a group to track their movements from a distance," said Ajati. "Their attack makes no sense though. When they took out our sentries they would have had time to scout us, to realise that we outnumbered them here, but they attacked anyway."

"Were they all Avernii?" asked Cutra. Ajati nodded. "Then that is why they attacked. Between being stranded in the jungle and picked off a few at a time, or attacking your enemy head on and dying in battle, the choice is not difficult. It would have been a good death. They had no plans to escape this battle alive."

"Given what I have seen of your people, I can believe that," said Ajati, talking to Cutra. "Without a map I doubt they would have been able to navigate their way out of here alive, even if they had wanted to. The direct route back west would have taken them straight through the Spider's Eye. You Avernii are a fatalistic breed. They seemed so committed to the fight that it took me off-guard when they withdrew."

"Killian gave them a good reason," said Dalton, "and now with the map, he's given them the means as well."

"Without the information on that data tablet this war will

drag on for another ten years, at least," said Ajati. "We'll need to find a way to re-power the source and make new duplicates. Getting our hands on those resources won't be easy."

"You won't have to," said Dalton. "Do you have another map?"

"There are others, yes, Eskela has one," said Ajati, struggling to his feet. "Why?"

"Because I have a plan," said Dalton, "I'm going after them."

* * *

"You're insane," said Eskela, glaring at Dalton.

"You wouldn't be the first to think it," muttered Blake.

The group had mustered at the edge of the camp. They were preparing themselves for the mission ahead. The Separatists had returned the group's confiscated weapons and gear, along with fresh supplies and ammunition salvaged from the recent battle. Dalton was strapping on his combat armour. He ran his fingers over the grooves and scratches that peppered the synthetic fibre plates. The left thigh-plate and chest-piece still had gouges in them from where he had been shot. That felt like so long ago now.

"This is your plan? Honestly?" asked Eskela.

He sighed, picking up his L7 and checking the magazine. "If you have a better one, I'm sure we'd all be eager to hear it."

"I'll forgive you for your ignorance, because you're a foreigner," said Eskela, "but what you're proposing is simply not feasible."

"I'm not proposing it," Dalton said. "I'm doing it. We're going through the Spider's Eye."

"You won't survive."

"We can't catch Killian just by following him. He has too much of a head-start on us, not to mention the carapace-walker watching his back," continued Dalton. "We know what route they're taking, though. We have the same map that they do. Killian knows about the Spider's Eye. He won't risk going through it. The only way for them to safely escape is to go around the southern edge of the region. So we'll go through the Spider's Eye. We'll cut the bend off the journey and intercept them on the far side."

"It makes sense as a theory," added Blake. "Going in a straight line is faster than travelling along a curve."

"You're not listening to me," stressed Eskela. "You will not survive."

Dalton shrugged. "What do you think, Cutra?"

The five transhumans were walking over to them, carrying the slack weight of their armour. The suits looked like rag dolls in their arms. Cutra set the suit's feet on the ground and Rolay helped lock the joints, until the armour was standing rigid, like a mannequin.

"This place that your people fear, it is a place that no one has ever conquered?" asked Cutra. Eskela nodded. "Then I think it would be good to try."

"I agree. There would be much distinction in it," said Rolay, setting up a second suit of armour. The transhuman turned a series of bolts and the back-plate unfolded, allowing the suit to be entered. There was the whine of servos as the suit sealed itself around Rolay, followed by the hum of building power. Blue light waxed behind the visor.

"Your friends, they're insane too," said Eskela bluntly. "Look, even if you do manage to cut through the Spider's Eye – and that's a big if – how could you possibly work out where Killian's group will be on the other side? This jungle is vast. You don't know how fast they're travelling, let alone if they're even taking the route that you've assumed. What if you make it to the other side only to find that you've missed the mark?"

"Cutra?" asked Dalton.

"Our carapace-walkers can achieve a maximum speed of

one hundred kilometres per hour, providing the circumstances are optimal," said Cutra. "However, in difficult terrain and having to keep level with infantry, I estimate a travel speed of approximately ten kilometres per hour. Based on that data I have calculated the necessary angle of approach from one side of this region to the other. If we maintain pace, we should come out approximately one hour ahead of them."

"Giving us enough time to figure out the hard part," said Dalton. "How to stop them."

"You think *that's* the hard part?" asked Eskela, incredulous.

"It's the only plan we have." Dalton turned his head to see Ajati approaching them. The man had a rocket launcher slung over one shoulder.

"Oh no, you are not going with them," said Eskela, stepping in front of him.

"They will need a guide," Ajati said, "and I will not ask any of my people to go into the Spider's Eye. I must do this myself."

"Mitera above! I'm surrounded by insane people," Eskela yelled. "You cannot go, Ajati. The movement cannot afford to lose you. It needs your guidance, it needs your vision."

"The Separatists existed before I was their leader, and they will continue to exist in my absence."

"Things are different now," stressed Eskela. "You're our captain, Ajati. You can't risk yourself on this fool's quest. It's selfish! You're needed here. You have a responsibility to your people. You are not going. I will not allow it."

"I have made up my mind, Eskela," said Ajati.

"Well I've made up mine!" She grabbed hold of the rocket launcher and yanked it from Ajati's grip.

"What are you doing?!"

"You are right," said Eskela. "These idiots will need a guide if they are to have even the slimmest chance of surviving. It cannot be you, though. So I will do it. I will take them through the Spider's Eye."

"You can't," said Ajati.

"Oh, and you can?"

"That's not what I mean," Ajati said. "I don't want to lose you, Eskela."

"That's the difference," she said. "You don't want to lose me, but I *can't* lose you. *We* can't lose you. It's my map and besides, who's the damn pathfinder here? I'm going. It's decided."

"Eskela…" said Ajati.

"Don't," Eskela warned. "Don't disrespect me in that way."

Ajati broke eye contact. He sighed, unslung the satchel of rockets from his back and handed it over. Eskela nodded gratefully.

"Be the first to do this," said Ajati, taking her in his embrace, "and then come back to me."

"Don't worry," she said, smiling and looking at Dalton. "If anyone's going to be the first to survive the Spider's Eye, I'm going to make damn sure it's because of an Ishradi."

* * *

"You know, we have a story amongst our people," said Harris, walking alongside Eskela and Blake. Dalton was up ahead with Cutra, out of earshot.

"A story about insane people doing insane things?" asked Eskela.

"Well, yes, actually," Harris said. "Our colonel, Lawrence Hunt, they call him The Storm of Landbreak."

"I'll bite," said Eskela. "Why do they call him this?"

"He led his fleet into a region of sea that was thought impossible to sail through. Because he was brave enough to take that risk, he managed to cut off his enemy and save a war that shaped our very nation into what it is today."

"You're making a parallel," Eskela said, "between this Colonel Hunt and James?"

"I'm just trying to say, sometimes it takes the biggest risk to achieve the greatest victory," said Harris, looking at Dalton's back. "And who knows, maybe at the end of this we'll all be calling him The Storm of Assahi."

Eskela scoffed.

"Do you know what the irony of this is?" asked Blake, leaning over. "Harris didn't even know that story until he set foot on Ishra. Now he's telling it like everyone ought to know it."

"Everyone should know it," said Harris, "and when we're through with this, everyone should know our story as well."

"It's a romantic thought, but I don't think this'll be a story that people will remember," said Eskela.

"And why not?" asked Harris.

"Because I'm not sure any of us will survive to tell it."

<h1 style="text-align:center">CHAPTER THIRTY</h1>

"It's a spineback," said Eskela.

Harris stared at the lacerated carcass. "A dead spineback."

"That's what worries me," she replied.

"Surely a live spineback should worry you more," said Blake.

"Think about it," the pathfinder said, "if this spineback is dead, that means something killed it. What are you more afraid of, the spineback, or the thing that kills the spineback?"

"Good point," said Blake.

"This is it, right?" asked Dalton. "We're in the Spider's Eye now, aren't we?"

Eskela nodded. "You can feel it, can't you? This place is cursed."

"There's certainly something about it," said Dalton, looking around. The canopy was thicker here, the shadows deeper. The trees seemed darker, their boles gnarled and their branches sickly. There was a weight to the air, beyond the usual, cloying humidity.

"There is a depression here," said Cutra.

"Tell me about it," Blake muttered. "Just being here is getting me down."

"You misunderstand. The terrain in this region is lower than it was a kilometre back. A physical depression. The incline appears to be continuous in a westward direction."

"Oh, right," said Blake. "I knew that."

"We have to keep moving," said Cutra.

They set off again, stepping around the mauled corpse of the spineback. Eight metres above them, something glinted in the dark and very slowly shifted its weight through the canopy, careful not to make a sound.

* * *

The stalk lurched forwards and hammered its spiked bulb against Rolay's arm. The transhuman paused and turned its head to look at the plant. Reaching out, Rolay took the barbed head in one armoured hand and crushed it. It squelched as it collapsed, releasing a stream of viscous, black liquid that made Dalton's nose sting.

"Did that plant just… attack you?" asked Harris.

"It tried," said Rolay, inspecting the armour where the barb had broken itself against the segmented plates.

"What is that?" Dalton asked, looking to Eskela.

"Scorp-reed," she replied. "They're rare, but lethal. In large enough doses the venom causes permanent nerve damage. If they grow here we're going to need to be extra careful."

"Why does a plant need venom like that?" Blake asked.

"Look underneath," said Eskela. Rolay crouched down and tore up a fistful of the thick roots that fed into the scorp-reed's stalk.

"Salty fucking eel balls," breathed Harris.

Hollow eye sockets stared up at them from out of the dirt. Beneath the roots were dozens of bones, the skulls and ribcages of small creatures.

"Carnivorous plants," said Blake. "Wonderful."

* * *

The scream was long and harsh. It grated on the ears, sent chills up the spine. The group came to a standstill, rooted by the wail as it tore its way through the jungle.

"What the fuck was that?" hissed Blake.

Dalton looked round at Eskela, searching for an answer. She looked back at him, her eyes wide, her lips half parted.

"You don't know, do you?" asked Dalton.

* * *

"It's getting too dark to see," said Dalton.

The light on his helmet had been smashed at some point, but he still had the torch attached to his rifle. His fingers hesitated at the switch. There were three moons in the sky that night and their glow had been strong enough to see by, but the further the group had travelled the thicker the canopy had become, until it blocked out all but the faintest light.

"Do it," said Eskela, snapping a glow-stick hanging from her belt and bathing the group in orange luminescence. "We can't risk moving through this area without vision."

Dalton nodded and flicked on his torch. Blake and Harris did the same, lancing the darkness with stark beams of white light. They played their flashlights across the trees to get their bearing.

"What was that?" yelled Blake.

"What was what?" asked Harris, tensing.

"You didn't see it?"

"See what?" Dalton asked.

"Something moved, over there," said Blake, his rifle at the ready.

Cutra strode to the front, surveying the way ahead from behind his flickering, blue visor. Dalton imagined that the transhumans had all manner of sight modes integrated into those helmets, including a night-vision function.

"See anything?" he asked.

"Nothing," said Cutra. "Let's move. We are already behind schedule."

Dalton nodded and they kept going, treading carefully as they went. Beyond the reach of their torches, concealed in the deep night between the trees, something watched, its limbs shivering and clicking.

* * *

The mud sucked and popped as Dalton pulled his boot free.

"What the salt?" growled Harris, stumbling back from the sodden earth.

Dalton played the torch over his feet, lighting up the water-logged ground that spread away before them.

"A swamp," he sighed, surveying the foetid soup of green and brown water. It swarmed with insects that skimmed the surface on long, spindly legs. As he watched, a small mouth broke the skin of the water and snatched an insect from the air, dragging it beneath the opaque surface.

"We have to go through that?" asked Blake.

Cutra looked left and right along the edges of the swamp. "Any detour would delay us to the point of mission failure. We must go through."

"This just gets worse and worse, doesn't it?" Harris said.

Dalton gripped his friend's shoulder. "We'll be free of this place soon, don't worry."

* * *

Blake swatted his neck for the fifteenth time and spat a curse. The insects were swarming up from the water, disturbed by the sloshing of the group's passage. The air was thick with buzzing wings. They invaded the eyes, the nostrils, the ears and the mouth, stinging and biting.

Dalton looked enviously at the transhumans as they strode through the muck, impervious to the assault of the bugs and the noxious reek of the swamp. The five of them were leading the way, forging a path through the reeds and between the trees that rose up out of the glutinous water.

"What I wouldn't do for one of those suits right about now," said Harris.

"I was just thinking the same," Dalton said. "Not a damn thing in this jungle could get through that armour."

It dropped out of the canopy, a shadow let slip from above.

One of the Avernii went down beneath its many legs. A wave of rancid water exploded from the impact and collapsed across the group, drenching them in webs of algae.

Dalton kept his balance and swept the sludge from his face. He saw it clearly then, perched amidst the reeling transhumans. The sight of it locked his thoughts with fear. It stood a foot taller than the Avernii, braced on six legs that terminated in sharp points. Its torso rose in front of its lower body, a dozen vestigial limbs twitching along its ribbed chest. Two sets of larger limbs spread beneath its shoulders, arched and bladed like the harvestman's scythe. The creature regarded them with sixteen eyes that lined either side of the broad, ridged crest of its head. That crest tapered down to a mouth which swarmed with clicking mandibles.

The horror screamed. Long and harsh, it was a wail that clawed against the senses and drove fear deep into the gut. The creature whipped sideways, raking its scythe-limbs through the air. Rolay couldn't move fast enough. The transhuman came apart, cleaved into pieces. Silver blood jettisoned from the riven segments of armour as they toppled into the swamp.

Dalton gathered his wits and dragged up his rifle, but there was no clear shot past the Avernii. Cutra and the two other transhumans opened fire. The blue flare of their rifles lit the horror from beneath, casting spectral light along its gnarled and hardened carapace. It reared, screeching as the rounds crashed against its body. The horror fled, skittering away on its six legs, disappearing between the trees. Eskela and the Islanders chased it with rifle fire, following the sounds of splashing water.

Cutra lifted a transhuman from the swamp, the one who had been pinned by the horror's ambush. The warrior was dead, its visor shattered and its armour punctured. Cutra let the body slip back beneath the water. The three Avernii locked away their rifles and pounced off amongst the trees.

"Cutra! Wait!" cried Dalton, but the transhumans were gone.

"What the fuck was that thing?" stammered Blake.

"Keep it together," Dalton said. "Form a circle, back to back. Stay as far from the trees as you can."

Eskela and Blake stood to his left and right, with Harris at his back. They shone their torches into the darkness and up towards the trees. The flash-light beams were weak beneath the canopy, faltering in the dense night, casting shadows that looked all too much like scrambling limbs.

"This was a mistake," said Harris. "We should have listened to you, Eskela. None of us are going to survive this place."

"I said keep it together!" snapped Dalton, playing his light along the boles of crooked trees.

"We should turn back, while we still have the chance," Harris continued. Dalton could feel the tension in the man's back, could feel the spring-loaded instinct to flee vibrating in his muscles.

"Don't run, Harris," he said, fighting his own sense of rising panic.

"Where did the mods go?" asked Blake. "Did they abandon us?"

"No. They wouldn't do that," Dalton said, trying to keep his voice calm.

"Are you sure?" Eskela asked.

"It's not in them to flee," said Dalton. "They're hunting it. I think."

"You *think*?" said Harris. The trooper's voice was trembling.

"As long as we have each others' backs, we'll get through this," Dalton said.

A splash echoed out of the trees. Another high-pitched scream followed. Their boots squelched as the four soldiers jostled closer together. The ferns rustled, just a handful of metres in front of Dalton. He pressed the L7 to his shoulder and squinted into the darkness.

"Ahead of me," he said. The others came round to face his direction, bringing up their rifles. "When it comes, aim for the eyes and the mouth."

A square of flickering blue appeared in the night. Two more followed. Dalton released the air from his lungs. Cutra and the other transhumans waded towards them through the calf-deep swamp. In one hand Cutra was holding the creature's severed head. Its crest was bloody and chipped, its lidless eyes staring, glinting like black pearls in the light of the torches. The nest of mandibles was still twitching in its mouth.

"Cutra," said Dalton, unable to form any other words.

"This place is full of good opportunities," said the transhuman.

"Did you kill it with your bare hands?" asked Blake, astounded.

"This thing killed Rolay and Arturo," Cutra said. "It proved itself a worthy foe. It was only right that we treat it as such."

"I'm sorry," said Dalton. Cutra looked at him, head cocked. "About Rolay. And Arturo."

"I do not understand," replied the transhuman.

Blood splattered against Cutra's scuffed, white armour. Dalton regarded the little beads of red as they rolled down the segmented plates. He heard a sound, like water rushing down a drain, bubbling and gurgling. The transhumans were moving, unlocking their rifles and diving aside. Dalton watched the creature's severed head tumble from Cutra's fingers, turning end over end in the air.

Someone was yelling. It sounded like Blake. Dalton looked sidelong even as desperate hands closed around his shoulders. He saw Harris. The man's eyes were wide. He was looking down at his stomach. There was a scythe protruding from his belly, glistening red with viscera. Harris turned his head and met Dalton's gaze. A bubble of something dark oozed over the man's lip and trickled down his chin.

The horror flung Harris aside, flicking him from its bladed limb. The trooper crashed against a tree and dropped into the swamp. The thick water crept up over his body and sucked him under.

Gunfire thundered close in the air. Dalton realised his finger was tight on the trigger. The L7 bucked in his grip as he emptied the magazine, hitting the horror with everything he had. Blake and Eskela were firing too, as were the Avernii. The creature crumpled under the weight of the barrage, its carapace breaking into pieces. It was dead long before it hit the water, its limbs severed and its body ruptured in a hundred places.

Dalton dragged his feet through the stinking water and collapsed to his knees. He ploughed his hands into the brackish muck and dragged Harris to the surface. There was swamp water in the man's mouth. Strings of algae covered his face. His eyes, locked wide in the moment of his death, stared towards the hidden sky.

"He's gone," said Blake, his voice choked.

Dalton let go. He let the body slip back into the water. He watched as the swamp rose up over Harris' face, seeping across the hollows of his cheeks, into his mouth and over his eyes. Then Harris was gone, dragged under by the weight of his combat armour. Dalton drew his knife and plunged it into the water.

"What are you doing?" cried Blake.

The blade found its mark and Dalton dragged the dead man's webbing free. He slung the string of ammunition pouches over his shoulder and stood up. With practised movement, he ejected the spent magazine and reloaded his rifle.

Dalton looked up at the remainder of his group.

"Let's move."

Chapter Thirty-One

"How far are we?" asked Dalton.

"I have adjusted our course to account for the delay," replied Cutra.

"That will take us deeper into the Spider's Eye."

"It will."

Dalton nodded. He looked behind him, at Eskela and Blake, and lowered his voice. "There's a chance we won't survive to see the end of this."

"We are not so easily defeated," said Cutra.

"You aren't, but us? Eskela, Blake, me? We're not like you, Cutra. We're not like the Avernii. We can't move as fast or hit as hard; we can't hunt monsters with our bare hands," he said. "I need to know that if we don't make it, you will continue the fight."

"I will," said Cutra, without hesitation.

Dalton narrowed his eyes. "Why?"

"You suspect my motives, James Dalton?"

"I don't *know* your motives," he said. "Back at the Separatist camp, I asked you why the Avernii are here on Ishra. You didn't give me an answer."

"Tell me first, why are the Islanders on Ishra?" Cutra asked.

"You won't answer my question," said Dalton, sighing. "You know how suspicious that is, right?"

"I will give you an answer, but first I must ensure that you will understand that answer."

"Fine," Dalton said. "The Privateers were sent here in response to the request for aid from Ishra's recognised government."

"Let us assume that what you have just said is true," said

Cutra. "You could, therefore, say that you were sent here to save Ishra, correct?"

"Alright."

"By merit of that assumption, I am also fighting to save Ishra," Cutra said. "Broadly speaking, that is also why my people are here."

"Are you being purposefully elusive?" asked Dalton.

"If you don't like the answer," said Cutra, "then perhaps, James Dalton, you are not asking the right question."

Dalton thought about that.

"I remember the speech that Colonel Hunt gave, before our deployment," said Dalton. "He claimed the reason for saving Ishra was so that its problems wouldn't become our problems. He said our moons could no longer pretend to exist isolated from one another, and we would need stable neighbours if Landbreak was to be strong. So, I guess the question I'm trying to ask is, why do the Avernii *want* to save Ishra?"

"That is the right question, and in asking it you have already answered it," said Cutra. "First you said that the Privateers had been sent here to save Ishra. That was not the true *why* of the matter though. The Privateers are not here to save Ishra, they are here to save Landbreak. There is a universal truth in that. Our motives are only ever self-serving."

"So, what, you're here to save Avernus?"

"No," said Cutra. "We are here to save the Avernii."

"Save them from what?" asked Dalton.

"Ourselves," Cutra said. "You say that the Avernii are not like you. That statement is true, but in more ways than you are aware of. How old are you?"

"Twenty-four," said Dalton, but hesitated. "Twenty-five? I don't know. I think I might have missed a birthday in the time I've been here. Why?"

"That's based on the Earth Standard?"

"Yup, three hundred and sixty-five, twenty-four hour days

to a human year," said Dalton. "Don't ask why we still use a two hundred year old dating system developed for a planet we no longer live on. I used to ask the same question all the time when I was in school."

"We use the same system on Avernus. The migrant ships provided us with many established metrics once used on Earth. In some circumstances it is easier to adopt them rather than change them," said Cutra. "Do you wish to know the true difference that separates you and I? By Earth Standard I am twenty-nine. However, while you will live for perhaps another eighty years, I will perish before three."

"Wait, what?" asked Dalton, coming to a halt. Cutra put a hand on his shoulder and steered him onwards.

"Our modifications, they make us strong and fast, they provide us with more benefits than I could quickly explain," said Cutra, "but they also kill us. They burn us out. In our desperation to survive Avernus, we exceeded the capability of the natural human form. Given more time and more resources, it is possible that we could have perfected our augmentation, but as it is, my people have an average life expectancy of thirty-two Earth Standard years."

"Cutra, I had no idea," said Dalton.

"Every transhuman on Ishra has between two to five years left in them," Cutra said. "By the time my generation is gone, one of two things will have happened. Either the cycle will have begun again, or we will have made a new home for our descendants, a place where they won't need to rely on augmentation to survive."

"Your government made a deal with the High Shekahn," said Dalton, his words spurred by realisation. "Land in exchange for your assistance in destroying the Separatists. The Avernii mean to relocate here?"

"It is true," admitted Cutra, "and you would do well to think more sceptically about your own government's stake in this.

The promise of destroying a foe who could one day threaten you is a good story to motivate disillusioned soldiers, but it doesn't stand up to scrutiny. Ishra is rich in natural resources, resources that I could guess are not present on Landbreak. If you do not believe that agreements have been made between your government and the High Shekahn, then you might want to question whether you can afford to be so naïve."

"Salt below, did no one come here to actually just help Ishra?"

"It is in the nature of a nation to benefit itself before others," said Cutra.

"So, why?" asked Dalton. "Why are you here, fighting alongside me? Isn't that betraying your people's best chance for a better future?"

"I have come to realise, James Dalton, that your vision is the purest of them all," said Cutra. "Regardless of what reasons motivated you to come here in the first place, regardless of whether or not they were ill-conceived, you have now determined your fight. You have seen both sides of the conflict and, unfettered by the shackles of misguided loyalty, you have chosen the side that you believe is right."

"And that's the reason?" asked Dalton. "That is why you're with me?"

"I still want a new home for my people," said Cutra. "I want my descendants to be raised on a moon that does not reject the existence of life itself. I want a future for the young that is defined by something more than just survival. We Avernii speak a great deal about being strong, but if these foreshortened lives – of which every minute is a struggle – are the only result of our strength, then I believe it is a mentality that we can afford to leave behind."

"And if the High Shekahn has his way, then soon Ishra will be no different from Avernus," said Dalton. "Barren and inhospitable."

"So you see, James Dalton, your fight and mine are aligned."

"I just needed to know I could trust you," said Dalton.

Cutra came to an abrupt halt.

"What is it?" asked Dalton, tensing.

"I heard a sound," said the transhuman. "There's something close."

* * *

They hunkered down at the edge of a sodden ridge. A bank of roots and clumped earth formed a natural dam, beneath which lay a wide basin. Streams gurgled over the muddy lip and trickled down the gentle slopes, feeding into the shallow lake that had pooled in the depression beyond. Seven of the largest trees that Dalton had ever seen rose up out of that water. Their canopies were so broad that they shielded the lake entirely, leaving the jungle roof unbroken and impenetrable to any eyes in the sky. Enough moonlight was filtering through the branches to illuminate the water, colouring the surface with a reflective, silver sheen.

Wading through the heart of that watery glade was a leviathan. A horror, like the ones that had attacked them in the swamp, but on a scale unseen until now. On its six pillar-thick legs, it towered at twenty feet tall. The ridged, fan-shaped crest of its head was chipped and scarred, shot through with streaks of blue and green. The mandibles that waved from its mouth were as long as a man's forearm, and the jointed, blade-limbs that sprouted from its chest were easily four times that length. Its carapace was covered in bulbous, fungal growths and twitching vestigial limbs.

"That thing," Eskela whispered, her green eyes wide, "it is the cancer at the heart of this place."

Blake was making odd noises as he struggled to form words.

"We need to get out of here," said Dalton. "Cutra, tell me we can go around."

"If we moved quickly, yes, we could circumvent this area."

"We should kill it."

Dalton looked at Eskela. Her eyes were locked on the creature lurking in the water-logged glade.

"We don't need to," he said quietly. "This isn't why we're here. Our fight is on the other side of this. We need to save what strength and resources we have left for when it counts."

"It'll just take a second," said Eskela, shifting her weight to indicate the rocket launcher strapped to her back.

"How many rockets do you have?" asked Dalton.

"Five. That leaves four to deal with the war-machine," said Eskela. "The way I see it, that's still overkill."

"We don't need to do this," Dalton stressed.

"I do," said Eskela. "This place, this Spider's Eye, it's been a place of fear and death for my people for as long as I can remember. I can end that, right here, right now."

Dalton looked down towards the silver lake and the leviathan that waded through its waters, each step it took with those tapered legs sending shivering ripples across the surface. The creature filled him with revulsion. He sighed. "Do it."

Eskela clambered out of the mud, bracing herself on one knee and pulling the rocket launcher over her shoulder.

"Load me," she said.

Dalton took a rocket from her pack and slotted it into the launcher. Eskela lined up her shot along the tube's iron sights.

"Clear!" she called, making sure the blast cone at her back was free.

The mud bank in front of them exploded. A horror reared from its burrow, brackish filth and water streaming from its carapace. Dalton jerked back, lost his footing and crashed into the swampy earth. The horror loomed over Eskela, its arm-blades stretched high. It slashed down, thumping into the mud with its front legs. Its forelimbs scythed across the pathfinder.

She toppled backwards. The launcher came apart in two cleaved pieces. The front half fell into the mud, still loaded with its rocket. Eskela looked down at herself, shocked to be unharmed, let alone alive.

Blue light flashed as the transhumans opened fire. The horror screamed, so loud that Dalton felt the pressure pop in his ears. Eskela splashed out of the swamp and grabbed hold of him. Together they stumbled through the mud, fighting to get away from the thrashing creature. All across the basin, more horrors were tearing free of their burrows, lifting their crested heads into the air as they sought out the source of the disturbance.

"Run!" bellowed Dalton.

The transhumans backed away, firing as they moved. The horror's legs went out beneath it, sending it tumbling down the slope. Two more scrambled over it, shrieking and clawing their way through the mud to reach the group.

"Go!" shouted one of the transhumans, lowering its rifle and striding back towards the ridge.

"Distinction is yours," said Cutra with a nod, easing off the trigger and turning to withdraw.

Dalton looked over his shoulder as they ran. The transhuman that had stayed behind threw down its rifle as it reached the top of the dam. Framed in the moonlight, the Avernii looked, for just a second, like the statue of some hero, cast in steel. Then the horrors rose up over the lip of the basin. The transhuman dived between their slashing limbs, rolled and came to its feet. In one hand it had the rocket from the destroyed launcher. It leapt at the horrors, the warhead held outstretched.

The detonation ripped a gaping hole in the dam and sent waves of swamp water gushing into the basin. The two horrors were torn apart, the blast shredding off their limbs and sending bloody chunks of carapace fountaining into the air. Of the transhuman, there was no sign.

Dalton fled with the four survivors. The horrors were slow to follow, dazed by the light and the sound of the explosion. When they regained their senses and scrambled up the slopes of the basin, the survivors had already disappeared into the jungle. In the pit of the watery glade, the leviathan arched back its head and let out a roar that sent ripples splashing across the lake, shivering the silver light of its surface. Its children took up the cry and filled the night with screams.

* * *

"Are we clear?" gasped Blake. "Did we lose them?"

Their crashing escape came to a stop and they fell against the trees for support, panting and groaning. Even the two Avernii looked rattled, their armoured chests heaving as they sucked in deep breaths.

"Hopefully they won't stray from their nest," said Eskela, her hair matted and her skin coated in mud.

"Hopefully?" exclaimed Blake. "Aren't you supposed to know these things?"

"We're in a place that no one has ever come back from," snapped Eskela "How could anyone know anything about such a place?"

"That's about to change," said Dalton, pulling himself upright. "Isn't it, Cutra?"

"It is," said the transhuman. "We're almost there."

"We are?" asked Blake.

"Not far now and we'll break through to the other side," Cutra said. "By my estimations, we will achieve our target window, but only just."

Dalton nodded. "Then let's go."

"It's pointless," said Eskela.

"Don't give up now," Dalton said.

"I'm not giving up," she said. "I'm stating a fact. There's just five of us left and we're going after a group that's what? Three times our number? With a war-machine supporting them, no less. And we don't have the rocket launcher anymore. How is that a fight we're supposed to win?"

"I don't know," confessed Dalton, and looked at Cutra. "What do you think?"

"I think it would be good to try," said the transhuman. "Do you still have the rocket pack?"

Eskela held up the satchel. "Four rockets. Not that we have anything to fire them with."

"It gives us options," said Cutra. "We may be outnumbered and outgunned, but we have something that they do not."

"The element of surprise," said Dalton.

"Exactly."

ACT IV

REUNION

Chapter Thirty-Two

"Ajati will not believe me when I tell him," said Eskela. "We have just done what no one in the history of Ishra has done before."

"Focus on the task at hand," Dalton said. "If we don't get through this next part, no one will ever know that we even survived the Spider's Eye."

"One day I will go back," promised Eskela. "I will find that beast and I will kill it."

"Focus," said Dalton. He turned to Cutra. "Do we know where we are? Are we where we need to be?"

Cutra was inspecting the map. "I cannot attest to the accuracy of this document. In fact, I am highly doubtful of it. That being said, I know how far we travelled and how long it took us. Based off of that and what I know about who we are hunting, I can estimate how far they would have travelled if they were hugging the edge of the Spider's Eye. We should be ahead of them, but by how much I cannot say, not with any accuracy."

"Then we can't waste time," said Dalton.

"What's the plan?" asked Blake. "Do we lay a trap? Improvise mines out of the rockets?"

"We have no idea where they're going to come through," said Dalton. "Their path could lead them right across where we're standing, or it could be a handful of metres that way, or that way. There's too much room for error with laying mines."

"Then what?"

"First, I think we need to find them," said Dalton. "We need someone who can move quietly and quickly in the jungle, someone who can find our target and report their movements back to us ahead of time. Then we lay our trap."

"You're talking about me, aren't you?" asked Eskela.

"No one else can do this," said Dalton. "You can move quieter than any of us in these trees. You're the least visible and you're the only one who knows how to track."

"You don't have to convince me, James," she said. "I'll do it."

"Thank you. Everything depends on this."

"I'll do my part," said Eskela. "Just be ready when I get back."

The pathfinder set off without so much as a nod, melting away into the final hours of the night.

"Right," Dalton said, turning to face the others. "This is the plan."

* * *

"Can't we move any faster than this?" asked Lieutenant Killian.

"Not if you want the support of the carapace-walker," replied Zirris. The war-machine was thumping along ahead of them, its mechanised joints humming and whirring as it traversed its bulk between the trees. Every now and then its rotary cannon would spool up, or it would flex the digits of its claw.

"There one of your boys in there?" Thompson asked.

"The carapace-walker is internally piloted by a directly interfaced transhuman," said Zirris.

"What the salt does that mean?" asked Scott.

"The pilot controls the machine through electrical impulses," Zirris explained. "Their thoughts are made manifest in the actions of the carapace-walker."

"What, like, psychically?"

Zirris regarded the Islander silently for a moment before replying. "The connection is maintained via a hard-wire link."

"So, how do you lot do that thing?" asked Thompson. "You know, where you talk to each other without actually talking."

"Do you understand how communication devices exchange

messages in text format?"

"Well, sort of, yeah."

"Then I do not understand why you are asking me the question," said Zirris.

"You're saying you've got a phone in your head?" asked Scott.

"I'm going to stop answering your questions now," Zirris said.

The group had been marching throughout the night. Dawn was only a couple of hours away now and the Islanders were wired from post-combat nerves and exhaustion. Including the carapace-walker, there were seventeen of them. Of the force that had launched their suicide attack on the Separatist camp, only five transhumans and the walker remained. Without their armoured suits, Zirris and the two other transhumans from the prison stood out from their kin.

Along with the Privateers, they had scavenged what weapons they could during their escape, but it had been a paltry effort. Killian had been lucky enough to retrieve his .44 Snapper, pulling it from the dead fingers of the Separatist who had confiscated it from him in the first place. Colt had one of the wooden-stock Ishradi rifles and Scott had picked up an Avernii weapon from one of the fallen, but Thompson and the four other Privateers in their group had not been so fortunate. With a third of their force unarmed and the rest short on ammunition, the carapace-walker was their best bet at surviving to link up with the remnants of the second wave.

"Tell me again what you discussed with your people," said Killian, nodding at the other transhumans.

"You Islanders have an irritating lack of data retention," said Zirris.

"Yeah, whatever," said Killian. "It's been a long day and I'm trying to get things straight here, so just tell me."

"They told me that the second wave lost its cohesion six

days after it was air-dropped into the jungle. After the first wave was shot down, the drop-ships pulled back on emergency orders and deployed their troops outside of the planned landing zones. There was a degree of confusion, to put it mildly. Along with the hostile environment and the organised resistance of the Separatists, the situation was irreparable," said Zirris. "Of the twenty strike forces in the second wave, only seven of them managed to reach their designated targets. Of those seven, only four succeeded in securing their objectives. Of those four, only a single strike force maintained communications with the bulk of the wave. The rest stopped transmitting, either due to the interference caused by the jungle, or because they were compromised."

"So, the whole operation has gone to salt," growled Killian. "What about this strike force, did they reach their objective?"

"They were hit by the Separatists almost from the moment they dropped in. For days they fought through ambush after ambush, all the while heading for their target. After the sixth day, on the rare occasion that they could manage to acquire a signal, they heard broken reports about a mass withdrawal to consolidate at a base that was being set up in the mountains. By then they were just short of their objective, so instead of falling back they opted to press on. When they arrived, it turned out to be a trap."

"And even so they decided to keep fighting," said Killian, nodding. "I can't fault you mods for your tenacity. Even if it is suicidal. So, now we're heading for this mountain base?"

"It's the shortest route we know of back to our forces," said Zirris. "If we keep heading west their patrols should find us when we reach the foothills."

The explosion tore up the undergrowth ten metres behind the group. A rippling shockwave flattened ferns and showered earth and bark over their heads. Servos screeching, the carapace-walker swivelled round, tracking its cannon across the terrain. The barrels squealed as they began to spin.

"Cover!" shouted Killian, side-stepping neatly behind the closest tree. Islanders were diving aside, burying themselves in the undergrowth. The Avernii surged towards the explosion. Even Zirris and his companions from the prison raced into battle, without armour or weapons.

The transhumans were already out of sight when Killian heard the gong of metal striking metal. It was followed by the frantic whir of straining servos. He looked back as the carapace-walker stumbled and crashed through the brush, fighting to regain its balance. No, not regain its balance, realised Killian, as he saw the figure on top of the walker's shell. The war-machine was swerving wildly, struggling to dislodge its attacker. That attacker was an armoured transhuman with a cracked and flickering visor. The mod was scrambling to find purchase on the walker's smooth chassis. It had a device in one hand, three rocket grenades crudely strapped together to form a makeshift bomb.

Lieutenant Killian didn't hesitate. He drew his .44 and, arm fully extended, aimed it at the transhuman. The revolver barked once, kicking back hard in his grip. Sparks fountained from the mod's chest as it was flung clean from its perch. The makeshift bomb slipped from its hand and turned end over end through the air. Killian only had time to think about jumping aside before the rockets hit the ground. He squeezed his eyes shut, his body instinctively curling away.

There was no plume of fire, no huge explosion. He cracked open an eye and breathed a sigh of relief. It didn't last. A volley of gunfire raked through the trees around them, kicking up dirt and splintering bark. Hard rounds ricocheted from the walker's armour. Killian switched to the other side of the tree, ducking his head even as he glanced about to find the source of the ambush.

"In the trees!" shouted Colt, firing into the canopy. The

trooper was right, rounds were coming down from above, ripping up the undergrowth, but Killian could see shots impacting directly against the trees too, fired at a horizontal angle.

"They're all around us!" replied Killian, risking another glance out of cover. This time he didn't pull back. His eyes had locked onto something through the trees. "I don't fucking believe it. That eel-shagging bastard!"

Past the carapace-walker, James Dalton was sprinting towards them out of the trees. A second trooper was laying down covering fire behind him. It was Private Blake Leland. The walker couldn't see them coming, it was too preoccupied with manoeuvring around the trees, trying to get an angle on the attackers above them.

"He's going for the bomb!" roared Killian. In that same second the carapace-walker opened fire. The chatter of its rotary cannon blotted out all other sounds as it lanced a stream of rapid fire into the canopy. A blazing line of high-velocity rounds punched through the jungle roof, raining severed branches and fronds all around them.

A shape toppled out of the trees, glinting black and white in the new shafts of moonlight that speared down through the punctured canopy. It hit the ground with a bodily thud. It was another transhuman, its armour shattered and glistening with silver blood. All gunfire from above had abruptly stopped. The walker's cannon was still spinning, its barrels glowing red hot, but no more rounds spat forth. It had expended the last of its ammunition.

Killian looked back behind the walker in time to see Dalton coming out of the undergrowth, the makeshift bomb clutched in his hands. The .44 boomed in Killian's fist. The shot went wide, but Dalton flinched, distracted. Killian heard the crash of armoured bodies tearing through the undergrowth. Zirris and the other transhumans were returning from the diversion.

They were racing towards the walker and towards Dalton.

The bomb left Dalton's hand, hurled in a final, desperate gambit. It arced through the air, struck the walker's rounded shell and bounced aside, lodging itself in the joint between the war-machine's torso and arm. Still, it did not explode.

"Blake!" roared Dalton, and leapt off of his feet. Blake Leland stepped out of cover, lined up his shot, and pulled the trigger. The trooper was no marksman. Killian had seen him on the firing range. He should not have been able to make the shot. The range was twenty metres, the target was small. The shot was true.

The bomb detonated. A blistering fireball ripped the walker in half. The war-machine's internal power supply cooked off in the same second. The blast atomised the walker, ejecting an incandescent wave of flames that engulfed Zirris and the rest of the charging Avernii. Killian was hammered off of his feet, his ears ringing, his vision filled with the eye-searing light of the molten discharge. He slammed into a tree and fell sideways. Pain burned in his back and his ribs. There was blood on his lips. Killian fought to stand, felt the rising sense of vertigo, and slumped into the earth.

* * *

Dalton felt cold, metal hands on his shoulders. They hauled him out of the undergrowth and set him on his feet. He looked up into a cracked and flickering visor. The transhuman pressed a rifle into Dalton's hands.

"You're alright," said Dalton, looking at the new crater in Cutra's chest armour.

"There's no time," replied the transhuman, already moving away. Blake was jogging over, his face still etched in awe.

"Did you see that?" he asked, ripping off his reticle goggles. Excitement was brimming in his words. "Did you fucking see that?"

Dalton nodded. His head felt light. There was a rushing sound in his ears.

"Come on," said Blake. They went after Cutra.

There was a scorched crater where the carapace-walker had last stood. Twisted chunks of blackened metal were all that remained of the machine. Small fires were burning amidst the ferns, or licking the sides of trees. More than half a dozen transhumans lay sprawled and incapacitated around the blast site. Cutra was walking amongst them, putting the muzzle of his rifle to their heads and pulling the trigger. His movements were calculated and efficient. There was no relish in it, but no mercy either. Each shot was a resounding crack that filled the close, night air.

"What are you doing?" yelled Dalton, stumbling through the wreckage. "You don't have to do this! We can take them prisoner!"

"They will not listen to you, James Dalton," said Cutra, shattering another visor with a point-blank shot. "They will not give you the time to explain. They are your enemies. They are my enemies. If we do not kill them now while we are able, they will kill us later. That would be a failure on our behalf. I refuse to fail."

Cutra thudded his rifle against the back of a fifth helmet. The helmet twisted before the trigger could be pulled. An armoured gauntlet snapped round and tore the rifle aside. The transhuman on the ground lashed out with both legs, sending Cutra stumbling for balance. It kicked its legs and flipped to its feet. The two Avernii barrelled into each other.

Blake lifted his rifle, but Dalton put a hand on the barrel. "Don't. You could hit Cutra."

Gunshots rang out. Dalton broke left, Blake went right. Bullets thumped into the trees as they took cover.

"It's Colt," said Dalton through gritted teeth.

"You saw him?" asked Blake.

Dalton nodded. "You go that way, draw his fire. Stay close to the trees. I'll flank him."

"Why do I have to draw the fire?"

"Do you want to fight him?"

"Point taken. I'll draw the fire," Blake said.

"Go!"

Blake sprinted off through the trees. Dalton heard the shots and ran the other way. As he sprinted round the blast site he saw Cutra and the other transhuman. They were hammering one another with punches that filled the air with the thunder of crunching metal. He kept going, keeping an eye on the muzzle flash coming from Colt's position.

Dalton came up on the tree where the trooper was braced. He could see the edge of Colt's back. The gunfire had stopped.

He edged through the ferns, L7 at the ready.

The undergrowth whispered around his boots.

Fallen branches snapped and crunched.

Colt swung out from behind the tree. He cracked the stock of his rifle across Dalton's face. Vision blurred red. Dalton felt the ground at his back.

Colt's face swam into focus above him. A nasty grin was smeared across his mouth. "Thought you could outsmart me, James? Thought you could out-soldier me?"

Dalton groaned. His left cheekbone and jaw pulsed with agony. His fingers groped for a rifle that was no longer there. He rolled over and fumbled amongst the ferns. Colt kicked him in the gut. Dalton spluttered, tasted blood in his mouth. Colt lashed out again, forced Dalton onto his back. The trooper crouched down, pressed his knee into Dalton's throat.

"How did you think this was going to end?" asked Colt. "Did you think someone like you could out-fight someone like me? Like Killian? You're not a soldier, James. You're a deserter. A traitor."

Dalton spat blood and strained to push Colt away. His head

was swimming.

"You don't have what it takes. That's just a fact. You're not a killer," said Colt. "I never did tell you why I joined up with the Privateers, did I? Commuted sentence. Murder charge. I was looking at life behind bars, until the world realised it needs men like me. Men who can take lives without breaking down and crying about it. That's what makes a real soldier, James."

Dalton was no longer looking at Colt. He was looking past him. Killian was striding towards them. In one hand, the lieutenant had his sleek, black revolver. In the other, he had Blake by the scruff of the neck. He was dragging the small man through the ferns.

"This is over, and you're going to drown for what you've done," said Colt, speaking right into Dalton's face.

"Drowning is an Islander's death," said Killian, pushing Blake down to his knees in front of Dalton. "These two aren't worthy that."

"No," said Dalton, through clenched and bloody teeth.

Killian put the barrel of his .44 against the back of Blake's neck.

"No!" choked Dalton, fighting to free himself.

"What did you think was going to happen, you stupid bastard?" asked Killian.

"Don't give up, James," whispered Blake. There were tears in the man's eyes. "Don't give up."

The gunshot echoed out across the jungle.

Chapter Thirty-Three

Eskela stopped. Her hands were raw against the bark, scratched and bloody from the climbing. There were Islanders beneath her, clustered at the base of the tree. Eskela released her grip and dropped the last two metres. She landed on Killian, both feet first. The lieutenant crumpled. She rolled to her feet, twisted round and snapped up her rifle. Colt stepped in, smashed the weapon from her hands. Eskela kicked him between the legs and punched him in the throat. He staggered back, dropping his rifle and gagging for breath.

"Don't try it, bitch," growled Killian. The lieutenant was back on his feet, the revolver levelled at her head. Eskela slowly lifted her hands away from the dropped rifle. Killian smacked the gun across her forehead, knocked her into the dirt. He stepped over her body, but paused. His gaze flicked away from her. Cutra was limping towards them. The transhuman's armour was cracked and cratered, the visor half shattered, revealing the pale face beneath.

"Die, you freak!" roared Killian, and shifted his aim. The revolver barked. The round exploded against Cutra's armoured spaulder in a shower of sparks and metal shards. The transhuman regarded its shoulder, flexed the joint, and then turned its unblinking stare back onto Killian.

"Just die!" bellowed the lieutenant and pulled the trigger again. The cylinder clicked dry. Killian howled and threw the revolver. Cutra swatted it aside and kept limping towards them. Colt and Killian fled into the trees. When the two men were out of sight, the transhuman stumbled to a halt, slumped to its knees and pulled off its helmet. Silver blood fell in strings from Cutra's mouth.

"James," sobbed Eskela, crawling through the dirt towards him. "James."

Dalton was lying on his side. His face was covered in blood. Most of it was not his own. He reached out a hand and curled his fingers into Blake's shirt. He tried to pull his friend close, but there was no strength in his arm. All he could do was stare into Blake's eyes.

Lifeless eyes, locked open in the moment of death.

* * *

"I'm sorry I wasn't there." Dalton looked over his shoulder and saw Broden approaching. The sergeant was unbound and walking freely amongst the Separatist fighters that were securing the area. Shortly after the battle, the scouts that Ajati had sent to trail Killian's escape had caught up with Dalton. They had sent a runner back, only to find that Ajati and a sixty-strong force was already on the move, trailing the southern edge of the Spider's Eye. Four hours later, Ajati and his fighters arrived.

"What are you doing here?" asked Dalton.

"Ajati came to me shortly after you set off," said Broden. "He told me what you were doing, but he also told me that the war was too important to leave in the hands of one insane mission. He wanted a contingency in place. That was me, apparently. We were to catch up with Killian, and it was going to be my job to talk him down, or at least distract his group long enough for the Separatists to surround them."

"And you would have done that?"

"Ajati said that if I didn't come with him, they would be forced to kill everyone in Killian's group. With the threat of the carapace-walker, they wouldn't have the luxury of holding back in their assault. He told me that if you failed, then I was the only chance our boys would have at surviving this jungle. Anyway, I'm sorry I wasn't there. To help you bury him."

"To help me bury him?" asked Dalton sharply. "Maybe if you'd been here I wouldn't have had to bury him in the first place."

Broden came close and put a hand on Dalton's shoulder. His grip was firm. "I know where you are right now. The anger. The hurt. I've been there. Blake was your friend. But listen to me, alright? You can't stop it from happening. You can never stop it. They don't die because of you. They die because this is war. It's a cruel thing to have to accept, but the only thing worse is carrying every death like it's your personal responsibility. I tried that. All it's ever done for me is almost get me killed."

"He's the only one I buried," said Dalton. "It doesn't seem fair on the others. Wright. Nelson. Moore. Harris. Where are they now?"

"They're dead, James. They're just dead," Broden said. "It doesn't matter where their bodies are. You got the chance to bury Blake, and that was a fine thing, but at the end of the day you didn't do it for him. You did it for you."

Dalton opened his mouth to speak, then swallowed his words and looked away, blinking hard.

"Have you thought about what comes next?" asked Broden.

"Killian. Colt. They got away. This whole mission, it was for nothing."

Broden sighed. "I hate having to do this, but…"

Dalton caught the sergeant's wrist before the slap landed. Broden raised his eyebrows and nodded slowly, not shying from Dalton's hard eyes.

"You're not the man you were when we came to this moon," said Broden, pulling his arm free. "So, I think you know what you have to do. In fact, I think this sulk you're putting on is for Blake's benefit. Maybe you feel like you have to show you're in mourning, to cover up the fact that all you really want to do right now is go out there and hunt down the man that killed your friend. There's no shame in putting anger before grief, you know? No one who was sad was ever motivated to get up and fight. You have to be angry to get things done. Don't be afraid to be that person."

"You sound like Colt," said Dalton.

"He might be your enemy now," Broden said, "but that doesn't change the fact that he's a soldier, and a damn fine one at that."

"He's insane," said Dalton bluntly. "He's a murderer. A psychopath. I won't become that. This can't be about vengeance. This has to be about doing what's right. This has to be about saving Ishra."

"Then get up and do it."

* * *

"I will not threaten you with death or torture," Ajati was saying as Dalton came to where the prisoners were being interrogated. Cutra had been adamant in executing the surviving transhumans, but Dalton had convinced him to spare the six Privateers who had been found unarmed or knocked unconscious by the walker's explosion.

"I wish only to make you see reason," continued Ajati. The Separatist leader was sitting across from Scott. Eskela and two other fighters were standing guard. "To see that, by telling me what I need to know, you will be saving not just the lives of your comrades, but those of every woman, man and child on Ishra."

"He won't talk," said Dalton, "and if he does, it won't be what you want to hear."

Scott glared and spat on the ground. Ajati looked over his shoulder. "James, I'm sorry we've not had time to speak yet. As I'm sure you can imagine, finding out where Killian is headed is of the utmost importance. He already has a head-start on us."

"I know," said Dalton, and nodded at Scott, "but you're

speaking to the wrong man. Scott won't talk. He's too bitter. Too hateful. He wasn't always that way, but this war has changed us all."

"Then who?" asked Ajati.

"Thompson. I don't know the others well enough. They weren't from my squad. But Thompson will talk to me."

Ajati nodded to his guards, who lifted Scott by the arms and began to drag him away. Dalton stopped them. "Take him somewhere else. Don't let Scott talk to Thompson before he's brought over. Don't even let them see each other."

"Why not?" Ajati asked.

"When I speak to Thompson, I don't want him thinking of that look Scott intends on giving him, that look which says, 'You better not talk. You better not betray us. You're less than dirt if you do'," said Dalton. "All it takes between brothers is one look to breed that sort of shame. I know that better than most. Trust me."

Ajati nodded, his blue eyes narrowed thoughtfully as he regarded Dalton. "As you say."

* * *

"What's that?" asked Dalton.

Broden stood and held up the revolver. "A Snapper. It's empty."

A fighter appeared from behind a tree, rifle trained on Broden.

"Ah, my personal bodyguard," said Broden. "Ajati's little reminder to me that it takes more than just a conversation for him to trust someone."

"Easy now," said Dalton to the fighter, and took the .44 from Broden. "This belonged to Killian."

"Oh," said Broden. "This is what he used to…"

Dalton nodded, turning the weapon over in his hands. "Have any ammo for it?"

"No, but he does," said Broden, nodding to his warden. "I know you've got my .44, buddy. I've seen it tucked into the back of your belt. You're going to blow your arse off, by the way, because the safety isn't on."

Dalton walked over to the guard. "Can I?"

The guard hesitated, then drew the revolver and handed it over. Dalton opened the cylinder and shook out the six rounds inside. He handed back the empty gun and began to load Killian's instead.

"Is there a difference?" asked Broden.

"This is the one he used to kill Blake," said Dalton. "So, this is the one I'm going to use to kill him."

"I take it you found out where he's headed then."

"The second wave made a camp in the foothills to the west. That's where the Avernii were taking him. That's where he's headed."

"Has it occurred to you that he might not make it?" asked Broden. "He's out there somewhere with Colt, both of them unarmed and without supplies, in this nightmare of a jungle. It's entirely possible that he'll just end up dying out there."

"He'll make it," said Dalton, flicking the .44"s cylinder shut and holstering it at his belt. "He's got too much anger in him to die out here."

"So what's the plan?"

"We head west. If we don't find them before they find the camp, then we'll hit the camp."

"Hit the camp?" Broden asked. "That would be fighting your own brothers, James, just to kill one man."

"This is a war, isn't that what you said? Besides, the Separatists will do the fighting. I'll slip in under cover of the battle. I'll find Killian and Colt. I'll kill them. I'll retrieve what they stole, and then I'll continue with the mission."

"I came out here to save Privateers, not to fight them," said Broden.

"I'm not asking you to help me," Dalton said. "Just don't get in my way."

* * *

Eskela slipped through the trees to where Ajati's force was hiding.

"It's clear," she said, and glanced at Dalton. "I don't know why your Privateers bother patrolling the jungle. They might as well be blind."

The group moved up, slipping behind the final line of coalition patrols and coming to the edge of the jungle. Trees abruptly gave way to broad, rocky slopes that curved up into the foothills of the Jungle Spider mountain range.

"There it is," said Cutra, hunkered down at the tree line alongside Ajati, Eskela and Dalton. They followed Cutra's pointed finger and saw the camp, roughly a hundred metres up the slope. The collection of tents was spread across a plateau, encircled by makeshift barricades and watchtowers made from newly-cut lumber.

"Hand me those," said Dalton suddenly, gesturing for Ajati's binoculars. The man handed them over. Dalton brought the camp into view, then tracked his sight down towards the trees. "That's Killian! Heading up the slope. He's with others."

"He must have been picked up by a patrol," said Ajati. "Then we were only just behind him. Unfortunate."

"Can one of your snipers get him from here?" asked Dalton.

"And the other one? Colt? Is he there too?" Ajati asked, but didn't wait for an answer as Dalton looked back to the binoculars. "Assuming they haven't already told that patrol their story, we'd need to kill them both to keep your cover intact. And then we'd still have to recover the data tablet. No, risking that shot now would only remove our element of surprise for an uncertain outcome. We will wait for cover of night before we attack."

"That could be too late," said Dalton. "If they call in a drop-ship then Killian could already be gone come nightfall."

"You want to attack up that hill in broad daylight?" asked Ajati.

"Doing it at night is going to be no less dangerous," said Dalton. "There's no cover on that slope, and no jungle to protect you from their infrared."

Ajati gave his polite smile and gestured to the slope. "Do you see how broken the rocks are? The cracks in the ground? You see that small ridge there, and that one over there?"

"What am I looking at, Ajati?" asked Dalton, growing impatient.

"Indulge me," he replied. "Watch."

"We don't have time for this, damn it," said Dalton. "Killian is travelling towards that camp as we speak, and we're just sitting here—"

He paused and frowned. There was a slight trembling coming up out of the ground, so subtle that at first he had ignored it, but now it was growing stronger. A sound began to accompany the vibrations, a rumble that was building from somewhere deep beneath their feet.

"What is that?" asked Dalton, wide-eyed.

Ajati pointed at the slope. "Just watch."

The rumbling reached a crescendo and the tremors became so violent that Dalton had to lean against a tree to keep his balance. On the slope, a plume of water and steam ejected from what Dalton had taken to be just a crevice in the rock. As if it were the catalyst in a chain reaction, the first eruption was followed by many more. Geysers began to flare off all across the slope, firing superheated jets of vapour six metres into the air. The columns of steam and water rose up, reached a momentary point of equilibrium, and then collapsed, covering the slope in a fine mist. The eruptions lasted for almost five minutes before stillness returned.

"So you see," said Ajati, "we will attack at night, under the cover of one such episode, and the garrison won't know we're coming, not until we're already on them."

* * *

Dalton sat in silence with Cutra, their backs pressed into the curve of a tree hollow. He knew the Separatist assault force was spread out around them, but he could no longer see them. They had blended seamlessly into the jungle, lying prone in the undergrowth or finding perches high up in the trees. It gave Dalton no comfort. They had been waiting so for over an hour.

"This is a mistake," he whispered, as the most recent geyser eruption subsided. They would occur frequently, sometimes one straight after the other. The constant tremors were making him feel sick. "Killian was there on the slope and we did nothing. We're still doing nothing. Just waiting for a patrol to stumble our way, or for a drop-ship to come over the mountains and destroy any hope we have of salvaging this mission."

"I too would prefer decisive action, but our options are limited," Cutra replied.

"I know that," Dalton snapped. "It just feels wrong, waiting like this. It's like I can feel Killian getting further away with every second. They could be sending a transmission to *The Moongate* right this minute for all we know, reporting everything that's happened back to High Command. The moment that happens is the moment this mission becomes impossible. I'll never get back to Landbreak if I'm branded a traitor, not as a free man in any case."

"I saw no long-range communication masts in that camp," said Cutra. "From what we observed it looks as though they have yet to receive support or supplies from headquarters. High Command is no doubt wary of flying in more transports, given how few anti-aircraft positions this assault managed to neutralise."

Dalton sighed. He felt frustrated, but more than that, he realised as he glanced around, he felt alone. For the first time since he had come to Ishra, he was separated entirely from his squad. Out of the two men whom he had counted amongst his closest friends, one was dead and the other would now happily kill him given half the chance.

He looked at Cutra. The transhuman was now his only companion from *The Moongate*. He would never have guessed that this was how things would turn out.

"Things have changed," he said, half to himself.

"It's darker," said Cutra.

Dalton nodded. "Yeah. This whole war gets darker by the day."

"No, it's getting darker," said Cutra, pushing out of the tree hollow. Dalton frowned and followed the transhuman. "Look."

Sure enough, a shadow was passing through the trees, blotting out the shafts of light that pierced the jungle canopy. Fighters were emerging from their hiding spots, looking up towards the sky or following the broad shadow as it crept across their position.

"What's happening?" asked Dalton.

"It's easy to forget, when you live in the jungle and so rarely see the sky," said Ajati, jogging towards them. The man was beaming.

"It's the eclipse," said Eskela. "I'd forgotten too."

"An eclipse," said Dalton, his brow furrowing. "I remember Sergeant Banks saying something about it, before…"

"This is fortuitous. No, more than that, it is preordained. You've got your wish, James," said Ajati. The man could barely contain his glee. The fighters were coming down from the trees and creeping out of the ferns, readying their weapons and checking their gear. "In ten minutes' time it'll be as dark as night."

"How long will it last?" asked Dalton.

"Not long," Ajati admitted, "but it should give us enough time to get into position. You remember the plan?"

"I'll flank around, wait for the shooting to start and infiltrate the camp under cover of the confusion," said Dalton.

"I don't have the numbers for a sustained assault," said Ajati. "We'll engage for as long as our advantage allows, but then we'll be forced to withdraw. You'll have to move fast, deal with Colt and Killian and recover the data."

"I'll get it done," Dalton promised.

"You realise this may be the last time we see one another?" asked Ajati.

"I'll stay true to the mission," said Dalton. "I'll find a way back home and deliver your message to every Islander on Landbreak. Cutra will do the same for Avernus. Everyone is going to hear about Ishra's plight. You have my word."

Ajati came forward and embraced him. Dalton hesitated, taken aback, and then patted the man on the shoulders.

"We won't ever forget you, James," said Ajati, pulling away. "You are the enemy who became our salvation. You are the foreigner who survived the Spider's Eye. You are Ishra's messenger."

"Let's get this done before we start singing praises," said Dalton.

"There may not be another chance," said Eskela, and came forward to embrace him as well. "Thank you, James. You were under no obligation to help us, but you did anyway. You are a true friend. I wish I could come with you."

"I reckon we'll manage," said Dalton, winking at Cutra.

Cutra stared back at him, expressionless.

"Right then," Dalton said. "Time's wasting."

Chapter Thirty-Four

The shadow swept over the trees and began climbing the foothills, throwing into darkness the broken slopes. Steam was rising from the geysers already, drifting down the rocky climbs that had been worn smooth from years of water erosion.

"It's coming," said Dalton, feeling the tremors growing beneath his boots again. A hundred metres down the tree line, he knew that Ajati's fighters were preparing to storm the camp. As soon as the geysers erupted they would move, hidden from the naked eye by the artificial twilight of the eclipse, and shielded from any infrared sensors by the super-heated water that would be venting around them.

"We won't have long," said Cutra. "Do you have a plan for how you're going to find Killian once we're inside?"

"I don't," he admitted. "I don't know the layout of that camp or even how many soldiers are inside."

"So what are you going to do?" asked Cutra.

"Focus on getting there first," said Dalton, "and worry about the details when they matter."

Cutra considered this. "That is a terrible plan."

"But I think it would be good to try," said Dalton, flashing his transhuman companion a smile.

Cutra looked at him. Dalton couldn't tell whether he was seeing the hint of a smile at the corner of the transhuman's pale lips, but he realised in that moment how unwell Cutra looked. The transhuman's skin was more translucent than Dalton had ever seen it, so much so that he could almost make out the shadow of teeth behind Cutra's cheeks.

"Are you—" Dalton's concern was cut off as the first of the geysers erupted, sending a column of sizzling water and steam roaring into the air.

"Move! Now!" said Cutra, and side by side they broke from the cover of the trees. The ground trembled beneath their feet. Waves of pebbles shaken loose from splintered rocks clattered down the slope towards them. They scrambled and staggered along the ascent, weaving between the columns of high-pressure water that were bursting from fissures in the stone. In the twilight of the eclipse, the geysers shone ghostly white and sent clouds of steam drifting through the air.

Dalton glanced over his shoulder, up towards the darkened sky. Where Patera had been shining only minutes before, a black orb now hung over Ishra. The light of the star streamed from behind the eclipsing moon, rays of pale light that waved and curled like the emerging tentacles of some deep sea hunter.

"Focus!" shouted Cutra, pulling Dalton aside as a geyser powered into the air just half a metre ahead of him. A mist of scolding water blew across his face as he struggled to keep his balance on the slippery rock.

"The eclipse is already ending," he yelled, having glimpsed the crescent edge of the star reappearing from behind the passing moon.

"Then move faster!" Cutra replied.

They ran sideways across the slope as they came level with the camp. Dalton tried to catch a glimpse of Ajati's assault force between the geysers, but the hill was veiled in a steadily thickening mist of steam, reducing everything in sight to a soft and hazy shape. He focussed on his approach to the camp, trusting that he would hear the shooting when the attack began.

The silhouette of the encampment resolved out of the mist, a ragged assembly of tents enclosed within low, wooden barricades and rickety watchtowers. He could make out figures in those towers and others patrolling the perimeter. It occurred to him that he too would be in sight of those guards, and there was precious little cover on the slope.

"Why hasn't Ajati started the attack yet?" asked Dalton, crouching to minimise his silhouette. The eclipsing moon was now half way through completing its passage across the face of the star. "We're running out of time."

A flashlight blinked on in the closest watchtower. The beam of light swept along the mist-wreathed slope towards them. A muffled voice shouted something in the distance, and other lights came on, cutting through the hazy twilight. The tremors were abating now, the rumbling fading as the most recent wave of eruptions bled out the last of its fury.

"We can't wait," Dalton hissed. "We need to do something, now."

The shadow that had fallen across Ishra began to lift. Patera's light washed in over the eastern horizon, lighting up the green ocean at their backs.

"Do you want to fight?" asked Cutra.

"If Killian has already told his story, we may not have a choice," Dalton replied.

Water sprayed across them as the last of the geysers gave out and the jets of water slapped down across the stone. The eclipse was slipping away, second by second, restoring the day.

"Damn it," growled Dalton. "We have to try."

He came to his feet, lifting the rifle in his hands.

Cutra hesitated. "Are you sure about this?"

"No," Dalton admitted, "but what choice—"

A salvo of gunfire lit up the eastern face of the camp. Sustained, overlapping fields of rifle fire ripped through the tents and filled the air with clouds of pulverised stone. A rocket spiralled out of the fading shadow and struck one of the watchtowers, ripping it apart in a blossom of fire and shrapnel. Cries erupted across the camp as Islanders and Avernii scrambled to the defence.

"Go," said Dalton, seeing the perimeter guards shift their

attention. They moved quickly across the final stretch to the camp, keeping as low as they could. Most of the soldiers on the perimeter were hurrying off in the direction of the firefight. The volume of gunfire was only increasing as the garrison mounted its resistance.

"Halt!"

Cutra and Dalton came up short, skidding on the slick ground as they reached the low barricade. Across from them stood a guard, his rifle raised. Dalton drew the .44 from his belt and brandished it towards the violent pulses of light that were coming from the other side of the camp.

"What are you doing, trooper?" he bellowed. "Get out there and fight!"

The guard hesitated briefly, squinting at Dalton through the settling mist. His eyes locked onto the revolver. "Yes, sir! Sorry, sir!"

As the guard raced away, Dalton glanced at Cutra, eyes wide. "Wasn't sure that would work."

"Why did it?"

"Only officers carry these," Dalton replied, gesturing to the .44 Snapper.

They moved into the camp, keeping their heads low. Another explosion rocked the hill. A fireball rolled through the rows of tents further down, engulfing them in roiling flames. Most of the soldiers were already at the front, leaving just a few stragglers in this area, none of whom paid any attention to Dalton or Cutra.

"It's time to address those details you were so eager to dismiss earlier," said Cutra.

Dalton was looking left and right, his brow furrowed in desperate thought. "We need to find the command tent. Every camp has got one. That's one of the first places Killian would have been taken."

"It's unlikely that he would still be there," said Cutra as they set off again, moving along a central passageway between the tents.

"That's true," said Dalton, "but the data tablet might be, and that's just as important."

A third rocket detonated, three rows away from them. Dalton watched as the flames boiled over the tops of the tents and sent canvas flapping into the air. A group of Privateers burst through the rows up ahead, fleeing the explosion. On their heels came an officer, his revolver held high.

"Get back to the fight, you squid-limp bastards!" the officer was bellowing. The man turned, catching sight of Dalton and Cutra in the newly returned light of day. He levelled his .44 at them. "You two! With me, now! The fight is this way!"

Cutra strode towards the officer. The transhuman took the man's head in both hands and yanked it sideways. Dalton heard bone snap. Cutra looked back at him as the officer's body slumped to the ground.

"Come on."

Dalton blinked. He looked from Cutra to the murdered officer, and back again. Then he nodded and carried on, stopping only to collect more rounds for his revolver. They found the command tent after that, situated at a crossroads between the main avenues of the camp. Ducking under the entrance flaps, they came into the shade of the much larger tent. There was no one inside.

Several supply crates had been pushed together to form a surface, across which were scattered the disembowelled components of a long-range radio set. A topographical map of the Assahi Territory had been unrolled beside it, and lying on top of that was a data tablet. It wasn't one of the sleek models carried by officers, but an older, clunkier version with a cracked screen. Dalton recognised it at once.

"Got it," said Dalton, scooping up the device and flicking through the data storage. "It's all here. The pictures, the propaganda material. It's intact."

"What now?" asked Cutra.

"Now you pay."

Dalton spun on his heel. Killian was framed in the light of the entrance. There was a rifle in his hands. It was aimed at Dalton. Killian's finger tensed on the trigger. Cutra moved, lunging towards the lieutenant, but the transhuman was too far away. In the instant before Killian pulled the trigger, a rocket struck the ground twelve metres from the command tent. The concussive kill-radius that rippled through the air ended two metres short of the lieutenant, but the resultant shockwave billowed into him, throwing off his aim.

A burst of rounds punched through the canvas above Dalton's head. He flinched and leapt aside. Cutra reached Killian. The transhuman plucked the rifle from the lieutenant's grip and hammered a fist into the man's chest-piece. Killian came off the ground with both feet, cleared the tent's entrance and thudded to his back, gasping for air. Cutra smoothly rotated the rifle and aimed it at Killian.

Gunfire cracked close by. Half a dozen rounds sparked from Cutra's beaten armour. The transhuman jerked back, clutching the side of its face. Dalton saw silver blood in the air. He drew the revolver and fired three booming shots out of the tent, grabbing hold of Cutra and pulling the transhuman away from the entrance.

Colt was striding towards them, errant flames flickering across the tents at his back. He was firing from the hip as he came, streaking the inside of the command tent with narrow beams of smoky light.

"Salt," hissed Dalton. A round had gouged the side of Cutra's face and taken off the top of one ear.

"Don't concern yourself," said Cutra, pushing Dalton aside to return fire. "There are more of them coming."

"Sounds like Ajati is breaking off the attack," said Dalton, noting that the sounds of battle were subsiding. "We'll get shredded if we're cornered in here."

"Then let's not get cornered," said Cutra, and moved to the back of the tent. The transhuman raised its arm, fingers extended, and cut through the canvas with the blade of its hand. They made their escape out of the tear and hurtled between the backs of two rows of tents. Guy ropes snapped and whipped loose as Cutra ploughed through them. Tents sagged as the taut support lines were cut. Dalton had to push himself to keep up with the transhuman's speed, and even then Cutra was well ahead of him. He could hear angry shouts behind them. It wouldn't take Killian long to realise that Dalton and Cutra had made their escape, at which point the lieutenant would waste no time in mustering a kill team for the pursuit.

They came out at the westernmost edge of the camp and vaulted the barricades. Up ahead, the foothills became steeper as they rose from the plateau and fed into the mountain heights. Dalton could make out jagged ravines further up, passageways that led deeper into the Jungle Spider network.

"We could loop around and return to the tree line," said Cutra, looking back east. Smoke from a dozen fires was pouring from the far side of the camp, but the sounds of gunfire had ceased entirely.

"I'm not going back," said Dalton, securing the data tablet in his webbing.

"You intend to pass through the mountains?" asked Cutra, following Dalton's gaze. A sharp wind was picking up, carrying raised voices from the camp.

"I don't have time to argue the point," said Dalton, "but I have to keep going. I have to find a way back to *The Moongate*, a way back home."

"Into the mountains, then," said Cutra.

Dalton nodded. They went west, forging a path off the plateau and onto the steepening slopes that led towards the imposing wall of the mountain above. The higher they went, the stronger the winds blew, funnelling up the curve of the foothills and driving into the many gulleys and canyons that defined the mountain facade.

Chips of rock peppered Dalton as he hauled himself up the craggy lip of an escarpment. He heard the throaty, staccato chatter of an L7 and rolled away from the ledge. More rounds cracked into the rocks beneath him. He risked a glance over the shelf. Ten Privateers were making their way up the hill after them. Killian and Colt were at the front, firing as they came.

"The Scour of Ishra," said Cutra.

"What?" asked Dalton, ducking back as another burst of rounds hammered the ledge.

"That is what the Ishradi call it," Cutra said, "the great dust storm that blows across the moon every year. The Scour of Ishra."

"What of it?"

"It's here," said Cutra, pointing to the east. Dalton followed the gesture, over the top of the camp, across the vast sprawl of the inner jungle, to the horizon beyond. He froze. A shadow was blotting out the eastern sky, a shadow that writhed and roiled and bulged. Bursts of light, purple and blue, pulsed in the depths of that shadow and, carried across the distance on howling winds, Dalton began to hear the muted rumbling of approaching thunder.

"I thought the jungle was supposed to be protected from the storms," said Dalton.

"It will be," Cutra said, turning and leaping up the next shelf of rock. The transhuman turned and held out a hand. "But we are no longer in the jungle."

"We need to get off this slope and into the cover of the mountains! Now!" yelled Dalton, raising his voice over the wind. He took hold of Cutra's hand and the transhuman hauled him up. They pulled themselves along the shattered face of the upper slope. Bullets whipped through the air above them, hitting the steeper climbs ahead.

The wind grew coarse against their backs as the air began to fill with dust. Their world started to shrink and grow dark as the storm surged in over the jungle's roof and struck the bulwark of the mountain. Dalton's vision was reduced to a handful of metres, boxed in by swirling clouds of dust that whirled around him.

"In here!" shouted a voice from up ahead, and Dalton staggered towards the dark shape that was Cutra. The sheer cliffs of the lower mountains resolved out of the storm. Cutra was disappearing through an opening in the stone, a narrow ravine that led deep into the spine of the mountain range.

Shards of splintered rock hit Dalton in the face. He ducked, glancing over his shoulder as more rounds bracketed the ravine entrance. Shadows were coming out of the thickening dust, the silhouettes of Privateers, framed by the flashing of their rifles.

"Come and get me then," Dalton growled, and slipped away into the dark of the ravine.

Chapter Thirty-Five

It made the tunnels scream.

The Scour of Ishra originated in the dune valleys far to the east of the Assahi Territory, given life by the slightest and most unassuming gusts of air, nothing more than a dust devil spinning up the sand into little pillars. But it grew and it grew, gaining strength and intensity, slaving the winds and the sand to its will, so that by the time it reached the easternmost edge of the Jungle Spider, it was a juggernaut that stretched for over three thousand kilometres in length, tearing across the land with inexorable momentum.

The storm front hit the eastern ramparts of the Assahi mountain network, an unstoppable force striking an immovable object. The greater majority of the storm's energy was crushed against the stone bulwark and diverted north and south along the flanks of the mountain line, but the force of the Scour was too immense to be so easily deflected.

An enormous wave of sand and dust thundered over the eastern peaks, powered up along the natural curve of the mountain slopes. The momentum carried the storm clean across the roof of the inner jungle, making the canopy thrash wildly, but sparing it from the full, destructive drive of the onslaught. This huge, overflowing force next met the westernmost line of mountains, where once again it was carried up and over the peaks.

On the far side of the Assahi Territory, the Scour of Ishra would reform in all of its might, the diverted wings of the storm recombining after their journey around and over the jungle mountains. From there, the Scour would rip its way uninterrupted across the open plains of short, yellow grass, engulfing the city of Ushura as it went.

Before that though, as it hammered against the westernmost mountain barrier, the storm would drive a thousand spears into the many winding tunnels and canyons that snaked through the stone. As the wind was drawn along these jagged passageways, it produced a howling shriek, a hair-raising scream that was repeated across the entire length of the mountain line.

Dalton could hear nothing else as he hurled himself along the ravine. Even with its momentum broken by the zigzagging passage, the wind was no less harsh against his back. Waves of grit and sand and even small stones were blasted along the corridor, rattling and ricocheting from the steep walls. As the airborne detritus pelted his armour or struck stinging blows against his fatigues, Dalton was under no confusion as to how The Scour of Ishra had acquired its name.

The air was so thick with dust and sand that Dalton didn't see the transhuman until it was almost too late. Cutra grabbed hold of Dalton's shoulder guard and stopped him from losing his footing as he veered to avoid collision. Dalton looked up at the transhuman, wondering why they had stopped moving. Killian and his hunters were surely only a few minutes behind them at most.

"A choice," said Cutra, staring ahead to where the ravine bifurcated, forming two distinct paths that angled away from one another. Dalton looked between the two passageways. Neither one seemed more promising than the other, nor more likely to deliver them swiftly to the far side of the mountains.

He looked up, following the sheer sides of the ravine to where the sky had been replaced by the rushing torrent of the storm. Then he looked back, squinting into the wind, half expecting to see Killian and Colt emerging from around the last bend, guns ablaze. There were alcoves and nooks in the wind-worn sides of the ravine, dead-end diversions and shallow caves. Many of them could provide refuge from the storm that funnelled down the main passage.

Dalton looked away, blinking grit from his eyes. His back ached from the non-stop trials of the past two days, his legs burned from running and his gear weighed heavy. He had lost track of the scratches, scrapes, cuts and bruises that plagued his body. The revolver in his hand, however, felt light. It reminded him of the anger that still lurked in his gut. It reminded him of Blake, and of the bastard who had killed him.

"Follow me," said Dalton.

"This way?" asked Cutra. "Are you sure?"

"I'm sure."

* * *

"Come on, keep up! They can't be far!"

Killian's words were half lost on the wind. The eight Privateers were stumbling along behind him, hunched against the storm at their backs. Colt had disappeared up ahead. The man was fury distilled. He had been the first into the ravine after that traitor, Dalton. Killian wanted that cur dead just as much, but the men behind were lagging. He needed to keep them close. After all, he would need all the help he could get if he was going to have a chance at killing Cutra.

It was true that there were Avernii in the camp that he could have brought with him, but he would be damned before he trusted some mod freak over an honest-to-salt Islander. Killian could tell these Privateers were rattled though. He couldn't blame them. They had just weathered a Separatist raid under the cover of an eclipse, in the midst of a mass geyser eruption, followed by the onset of a gargantuan storm and now a lieutenant – who had crawled out of the jungle just over an hour ago – was leading them into the mountains on a mission that they knew nothing about.

There had been no time to explain though. He hadn't even

been in the camp long enough to bring the garrison commander up to speed on his story, let alone brief a squad on the specifics of why they were hunting down one of their own.

Damn that bastard, James Dalton. Killian still had no idea how the traitor had managed to get ahead of them in the jungle. Dalton was no seasoned soldier, no hardened guerilla fighter, and yet killing him was turning out to be nigh impossible. How could one man be so lucky?

Killian had escaped the jungle alive and reached the safety of a defensible camp, yet somehow events had still aligned themselves to give the Separatists – to give Dalton – the advantage. It was as though the bastard had willed that moon across the very skies to blot out the light of Patera, as though he had summoned the storm itself to cover his escape.

The lieutenant squashed those thoughts. He knew he was allowing frustration to get the better of him. Right now he needed the cold, killing edge of focus, not wild thoughts born from bitterness and anger. He would chase Dalton and that mod freak across the length and breadth of the mountains if he had to. He would find them and when he did, he would dispense immediate justice from the barrel of a gun, as he had done for that worm, Blake Leland.

They found Colt standing at the mouth of a fork in the ravine.

"Give me four men," said Colt. "I'll go that way. You take the rest and go the other way."

"You want to split up?" asked Killian.

"There's just two of them, lieutenant," snarled Colt, "and this time we're fully armed and ready."

"Alright," said Killian, "keep following the passage, but if you find another fork, turn back and wait for us here. We'll do the same. I'm not getting us lost in these mountains."

"You'd let him escape?" asked Colt, a dangerous look in his eyes.

"I'll catch him if I can," said Killian, "but letting him starve out here is second best. If you find him, bring me his head. Now move, private!"

Colt nodded and picked out four men. Killian took the rest and they pressed on down the left branch of the ravine. The corridor became even narrower. They had to travel in single file as it was, but in some places Killian now had to turn his body sideways to slip between the walls. The narrowing passageway only served to amplify the wind. It roared past them, clawing at their fatigues and hounding them with coarse grit and tiny, stone fragments that drew blood where they found bare skin. The back of Killian's neck was raw from exposure. He ignored it and put all of his focus into moving forwards.

****

Behind the lieutenant, back where the ravine divided, Cutra and Dalton watched the hunters split up. The two warriors emerged from the shadows. Dalton squeezed his way free of a crevice in the rock. On the other side of the ravine, Cutra crawled out from a hole at ground level, armour scraping against stone. They came to stand before the fork. They said nothing, only shared a nod.

Cutra went right.

Dalton watched the transhuman go. He drew his revolver, emptied the three spent cases and thumbed fresh shells into the cylinder. He flicked it shut and set off, down the left fork of the ravine and after Killian.

****

The pass ahead had collapsed. Colt looked up at the boulders and chunks of fractured rock that had fallen from the steep walls and clogged the ravine. Given time and effort, it may have been possible for someone to climb the blockage.

The rubble had formed an uneven slope, up which the wind continued to stream.

He wasn't looking at the slope though, because if Dalton had come this way, there was another path that the traitor might have taken. A cleft in the right-side wall led beneath the mountain, though in what direction or for how far was impossible to tell. Colt's flashlight illuminated only so far into the shadowed tunnel.

"This way," he said, turning sideways to get his broad shoulders through the cleft.

"The lieutenant said we were to turn back if the path split again," said a Privateer.

"What did you say?" snapped Colt.

"I said, the lieutenant—"

"Does this look like a fork in the road to you?" asked Colt.

The Privateer hesitated and looked from the cave entrance to the blocked corridor. "Well—"

"Because I just see one way forward," said Colt, cutting off the soldier again, "and I intend on taking it. So, the only question is, are you some squid-limp coward who's afraid of the dark, or are you a damn Islander?"

"It would be a perfect place to lay an ambush," said a second Privateer, nodding at the cleft. "No telling what's waiting for us in there."

"Cowards it is, then," Colt snarled, and pressed on into the cave. The four soldiers shared a glance and reluctantly followed.

The cleft was so close that once the soldiers had entered it, they could not even turn their heads to look back, for risk of grating their faces against the craggy rock. Soon the howl of the storm was behind them, replaced by a dense, subterranean silence.

Colt came free of the tunnel. He brought his rifle up, cutting across the pitch black with the beam of his flashlight. Colt knew the soldier was right about this being a prime ambush spot, but in truth he didn't care. All that mattered to him was finding Dalton and that mod freak, and putting an end to this charade.

As the others worked their way out of the cleft, Colt ventured further into the cave. He could hear the unmistakeable rushing of a river, somewhere in the darkness ahead.

"Don't get lost," called a Privateer behind him. "Raymond is still in the tunnel."

"Well, if they didn't know we were here already, thank you for announcing our presence," said Colt. "Get a move on."

"Raymond? You back there?"

Colt sighed and pressed on, tracking his light across the floor. One of the Privateers caught up with him, his boots clattering on the stone.

"I think Raymond is stuck in the tunnel," said the soldier.

"Who's Raymond?" muttered Colt.

"So, I was thinking," the soldier continued, "we saw a lot of horrible shit in the jungle."

"Some of us more than others," said Colt.

"Just makes me wonder what could be living up here, in the mountains and the caves."

"Keep your focus on the damn mission," Colt said. By the sounds of it, they were getting closer to the river.

The Privateer shone his light behind them. "We should stay together."

"Then the others should keep up."

"Wait a minute," said the soldier, coming to a halt. He lowered his voice to a whisper. "I don't see their lights."

Colt stopped. The hairs on the back of his neck pricked up. Slowly, he turned around, dragging the beam of his light through the thick darkness that surrounded them. The soldier was right. The flashlights of the other three Islanders were no longer visible.

"You reckon Jones went back into the tunnel, after Raymond?" asked the Privateer.

"Shut up," said Colt quietly. "Get your safety off. Keep your eyes peeled."

"You think the enemy is in here, with us?"

"Shut. Up." Colt turned gently on his heel, finger ready at the trigger of his newly requisitioned L7. There was a meaty thud behind him and something hit the floor with a crack and a clatter. Colt spun round, torch probing the dark.

There was nothing. Nothing was precisely the problem. The other Privateer had disappeared. Colt shone his light along the ground and found a rifle lying there, its under-slung flashlight broken. He backed away rapidly, switching his light left and right.

"You bastard," he shouted into the dark. "You coward! Where are you?"

The ground went out from underneath one of his boots. He teetered on the edge before regaining his balance. The river was at his back. Water splashed against his calves, icy cold, churned up by the swift current. His finger was tense on the trigger. A bead of sweat rolled off his brow. The pounding of his heart was loud against his ribcage.

The transhuman came out of the dark. It had the face of a wraith. Its skin was so translucent that Colt could see the ridges of its eye-sockets and the shape of teeth behind the taut skin of its cheeks. It launched itself into the light, mouth drawn wide in a silent scream, armoured hands outstretched.

Colt pulled the trigger. The transhuman disappeared from sight in the blinding muzzle flash. Then the L7 was wrenched from Colt's hands. Something hard crashed into his sternum, drove the breath from his lungs. His boots slipped out from beneath him. He hit the water, every muscle in his body seizing as the ice-cold water drove in around him. Colt surfaced, gasping for air and thrashing for purchase as the current swept him into the darkness.

* * *

Cutra, who could see better in the dark than any Islander, watched as Colt was dragged away, spluttering and fighting hopelessly against the force of the water. The transhuman drew its fingers up along the armour of its abdomen, feeling the edges of broken metal where the point-blank rounds had punched clean through. Thick, silver blood was oozing from those bullet holes. Cutra could feel the blunted rounds in its flesh, could feel the pain of its muscles and organs contracting around the wounds.

Distantly, the transhuman was aware of its knees hitting the ground. A weakness was reaching up through its body, like vines wrapping themselves around its limbs and pulling them down. Vision threatened to fade, but the transhuman fought against the dimming of its eyes.

Cutra was not ready to die.

* * *

Dalton clinched his arm around the Privateer's throat. His other hand clamped around the soldier's trigger finger, bending it away from the rifle. The Privateer struggled to break free, but panic and fear diluted his efforts. His grunts and choked pleas for help went unheard by his comrades ahead, covered by the shrieking winds. The Privateer fell limp, his head drooping. Dalton stashed the unconscious soldier in a nearby alcove, taking his rifle and ammunition.

"Sorry about this," he muttered, as he stripped the soldier of anything that could be used as a weapon. Dalton peered back into the ravine. The tail end of Killian's group was disappearing into the storm. They hadn't noticed their missing comrade yet. The wind and the grit that it carried meant the soldiers were reluctant to look behind them. It was an advantage Dalton intended to use to the fullest.

He set off again, keeping low as he ran up the corridor. The revolver was holstered at his belt and the rifle strapped tight to his back, leaving his hands free. He only had quarrel with one man here, and he wouldn't kill the others, not if it could be helped. Unfortunately, that still meant he had to hurt them.

Dalton came up on the group again. He caught the next soldier and drove the man's head sideways into the ravine wall. Dalton put the weight of his shoulder behind the attack. Over the storm, he could barely hear the crack of the Privateer's helmet striking the rock. The soldier slumped to the ground, a trickle of blood running from his hairline. Dalton liberated the man of his ammunition and continued onwards.

The last three soldiers, oblivious to Dalton's presence, were rounding a bend in the ravine. He stalked them as the steep walls of the corridor fell away, and the path ahead opened onto a plateau. The jutting tongue of rock overlooked a valley enclosed by the mountains. Partially obscured by the storm, the valley floor was dotted with hot springs and geysers.

Dalton moved quickly. The two Privateers behind Killian, now free of the narrow passage, had come shoulder to shoulder. It would only be a second before they realised their comrades were missing. He stamped his boot into the side of one Privateer's knee. The soldier yowled and crumpled. Dalton drew his .44 and struck the kneeling man in the back of the neck, putting him out cold. The second Privateer looked round and received the grip of the revolver to his face. He staggered back, gushing blood from his nose. Dalton kicked the soldier off his feet.

Killian was turning, lifting his rifle. Dalton caught the L7 before it could be aimed and shoved it down and away. He brought up the revolver, but Killian jerked forwards, smashing his helmet into Dalton's face. He reeled. Light bloomed before his eyes and he felt warm blood on his lips. The revolver tumbled from his fingers, but he kept his other hand tight on the lieutenant's rifle.

They grappled, pushing and shoving, their feet skidding further and further out along the plateau. Killian hammered a fist into Dalton's cheek that split skin. Dalton drove his knee into Killian's ribs and knocked the air from the lieutenant's chest. Killian slackened and Dalton ripped the rifle free. Before he could bring it to bear, Killian staggered forwards, body-tackling him to the floor. The back of Dalton's helmet cracked against the stone and the rifle clattered away.

Killian tore off Dalton's helmet and hurled it aside. He ploughed in with his fist, battering Dalton across the face again and again. Dalton felt numb. His head was pounding. There was a ringing in his left ear that wouldn't go away. The storm howled around the two men, billowing out of the ravine and sweeping the plateau, blasting them with waves of grainy dust.

Dalton gathered his wits, clenched his fist and swung it off the ground in a ninety-degree arc that crashed across Killian's jaw. The lieutenant fell sideways, his head drooping. Dalton sucked in air through bleeding lips. He fumbled with the strap that was keeping the L7 firm against his back. Trembling fingers loosed the weapon and he groaned as he pulled it over his shoulder.

Killian came back. He kicked the rifle out of Dalton's grip with such force that it went over the edge of the plateau. The next kick took Dalton in the gut. The next one in his hip. The next one in his spine as he rolled to protect his stomach. Dalton coughed and blood splattered from his lips. He dragged a shivering hand to his thigh and worked loose the combat knife sheathed there.

"It's over, you bastard," screamed Killian, and stamped down on Dalton's hand, crushing his fingers against the knife's handle. Dalton cried out and received another kick to the gut.

"This is where you die, you traitorous son of a bitch. This is where it ends!"

Dalton knew the next kick was coming. He had suffered enough of them to know how to catch it. He rolled into the attack and yanked Killian off balance. The lieutenant went down hard on his side. Dalton groaned, blood stained saliva dripping from split lips, and dragged himself away. Elbow over elbow, he crawled across the plateau, bending his head against the dust that billowed over him, coating his bloody skin and stinging his eyes. He could already hear Killian getting to his feet, could hear the man's footsteps as he bore down on him.

"This is where it ends," Killian repeated, lurching from the storm.

Dalton rolled onto his back. The .44 Snapper was gripped in both hands. He didn't hesitate, didn't waste time with words. He just squeezed the trigger. The sleek, black revolver slammed back in his grip as it fired. The boom of its discharge was loud even against the roar of the storm. The round hit Killian square in the chest-plate, stopped him in his tracks. Killian's eyes were wide, his mouth half parted in shock.

Again, the revolver barked. Killian staggered back as the second round hit home. Dalton pulled the trigger. He pulled the trigger again. Then again. Each shot knocked Killian back across the plateau. The lieutenant swayed on the edge, blood trickling from his open mouth, his back hunched, his fingers bent like claws.

Dalton looked into Killian's eyes. He saw the hate there and the anger, twisted and cruel. The revolver, the gun that had been used to kill Blake Leland, barked for the sixth and final time. The shot was off-centre. It tore through Killian's shoulder and spun him off his feet. His arms reached out, but there was nothing to hold onto, nothing to save him. His boots slipped off the edge of the plateau. Lieutenant Killian plunged into the storm and was gone.

The revolver, its barrel streaming smoke in the wind, slipped from Dalton's fingers. He let it go. He didn't want to touch it ever again. All he wanted to do was lay back his head and let sleep take him. His face was raw and swollen. His ribs and stomach and back screamed with pain. But he knew he couldn't sleep, not yet.

James Dalton rose to his feet and limped away, leaving the plateau behind him.

Chapter Thirty-Six

The Scour of Ishra did not relent. For the eleven days that it took Cutra and Dalton to cross the mountains, the storm continued to rage, relentless. It laid siege to the barren heights, tore through the valleys and the gorges, hauled on crumbling ledges and dislodged boulders that weighed tens of tonnes. Too often the sheer strength of the winds forced the two warriors to turn back and find another route, or risk being plucked from the edges of cliffside paths.

Their journey, for the most part, was spent in solemn silence. They reunited at that first fork in the ravine. No questions were asked. A simple nod passed between them and that was all either one of them needed, to know that the job had been done. They scavenged what supplies they could from the incapacitated Privateers: ammunition, water flasks, ration packs and rudimentary medical kits. Afterwards, they found shelter in one of the many caves, to rest and tend to their wounds as much as possible.

When some strength had returned to them, they ventured back into the storm. Cutra led them up the right fork of the ravine and they dragged themselves over the rubble of the blockage. From there, they followed the winding corridor until it opened onto the broad, sloping flanks of the inner mountain range. They pressed on due west, traversing the wind-blasted ascents and hugging the narrow walkways that criss-crossed the faces of sheer-sided cliffs.

As the pain of his wounds began to subside, Dalton gradually became aware of the beauty hidden within the folds of the mountain range. They were barren of vegetation, it was true, scoured clean of trees, plants and even grass by the savage winds and annual storms, but there was a rugged beauty in the monolithic structure of the cliffs, and in the wide valleys that were wreathed in steam from hot springs and geysers.

If the harsh environment of the mountains allowed for fauna, Dalton saw none of it. It was possible that the onset of the storm had driven any animals into the shelter of caves and tunnels. For this reason they refrained from venturing too deeply into the underground places, taking refuge in only the shallowest of caves. If their journey through the Spider's Eye had taught them anything, it was that the wildlife of Ishra was to be rightly feared.

Progress was slow. The storm sometimes blew so fiercely that they were confined to shelter, and their wounds made the going no easier. This would not have been such a concern if not for the dwindling of their already meagre supplies. The ration packs didn't go far, but water was the true issue. There were freshwater streams to be found in the mountains – from which they would gratefully replenish their canteens whenever they were lucky enough – but in the unrelenting storm the springs and creeks were difficult to spot.

On the eighth day, they stumbled upon a rapidly-flowing river that cut west through the rocky climbs, tumbling over the ledges and steep drops as it made its way out of the mountains. They found a hollow in the river bank and, sheltered from the storm, splashed themselves with handfuls of clear water, washing away the layers of blood, sand and grit that had adhered to their bodies over the past two weeks.

They followed the river as closely as they could in the jagged terrain, and on the twelfth day emerged onto the west face of the mountain range. Dalton had never been so happy to see the sprawling green ocean of the Assahi jungle, even if it was partially obscured by the dust storm that howled over its canopy. The river cascaded down the west-facing slopes in waterfall after waterfall, until at last it reached the jungle floor.

Dalton realised that they had been following the Sadari River from its source.

If they could find some way to travel along the river, it would cut their journey time out of the Assahi Territory by days. Then would come the hard part. They would have to find a way to secure transport off of Ishra. Dalton had been putting that part of the plan from his mind. Right now, getting clear of the jungle would be a victory in itself. Fortunately, the answer to that challenge lay ahead of them.

They set off down the mountainside, following the descent of the Sadari River.

** * **

"Why is nothing ever simple?" muttered Dalton.

Alongside Cutra, he was concealed in a cluster of large ferns. Ten metres in front of them, the river crashed down out of the foothills and gathered in a deep pool, before feeding west into the jungle. It was also the site of a military encampment. It looked to have been established some time ago, its tents and pre-fabricated structures enclosed in a perimeter of barbed-wire and fortified gun-posts. The pool itself had become a depot. A Seahound tank and two Wave-Rider transports were moored in the water, alongside an open-deck patrol boat that belonged to the Ishradi army.

"If they're this far up the river, it probably means the Separatists have been pushed back across the mountains entirely," said Dalton, trying to count the number of soldiers on patrol. There appeared to be a sizeable garrison in the camp, a mix of Privateers, Avernii and Ishradi.

"We could just walk in there," said Cutra.

"You don't think they would take issue with two random soldiers strolling up to their doorstep?" asked Dalton. "Two soldiers, I might add, who may very well have a wanted status on them."

"They couldn't know," said Cutra. "Killian was in that camp for just over an hour when the storm hit. Even if he had been able to report to the garrison commander in that time, I doubt that they would have contacted High Command straight away. I doubt that they even had the capability for long-range transmissions."

"There was a disassembled radio in the command tent," said Dalton, thinking back. "They may have been trying to boost the gain to get a message across the mountains, or directly to *The Moongate*. In the time it's taken us to get here, they could have fixed their radio."

"No transmission would survive this storm," said Cutra. "Besides, even if it did, I doubt there is a single person in this camp who could verify our identities."

"You're suggesting we lie about who we are?"

"When we were infiltrating the last camp, you managed to convince the guard that you were an officer, just by holding a revolver," Cutra pointed out.

"Those were very different circumstances," Dalton said. "The camp was being attacked and the man could barely see me for the mist. I doubt the same trick will work here. Besides, I don't even have a revolver anymore."

"As I said, I reckon there is a negligible chance of there being anyone in that camp who could verify who we are," said Cutra, "which means they would have to send us to someone who could. It would get us out of the jungle, at the very least. Besides, they would have no reason to believe we were lying. They have no idea what's happened on the other side of these mountains."

"I sincerely hope you're right about this, Cutra," said Dalton, "or else we'll be leaving this jungle in shackles."

* * *

They came out of cover and approached one of the entrances in the perimeter. The guards noticed them immediately and raised their rifles. Dalton could see they were hesitating, confused by the sight of a Privateer and a transhuman, both beaten and tattered, appearing out of the trees side by side.

"Halt!" called one of the guards. Dalton made to slow his pace, but Cutra nudged him onwards.

"Right," muttered Dalton. He mustered the little energy he had left and put it into making his voice as authoritative as possible. "Stand down! Lieutenant Killian, 9th Company, 4th Platoon! I need to speak to the garrison commander right away!"

The guards shared a glance, but didn't move aside. One of the soldiers looked Dalton up and down, checking his shoulder and chest for rank markings. Before he had come into the open, Dalton had made sure to strip himself of his name-tag and rank indicators.

"Sorry, sir, you're… lieutenant?" asked the guard cautiously.

"Killian. 9th Company. 4th Platoon," said Dalton, clipping his words in the fashion that officers were so typical of adopting. The guard glanced him up and down again. Dalton took advantage of the man's uncertainty. "Are you going to make me wait, private? I've just come half way across this damn moon to deliver vital strategic information to High Command, and you're going to keep me standing in this shit-salt jungle?"

"No, sir," stammered the guard, his nerve failing him. "Sorry, sir. I'll have you escorted through."

The guard flagged down a patrol and quietly explained the situation. The patrol leader, a burly corporal with fisherman tattoos on his face, kept his eyes on Dalton as the guard spoke to him in hushed tones.

"Come on in, lieutenant," said the corporal, and walked them through the camp towards one of the pre-fabricated structures. The corporal politely asked them to wait and went inside the metal trailer. Several minutes passed in silence. The three Islanders in the patrol were standing close, rifles in hand. Dalton could feel their eyes on him, could feel their curiosity. He swallowed and glanced at Cutra. The transhuman was staring ahead, expression unreadable. If they were discovered, Dalton wondered how Cutra would respond. Would the transhuman try to fight?

"The lieutenant will see you now," said the corporal, appearing in the doorway.

"Excellent," said Dalton, and stepped up into the pre-fab.

"Lieutenant Killian, is it?" asked the officer, standing at the far end of the room. A large plotting table took up most of the space inside the cramped trailer, along with a few foldable chairs, a weapon's locker and a sleeping cot shoved into the far corner.

"9th Company. 4th Platoon," said Dalton, trying to sound confident about it.

"Now hold on a moment," said the officer, his brow furrowing. "9th Company? 4th Platoon?"

Dalton's mouth was suddenly very dry. He cleared his throat. "That's right."

"I know you," the officer said, narrowing his eyes. The man strode across the trailer and stood in front of Dalton. Cutra tensed, ever so slightly, but Dalton had spent enough time in the transhuman's company to recognise that reflex.

"Well, not you specifically, but I'll be damned if I've forgotten your unit," continued the officer. "I'm Lieutenant Hayes, 12th Company, 5th Platoon. One of your squads pulled my boys out of the fire, back when this all started, in the tunnels under Ushura. They led a flank behind enemy lines and saved all our arses."

Dalton froze. He remembered Lieutenant Hayes. He had stood face to face with him, just as they were now. He had shaken the man's hand.

"I never did get to catch up with you boys after that battle, things being what they were," said Hayes. "This is a damn, pleasant surprise though. I owe your unit a debt, Lieutenant Killian. What can I do for you?"

Dalton blinked. The man didn't recognise him. It had been dark in Ushura's sewers. It was possible that Hayes hadn't got a good look at him in the tunnels, or that the encounter had been fleeting enough that he hadn't committed Dalton's face to memory. James spared a glance at Cutra, which the transhuman pointedly did not return.

"I'm..." began Dalton, and cleared his throat again. He pulled the data tablet from his webbing. "I'm on a mission of the highest importance, lieutenant. I have strategic information that I have been personally charged with delivering to High Command."

Hayes eyed the data tablet curiously. "Wasn't 9th Company deployed in the vanguard?"

"We were," said Dalton, unable to think of anything better to reply with.

"Salt, we haven't heard a damn thing from the assault force since the first drop-ships were gunned down," said Hayes. "What's it like over there?"

"A damn mess," Dalton said, "and it'll only get worse unless I deliver my report to High Command as soon as possible."

"I'll make sure of it," said Hayes, pouring two cups of water from a flask on his table. "I'm sorry I don't have anything stronger. Excuse my frankness, but you both look like shit. You've come across the mountains, haven't you? How many of you are there?"

Dalton gratefully accepted the water and drained the cup before replying. "There were more of us. Only me and Cut- only the mod here survived."

"Damn," breathed Hayes. "It really is that bad, isn't it? I'd heard rumours about the botched assault, but I didn't think we were in it this deep."

"You'll understand my need for haste then, lieutenant," pressed Dalton.

"Absolutely," said Hayes. "I've got a boat full of wounded scheduled to go down the river. It was meant for tomorrow, but I'll bump it up."

"Thank you."

"Like I said, I owe your unit a debt. Hopefully, this goes some way to repaying it."

"Is there somewhere we can rest until the boat is ready?" asked Dalton.

"I'll see to it all, lieutenant, get a medic to check you over too," said Hayes. Dalton nodded and turned to leave. "One more thing, before you go."

Dalton looked over his shoulder.

"I remember one of your men, the private that led the flank under Ushura," said Hayes. "Dalton, I think his name was. James Dalton. What happened to him? Did he survive?"

Dalton turned away.

"No, lieutenant, I don't think he did."

* * *

"You're not the first ones to come limping out of the jungle," said the medic idly, as he swabbed at the many cuts on Dalton's face. "Half the time the patrols come in all mauled, and sometimes we get groups from the checkpoints further down the river, who've got turned around and ended up wandering the wrong way. A couple of days ago we even found a lone Privateer out by the edge of the foothills. Man was half dead. Still hasn't said a word."

Dalton winced as the medic continued to apply disinfectant to his wounds. "Still, I reckon you're the first to have made it across the mountains. I wonder if there are other groups out there who tried to cross back over, after the ambush. I can't imagine what that's like, especially in the middle of this storm. What's it been now, twelve days? And no sign of it dying down either."

"You talking another patient to death, saw-bones?" asked the tattooed corporal, poking his head into the triage tent.

"It's called bedside manner, corporal," replied the medic, "and it's a fucking art, I'll have you know."

"As long as you believe it, doc," said the corporal. "Anyway, I'm supposed to tell the lieutenant here that the boat is ready and waiting."

"I'm not done yet," protested the medic, but Dalton pushed himself to his feet anyway.

"Thank you, but my mission really can't wait," said Dalton, and turned to look at Cutra. The transhuman was lying on a nearby cot, its armoured suit folded down to the waist. A second medic was bent over Cutra's stomach, fastidiously inspecting the gunshot wounds. "You coming?"

Cutra swung off the cot and sent the medic reeling.

"You can't be serious," complained the man. "I've just pulled five bullets out of his gut!"

"Are there any more?" asked Cutra.

"Well, no, but—"

"Then that should do," said Cutra, locking the battered armour back into place.

"Mod freaks, eh?" said the corporal, winking at Dalton.

"Watch your damn mouth," Dalton said, and shoved his way out of the tent.

* * *

Medics transported the injured from the triage tent out to where the patrol boat had been moored at the edge of the pool. The more grievously wounded soldiers had been stabilised in the forward cabin, where the pilot steered from. Those who could at least move unaided were clustered in the flat-bed to the aft of the boat.

One of them was a Privateer that a patrol had found half dead out by the edge of the foothills. The man had been treated for a dozen cuts and bruises, as well as a strained ankle, a broken nose and a fractured skull. His condition had been deemed too critical for active duty. The medics were especially troubled by the soldier's refusal to speak, and feared that he may be suffering from a concussion or some form of mild brain damage.

This soldier watched as the boat's final two passengers were escorted over. A Privateer and a transhuman.

"Here you are," said the corporal who was escorting them. "Have a safe trip, Lieutenant Killian."

The soldier buried his lower face in the collar of his jacket and sunk back between the wounded men to either side of him. He lowered his head, but kept his eyes on the final two passengers. The corporal had called one of them Lieutenant Killian, but the soldier knew Lieutenant Killian, and the Islander boarding the boat was most certainly not him.

That man, that traitorous bastard who barely deserved to be called a Privateer, was James Dalton.

Chapter Thirty-Seven

"I think we're coming up on the edge of the jungle now," said Dalton, leaning over the edge of the boat and peering along the shadowed river. He held out a hand to Cutra as he pulled back. "You done with that now?"

Cutra turned over the data tablet and Dalton tucked it reverently back into his webbing.

"The information that Ajati has compiled on that device is significant," said Cutra. "It has been arranged in such a way as to be… poignant. I believe that it will rally even my people to the cause. A great many of them, at least."

"That's the dream," said Dalton. They were on the deck atop the pilot's cabin. Removed from the rest of the passengers, Cutra and Dalton had spent the two day journey alone, watching the trees slip by on either side as the patrol boat made its way down the Sadari River. Dalton found that the jungle was by far more beautiful when he wasn't stranded on foot in the middle of it, with a dozen things trying to kill or eat him all at once.

Sometime during the night the Scour of Ishra had at last expended its strength, and finally relented. The rushing howl of the storm had become such a part of the background noise for the past thirteen days, that its sudden absence left the world strangely quiet. The storm's passing was fortunate, for all the while it had raged Dalton had known that getting a shuttle into orbit would have been an impossible task.

Now there was one less obstacle between Dalton and the completion of his mission. That knowledge filled him with confidence. Ever since they had found the Sadari River and followed it clear of the mountains, Dalton had felt as though things were at last falling into place. The path ahead was not yet fully known to him, but he felt ready to walk it nonetheless. The closer he got to being free of the jungle, the more excited he became about returning home.

"Do you have a plan for after we leave Assahi?" asked Cutra.

"I have," replied Dalton, keeping his voice low, "but it's risky."

"None of this has been without risk," said Cutra.

Dalton nodded. "Sure, but what comes next is of a different magnitude. I think we have to sabotage *The Moongate*. Not enough to cripple her, but enough to warrant a return home. Pass it off as a Separatist attack or something. I don't have the details worked out yet."

Cutra said nothing.

"Bad idea?" asked Dalton.

"Probably," said Cutra, "but I can see no other way of convincing *The Moongate* to leave Ishra."

"That just leaves actually getting aboard," said Dalton.

"First, let's focus on getting through this next camp," Cutra said. Dalton followed the transhuman's gaze. Camp Alpha had come into view, straddling the Sadari River at the edge of the jungle. Two reinforced towers with mounted machine guns overlooked the water on either side. A bridge had been bolted into place between the towers, from which a barrier had been lowered over the river to block access to even the smallest of boats.

During their journey down the river they had passed through several checkpoints, none of which had posed a serious challenge to their passage, but Dalton had a feeling that security would be tighter leaving the Assahi Territory. He wasn't sure how well his impersonation of Killian would hold up to deeper scrutiny, but if they ran into even a single Privateer that knew the lieutenant personally, the game would be over.

The patrol boat cut speed as it approached the barrier. Gears clanked and chains rattled as the heavy, steel beam was raised, allowing the boat to drift between the towers and gabion walls. They came into a holding area, with gun nests to either side and a bolted gate ahead of them. Once they were clear of the bridge, the pilot brought the boat to a stop and the barrier was lowered behind them. Water sloshed against the hull as a metal gangplank was extended to the boat's gunwales.

"Too late to turn back now," breathed Dalton, as three Avernii marched up the gangplank. One of the armour-clad transhumans met with the pilot, who was holding out a data tablet displaying his travel permit. The other two stepped down onto the deck and swept their visors over the passengers. One of them looked up to where Dalton and Cutra were perched above the cabin.

"Just wounded aboard," the pilot said as the Avernii meticulously checked his documents. "Nothing critical, but it'd be nice to get them to Ushura as quickly as possible."

"There's an armour convoy scheduled to come up the river any day now," replied the Avernii. "We're holding all non-essential vessels here to keep the waterway clear."

"Seriously?" asked the pilot. "I need to get these men off-loaded and head back upriver. I can't be stuck here."

"As I said, non-essential," repeated the Avernii, handing back the data tablet. "There are medics here that can take care of your wounded, but this boat needs to stay off the river until the convoy has come through."

"Wait a minute," said the pilot as the Avernii turned to leave.

"Oh shit," muttered Dalton.

"I forgot to say," the pilot said, pointing up at Dalton, "I've got a lieutenant aboard who has urgent information from the front-line that needs to be delivered directly to High Command."

The Avernii turned back.

"Is this true?" one of them asked.

"It is," said Dalton, patting his chest where the data tablet was secured. "I have to deliver it personally. It's vital to the war effort."

"And you are?"

Dalton swallowed. "Lieutenant Killian, 9th Company, 4th Platoon."

"Where are your pips?" asked the transhuman.

"Lost them," said Dalton quickly. "This isn't even the same uniform that I went over the mountains with. Gets messy out there, it being a war and all."

"Your heart rate is elevated, lieutenant," said the transhuman. "Are you afraid?"

Dalton faltered.

"Post-traumatic stress, wounded and starving to the point that he's metabolising his fat reserves," said Cutra, "and you think his heart rate would be anything but elevated?"

"Of course," replied the other transhuman. "It is easy to forget that these Islanders are… more easily affected. Fine. We'll seek authorisation for you to proceed."

The three Avernii moved to the gangplank. Dalton breathed a sigh of relief.

"Wait."

Dalton froze. The voice that had spoken was familiar to him. He looked down onto the boat's main deck, where the wounded were clustered. It was difficult to distinguish between the soldiers, in their filthy uniforms and bloody bandages. One of them stirred, drawing Dalton's eye.

"Son of a bitch," hissed Dalton.

"They're not who they say they are," said the Privateer, clambering to his feet.

The Avernii turned sharply.

"I'm Private Colt Bridger, 9th Company, 4th Platoon, under Sergeant Broden's 2nd Squad," he said, then pointed at Dalton, "and that man is an imposter. His name is James Dalton and he's a traitor to us all."

"What the fuck is going on?" asked the pilot, bewildered.

"Confirm your accusation," said the lead transhuman, drawing its rifle.

"Cross-check that man's face with Lieutenant Killian's records and confirm it for yourself," said Colt.

One of the Avernii crouched and launched itself from the gangplank to the top deck, landing with such force that it dented the metal. Cutra stepped up and kicked the transhuman square in the chest, sending the armoured warrior off the side of the boat to crash into the river. The other two Avernii pounced. Cutra caught the first by the torso and threw it across the boat's prow. The second slammed into Cutra and the two transhumans went down, grappling with one another.

Dalton lifted his rifle. Something caught his ankle and pulled hard. He slipped sideways, smacking his head on the deck. Colt came up the ladder and ripped the rifle from Dalton's grip. He put a knee in Dalton's chest and pressed the muzzle of the L7 to his head. The other two Avernii had recovered and were climbing back up.

"You're not getting away this time," snarled Colt.

* * *

The zip tie was tight around his wrists, enough to cut into the skin. The Wave-Rider bounced again, kicking its passengers an inch off of the benches. Dalton could hear the transport's tyres tearing across the plains and the growl of its engine revving at full speed. He looked up and glared at Colt. The soldier sat on the bench opposite him, flanked by two Privateers. Colt met Dalton's stare and grinned.

Cutra was on the bench beside him, and sat to either side of them were two Avernii. They had taken away Cutra's armour and done the same for all of Dalton's gear, including confiscating the data tablet. Before they had been loaded into the Wave-Rider, Dalton and Cutra had been kept under armed guard, while the garrison commander had questioned Colt and contacted High Command. That had been three hours ago. Now they were somewhere on the low, open plains west of Assahi, with no idea what was to become of them.

Dalton lost track of how long they travelled for, but eventually the Wave-Rider began to slow. Shortly after that, the transport came to a complete stop and the rear ramp was lowered. Dalton and Cutra were escorted out of the vehicle and onto the streets of Ushura.

The city looked nothing like he remembered it. The roads and tiled pavements were buried beneath a layer of sand that was a foot deep. The windows and doors of the round, squat domiciles had been barricaded with boards that were only now being removed. Awnings had been taken down, or else ripped clear by the storm to join the rest of the debris that littered the streets. Even some of the short, spiky trees that were planted along the pavements had been torn up, their thick trunks snapped clean through.

They left the Wave-Rider behind, parked off of the road, and trudged through the sand towards one of the many bridges which crossed the Sadari. The heavy, stone parapets that had once bordered the bridge were no longer in place, having been shattered by the force of the storm and blown into the river below. A crew of workers had blocked vehicle access to the bridge while they evaluated its structural integrity.

When they reached the palace square, the sheer force with which the Scour of Ishra had struck the city became apparent. The walls of the huge, circular halls were scored and pitted as if by hails of gunfire, and the colonnades of the upper floors had been blown in entirely, causing the facade rooftops to have collapsed. The domes had been stripped of their roof-tiles, which now lay shattered in piles around the palace. Scores of workers were already assembling scaffolds to begin the restoration.

"Just as Ajati said," murmured Dalton.

There were three Herdsman Class drop-ships in the plaza. Someone had made an attempt to protect the aircraft from the storm, anchoring them down with steel cables and covering their hulls with canvas sheets. The latter had been shredded and were now in crumpled heaps on the floor. The steel cables had at least worked for two of the drop-ships. The lines holding down the third one had been wrenched out of their anchor-points, and the aircraft itself had been pushed across the plaza to crash into the foot of the palace wall, where it still remained, half buried in broken masonry. Teams of engineers were at work on a second aircraft, lowering a new windscreen into place.

Something occurred to Dalton as they were led across the plaza, towards the only functional drop-ship. He turned to one of the Privateers assigned to guarding him.

"Why are we here, and not at Fort Alliance?" he asked.

The Privateer looked at him, taken aback by the question. "Fort Alliance didn't survive the storm. No one was ready for it. High Command had to relocate to the carrier."

"That's where you're taking us?" asked Dalton. "To *The Moongate*?"

"Don't talk to him, you idiot," snapped Colt. "This man is a traitor. Anything you say to him compromises our security."

"Thought you said I wasn't getting away," said Dalton, "so what's there to be worried about?"

"Oh, I'm not worried," Colt said, grinning, "but you should be."

"And why is that?" asked Dalton.

"Colonel Hunt has asked to see you," said Colt. "The Storm of Landbreak himself is going to hold your court martial. How do you think the colonel is going to deal with a traitor? All the way out here away from Landbreak, with no one to enforce the ban on capital punishment, except the colonel himself, that is. He'll blow you out the damn airlock for what you've done, James, mark my words."

Dalton glanced at the sky as he was shoved towards the embarkation ramp. He gritted his teeth. "We'll just have to see about that, won't we?"

Chapter Thirty-Eight

"Did we really lose?" asked Dalton, putting his head against the cold metal of the bulkhead. "Did we really come all this way just to end up here?"

Cutra said nothing. The transhuman sat in the corner of the cell, shoulders hunched, its translucent flesh visible in patches beneath the tattered body-glove. The bionics beneath the skin were more visible than ever, and Dalton could see the shape of Cutra's skull beneath its face.

"Are you alright?" he asked.

Cutra stirred and met Dalton's gaze. "Do not be concerned. I am recovering."

"Are you? Because you look… bad."

"My body is working to repair the damage," said Cutra. "This will not kill me."

Dalton nodded. "Good, because at this point, you're my last friend in the galaxy, Cutra."

"We cannot force *The Moongate* to return home anymore," said Cutra.

"I was trying to have a sentimental moment, but sure, we can discuss our failure if that makes you happy," said Dalton.

"You asked whether we had lost this fight," Cutra said.

"It was a mostly rhetorical question."

"One failure does not lose a war, James Dalton."

"This is a pretty big failure, though," said Dalton, "given the circumstances. We've lost the data tablet. We're behind bars. I'm pretty sure there's a military execution on the horizon. I don't see a way out of this, Cutra. Not this time."

"You have lost the data."

"Alright, there's really no need to go pointing fingers," said

Dalton.

Cutra raised a finger and pressed it against its temple. "*You have lost the data.*"

Dalton sat up, his eyes widening. "I forgot. I forgot you… downloaded it, when we were on the boat."

"So you see, one failure does not lose a war," Cutra said, "and we still have opportunities."

"We can't turn this ship around, we can't force it to leave Ishra," said Dalton, his brow furrowed, "but maybe we don't need to. Maybe there's still a victory to be had here, but of a different kind."

"You have a plan?"

"I do," said Dalton. "This ship was designed for deep space, long duration missions, so it has long-range communication equipment. Powerful broadcasting capabilities. It would take too long to try to send the data back to Landbreak or Avernus from here, and besides, the information would only be intercepted on the other side by military satellites. It would never reach the people."

"You want to broadcast it here, across Ishra," said Cutra.

"Exactly," Dalton said. "Ajati told me that when they reached out to the people with this information, recruits flocked to their cause in droves. It was only when they stopped being able to reach people that support wavered, because of the security around the bigger cities, and the government's control and censorship of Ishra's media. Would it be possible, to get through to Ishra's information network using *The Moongate?*"

"I think it would be good to try," said Cutra.

"I don't have the faintest clue about how to get this done though," said Dalton. "Do you?"

"We will need to reach a terminal with unrestricted access," Cutra said. "The bridge, or possibly one of the smaller control and communication nodes."

"Trying to get into the bridge would be suicide," said

Dalton.

"The nodes, then. If we can get to one of those, I will do the rest," Cutra said.

"Are you sure?" asked Dalton. "Have you done this sort of thing before?"

"I am connected," said Cutra simply. "Augmented. *Modified.* Accessing a computer network is no more difficult for me than it is for you to blink."

"It can't be that easy. Won't there be protection? Encryption?"

"There is. One of the first things we did, when we came aboard, was analyse your carrier's cyber network. It is safeguarded well enough from external threats, but from within it is vulnerable," said Cutra.

"What does that mean?"

"It means I cannot access the ship's systems wirelessly, which is why we must find a node," explained Cutra. "Once I have direct interface it should only be a matter of time before I can integrate with the ship's computer. You Islanders have constructed an impressive vessel, but you have never had access to Avernii technology. It is difficult to protect against something that you do not understand."

"That just leaves one problem, then," said Dalton. "Getting out of this cell."

* * *

"I hear they've got a mod in there."

"Salt, Daniel, don't sneak up on me like that," said the security guard, standing outside the brig.

"Sneak up on you?" said Daniel. "Wayne, I practically strolled down the corridor in full sight. Which genius put you on guard duty?"

"Whatever," snapped Wayne. The two guards were dressed in the neatly-trimmed, khaki uniforms of *The Moongate's* security crew. Their badges indicated that they held the rank of Shipmen, the basic corps of guards that formed the backbone of the carrier's defence force. Daniel and Wayne were what the Islander Navy referred to as "jams". It was a derogatory term used to refer to enlisted personnel who had hit the metaphorical roof of their career potential. They were jammed in their current rank, just competent enough to fulfil their functions, but entirely incapable of advancing their pay grade.

"So, is it true?"

"Yeah, there's a mod in there," Wayne said. "One of ours too."

"An Islander? Behind bars with a freak? Salt. Now that sounds like a story worth hearing."

"Well, tough, because I don't have a damn clue what it's all about," said Wayne. "Just some rumour about a band of soldiers that went into the deep jungle, down on the moon. These two were the only ones to come back out, but when they did, they were changed."

"Changed?" asked Daniel. "Changed how?"

"Some are saying it was something in the jungle," said Wayne, warming to the topic. "Something that got into their heads. You should see the mod."

"Why? What about it?"

"You think the regular ones look ugly?" asked Wayne. "This one is something else. Looks like a ghoul out of some horror film. You can see its bones and everything, under the skin. Horrible."

"I've got to see it, Wayne," said Daniel. "Let us in for a peek. Just quickly."

"You're kidding me, right?" Wayne asked. "I've got strict orders. No one in or out till the court martial."

"Who's going to know? Come on, Wayne, don't be a prick!"

"Can't do it. Orders."

Daniel paused. "What's that sound?"

"Oh, please," scoffed Wayne. "You must think I'm stupid to fall for that."

"No, seriously. You can't hear that?"

Wayne cocked his head and heard it too.

"Oh shit," he muttered. "That's coming from inside the brig, isn't it?"

"Well, are you going to check on it, or what?" asked Daniel.

Wayne groaned and punched in the door code. It slid open and the two guards rushed into the room beyond. Behind the bars that partitioned the brig was an Islander and a transhuman. The Privateer's face was currently being squashed against the bars, held there by the Avernii.

"Get this mod freak off me," slurred the Privateer.

"Hey!" shouted Wayne, drawing his baton and stepping in. Daniel put a hand on his arm and pulled him up short. "What are you doing?"

"Seriously, Wayne?" asked Daniel. "The prison fight? You're going to fall for the prison fight?"

"What are you talking about?"

Daniel sighed and walked up to the bars, jabbing a finger at the occupants. "Two prisoners in a cell. They both want out. How do they do it? They fake a fight, the guards burst in to break them up, and the prisoners turn on them when the door opens. Oldest trick in the book."

"Oh well," said the Privateer in the cell, straightening up. "Was worth a try. Cutra?"

The transhuman's arm shot between the bars and locked Daniel's head in a vice.

"Hey! Stop!" cried Wayne and rushed forwards, baton raised. The Privateer reached out and grabbed Wayne's head in both hands, yanking it in to crash against the bars. The guard went limp and slumped to the deck.

The Privateer crouched and pulled the key-card off of Wayne's belt. He held it between the bars and swiped it against the sensor. The gate rattled as it slid aside on its automated track. Daniel cried out and stumbled as he was pushed into the cell, alongside the unconscious Wayne. The Privateer swiped the key-card again and the cell bolted shut behind him.

"Sorry about this," said the Privateer, before following the mod out of the brig.

Daniel nursed his neck and looked down at his friend, out cold on the deck.

"Well done, Wayne."

* * *

Four of the ship's security personnel in their khaki uniforms came jogging down one of the narrow, metal corridors. They had been authorised to carry emergency firearms by *The Moongate's* captain, and had equipped themselves with the low-velocity, square-barrelled SMGs designed for room-to-room fighting.

They reached a junction, turned a corridor and ran straight into a stream of white powder. The first two guards stumbled back, groping at their eyes. The second pair raised their weapons, struggling to push to the front. Cutra stepped out behind them. The transhuman moved through the four surprised guards with mechanical efficiency, putting them down with solid strikes to their ribs and their throats.

"I'm quite fond of these," said Dalton, hefting the fire extinguisher.

"These are better," Cutra said, picking up two SMGs. Dalton dropped the tank and gathered up the other two guns and their spare magazines.

"They're onto us now," said Dalton, nodding to the downed guards. "It's only a matter of time before they surround us."

Cutra was moving again and Dalton hurried to keep pace.

"How do you know where we're going?"

"During the voyage to Ishra we were instructed to commit

the layout of this ship to memory, should the need arise to secure it," said Cutra.

"Secure it?"

"Yes," Cutra said. "In the event that a breakdown in diplomacy occurred between our peoples."

"You Avernii are always ready for the next fight, aren't you?" asked Dalton.

"At the time, we could not be sure that your people were trustworthy."

"And now?"

"I trust you, James Dalton," said Cutra. "I cannot speak for my people. It's this room."

They swept into the cramped, hexagonal room, securing the narrow spaces between the computer stacks. With the ship locked in orbit and the assault force deployed to the ground almost in full, *The Moongate* was running on the bare essentials, to conserve energy and keep the crew rested in preparation for the return journey. Many of these secondary control and communication nodes were unmanned, their systems shut off entirely or idling in low power mode. Cutra set about re-activating the necessary consoles.

"I'll keep watch," said Dalton, moving back to the hatch. "How long will this take?"

Cutra didn't reply, immersed in the task ahead.

"As long as it takes, then," muttered Dalton, edging out of the doorway to peer left and right along the corridor. With the amount of cameras in place around *The Moongate*, Dalton had no doubt that the ship's security knew exactly where they were. By now, teams would have already been dispatched to cordon them off and smoke them out. He only hoped that the bridge crew wouldn't realise what they were trying to do here and shut down power to the node.

A head poked round the corner at the far end of the corridor. Dalton put the SMG's wire stock to his shoulder and pulled the trigger, peppering the distant junction with a short burst. The chatter of the weapon echoed loud in the close space. The guard pulled back out of view.

"Things are about to get very busy out here," said Dalton, looking down the right side of the corridor. For now, the guards were only moving up from the left, but he knew it would only be a matter of time before they closed off both approaches. "What's our progress like?"

"Still integrating with the software," said Cutra idly. "Then I have to find a compatible format to upload the data, determine the best way to globally disperse the information across Ishra, and account for any virtual security in use by the Ishradi government."

"Salt's sake, Cutra," said Dalton, pausing to fire off another burst as one of the guards peered out. "You didn't make it sound this difficult before."

"I didn't want to put you off," said Cutra.

"Just hurry up," Dalton said. He leaned away as the barrel of a weapon jutted round the corner. The angle was bad and the rounds clattered against a bulkhead further up. He returned fire to dissuade the guards from advancing. "I've only got so many bullets."

"Take mine," said Cutra, kicking the SMGs across the deck.

"You won't be joining me any time soon, I take it," he growled, tilting away as another volley came his way, closer this time. He leaned back out to trade shots. A cry of pain echoed down the corridor.

"Damn, I think I hit one with a ricochet."

"That is a good thing, surely?"

"I don't want to have to kill any of these men," said Dalton, "and I'd rather not motivate them to kill me either."

"I think we're past that point now," Cutra said.

"Don't you have work to be doing?" Dalton snapped.

"I'm transferring the data now."

Dalton glanced back into the room. Cutra was sat at the main terminal. A bundle of wires had been torn from the console and spliced directly into a slit in the transhuman's wrist. The screen was flashing and streaming with reams of data, but Cutra's hands were not at the keyboard. Dalton tried not to think about it and turned his attention back towards the corridor.

Another hail of rounds crashed along the bulkheads, but this time it came from the right side of the corridor. Dalton leaned out to return fire. A second hail of shot came from the left and he jerked back into cover.

"Well, shit," he said and scooped up a second SMG. He leaned out, a weapon in each hand, one facing left, the other facing right, and pulled the triggers. The chatter was deafening and his arms shuddered as he fought to control the recoil. His accuracy was laughable, but the storm of gunfire pressed the guards deep into cover.

"Any second now would be great," yelled Dalton.

"I need more time," said Cutra calmly.

"I've just realised something," said Dalton, throwing down the empty SMGs and picking up the other two. "Even if we do this, even if we succeed, there's no getting out of this. We're surrounded. There's only one way out."

"Then let's make it count," Cutra said.

Dalton stuck the SMGs around the door frame again, tapping the triggers to fire three-round bursts, instead of spraying out the entire magazine in a single barrage. It would buy them a few more seconds at least.

"Smoke!" yelled a guard. A canister bounced off one of the bulkheads and rolled across the deck. Smoke began to spew from the grenade, quickly obscuring the right corridor with thick, grey clouds. All gunfire from the left suddenly stopped. Then he heard the drumming of boots on a metal deck, growing louder with every second.

"They're coming," whispered Dalton. "Cutra, they're coming."

"If you don't stop them," said the transhuman, "this will all be for nothing."

"You haven't finished, have you?"

"No. I need more time."

Dalton closed his eyes.

I didn't want it to end this way.

He stepped out into the corridor, an SMG in each hand. He faced the smoke, locking his elbows to his sides, bracing his fingers on the triggers. There were shapes moving in the smoke, the shapes of men, Islander men. His kin.

This wasn't how it was supposed to end.

He pulled the triggers. Tongues of flame licked from the muzzles of the SMGs. Bullets punched through the cloud, knocking ripples and curling tendrils into the smoke. The closest shapes bucked and writhed and collapsed against the bulkheads. Men roared in anger, in fear and in pain. Then Dalton's fingers were flat against the trigger guards, and the SMGs clicked silent. He was all out.

"Open fire!" yelled a voice from the smoke. Dalton was already leaping aside, leaving the guns to fall from his fingers as he dived through the hatch. A salvo of gunfire hammered along the corridor, pounding on the bulkheads. Rounds screamed as they ricocheted from the reinforced walls.

Dalton scrambled on the deck to reload the empty SMGs. Out in the corridor, the firing had stopped. He tore the empty magazines free and fumbled fresh ones from the pockets of his fatigues. Boots drummed on the metal floor. Dalton spun round, a newly loaded SMG in his hands. He never got the chance. It was knocked from his grip. He looked up into Colt's rage-contorted face. The rifle stock crashed into Dalton's nose and sprawled him on his back. Hot blood trickled from his nose and lips.

His vision blurred and faded to black. It came back, fuzzy around the edges, clearing and fading in turn. Cutra was still at the console. The transhuman hadn't even turned around, as though the storm of gunfire and the enemy at its back were irrelevant.

"Get up," snarled Colt, aiming his rifle at the back of Cutra's head.

Dalton struggled to rise, but his skull pounded with the effort. A wave of nausea flooded through him. He sagged back to the floor.

"I said, get up," hissed Colt.

Cutra didn't move. The wires were still attached to its flesh, the screen was still flashing.

"Have it your way," said Colt.

The rifle barked once. A spray of blood splattered across the screen. Cutra's body went limp. The transhuman fell against the console, eyes open, a trail of silver running from the hole in Cutra's brow.

Chapter Thirty-Nine

The Miteran Jewel dominated the screen. It was not a true window, not like the tempered glass panels of the ship's observatories, but rather it was a simulated picture of space, fed to the screen via external cameras on the carrier's hull. It occupied the entirety of the far wall, filling the room with Ishra's reflected light.

Framed against the moon's bright continents was Colonel Lawrence Hunt. The man looked as if he were standing at the edge of a portal into the void, the broad, angular frame of his shoulders silhouetted by the screen's crisp glow. It was the first time Dalton had seen the man without his greatcoat or iconic bicorn. He wore a dark blue shirt with the sleeves rolled up, emphasising the thickness of his forearms. Hunt was a bear of a man, large in the way that only an older man could be. His greying hair was cropped close to the skull and his face was craggy, lined and leathery from a lifetime of facing down the wind and the ocean.

There was a .44 Snapper in the centre of the desk, behind which stood the colonel. He was half turned away from them when they entered the dark office, hands clasped behind his back, shoulders slightly hunched.

"Where's the other one?" he asked.

"The mod put up a fight, colonel," lied Colt, "had to put it down."

Hunt took a deep breath, his broad chest rising, and turned his head to study the face of Ishra.

"I have seen the contents of the data tablet you brought with you," he said, still looking away. "I think I understand what your intentions were."

"We're on the wrong side of this war," said Dalton, cleaving to what sounded like sympathy in the colonel's voice. "If you allow me to—"

"Quiet," said the colonel firmly. "I never imagined that naivety could carry a man so far. You are young and impressionable, and because of this I can at least understand your motivation. What I cannot do, however, is forgive your actions. You turned on your kin, fought against your brothers, betrayed your own, and for what? To further the agenda of savages who skulk in the jungle?"

"Savages?" said Dalton, appalled. "Colonel, these people are—"

"Do not speak," Hunt commanded. "Our presence here is about more than you could imagine. This isn't about ending a civil war, this isn't about killing Separatists or even earning Ishra's favour. This is about the future of our people. This is about protecting Landbreak from the wars to come."

"Wars to come? What are you talking about?" asked Dalton.

Colonel Hunt turned slowly and picked up the revolver on the desk. His thumb pressed back the hammer.

"You think I'm going to stand here and explain this to you," said Hunt. "You still don't realise how far you've gone. That does not surprise me. Only a man blinded by childish idealism could do the things that you have done and still stand here convinced of his righteousness."

Hunt levelled the revolver. Dalton looked down the barrel of the gun. In that moment he realised that Cutra had been right. Landbreak had entered this war not as a favour to Ishra, but to help itself, just as Avernus had. Whatever the reason, resources, land, trade, even access to the damn sap, Dalton knew Hunt would never admit it. He couldn't. There was something in the colonel's eyes, a flicker of hesitation despite the man's legendary iron will.

"You know," said Dalton, realisation dawning. "You know

this is wrong. I can see it. You know our agenda here is dishonourable. You hate it, but you're too proud to do anything but your duty."

"What would a traitor know of duty? I won't waste time on a trial, on a drawn-out punishment or an attempt to make you see the truth," said Hunt. "You are a wild beast, and for that there is only one cure."

Dalton fought against the urge to squeeze shut his eyes. He met Hunt's glare with one of his own. Every muscle in his body was tensing, urging him to leap away, to do something, anything, to survive. Instead, he decided that he would not shame himself in this final moment with futile cowardice.

He had signed on with the Privateers out of childish frustration, without thought or valid motivation. It had been an act of rebellion against a tame life, the sort of stupidity bred in young men by too much testosterone. If he had been able to, he would have turned back, but by the time he had realised his mistake, *The Moongate* had already been underway. So he had come to Ishra by the path of the fool, but that path had led him to truth, to purpose. He would stand by that to the end.

"Colonel," said an urgent voice from the hatch.

"Not now," said Hunt, his gaze still fixed on Dalton.

"I'm sorry, colonel," said the crew-man, "but it's urgent. Ship-captain Reed requests your presence on the bridge."

"What is it, man?" asked Hunt, sighing and lowering the revolver.

"The ship is… transmitting, colonel."

"What are you talking about? Transmitting what?"

"A data parcel to Ishra, colonel, but it's not authorised," said the crewman. "It's using the full communications array for maximum broadcast, but we can't locate its onboard source."

"This is his doing," snarled Colt, stepping up and jabbing his rifle into Dalton's back. "They were doing something when I caught them, on one of the computers."

"What is this?" asked Hunt, his lip curling.

"It's… Cutra," said Dalton, his voice at the cusp of laughter. "I don't believe it."

"Cutra? What's Cutra?"

"The mod, colonel, the one that was with him," said Colt.

"You're going to stop this, right now," warned Hunt, levelling the revolver again.

"This is out of our control now," Dalton said, smiling despite himself. "He did it, he did it before the end."

"Colonel," the crewman said, raising a finger to his ear as a transmission came across his headset. "Colonel, we've received a hail from an Ishradi corvette. It's demanding that we stop the transmission immediately."

"You're telling me we can't just switch this thing off?" asked Hunt.

The crewman gave a pathetic shrug. "We can't find the source of the transmission, colonel, and all of our attempts to shut down the array are being jammed from the inside."

"What do you think this is going to achieve?" snarled Hunt, looking back to Dalton.

"Revolution," he replied.

"Colonel, the Ishradi corvette is threatening to open fire if we don't stop transmitting."

"They what?" growled Hunt, incredulous. "The bastards wouldn't dare!"

"Do you wish to compose a response, colonel?"

"Tell them to stand down immediately!"

"I'll relay word to Captain Reed."

"Do you really think this is a victory?" asked Hunt. "This doesn't change how this ends for you. Are you so committed to their cause that you would die for it?"

"You've made it perfectly clear that you're going to pull the trigger either way," said Dalton, "so I might as well die for a worthwhile cause."

"Colonel! The corvette has just fired a warning shot off our bow!"

"They dare?" shouted Hunt. "Make it known that if they discharge their weapons again, even if it's to shoot in the opposite direction, *The Moongate* will return fire!"

"Yes, colonel!"

"If you know how to stop this, it could save your life," said Hunt.

"Even if I could stop this, I wouldn't tell you how," Dalton said.

"Have it your way, then," said Hunt, tensing his finger on the trigger.

The deck bucked under their boots. Dalton staggered. Hunt reached out to steady himself against the desk. The crewman and Colt were braced against the bulkhead. Emergency lighting thudded on in the corridor outside. Somewhere, a klaxon was wailing.

"Colonel, we've been hit! Starboard impact. Hull integrity is intact," said the crewman, repeating the report that was coming across his headset.

"What the salt are they thinking?!" bellowed Hunt. "They would open fire on us over a transmission?"

"The truth is a powerful weapon," said Dalton, "one that the High Shekahn fears above all others."

"Enough!" shouted Hunt, lifting the revolver.

The screen went black, plunging them into total darkness. It flashed. Dalton blinked. The screen flashed again. Had he seen that right? For the third time the screen flashed and this time Dalton was sure. In large, bold, white font the word 'RUN' had flickered on the screen.

"Cutra?" he said, his voice distant.

RUN.

The ship shuddered again.

RUN.

"Return fire, damn it!" Hunt roared. "Return fire!"

RUN.

Dalton threw his elbow backwards into Colt's face. The trooper smacked into the bulkhead. Dalton turned and barrelled past the crewman. A revolver boomed behind him, but he didn't stop. There were guards in the hallway. Shocked by the juddering of the ship and the wailing of the alarms, they barely noticed Dalton's escape.

"Cutra, if you're there, somehow, then I could really do with directions right about now!" he yelled, switching left into an empty corridor. He reached a t-junction and skidded to a halt. "Come on, Cutra!"

The klaxons wailed. The emergency lighting bathed the corridors in red. Nothing happened. He could hear shouts rebounding from the bulkheads. It would only be a matter of minutes before someone regained their senses enough to come after him.

"Of course you're not there," said Dalton quietly. "I watched you die."

Dalton blinked. The lights in the corridor ahead had returned to normal, but behind and to the right the emergency lights were still flashing.

"You're in the ship, aren't you?" asked Dalton, seeking out one of the security cameras. "How did you do it, Cutra?"

The lights ahead started blinking rapidly, on and off.

"Time to move, I get it, I get it," said Dalton. He started running, following the corridors not drenched in red light. Around him, the ship shivered and groaned, and the plaintive cry of the klaxons echoed around every corner.

* * *

The Moongate hung in Ishra's orbit, its slab-sided hull bathed in Mitera's fiery radiance. Four ochre-painted corvettes flanked the carrier. One of the attack craft had turned its tapered prow parallel to *The Moongate's* starboard side. In this position it could bring ten of its twin-barrelled cannon pods to bear, though only one of them was currently firing.

A stream of shots, burning white in the vacuum, exploded against the carrier's flank. The ablative, armoured plates between the prow and the midship hangar bay took the brunt of the attack. Flattened, shattered warheads spun away from the impacts, along with shards of torn hull plating.

At *The Moongate's* prow, the fifty-metre long railgun lit up as its mechanisms were fed with power. The huge weapon turned through ninety degrees, to aim off the starboard side. It acquired target-lock on the offending corvette and opened fire. The electromagnets activated in sequence along the conductors and accelerated its two-thousand pound tungsten projectile at a velocity which exceeded four-thousand metres per second. The shot crossed the void between ships in less than two seconds. It struck the corvette's gun-prow and tunnelled clean through. The sheer amount of imparted kinetic energy did the rest, shattering the tapered bow of the ship and sending its aft bridge section spinning away. A blinding flash of light bloomed from the impact, before the corvette came apart in a series of smaller explosions, shredded internally by its detonating magazines.

It took a few moments for the remaining corvettes to respond, as their captains and crews watched in abject horror at the almost casual destruction of one of their squadron. Perhaps they had believed that their bullying jabs against *The Moongate* would have been sufficient to make her submit, that the larger ship would never even consider retaliation. When they recovered from their shock, the three corvettes powered into motion, bringing as many of their guns to bear as they could. They flew loops around the carrier, not eager to be targeted by the devastating power of its railgun.

In response, *The Moongate* opened up with the dual-barrelled cannons on its port and starboard sides, filling the vacuum around it with exploding shells.

* * *

Dalton grabbed hold of the pipes that lined the wall and held on tight, as the most recent bout of tremors rocked the ship. He had tried to keep moving through the last one and ended up flat on his face. His nose was still bleeding, or maybe that was from when Colt had struck him. He couldn't tell. Pain had become such a constant in his life that he barely paid attention anymore.

"What the salt is going on out there?" he asked, gaining his feet as the tremors subsided. "Are the Ishradi really trying to sink us?"

The lights began blinking rapidly again. Dalton switched left along a starboard maintenance tunnel, following the path that Cutra was lighting for him.

"I get it, you can't answer," said Dalton. "Are you even alive? Just blink twice for yes."

The lights blinked twice. Then a pause, followed by a third blink.

"What does that mean? Yes and no?"

Two blinks. That was a yes.

"Can you get out? Back into your body?" asked Dalton, panting for breath as he sprinted down the cramped tunnel, ducking his head to avoid low hanging pipes. The lights blinked once. *No.* "Shit, Cutra. What does that mean? Are you stuck in the ship forever?"

No.

"So there's a way you can get out?"

Dalton clung to a pipe, then yelled and recoiled from the hot metal. The tremors had begun again. A rumbling was echoing through the ship, like distant thunder. The lights blinked once. *No.*

"You're not stuck in the ship forever, but you can't get out. What does that mean?" asked Dalton, raising his voice to be heard by the microphone in the closest camera. "Cutra? Cutra, does that mean you're dying?"

No response. The tremors calmed and Dalton set off again.

"Cutra? Cutra, what does that mean? Are you dying? Answer me!"

The light blinked once, almost slowly. Then again. *Yes.*

"There's got to be a way I can help you, a way to get you out," yelled Dalton, hauling on a door crank and stumbling into one of the main corridors. He looked right. At the end of the corridor the emergency lights were on. He went left instead. "Cutra? Respond, damn you! Is there a way I can get you out? A way I can help?"

Dalton stopped in his tracks. The hatch ahead of him led to the prow hangar bay. Standing in front of it was Colt. The trooper put his rifle down against the hatch and drew the combat knife from his thigh.

"Let's finish this, then," Colt said, flipping the blade into an underhand grip.

"Are you fucking serious, man?" asked Dalton, as another tremor ran through the deck. For a moment the sound of ship-grade projectiles could be heard drumming against the hull. "The ship is coming apart and you want to do this now?"

"All this," said Colt, "all this is because of you, James. You're the one to blame. The way I see it, if you die, all this goes away."

"We used to be friends, Colt," said Dalton.

"My mistake," Colt replied, and dived towards him. Dalton cried out and leapt away. The black oxide blade swished through the air an inch from his stomach. Colt reversed the knife in his grip and slashed again. Dalton stumbled. Hot pain splashed across his shoulder as the blade sliced through flesh.

The deck bucked. Colt staggered. Dalton hurled himself forwards. He caught Colt's wrist in one hand and punched him in the forearm with the other. Colt yelled, the blade slipping from his limp fingers. He kneed Dalton in the ribs and they both went sprawling as the ship rocked sideways.

Dalton crawled across the deck, wheezing. Colt's rifle had fallen by the hatch. It was barely three metres away. The floor was trembling, vibrating against his aching body. The ship tipped and the rifle slid towards him. His fingers brushed the barrel. He felt a grip on his shirt and flailed as he was pulled into the air. Colt lifted him up and slammed him back down into the deck. Dalton heard something crack as his cheekbone smacked against metal. A boot crashed into his gut and he curled up, spitting blood.

With both boots he lashed out, catching Colt in the ankles. The trooper lurched against the bulkhead and toppled from his feet. Dalton clawed himself to his knees. Something caught his eye. A small, blue bulb set into the bulkhead was flashing rapidly. Beside it was a fire extinguisher, supported against the wall in its bracket.

"Now is not the time to develop a sense of humour, Cutra," croaked Dalton, but crawled towards it anyway. Colt's heel thudded into his tailbone and sent him skidding across the deck. Dalton groaned and rolled onto his back. Colt was approaching, slowly, racking the slide on his rifle.

"Everyone's luck runs out eventually, James," he said, closing the distance between them with every step.

The emergency blast-door came down out of the ceiling, directly on top of him. Colt didn't see it coming. It crushed him flat into the deck. Dalton jerked back, wincing as a wave of blood squelched out from beneath the thick door.

The small, blue bulb was flashing in the corner of his eye. Dalton looked up at the fire extinguisher beside him. He slumped back and drew in a shuddering breath.

"Thanks, Cutra."

* * *

Colonel Hunt stormed onto the bridge. He still hadn't put on his coat or his cap. There hadn't been time. The bridge was trembling. The deck heaved beneath the crew as a fresh volley of projectiles battered the hull. Hunt steadied himself on the back of the nearest console stack and fought his way towards the captain's dais.

Crewmen scrambled to get out of the colonel's way. There was a fire in Hunt's eyes, a fury that none of them had ever seen before. His craggy face was apoplectic, his brow was thunderous. At some point during his journey to the bridge, his shirt had caught on something and torn at the shoulder. It made him look as though he was swelling with rage, as though he was bursting out of his uniform.

"Order them to cease fire! Now!" bellowed Hunt over the hive of noise that engulfed the bridge. Deck officers were strapped into their stations, their eyes glued to their screens as they called out curt fragments of information or yelled for verification. Those amongst the crew who weren't seated were lurching from station to station, desperately working to contain the situation. Emergency lighting and the cold glow of screens cast the bridge between stark beams of light and sharp shadows.

"I have tried, Colonel," replied Ship-captain Reed. The master of *The Moongate* seemed oddly out of place amidst the madness of the bridge. She was a portly woman, whose dark green uniform seemed to have been tailored for a leaner body. Reed was reclined in her command chair, her fingers hovering over the keypads built into the armrests. A shell of nine screens hung above her head, suspended from the ceiling on mechanical arms. Each screen showed something different, a view from one of the carrier's external cameras, a readout of technical data concerning the ship's performance, a wire-frame schematic of one of *The Moongate's* decks, and so on. There seemed to be too much information present there for one person to assimilate by themselves, but Reed appeared unaffected as she flicked her eyes across the screens with an almost idle ease.

"Try again, damn it!"

"You realise we're engaged in an exchange of ordnance, don't you, colonel?" asked Captain Reed politely.

Hunt glanced around the bridge. Thick blast shields had been lowered across the wide view ports that normally looked out into space. Three dozen screens situated throughout the bridge showed snippets of the battle unfolding around them, but Hunt couldn't piece them together.

"What's the situation?" he snarled, hating the feeling of helplessness that was creeping over him.

"Three hostiles, corvette class," said Reed, as if she were reading the words off a report. "We are struggling to bring them into our firing arcs. They have a considerable speed advantage on us. The ship won't be able to survive this sustained level of damage for much longer."

"What is much longer?"

"By my estimations? Eight minutes, should the Ishradi corvettes continue to target our most vulnerable sectors."

"You don't seem concerned, ship-captain."

"That's because I'm not, Colonel Hunt," muttered Reed. "Please find a seat somewhere, you're being terribly distracting."

"Ship-captain, you've put through an order to prime all keel thrusters along the bow," called a deck officer. "Requesting verbal confirmation!"

"Confirmation given," said Reed.

The deck officer hesitated a second. "Ship-captain, that manoeuvre would put considerable strain on the carrier's support structure, not to mention increase the probability of a collision vector."

"Well, yes, that's the intention," Reed said, only half paying attention.

"What are you doing, Alicia?" growled Hunt, gripping the back of her chair as another violent tremor rocked the ship.

"Levelling the playing field, Lawrence," Alicia Reed replied. "Be a dear and don't get in the way."

* * *

The three corvettes raked *The Moongate* with salvoes of flickering gunfire from their broadsides, looping around its hull like sharks hunting a whale. The carrier bled smoke and oxygen from a dozen punctures, a score of chambers and corridors venting their atmosphere into space. It tried to turn in concert with the smaller attack ships, to keep them in its firing arcs, but *The Moongate* was cumbersome in comparison to their nimble movements.

One of the corvettes came over the carrier's forward hull, daringly close. The attack ship's cannons breathed fire into the void, savaging *The Moongate's* dorsal plating. It was in that moment that Ship-captain Reed ordered all keel retro-thrusters along the bow to full burn. The huge ship swung forwards with sudden momentum and hammered against the corvette. Metal ground against metal. Inside the carrier, the crew ducked their heads instinctively as the ship groaned, so loud it sounded as if it might split apart at the spine. Clouds of sparks and scraps of sheared armour billowed into space. The small corvette was dashed apart against the carrier's slab-sided hull, leaving its broken frame to drift away, end over end.

A second corvette veered wildly to avoid the reckless move. The attack craft sailed straight into the arc of *The Moongate's* broadside turrets. It was blasted apart in an expanding ball of fire that was extinguished in the void as quickly as it blossomed. The third and final corvette turned to make a run for the nearest space station. *The Moongate* gently came about as the Ishradi vessel fled. The corvette had put thirteen-thousand kilometres between it and the carrier when the railgun fired. The projectile burned through the void, leaving a brilliant scar of light in its wake, so bright that it was visible from the surface of Ishra. The shot reached out across the distance and caught the corvette, coring it from aft to prow in a millisecond.

That night, as the Ishradi stared up into the sky, they would see showers of shooting stars in the heavens.

* * *

"Fly, now," said Dalton, leaning against the cockpit's hatch and pointing the rifle at the pilot's head. He had found the pilot strapped into his seat, his Herdsman clamped to the deck.

"What are you doing, soldier?" asked the pilot, twisting round to look at Dalton. He faltered as he saw the rifle.

"Get us out of here," said Dalton.

"What? Why? Are you pointing that gun at me?"

"Do it. Fly," said Dalton. "I don't want to have to kill another Islander today."

"You what? You're insane."

"*Now.*"

"You want me to fly out there, into that storm?" asked the pilot. "We're under attack, for salt's sake!"

"I've been through worse," Dalton said, spitting blood. "Reckon I'll survive."

"Even if I wanted to, I couldn't," said the pilot, nodding through the armoured windscreen. "Hangar doors are sealed. Combat protocol."

"Cutra, open the hangar bay," shouted Dalton.

"Who are you talking to?" the pilot asked, his eyes wide with concern. He fell quiet as a warning chime sounded across the hangar bay and the huge blast-doors began to grind open. "How did you do that?"

"Fly," growled Dalton. "Take me over the Assahi Territory.

The inner jungle."

"You're mad."

"Cutra, give him incentive."

Red lights flashed on across the dashboard as one of the hangar's inner defence turrets swivelled to target them.

"What the salt is going on?!" cried the pilot.

"Fly, or we both die here," said Dalton. "At this point, I couldn't give a damn either way."

The pilot began scrambling at his controls.

"Thought so," said Dalton, strapping himself into the co-pilot's chair. "Assahi Territory. Inner jungle. Don't stop for anything. And you're going to need to show me where the radio is, unless you want to get shot out of the sky."

"You're out of your mind," said the pilot, sealing the cargo hatch and feeding power to the thrusters.

Dalton put his head back against the leather chair.

"Cutra, if you can still hear me, I want to say thank you, and goodbye," he said to the air. "Distinction is yours."

Chapter Forty

The Herdsman dropped through the clouds, parting wisps against its belly and broad wings. Dalton gazed across the open plains of low, yellow grass and the winding, glinting length of the Sadari River. Ahead was the great, green expanse of the Assahi Jungle Territory, and the barren, wind-blasted heights that divided it.

"I didn't expect to be returning here so soon," said Dalton quietly, "somehow it feels like coming home."

The pilot wasn't paying attention.

"We're being chased," he said, one eye on the dashboard instrumentation.

"Get to the jungle," Dalton said calmly, "we'll be safe there."

"You're crazy," said the pilot.

"So you've said," Dalton replied, lifting the microphone from the radio panel and setting the dial to general broadcast. "Just get us there."

The drop-ship shook as its flight path steepened towards the jungle and the wind howled around them. A burst of light flashed over the cockpit, bringing with it the thrumming rush of sundered air.

"That was a warning shot!" yelled the pilot. "We've got two Hurricanes on our six! Next time they won't miss! I'm taking us back up!"

"Do that," said Dalton, shifting the rifle across his lap to aim at the pilot's head, "and I'll land this ship for you."

The pilot scoffed and hauled on the controls, swerving the drop-ship out of its current trajectory. Dalton shrugged, jerked the rifle and pulled the trigger. Were it not for their earphones the shot would have deafened them both. The round punched through the pilot's side-window, crazing the glass. Half a dozen warning lights flashed across the dashboard as the pressure in the cabin began to drop. The atmosphere inside the cockpit was venting out of the breach, screeching as it went.

"Fuck! Fuck!" screamed the pilot. "Alright! Alright! I'm doing it! I'm taking us down! Don't fucking shoot!"

The pilot slapped a suction pad over the bullet-hole and readjusted their course. The jungle canopy was streaming by beneath them now as they flew over Assahi's furthest reaches. The Hurricane fighters flanked them on either side, drawing level with the cockpit and flying so close that their wings were grazing against those of the drop-ship.

"If any Separatists are reading this, my name is James Dalton," he said, speaking into the microphone. "I am a friend of Ajati. Do not fire on the drop-ship. I repeat, this is a friend of Ajati, do not fire on us."

"If I don't turn us skywards, those fighters are going to stop asking nicely," said the pilot.

"Flip their wings," said Dalton. "Make them chase us. Make them shoot at us."

The pilot looked at him, eyes wide.

"I know, I know, I'm crazy, I'm out of my mind," Dalton said. "Just do it."

The pilot hesitated, so Dalton shrugged and shifted the rifle's aim.

"I'm doing it!" yelled the pilot. "Salt's sake, I'm doing it!"

The drop-ship rolled its wings and forced the fighters to veer aside. The sleek jets cut speed and dropped behind, bringing the transport into their arc of fire.

"They're going to kill us," yelled the pilot.

"Maybe," said Dalton, his voice devoid of emotion, "or maybe we'll get lucky."

He leaned into the radio and repeated his message. The westernmost mountain range was behind them now as they cut a path over the inner jungle. A ripple of cannon fire zipped across their port side. One of the shots blew through the left wing in a welter of smoke and flames. The drop-ship wobbled violently.

"I repeat," he said, "this is James Dalton. Ajati knows me. I'm aboard the drop-ship and I'm being pursued. Help me!"

A tongue of light and flame tore free from the jungle canopy. It burned a path towards them, but missed the drop-ship by several metres. Behind them, one of the fighters was struck dead on. The anti-aircraft fire tore its chassis down the middle, sending its bifurcated wings spiralling away on trails of flame. The second Hurricane sharply banked away and made for orbit, weaving left and right as more rounds chased it across the sky.

"Bring us down right there," said Dalton, jabbing his finger against the windscreen. "There! Where the shots came from!"

The drop-ship soared down towards the jungle canopy, spewing a trail of black smoke from its punctured wing.

* * *

Dalton came down the ramp as it was lowered to the ground. Daylight streamed into the jungle clearing, now that the camouflage netting had been torn away. Squinting against the brightness of the day, he could make out a line of rifles facing him from the foot of the ramp.

"My message," he called, "did you get my message?"

"What message?" replied one of the Separatists.

"I'm James Dalton, friend of Ajati. I broadcast a message to let you know I was aboard."

"Didn't get it," said the Separatist.

"Then how did you know not to shoot us down?"

"Was going to," admitted the Separatist. "Then we saw the jets open fire on you. Reckoned you were an enemy of our enemy."

"I need to see Ajati," said Dalton.

* * *

It took Dalton nine days to reach Ajati and the bulk of the Separatist army. It took twice that long again for news to start trickling in through the dense barriers of the jungle, brought to them by the scouts and runners that were their only link to the rest of Ishra. Fragments of rumours from a dozen sources began to paint a picture of what had occurred, and of what was to come.

Cutra's broadcast had cut through the firewalls and censor filters that shackled the moon's public information network. It had been dispersed via satellites and radio towers, fed into the televisions and personal computers of every civilian in every major city across Ishra. For seven hours the broadcast had looped, before the High Shekahn's administration managed to completely shut it down on their end. By that time, Ajati's propaganda footage and information had been copied and propagated a million times over.

The truth had been irrevocably revealed.

It wasn't long before people began flocking to the streets, protest en masse upon their lips as they marched on administration centres and government buildings. When the protests were met with force, they turned into riots. Years of smothered anger and dissatisfaction were reawakened. The High Shekahn's oppression would be tolerated no longer. The lies and the false coverage about the civil war fell away, and became further fuel for the people's rage.

Ishra had awoken.

More stories still came from Ushura. Messengers told of how the Privateers and the Avernii garrisoned in the city had turned their guns inwards and laid siege to the palace. Coalition soldiers were withdrawn from their camps in and along the jungle, rerouted to join the siege and secure the city.

One rumour told of how the High Shekahn had ordered his entire space fleet against *The Moongate*, and that a battle of huge proportions had raged in orbit. When the siege had finally broken through the palace defences, the High Shekahn had been forced at gunpoint to call off his attack craft.

A revolution had been set into motion and there was not a soul upon Ishra that did not know it. The High Shekahn's power had been broken, his manipulations uncovered. The people marched in their millions, demanding justice for the crimes that had been perpetrated against their nation and against the moon that they called home.

There was no more fighting between the coalition soldiers and the Separatists after that. The off-world forces began their slow departure from the jungle, unopposed by the Separatists. It seemed as though the civil war on Ishra had finally come to an end.

***

Dalton stood alone amongst the trees. There was a knife in his hand, one of the curved blades wielded by the Separatist jungle fighters. He drew it along the bole of a tree, carving letters in the bark. When he heard the footsteps approaching behind him, he did not stop or even turn. He had become accustomed to the sounds of the jungle, of what noises a human made when they were travelling through the undergrowth, even when they were trying to move quietly.

"Hello, Eskela," he said, not turning.

"There you are," she replied. "Ajati has been looking for you."

"Is it time?" Dalton asked.

"He believes so," Eskela said. "Time to return to the light, he says. Time to show our true face to the people we've been secretly serving for so long."

"I wonder what happens now," said Dalton, chipping away

at the bark. "Now that the war is over, what becomes of the soldiers?"

"The fighting may be over," said Eskela, "but the war is still to be won. There will be those who oppose our coming, those who still cling to the High Shekahn's regime. It will be a different kind of war, but one that will require soldiers nonetheless."

"It's strange," Dalton said. "I never considered myself a soldier, not really, not until the fighting was done with. I didn't come here a soldier."

"It doesn't matter what you came here as, James," Eskela said. "It doesn't even matter why you came. All that matters is what you chose to do when you arrived."

Dalton pulled the blade from the tree and sheathed it at his belt.

"Come on," he said, turning to face her at last. "We wouldn't want to keep Ajati waiting."

"We wouldn't want to keep the world waiting," said Eskela, and side by side they walked away between the trees.

Behind him, Dalton left a list carved in the bole.

WRIGHT
NELSON
MOORE
ROLAY
HARRIS
BLAKE
CUTRA

Harry Elliott is a British author with a passion for the fictional and the fantastic. Born in England and raised in Cyprus, it was there that Harry got his first taste of military life serving in the National Guard. A generally unpleasant experience that he would happily repeat, it informed a great deal of the work in his debut novel, *Warrior Errant*. He makes his home wherever there's a flat enough surface to write on. His hobbies include reading and impressing upon people the importance of reading, especially his own work.

www.ingramcontent.com/pod-product-compliance
Lightning Source LLC
Chambersburg PA
CBHW070815190726
48292CB00006B/2027